D0049224

THE RENDING
AND THE NEST

The Rending and the Nest

A NOVEL

Kaethe Schwehn

B L O O M S B U R Y

NEW YORK · LONDON · OXFORD · NEW DELHI · SYDNEY

Bloomsbury USA
An imprint of Bloomsbury Publishing Plc

1385 Broadway	50 Bedford Square
New York	London
NY 10018	WC1B 3DP
USA	UK

www.bloomsbury.com

BLOOMSBURY and the Diana logo are trademarks of Bloomsbury Publishing Plc

First published 2018

© Kaethe Schwehn, 2018

ISBN: HB: 978-1-63286-972-2
       TPB: 978-1-63557-194-3
       ePub: 978-1-63286-974-6

LIBRARY OF CONGRESS CATALOGING-IN-PUBLICATION DATA

Names: Schwehn, Kaethe, author.
Title: The rending and the nest : a novel / Kaethe Schwehn.
Description: New York : Bloomsbury, 2018.
Identifiers: LCCN 2017012311 | ISBN 9781632869722 (hardcover) |
ISBN 9781635571943 (softcover) | ISBN 9781632869746 (e-book)
Classification: LCC PS3619.C4926 R46 2018 | DDC 813/.6—dc23 LC record
available at https://lccn.loc.gov/2017012311

2 4 6 8 10 9 7 5 3 1

Typeset by Westchester Publishing Services
Printed and bound in the U.S.A. by Berryville Graphics Inc., Berryville, Virginia

To find out more about our authors and books visit www.bloomsbury.com.
Here you will find extracts, author interviews, details of forthcoming events, and
the option to sign up for our newsletters.

Bloomsbury books may be purchased for business or promotional use.
For information on bulk purchases please contact Macmillan Corporate and
Premium Sales Department at specialmarkets@macmillan.com.

for Peder
and
for Anjuli

in memory of
George Thorkelson and Graham Thorkelson

Now hope that is seen is not hope. For who hopes for what
is seen?

—Romans 8:24

I gave my love a cherry that had no stone
I gave my love a chicken that had no bone
I gave my love a baby with no crying
I gave my love a story that had no end
How can there be a cherry that has no stone?
How can there be a chicken that has no bone?
How can there be a baby with no crying?
How can there be a story that has no end?

—"The Riddle Song"

There is a gold light in certain old paintings
That represents a diffusion of sunlight.
It is like happiness, when we are happy.
It comes from everywhere and nowhere at once, this light,
 And the poor soldiers sprawled at the foot of the cross
 Share in its charity equally with the cross.

—Donald Justice, "There Is a Gold Light
in Certain Old Paintings"

THE RENDING
AND THE NEST

THE MOST DANGEROUS thing of all is the absence of a story, a narrative to explain what is happening to you. A why with no edges. Because someone will always arrive to invent one. Then you will be at the whim of someone else's story, you will be swept into a current that is not of your own making.

It wasn't fire or ice. Wasn't a virus or global warming or a meteor. Wasn't an atomic bomb or a tsunami or a sulfurous-smelling ape. It was a Rending, a split. Ninety-five percent of the earth's population and the vast majority of the animals, food, and goods—gone. We were left with each other and the Piles. Later, the Babies. And we were left without an explanation.

PART ONE

CHAPTER ONE

I T WASN'T A surprise, exactly, that Lana got pregnant first. In fact, it was something of a surprise that it took three years for anyone in Zion to show the signs. In all our searching and scavenging, we'd discovered very few condoms and those had been used quickly. On the day Lana told me she was pregnant, after her quick and fairly ambivalent declaration, she followed me out to the Piles. She mumbled something about needing to release negative energy.

I wore a pair of white Keds for scavenging, the sole thick enough to give me cursory protection from exposed edges and thin enough to squeeze into narrow gaps between the objects. Lana stood at the base of the Pile while I worked, her arms wrapped around her gray Dodgers sweatshirt, kicking, half-heartedly, at a hard-sided suitcase with one of her mustard-colored flats.

"Fuck," she said. "Fuck. Fuck. Fuck." The suitcase made little echo-grunt sounds in return.

I was ten feet above her, trying to free a piece of PVC pipe from between a child's scooter, a lawn mower handle, and a faux-distressed wood sign with an inspirational saying. I assumed it was inspirational. All I could read was TIME IS A ROAD THAT. Asher, the closest thing Zion had to a plumber, had asked me to be on the lookout for pipe or things that could be used as pipe, since our water catchment system was leaking.

"Mira, are you even listening?" said Lana.

"Yes." I was lifting the sign with my right hand while trying to make sure that the strain of pulling the PVC out of its hiding place didn't upset my center of balance. "You were saying something about fuck."

"Not funny," she said. She started to pull the suitcase from its position.

"Lana, don't mess with that, please."

"It's not your Pile, Mira. The Pile does not belong to you."

"I know. But I'd rather not have the Pile start sliding. It's a balancing act."

"Yes, I know, a gigantic Jenga game," she said, putting her hands on her hips and nodding her head forcefully as, apparently, I did when I described the Piles as a gigantic Jenga game.

"Here, put this in the buggy," I said, tossing the PVC pipe toward her.

"It's really more of a *perambulator* than a buggy," she said. "Something out of *Peter Pan*. Remember *Peter Pan*?"

"Yep," I said. To my right, a length of some kind of flexible tubing dripped flaccidly out of the mouth of a ceramic cookie jar. I inched my hand toward it.

"I always wanted to be Tinkerbell," she said. "I suppose every girl wanted to be Tinkerbell."

"I wanted to be Wendy," I said. "Oh, fuck me!"

"Are you OK?" asked Lana, cupping her hand over her eyes to shield them from the sun. As if there was a sun.

I took my hand out of the jar so she could see the blood running down my palm. "It's nothing. My own fault. I should have looked." I wiped the blood on my shirt as best I could and climbed higher so I could see the jar from above. "Knife," I said, pulling the blade from the jar and dangling it between my thumb and index finger.

"Come down," she said. I did, the handle of the knife clenched in my mouth, enjoying the way the fibers of the wood gave in slightly to the pressure of my teeth. She took it from me and studied the handle. "It looks hand carved."

Two years ago one of us would have wondered aloud who the knife had belonged to, who had carved the undulating sea serpents, the tiny crests of wave. I would have guessed salty fisherman and she would have guessed CEO taking a "whittling as meditation" class. We didn't spend the energy wondering anymore.

"At least the blade's not rusty," Lana said. I sat down next to her and she dabbed at my injured hand with the corner of her sweatshirt. "Rodney will be glad to see it. You gonna deliver it personally?" She nudged me suggestively. I ignored her.

She stopped dabbing and sighed. "Mira, what am I going to do with a baby? What if I die giving birth to a motherfucking baby?"

"You're not going to die," I said, though the thought had crossed my mind.

"Do you think Ida and Sylvia could get rid of it?"

"*Would* they get rid of it if they could?"

"Fuck," she said. This time her voice was clogged with sadness. I rubbed some slow circles into her upper back with my uninjured palm. She bent over to let me rub lower, her head with its twelve neatly coiled knobs of hair almost touching the earth. Even as I touched her back, felt in myself the fringes of her grief and fear, I was jealous of the way her body could bend so effortlessly, a svelte Gumby doll. The tiniest shard of me smiled in anticipation of the way she'd have to learn to carry more weight than she desired, glad she'd need to alter the way her body moved, to adjust to its new boundaries.

"Do you know whose it is?"

She shook her head, then named a few of the men, her regular clients, the words muffled slightly by the ground below her.

For the rest of the afternoon she lingered at the bottom of the Pile, occasionally easing herself into Downward Dog or Warrior Two, sometimes watching me, calling out objects she wasn't sure I could see. As the sky sullied from gray into darker gray she began singing "Hush Little Baby," trying on different accents, though they sounded imperfect, distant, strange. Had there been an England, an Ireland, an India? Then she replaced the objects in the song with ones she could see in the fissures of the Pile. "Mama's going to buy you a window screen, a ceiling tile, a crap shoe rack." From the top of the Pile, forty feet above her, I studied her splayed legs, the knobs of hair on her scalp, the skirt blooming around her. I closed my eyes and her wavery voice came to me. Accents and silly words forgotten, she was trying on nostalgia and intimacy, fear rubbing against a sliver of hope.

When the buggy and my backpack were full we walked the objects over to the area behind the Clinic, where Rodney and Asher were attempting to install a cistern that would direct water to a sink in the examination room. Rodney had the cistern (actually a stainless-steel garbage can) tipped back against his body, holding it so that Asher could attempt to work the end of a vacuum cleaner hose into the hole he'd cut at the base of the can. Behind them, through the pane-less window of the clinic, I could see the curve of a man's head and Sylvia's profile, bent to study something along his hairline. Rodney tipped the can back down when he saw us and rested his arms across the top. In the gloaming the inked branch along his jaw was barely visible so it was simply the outline of his form—breadth of shoulders, hulking height—that struck my chest like a soft mallet and would, continually, until I walked away from him.

"What'd you find? Anything good?"

Lana bumped my shoulder. "Something in here should work," I mumbled.

Asher sauntered over, lifting his hat to run his fingers through his curly red hair. He chose a couple items from the buggy, the PVC pipe and the flexible tubing from the cookie jar. "Thanks, Mir," he said, kissing me on the cheek. Asher had changed the least in appearance since the Rending. He still wore the same pair of khaki pants he had on the day I met him, though now they were considerably frayed along the bottom and patched at the crotch with a candy-cane print fabric. The baseball hat was the same, too. Minnesota Twins. The white inside band had darkened to gray and stalagmites of salt reached up the contours of the middle. He basically looked like an older, impoverished version of his former preppy self. Of all the men in Zion, he was the most openly flirtatious with me, but he was also gay, so it was an easy relationship for both of us.

"Anything else?" I asked. "If not we'll take the rest to the Sorting Stations."

"I think we're good," said Asher.

"We're good," said Rodney, looking directly at me, his stare carrying far more weight than his words. I had to turn quickly, the blush creeping up my neck.

"For tomorrow?" I plucked the pen from the coil of the small spiral notebook that hung around my neck.

Asher shrugged. "More of the same."

"Maybe one of those recliners. The kind that give you a massage," said Rodney.

"Yeah, and maybe a couple beers," added Asher.

"Maybe a keg."

"Maybe the two thousand nine NFC championship game on a flat-screen TV."

"Maybe just Brett Favre."

"Yeah, Mira, maybe just find Favre so we can talk to him about why he threw the ball directly into Porter's hands."

From inside the Clinic, the edge of Sylvia's voice interrupted the banter: "This window has no glass, you know."

Lana made a tsk-tsk sound. In the frame of the window, the wide moon of Ida's face appeared.

"Visitor?" I whispered.

Ida nodded before rolling her eyes at us and draping a curtain over the empty hole. As though bunnies parading across flannel would protect the visitor from our commentary. But in the split second before the curtain closed, the visitor turned his head toward us and I saw his eyes. They looked shallow. Dead. The scrubbed bottom of a cast-iron pan.

I grabbed the handles of the buggy.

"And . . ." prompted Lana, clearing her throat and plucking at the front pouch of the backpack where I'd stashed the knife.

"Oh," I said. I turned so that the backpack was facing Rodney and then backed up until the front pouch was right in front of him. "Here."

He slid the zipper open. "Thanks," he said. "I'll put it—"

I turned and nodded severely in the direction of the flannel curtain.

"I'll put it where it belongs," he finished.

"And I'll push," said Lana, taking the buggy handle from me. "It's good practice."

"Ha."

"Ha."

*

At the Sorting Station we placed the remaining objects in the appropriate areas: household, construction, apparel, et cetera. I left the buggy there and we headed over to my room so I could change out of my gathering shirt and into something with less odor worked into the fibers below the arms. While I changed, Lana bent from the waist and swayed side to side, letting the backs of her knuckles sweep the floor.

"How long do you think it will be until I can't bend over anymore?"

I shrugged. Realized she couldn't see the shrug. "Who knows. How far along do you think you are?"

"Three months. Maybe four. My periods aren't very regular."

"You have to let Ida and Sylvia check you out."

"I know."

"Tomorrow."

"Soon."

She stood, face flushed with blood. "You're getting buff, Mir."

"You're changing the subject."

"You are."

I rarely got to see the entirety of my body anymore. Lana had a mirror in her room, one of the few in Zion. There was another in the Center and a third in the Clinic. Lana's claim was that she needed it to correct her yoga poses but I knew she also used it when she entertained, knew that men liked to watch themselves enter her, the smoothness of her back before them, her face reflecting the fervor of theirs. One man liked to drape a paisley scarf over her back, to set a portrait of his wife in a tiny frame on top. To enter and exit her body slowly enough that the portrait of his wife didn't tip, remained steady and smiling. She wouldn't say who. She was generous with details but always circumspect about identity. I admired this about her.

I didn't have a mirror and most of the time dressed quickly, not paying attention to my body, thinking about the Piles, committing to memory the location of a set of bedsprings or a lampshade or a sheet of corrugated tin. Part of my job was knowing where things were located so that when a need arose, I could fetch what was necessary. I carried that inventory of objects in my head, saw them the same way

I carried Rodney's body, what I'd seen of Rodney's body: back of the neck, swell of the biceps, curve of the calf.

But Lana was right; I wasn't buff exactly, but my body had changed since the Rending, narrowed by the scarcity of the first few years and then tightened by climbing the Piles. My thighs and breasts were still "womanly" (as a friend of my father's had said once after two rather stiff Manhattans), but the flesh around my bones didn't ripple when I moved. It stayed steady, fixed by muscle to my frame. Ironically, I would have killed for this version of my body when I was seventeen. GOD MADE YOU PERFECT, ONE OF A KIND! said a poster in the youth-group room of my father's church. My church too, I guess. The words were in black script over a sloping green hillside speckled with lavender. A blue sky brushed easily overhead. Back when a blue sky was an easy thing, something that appeared overhead eventually, if you waited long enough.

I hated the poster. I was a junior in high school and the only reason I agreed to the weekly youth meetings was because of the new youth minister who wore Chaco sandals and Carhartts rolled up to reveal his muscled calves. He often asked me to turn the pages of the sheet music while he strummed his guitar. I couldn't bring myself to look at him—we were too close—so I'd stare at his ankles and calves; the brown hairs curling there looked so old and masculine. His breath smelled faintly of coffee and he picked songs that only skirted the edges of Jesus: U2 or Mumford and Sons. His name was Tony. Or Tory. Or Toby. I can't remember. Only Tony/Tory/Toby's abrupt disappearance from youth group and his disappointing replacement (a man named Kurt, who was bald and insisted that we start each gathering by talking about the high point and low point of our week).

The week Tony/Tory/Toby left I went to my first high school party with my friend Kat. She handed me a red plastic cup, whispered "jungle juice" like a secret password, and promptly settled herself in a La-Z-Boy recliner with a boy named Zach who wanted to show her a meme of cats playing pianos on his iPhone. I didn't know anyone else very well so I tried to look haughty and cool instead of pathetic and lonely. The party wasn't nearly as full or busy as I'd anticipated. I'd imagined bodies pressed to bodies inside a sauna of pot smoke and cheap perfume. Instead it was mostly just people hanging out, their actions made dumber and louder by the alcohol. A few guys from my Spanish class were watching a football game, throwing pretzels at the screen when a player made a particularly dumbass move. In the kitchen, a guy and girl stood over a cookie sheet lined with rows of Dixie cups. They were trying to figure out the best way to get the Jell-O out of the cups but from a distance they looked more like they were collaborating on a science lab.

"Oh my God is that a DICK?!" Kat suddenly shrieked and everyone turned and laughed and she slapped a hand over her mouth and burrowed her head in feigned embarrassment in Zach's shoulder.

"Can I bum a cigarette?" I asked her. She handed me one and a lighter with She-Ra on it without taking her eyes off Zach's phone, where apparently the dicks were growing bigger by the second. Likely, Zach's was too.

Out on the back patio I lit the cigarette, took a drag, and tried not to cough. Beer bottles sprouted like a field of beheaded daisies from the cement. At a table, one guy stared up at the underside of the patio umbrella while the other held up the paw of a tabby cat, making it wave at a girl who was busy not looking at either of them, lost behind a curtain of hair. I couldn't see her face but I could see her hands, spinning a blue lighter in circles on the table. The guy with the cat finally noticed me. He turned the cat toward me and directed the wave at me. "Hey pretty lady," he said.

"Hey," I said, avoiding eye contact and blowing out a thin stream of smoke. The one who'd been staring at the umbrella stood up from his chair and walked over to me. Curtsied, holding out an invisible skirt.

"You're supposed to bow, fag," said the guy holding the cat. The curtsying guy took my hand, kissed it, and looked up at me. The ring through the middle of his nose made him look like an emaciated ox; I suddenly longed for the boys throwing the pretzels at the television screen.

Then the guy with the cat stood. "Want a little pussy?" His walk toward me was almost graceful in its awkwardness, as though he were performing a dance about a prima ballerina who goes suddenly lame. It wasn't until he was a few feet away from me that I realized the cat was dead. He held it by the scruff of its orange neck; its lower legs splayed out and a few pink nubs dotted its sagging belly. There were no noticeable gashes or broken bones, its eyes hadn't been plucked out or invaded by curious ants—and the body wasn't stiff.

"Pet it," he said.

The girl at the table did not look up. She picked up the blackened spoon beside the lighter and raised it almost all the way to her lips before she realized it wasn't a cigarette.

"Pet it," he said again. I reached out and gently stroked the cat between the eyes. In my memory, the body feels warm, though I couldn't have known that from those two seconds of contact.

"See? You think it's a good kitty, don't you?"

The boy with the nose ring took the tail of the cat and ran it along his own cheek. "Soft."

"But then . . ." And at this point the boy holding the cat switched his grip, grabbing it around the throat with one hand and using the other to peel back the upper edges of its lips. The upper canines were clean and white. "Bad kitty!" He thrust the cat at my face. I took a step backward and they both laughed. At the table, the girl laid her head in her arms.

I took a shaky drag of my cigarette in an attempt to regain my composure and realized my smoke was almost gone. Unfortunately the boy realized too. "Show her the perfect ashtray," he said to the other boy, who dutifully tugged out the cat's tongue. It was pink except for the places they'd already smudged with ash. "At your service," said the nose ring boy.

Nothing my parents had talked about had prepared me for how to deal with this. The question of whether to deface the body of a dead cat in order to get away from potential rapists had never come up at dinner. Music from the party pushed through the screen door, its own heartbeat. No one was going to come. I wasn't even certain I was in danger. Wasn't sure whether the threat of these boys was real or I was a goody-goody, overreacting.

I said a little prayer for the cat and pressed my lit cigarette against its tongue. I closed my eyes at the moment of contact but I heard the sound, that small dying fizz. "Nice," said one of them. I turned and went inside.

My prayer for the cat, which went something like, "Dear God please forgive me for hurting this dead cat," was the last prayer I said.

The next morning, at church, I passed the offering plate, its smooth felt bottom like a little putting green. I watched a pink polka-dotted dress ride up the belly of a toddler as she squirmed in her mother's arms, noted the short, feathered haircuts of the women and the neatly tucked shirts of the men; I mouthed the hymns, each verse returning to the same melody with slight alterations in content, words like *risen* and *faithfulness* and *grace* on my lips without any breath behind them. And the distance—between this world and the one I'd been in the night before—it was so far that I had to put my head between my knees. That my father was the one wearing the alb made me feel doubly remote from him.

As a pastor's kid, religion had always been a singular, predictable landscape, the backdrop wherever we traveled. But that day the landscape felt constructed; the rituals and liturgy and readings felt like flimsy set pieces meant to make suburban parents feel right about their lives.

My father preached that Sunday on the text where Jesus walks across the water, saves a drowning Peter. Half that story spoke to me. I was Peter, the water clogging my throat, wind breaking the sky. But the previous night there had been no hand that I could see, reaching down from above, no grip on my forearm raising me up, showing me how to float above it all to some enclave of safety. For the first time in my life, God felt distant, unreachable.

Three weeks later came the Rending, and along with it the departure of my belief in God altogether. Before the Rending I lived in a world of unconditional love: God's love, my parents' love. "No matter what!" my mom would say. "Even to the end of the world!" my dad would add.

But here I was at the end of the world and that promised unconditional, abundant love did not prop me up, did not cover me at night with feathered, metaphorical wings.

The first thing we did when we started Zion was to create the Rules. The Rules were the only Gospel I lived by now.

I hung my scavenging shirt on a nail and slipped on a pale pink sweatshirt with rhinestones bedazzled around the collar and the cuffs. I was almost certain that everyone knew I wore the sweatshirt ironically (and practically, because the fabric was warm), but I always felt a little vulnerable in it. Like other Zionites were making snide remarks about it over their lukewarm tea in the Center. As if anyone cared anymore. That I even thought about that kind of thing now, three years after the Rending, twenty years old, embarrassed me further. On the floor, Lana rocked on her back, holding her feet in the air above her in the Happy Baby yoga pose. The tulle of her skirt fell over her chest, revealing her Superman underwear. Her lucky underwear that she only wore on days she didn't see clients.

"What if I don't have a happy baby?"

"Look around, Lana. There are no babies. Cal is the closest thing we have in Zion to a baby and he's now seventeen. Everyone will go gaga over it."

"What if it doesn't like me?"

"Babies are genetically programmed to like their mothers."

Her feet made two muffled thumps as she released them to the floor. "What if I don't want to be a mother, Mira? I'm supposed to have my own mother, here, to tell me how to do this. People are supposed to give me bibs and pacifiers. There's supposed to be a class where they give me a baby doll and I learn how to hold it and feed it. I'm supposed to have a charming husband who feeds me ice chips and reminds me how to breathe. And it's all supposed to be on purpose."

I lay down on my back on the floor next to her. Took her hand. Tears slid from the corners of her eyes.

"Why isn't anything on purpose anymore, Mira?"

"I don't know."

When I was thirteen, my mother and brother and I had to go with my father on a hospital visit. We'd been at a waterslide park. I loved swaying side to side down the chutes, the shriek of the child behind threatening, at every turn, to catch me. Then my father got a text. Two of his elderly parishioners had been in a car accident, then rushed to a hospital midway between the water park and our home. So my parents wrapped us in beach towels and scuttled us to the station wagon. My father disappeared into the hospital in flip-flops and swim trunks and a CROP Hunger Walk shirt. We sat in the car, windows rolled down, my mother trying to assiduously dole out the remaining snacks in the cooler: string cheese, graham crackers, juice boxes, fruit snacks. After an hour she took us inside, to the waiting room. Deposited us in chairs near a Lego table made for four-year-olds and told us not to move, not to bother our father. He was on the other side of the waiting room, beside a woman who wore glasses on a chain around her neck and whose flesh bubbled over the top of her compression socks. While my mother thumbed through a *Redbook* and six-year-old Bim divided the Legos by color, I watched my father. How he held the hand of the woman but didn't say much. Just nodded. Nodded and nodded. He opened his mouth to say things occasionally, though I couldn't hear exactly what. It was the same look he gave us when we hurt ourselves, when he told us to look him in the eye, not at the wound, his hands masterfully peeling the wrapper off bandages or unscrewing ointment bottles without unhinging his gaze from ours.

I squeezed Lana's hand. Lay beside her as quietly as I could.

Hours passed. Likely only minutes but it felt like hours, because I was not as patient as my father, not as comfortable with silence.

"Since you don't know who the father is, maybe you could just give birth, name the baby something horrible, and give it to your least favorite former client."

Lana made a wet, snorting sound. "Here is baby Heimlich."

"Here is baby Guttersnut."

"Here is baby Grendel."

"Let's ask Chester," I said, pulling her to her feet.

I shared my walls with Chester (to the right) and Asher (to the left). Asher and Rodney and Tenzin had designed the living quarters two and a half years earlier when we needed something fast. We expected we'd expand and remodel—but those were words from the Before, words that assumed that you existed in a world where basic necessities were taken care of, in a place where you didn't have to use vacuum hoses and garbage cans to provide water for a clinic or roam spiderlike over Piles of objects in order to find something to patch a roof or bandage an arm. The rooms were like a scrawny version of the townhomes or row houses of the Before. A long rectangle divided width-wise into rooms, each with a door and window at one end that faced the Center and a fireplace at the back. Ten feet by fourteen feet. Asher wasn't religious but he decided after the Rending that even numbers were best.

Separating Chester from the rest of the world was a beaded curtain he'd fashioned out of junky necklaces from the apparel Sorting Station that no one else wanted. I often told him it made it look like he was a cheap hooker, though not when Lana was around. Chester claimed the necklaces would be gorgeous in the sunlight. All those beads acting as prisms. "There will be rainbows everywhere," he'd say, gesturing around his rather barren space, "as soon as we get some sun." This was Chester in a nutshell: 70 percent sarcasm and 30 percent wisdom. His portent of rainbows was both cheesy and ridiculous (we hadn't had direct sunlight for three years) but the image, flecks of rainbow stippling the walls, the imperfect remains of beauty, this was appealing; there was something true and possible in that image. Chester, on rare occasions, offered the closest moments to hope I'd had since the Rending.

The click of the flimsy beads announced our arrival.

"Lana's pregnant. We need awful baby names," I said by way of introduction.

Chester nodded, as though he'd been expecting all of this—our arrival, the pregnancy, my request. His blue eyes bulged slightly from his skull below an uneven bowl cut; even though some of the softness had gone from his cheeks in the past three years, he still looked boyish. He rose from the rocking chair where he'd been reading *Marriage in the Balkans* and turned to his bookshelf. Books were hard to come by in the Piles and we had yet to find literature of any sort. Anything medical in nature went to Sylvia and Ida, anything related to building or architecture to Asher. Anything mechanical to Tenzin or Rodney. Gardening to Marjorie and Sven. "Fun" reading went to the library in the Center. Chester got everything else.

He brought *The Danish Monarchy, Brewing Tea on Your Own Time*, and *Dogs Without Borders* over to the coffee table. We flayed the pages to find names for Lana's baby, calling them out as we held up the scraps, our voices buoyant as Santa calling his reindeer by name: Valdemar and Canute and Darjeeling and Bluetick! Basenji and Chow-Chow and Sencha and Earl Grey!

None of us knew then what the Baby would be. Our minds swung back and forth between genders; we imagined a being that would cry, shit, suckle. But when we grew tired from tearing and laughing and Lana fell asleep on Chester's rug and Chester went out for a walk, I collected the scraps, the names. I put them in a wallet with a fluorescent sunset on the side, ARIZONA spelled out in the rays of the falling sun.

CHAPTER TWO

I HADN'T YET FOUND an examination table in the Piles but I had found a massage table and this is what Lana stretched out upon for her first prenatal exam. Ida and Sylvia's Clinic was small but its own structure, apart from the Center and our rooms. Rodney and Asher and Tenzin had paid more attention to the infrastructure of the Clinic than the other buildings. Large windows in the exam room, lanterns for adequate light, attempts at plumbing that were still in progress. And many of my best finds went to the Clinic: a small pot-bellied stove, an industrial aluminum sink, a little IKEA table on wheels for the hodgepodge of instruments we'd managed to collect. On the other side of a floor-length curtain, the waiting room boasted three blue plastic stadium seats and a wicker rocker with an embroidered pillow (A GOLF PRO SITS HERE!). On a coffee table, *Popular Mechanics*, *Bathroom Interiors*, and *Model Train Enthusiast* were fanned out in an artful way that made it look like they'd never been moved. Behind the magazines, a ceramic sheep sprouted three fake daisies out of a hole in its back. The only comforting decorating choice was a rag rug, scraps in varying shades of yellow and orange, coiled tight as Sylvia's interior. I was staring at the rug and Lana was rubbing her thumb over the ceramic bumps of the sheep when Sylvia pulled back the curtain and said, "We're ready for you."

Lana rolled her eyes at me and stood. "And I am ready for you." She nodded her head demurely at Ida and Sylvia, while she held out the skirt of her Fourth of July–themed June Cleaver dress (navy, white polka dots, American flags on the lapel). Along the back of the dress, big silver safety pins coaxed the extra-large dress around her narrow frame.

Ida smiled and Sylvia opened the door of the stove and fed another log into the flames. I touched the small of Lana's back to guide her to the table.

*

The small of the back. The place on a human where a rudder should be. Or a tail. A point on the body that requires little pressure but moves the whole being forward and ahead. I'd seen men at church do it mostly, guiding their wives into a pew or through an open door. A couple my parents knew were walking hand in hand along a sidewalk when a car jumped the curb, killing the husband but leaving the wife perfectly unscathed. You can hold hands and still be two arm-lengths apart from a person. But the middle of the lower back, that point requires closeness, suggests intimacy, familiarity. It was the first place Rodney touched me: his hand, my back, only an hour after the Rending.

I'd woken alone, on the floor of H&M, tucked between rows of cheap jewelry. The displays looked picked over, as though a massive horde of zirconium-hungry locusts had passed through while I took a nap on the tile floor. I reached up and touched a pair of earrings hanging slightly above my head and to the right. Huge gold hoops strung with enough baubles to drag a person's ears to the floor. *Do your ears hang low? Do they wobble to and fro?* I giggled. I was like a gigantic baby pawing at a dysfunctional mobile.

These were the few observations I managed before a face appeared over my face, a drop of sweat from that face falling directly onto my chin.

"Get up," said the face. The face was bristly.

It suddenly seemed strange that I wasn't standing. Why wasn't I standing? The face belonged to a man in a navy security uniform, walkie-talkie clipped to a pocket over which a gold badge read DOUG. I took his hand and stood. From my upright position I noted that the rest of the store looked like it had suffered a plague as well. Nothing was overturned. Nothing rumpled or broken. A turquoise blouse peppered with white elephants lay folded neatly on a display table next to me. In a mirrored alcove across the mostly empty room a single trench coat swayed in front of its own reflection, belt still neatly cinched. Everything else had vanished. There were no clerks behind the registers. There were no registers. No socked feet twisting and pirouetting below the changing room doors. No shhhhhtk shhhhhtk of hangers sliding over metal bars.

I patted the pockets of my cargo pants reflexively as though maybe I had taken something. I had twenty dollars and a Burt's Bees sparkling lip shimmer in one pocket. In my right hand I held the necklace I'd been admiring just before I decided to take a nap on the floor.

"Something's happened," said Doug.

"OK," I said.

"Come with me," he said.

"OK," I said.

Doug seemed to be in the know about something I had yet to grasp. A lone gunman or a terrorist attack. I couldn't quite put the pieces together. Each thought had to be pressed through my brain like Play-Doh in Bim's spaghetti maker.

Bim.

"I need to find my brother," I said. I don't remember being worried. I remember thinking my mother would be very angry with me. I imagined her in the food court, turning her thin silver watch around and around on her wrist.

Doug nodded. "Description?" I rattled off a strange, abstract description of Bim that Doug repeated phrase by phrase into his walkie-talkie. When he released the button, static crackled back at us.

"We'll find him," said Doug. He grabbed me by the upper arm and we began our procession around the mall. One store after another. Emptiness after emptiness. In Ann Taylor he took a pen with a daisy at the tip and stuck it behind my ear. "Puuuurrty," he said, winking. His lips were big and red, almost purple; I was afraid they would burst, that whatever was inside his lips would get on me and I'd never get it off again. As we passed Bath and Body Works he yelled, "Get down!" I dropped to my belly and he lay on top of me, his growing erection pressing against my thigh. From Doc Popcorn he took a handful of caramel corn, made me eat it from his hand. "Sustenance," he said and I could tell he was proud of the word. The caramel corn carried traces of whatever he'd been eating before, Funyuns or Fritos.

And then there was Lana, or the back of her knobbed head. The two points where her shoulder blades pierced the film of her blue blouse. Elbows making flesh-colored punctuation marks in the air as she worked the espresso machine at Chilly Italy, a gelato stand outside Macy's. Beside the café, generators moved a set of escalators up and up toward the amusement park at the center of the mall, where faux foliage framed roller coasters clicking around curlicue tracks. Earlier that day I'd plucked cotton candy off a paper cone while Bim rode the Infinity Coaster. "I guess that's a sexy way of saying figure eight," I had said to him and he was gone. Not Gone gone, just gone in the way people left before the Rending, when we assumed invisible strings, when we thought we could wind anyone right back to us.

Yes, there was Lana puttering at the espresso machine and Rodney sitting at a little table on a patch of faux marble tile in front of the long row of gelato coolers. I guess the table wasn't little; Rodney's frame was simply big. But in my memory it's as if he had been sitting at a toddler's play table. His face was in profile so I didn't see the branch tattooed across the right side of his jaw, thicker near the ear and tapering to a fragile twig near the corner of his mouth, three tiny buds at its tip, clustered near his bottom lip as though he were about to be fed.

It was only when I saw them, when Lana turned and wiggled her fingers, when Rodney offered a half-smile, that the enormity of the wrongness of the situation began to appear at the edges of my consciousness. I couldn't face it yet, but I knew something terrible had happened and I knew that the man holding my arm was not a good man. Later Rodney would tell me there had been mascara tracks down my cheeks. I don't remember crying, but when I saw Lana and Rodney I started to shake. My insides parched, scabbed, everything green scythed down to nubs. I rattled. I quaked.

And Rodney stood and walked to us. He looked at me. While he unclenched Doug's hand from my arm, while he straightened my scarf, while he took my hand gently. He looked at me. Like my father's gaze when I was wounded but he didn't want me to feel the pain of the injury.

Doug didn't resist. He turned and whispered something into his walkie-talkie and walked away. As though he hadn't spent the last hour forcibly carting me around the mall, occasionally using my hand to wipe the sweat from his forehead.

Doug was gone and there was only the warmth of Rodney's hand on my lower back, guiding me to the chair where he'd been sitting. And Lana, setting a cappuccino in front of me, cinnamon dusted across the top. My very first cappuccino. And, of course, my last.

On the edge of the exam table, Lana swung her legs as though she were sitting on a dock, the water spitting shards of sunlight into her eyes, fish swarming and darting below the balls of her feet.

"Lie back, sweet pea," said Ida.

"Ouch," said Lana.

Sylvia looked vaguely concerned.

"It's the pins. Digging into my back."

"Oh," said Sylvia. "You'll have to take your dress off so I can palpate your stomach. Your uterus."

Ida and I undid the pins. Lana stood up, pulled her arms through the holes, let the whole thing fall, a drop cloth used to hide the statue beneath. No bra or underwear. She was more like a column than a woman: tall, thin, pale, small breasts, large nipples, hips barely interrupting the line between ribs and thighs. Her pubic hair was neat, the clipped yard of a house trying to keep in step with the rest of the neighborhood. Her nakedness was sudden and therefore strange, though I'd seen Lana naked before. It was too much for a prenatal exam; removing her dress had made her overly vulnerable.

"OK," said Sylvia, always articulate, "OK."

"That will certainly give us the access we need, sweet pea," said Ida, coaxing her back onto the table, covering her breasts with a knit blanket, its spaces wide enough for her nipples to poke through.

"Should I be here?" I asked, suddenly. I felt a blue flame of panic between my lowest ribs. This happened occasionally, a flash of how absurd we were, how ill prepared for anything, really. Most of the time I puttered along, spidering over the Piles, trying to keep the usual kinds of longing and worry at bay. And then suddenly I would have a second of deep clarity, I would see us the way we actually were, Ida and Sylvia like two children still playing at doctor: Sylvia rolling back the sleeves of her XXL pastel green men's sport coat to wash her hands and Ida pressing her fingers to the inside of Lana's wrist as if she'd have any idea what to do if the pulse she found there was actually irregular. A counter with scissors and thread, scalpel and rags, a box of Hello Kitty bandages, a bowl with clean water and a bowl with soapy water. The window holding a rectangle of tired grass and the outlines of the Sorting Stations. The aluminum sink on the ground, tipped like a paralyzed man, the hole in the wall from which water would theoretically spill. And Lana, the pretend patient: white, goose-bumped legs, mound of pubic hair, baby blanket stretched over her midsection.

Ida began to whistle "What a Wonderful World." The flame between my ribs rose higher. I tried to blow it out slowly, between my lips. A thin stream. We practiced this the one time I'd gone to Lana's yoga class.

"Yes," Lana said, grabbing my hand. Though by now I'd forgotten the question. "This is happening, Mira," she said. Then she turned to Sylvia. "Let the palpating begin."

The exam consisted mostly of Ida wiping Lana's midsection with a washcloth and then Sylvia kneading around like a cat until she found, a little above the pubic bone, the place where she thought Lana's uterus ended.

"Measuring tape," she said, holding the place on Lana's belly with two fingers on her right hand and hanging her left into the air, a perfect replica of every medical show ever invented.

"Tape," said Ida, playing along. Only the measuring tape wasn't the long flimsy kind you'd use for fabric or for circumnavigating your ribs to check for cup size. It was the kind used for carpentry, the kind that curls like a snail inside a metal square and goes snapping and sizzling back to its home when a job is complete. Sylvia looked ridiculous trying to unspool it from its shell and then trying to lay the flat plane across Lana's (only slightly) rounded belly. The flame of panic rose again.

Lana squeezed my hand and rolled her eyes. "This is happening," she mouthed.

"Eighteen centimeters" proclaimed Sylvia. Ida dutifully wrote the information down in a college blue book (I'd found a box the previous week and they'd decided to use the books for patient files). "That means you're about eighteen weeks along." Lana stared at her blankly. "There are forty weeks in a pregnancy, so you're probably a little over four months."

"Goodie," said Lana. "Can I get dressed now?" Sylvia nodded.

While Lana slipped back into her 1950s housewife attire, Sylvia asked her a few standard pregnancy questions. Date of last menstrual period (Lana shrugged), morning sickness (no), other symptoms (I have to pee all the time), any movement (no), any questions (no).

"We'll see you in another month," said Sylvia.

"I think you'll see me before then," said Lana.

"You know what I mean," said Sylvia.

"Sure," said Lana.

"Everything looks good," said Ida, cheerfully.

"Would you know if everything wasn't good?" asked Lana.

Sylvia's response was the sound of the curtain, pulling back over the rod, revealing an empty waiting room, no one hoping to be seen.

I don't know when Sylvia knew something was wrong, or Ida for that matter. I don't think it was that first visit, but maybe she had an inkling, something quivering below her own skin indicating the lack of what was quivering below Lana's. I did note the crease in her brow that quickly erased itself when Lana still reported no movement at twenty-two weeks and still none at twenty-six. Lana herself seemed unperturbed, partly because she was ambivalent about the baby and partly because she was twenty-one. When the Rending happened she was waiting to go to Yale on a dance scholarship. She'd been spending her last summer pirouetting and pas de bourrée-ing her way across her parents' basement, the mirrors and barre a gift from a foundation that provided for kids with nonterminal cancer. "Essentially, getting cancer as a ten-year-old was the best thing that could have happened to me," Lana had explained to me about a year ago, in her brushing-lint-off-a-pea-coat kind of way.

But the point is that she hadn't read books on pregnancy or labor, had no idea when the fetus should grow fingernails or nostrils, when it would begin to register light behind its closed lids or to hiccup against its cavern walls.

CHAPTER THREE

"COME HAVE A cup of tea with me before you go back to humping the Piles," said Lana as we left the Clinic.

"I don't know if I can put up with Talia right now," I said.

"Maybe she'll be taking a break. We can play Candy Land. I have to learn this kind of shit now, Mira. I'll even let you win. See how my mothering instincts are already coming through?"

Halfway across the quadrangle, off to the right, I could see Kristen talking to Chester outside of his room, her brown ponytail marking the air for emphasis. I tilted my head in the direction of Lana's room where a red bandana fluttered above her doorframe. "It looks like you have someone waiting for you anyway."

"Oh, he can wait. I think they like to wait, even though they whine about it. Plus, the longer they have to think about it before I arrive, the less I have to do after I arrive."

I didn't say anything. I'd slept with two boys before the Rending, one to spite my parents and one I really liked. I'd slept with one man since the Rending, early on; because the men in Zion outnumbered the women almost four to one it was easy, initially, for sex to become a form of currency. Those exchanges got old quickly, for the women at least, so we developed the Rules, decided to share resources, assigned communal tasks. But Lana insisted on offering her own body as her contribution to communal labor. The community tried to dissuade her publicly and I tried privately; she just shrugged and then baldly observed that if the men couldn't get sex here they'd leave, they'd go elsewhere in search of it. Plus, she noted wryly, it was unlikely that any of the women were going to willingly spread their legs for Oscar or Zephyr anytime soon.

We didn't talk about Lana's job all that often but when Lana did start to banter about sex I felt awkward and stodgy; I tried to fill in the gaps in conversation without revealing my limited knowledge. Luckily, Lana never really seemed to notice; her attention span was short enough that she was on to the next topic before the blush that began at the tops of my breasts could work its way to my neck and cheeks.

"Wasn't Marjorie talking at the last community meeting about doing little stones or fences or something?"

"What?"

"Here," said Lana, "in our glorious quadrangle!" She did a little hills-are-alive-with-the-sound-of-music spin, her Fourth of July dress turning briefly into a navy blur around her.

"Fences? That seems weird."

"Cobblestones could be cute though."

"If we had a bunch of cobblestones."

"Oh, you'd find something. Not cobblestones but something better."

"Lana, the water containment system is leaking, the roof over Tenzin's room is turning to shit, and about thirty community members still don't have enough stuffing for their beds."

"I know, I know. The List! I'm saying that with a capital 'L,' Mira, can you hear it in my voice? The List!" She grabbed the small black notebook that dangled against my chest, its neon shoelace strung through the spiral and knotted at the back of my neck. Then she bent her head and kissed it reverently.

"You're so funny," I said.

"People need beauty, too, Mira."

"I don't know if cobblestones qualify as beauty."

"You know what I mean."

I did know what she meant. The quadrangle was the open space at the center of Zion. The Clinic at one end faced the Center on the other, the length of a football field between them. Our rooms— barracks in form but shantytown in appearance—lined two sides of the quadrangle, thirty rooms on each side. A few couples shared a room, like Marjorie and Sven, and a few Zionites, like Rodney, had decided to construct their dwellings in other areas of the community.

The matted brown grass and weeds of the quadrangle were interrupted by packed paths, some darker and more worn than others, but all of them giving the space the appearance of a spiderweb gone wrong or a wheel with broken spokes. An uneven road encircled the buildings and the Sorting Stations. Beyond the road to the east lay the ghost fruit orchard, to the north the fields where we grew root vegetables, and to the west the river. Beyond the road to the south, about three quarters of a mile from where we stood, the Piles rose up, jumbles of color against the gray. On good days, I could manage to find hints of beauty or comfort in Zion—in the Formica of my favorite table in the Center or the juxtaposition of corrugated tin, shingle, and green awning that marked the top of the rooms where Asher, Chester, and I lived. The amiable puttering of the river was a comfort. Even the sensation of ghost fruit, crumpling to a sweet skin of nothing on my palm, was fascinating, at least. But I couldn't walk across the quadrangle without the word *desolation* pinging around in my head.

"Someday. Cobblestones. Definitely," I said. Lana linked her arm through mine. "Plus, your baby will need a job," I reminded her.

"True. Cobblestone installer."

"You could name him Cobblestone. Or her."

Lana nodded thoughtfully; her face moved from light to shadow as we entered the Center.

A small voice chirped across the darkness. "Name who what?"

"Talia," Lana sighed under her breath.

"Please don't name the baby Talia," I said.

"Never," said Lana.

Talia was the reason we had stopped walking. After the Rending, after Lana and Rodney and Chester and Ida and Sylvia and I found each other, after a brief stay in IKEA and a few weeks of scavenging what was left to be scavenged in the Cities, we had left, following the trail of abandoned cars down Highway 77. We crossed the Minnesota

River, spotted a single heron in the reeds and took it as a talisman, a sign. At night we slept in cars. Usually Ida and Sylvia in one, Lana and I in another, Chester and Rodney in a third. One night we slept in a greenhouse, chewing the leaves of mint, stuffing our pockets with the few remaining seed packets on a rotating stand. The next day we sounded like rattles as we walked, like we were being shaken by an invisible fist. Another night Ida and Sylvia stretched out in the back of a Volvo station wagon and Lana and Chester and Rodney and I curled up like puppies in the back of a minivan. Rodney had a bottle of whiskey and we were drinking—because we were seventeen and eighteen and twenty and didn't grasp that the end of this particular bottle was the end of alcohol altogether. Ida and Sylvia didn't drink so they went to bed early. After we'd downed half the bottle the four of us crept the fifty feet from our vehicle to theirs. We were going to play a prank, I think; we were tipsy and wanted to inflict something on someone. But when we reached the back window of the station wagon, we just stood and stared. This was before Sylvia and Ida changed, when they were still identical: brown shoulder-length hair, still shiny in spite of the days walking, with bangs cut straight across their matching foreheads. The both slept on their backs with a tartan blanket pulled up under their armpits, bare arms lying on top, as though preparing to give blood. The only difference between the two was Ida's half-smile, a softness around her mouth and eyes, and Sylvia's tight lips that changed quickly, abruptly, with an occasional twitch, then went back to a line so perfect that you wondered if they'd twitched at all.

"OK, that's creepy," Rodney whispered quietly.

"They're so strange," said Chester.

"They look like American Girl dolls," said Lana.

We turned then and went back to the van. Rodney was beside me that night, asleep as soon as we lay down in our nest of coats and blankets. I pretended to fall asleep too, but I couldn't sleep, not with his body that near. So I closed my eyes and dedicated myself to turning, every once in a while, in my supposed sleep so that I could curve my spine along his rib cage, test the fit of my head in his armpit. He turned, in the middle of the night, on his side, away from me, and then I brought my body against his, breasts to his back. He reached behind him, cupped the back of my thigh. We slept like that for a long time. It is easy to be brave with your body when you're not supposed to be in charge of it, when you can blame your unconscious for pushing you toward warmth or touch or breath. Not that I had to explain myself, not that I ever had to defend what my body wanted from Rodney's.

Most of the other survivors we met were walking toward the Cities, rather than away from them. It was the obvious choice. The lure of supplies, dwellings, companionship. But most of the supplies were gone. We'd walked the mall, then IKEA. We'd hiked to Kmart and Cub. Each store looked raided, purged—at first we thought other survivors had simply been faster, more aggressive—but the remaining objects were perfectly aligned, undisturbed. A bottle of Pert Plus and a box of razor blade refills sitting seven feet apart. Or all the Hallmark cards gone except for one, "Happy 5th Birthday to My Darling Grandson." Chester plucked the card from the rack and read the poem inside repeatedly that day. We collected an odd assortment of foods: a box of Lucky Charms, a mango, a mostly thawed bag of Ore-Ida hash browns. Some of the buildings and houses were damaged too—though again, not damaged in the way we had witnessed damage before the Rending—simply missing parts. Shutters, frames, and ivy missing from the right side of a Victorian mansion on Lake Harriet. Bricks stripped from a squat apartment complex in Bloomington so that the building looked naked, plucked. Rodney worried about internal absences; he knew enough about how a building was made to imagine the lack of support beams and joists. "A body without veins or nerves," was how he described it. "Or a body without bones. You don't want to be living in a body without bones." Ida and Sylvia nodded—they always did when Rodney spoke—and then Ida took Sylvia's hand and shuddered a little.

Even with the metaphor, I didn't understand enough about building construction to truly realize the danger of living in a house without bones, but I did hate the idea of living in the wispy remains of other people's lives. The people who had survived the Rending did not seem remarkable, special, or—oftentimes—sane.

We met Talia when we walked into a Zen Buddhist center with a gold-domed roof. The building was mostly empty. A few faded pillows, beige, bore the imprints of knees. The spice of incense lingered. A lone figure whirled up from kneeling as soon as we entered. She wore a black peasant skirt and a black shirt with embroidery that hung baggily across her chest. Her nose was pierced on both sides and she kept tucking her short, fine hair behind her ears as she talked. "I've been waiting for so long for someone to come and now here you are! Now here you are! I'm Talia."

"I'm Ida." Ida reached out her hand and Talia took it, rubbing her thumb over the knuckles.

"Look at your skin, Ida. It's soft. And you must be her twin." Talia took Sylvia's hand too. "The skin is the same." She raised each hand to her nose. "The smell of your skin is the same." She smiled brightly at both of them.

Lana was straightening a painting of a cloud-haloed mountain on the other side of the room. Rodney, head tilted back, studied the rafters. Chester lifted his own hand to his face and made a mock sniffing noise in my direction.

"It's very nice to meet you," said Sylvia stiffly. She'd pinned her bangs back that day and her high, white forehead made it look like she was wearing a headlamp.

"Would you like some something to eat?"

"Sure," said Chester.

Talia scurried away and came back with two Costco-size plastic jugs, one of raw almonds and one of wasabi peas. "This is all that was left. And some water. And a smidge of soy milk." She held her fingers a half inch apart. We all took a handful of the almonds. "I've eaten so many almonds. My tongue starts to tingle on the back when I eat too many but I have to eat a lot, to stay alive, so I've gotten used to the tingling. There were pears too. A crateful. We were getting ready for the Dharma talk, just laying out the food and then—Bam!—I was the only one laying out the food but there was no food. No food but this"— she gestured at the Costco jugs—"and the pears. The pears I ate pretty quickly—which was not the best for my digestion. By quickly I mean in a couple days, not like, an hour or something."

The sound of crunching filled the space. It was unclear whether Talia was always this chatty or whether being devoid of human companionship for three weeks had turned her a bit verbally manic. We ate more almonds. She continued.

"I don't know what I thought afterward. I thought maybe it was a joke? Did you think it was a joke? Or maybe a test? Anyway, I walked around a little outside." She gestured vaguely toward the windows with her hand. "And there was no one. I walked down the road to a gray Mazda and then I walked the other way to a Plymouth minivan. I sat in each for a while. I pressed all the buttons on the dash. Then I came back and ate more pears." She paused as if trying to conjure the taste of a pear. As if the experience were already years in the past.

"Thanks, Talia. The almonds were delicious." Rodney smiled at her, the branch moving slightly up his cheek.

Talia reached up. "I love this," she breathed.

Rodney tilted his head to the right to crack his neck and Talia pulled her hand away sharply. "We should go," he said.

Chester looked at his watch, sighed, and nodded as though we had a babysitter waiting. Lana and Ida and Sylvia mumbled thank-yous and followed Chester and Rodney. I was screwing the lid back on the almond container politely when Talia covered my hand with hers. In a quiet voice with none of her earlier squeaky modulations she said, "I have to tell you about the other thing that happened." She must have seen my eyes dart toward the others because she squeezed my knuckles and said, "Please."

"OK," I said.

"A man came here with a woman while I was out walking around. I heard their voices when I came back in and I was going to introduce myself when I heard her start to cry and scream. So I hid instead. Over there." She gestured toward a supply closet. "I hid in there for a full day and listened to what he did to her and I didn't do anything. Do you know what I thought about? I thought about how if he opened the door of the closet he would see me and he would do to me whatever he was doing to her and then when I peed myself I worried that he would smell me. And I pretended the noises she was making were other things: bird calls, a baby, an electrical saw, a little boy singing. Finally I fell asleep and when I woke up they were gone. I didn't help her and I didn't even let myself *hear* her. I need you to know the kind of person I am."

I took her hand between both of mine. "You were afraid. You didn't know what to do," I said. "None of us really knows what to do. We're doing the best we can."

"But I wasn't. I mean, I didn't do the best that I could have. It turns out that's the kind of person I am."

I thought of all the things my father might have said: that God keeps giving us opportunities to do the right thing; that we are all both sinners and saints; that courage takes practice.

Instead I said, "I'm glad you're coming with us," and led her out.

As soon as we emerged below the blowsy gray sky the sliver of vulnerability I'd seen disappeared and her wheedling crystal-vendor voice returned. "Is there a plan exactly? Do we know where we're going?"

"No. I'm Mira and I don't know where we're going," I said, trying on the cadence of an AA meeting.

Talia didn't catch on. "Well, no worries, Mira, because I'm Talia and I don't know where I'm going either! I used to have a bumper sticker on my Jeep. My Jeep that was right here, in fact," she said, gesturing at a parking place where a spot of motor oil still held its shape, "and the sticker said NOT ALL WHO WANDER ARE LOST. Maybe that would be a good thing to hold at the front of our thoughts as we walk."

Chester and Rodney and Lana were at least fifty feet down the road already. Lana looked over her shoulder and wiggled her fingers at me.

"I lead meditation here. I did. So if people want me to lead medi-tation as we walk, just say so. I'm also excellent at brewing tea. I can make a mean tea out of almost anything. Truly."

She was right about the tea and the meditation. These were the only two things Talia was really qualified to do. Well, three things: tea, guided meditation, and incessant talking.

We stopped walking because none of us could stand Talia anymore. Because we wanted to build a room and put her inside it and close the door.

Inside the Center, at a long rectangular folding table near the fire, the three current visitors were helping Talia with food prep. We were generally in charge of our own food preparation; or rather, if we wanted to eat our chosen root vegetable in some version other than Recently Untucked from the Coals of a Fire, we had to do it ourselves. But occasionally, in order to keep visitors occupied, we asked them to mash turnips as their contribution to community life. We didn't let the visitors use knives, however, so their efforts were often slow and pathetic.

The visitor with the cast-iron eyes I'd seen in the Clinic was peeling sweet potatoes with his fingernails, pulling down the skin in slow vertical motions like a cat at a post. He didn't look at the potato while he worked; his eyes flitted around the room, resting on me then Talia then Lana then Cal (reading a magazine on an inflatable pool float in the corner). Then he'd scan the objects in the room: the haphazard collection of tables and chairs, the huge bin full of vegetables, the three different pots raised just above the tendrils of the fire, the collection of ceramic mugs, the pile of burnable objects, the glass ashtray Massey, another visitor, was using to mash the potatoes, the cookie tins filled with spice bottles in front of the visitor beside him. I couldn't tell whether his spastic glancing was some kind of nervous tic or he was cataloguing, the way I did with the Piles, taking stock and making notes inside his squirming brain.

Massey stood on his right. He'd been in Zion six nights already so tonight would be his last. He looked like a man auditioning for the role of Navy SEAL in a movie: shorn blond hair, square face, muscled girth straining against a gray army sweatshirt. He'd come to Zion looking for his daughter.

"Wait, don't tell me," said Massey, setting down the ashtray. He pointed to me. "Myrna?"

"Mira," I said politely.

"Mira! Yes! And La—. La—"

"Lana," said Lana, turning away from his obvious wink and toward the bookshelf where we kept puzzles, games, and other sundry distractions.

"How're you ladies doin'?" He had the edge of a Texan accent but we couldn't tell whether it was real or affected.

"Fine," I said.

"Candy Land," said Lana, holding up the box before nudging me to the table farthest away.

"Well, don't let things get out of hand with those marshmallow houses or whatnot. Some of us got work to do over here."

I offered a half-hearted military salute in response.

"I know Massey. Who are the other two?" whispered Lana as we sat down.

"The short one with the spices came two days ago. He's got a mangled hand and hasn't spoken much; won't say his name. Ida calls him Starfish because that's what his hand looked like all splinted out. He seems harmless." I shrugged. We paused to watch Starfish cup a spice bottle to his side with his thickly bandaged hand so that his good hand could unscrew the lid. He was responsible for adding flavor to the mostly obliterated potatoes after Massey worked his magic with the ashtray.

"Is he using basil?" Lana made a face. Pulled up her legs so she was sitting cross-legged. *Spine a line to the clouds,* as she liked to say at yoga. "How about the other one? Who we saw in the Clinic with Sylvia?"

"Neither has tried to see you?" I asked, surprised. Lana refused to see visitors as clients. Too risky. But almost all of the male visitors seemed to intuit her chosen occupation, even before they noticed the red bandana that periodically waved from the hook beside her door. Even from across the room, I knew how different our bodies looked, hers lifted, statuesque, graceful, and mine compact and practical. She was a swan and I was a Geo Metro. She belonged on an urn; I belonged on a MISSING CHILD—TWENTY YEARS LATER poster, the computer-generated kind in which you can still see bits of the child pressing through the features but the adult version looks strange, never quite beautiful. This is what I thought every time I caught my own reflection in Lana's room, even as Lana tried to convince me of the appeal of the strafing of freckles across my nose or the way, no matter how I pulled my chestnut hair back, small wisps crept out and curled around the edges of my features. She said it looked angelic, but I didn't want anything to do with angels or their aesthetic representations.

"Massey came nosing around but not the other two. Your turn."

I moved my game piece down the colored path toward a gummy-looking cartoon girl clutching a fist full of lollipops.

"He came to my room. Stood outside. Showed me the picture of his daughter."

"Lexie," I supplied.

"Whatever. He showed it to me again. Said he was feeling sad. That it was hard not to have a loving woman's touch."

"He did not use the words 'loving woman's touch.'"

"He did! So I told him I'd heard there were a lot of children somewhere south of here. Near a large body of water."

"You didn't say that."

"I did." Lana drew a card and then moved her marker two pink spaces forward. "His eyes got kind of sparkly when I said it and I felt a little bad. But he's been looking for her for more than three years. It's what he's going to keep doing anyway. Why not throw him a little hope."

"False hope."

"Who cares anymore?"

"I do."

"Of course you do, my highly ethical friend," she said, reaching over and pinching one of my angelic cheeks, "but the real kind of hope isn't exactly forthcoming, is it?"

Her pinch was slightly harsher than it needed to be—though whether out of a personal sense of desperation or a desire to chastise me I wasn't sure. Her fingers smelled like the guava-coconut body lotion I'd found a few weeks earlier.

I felt the stillness of the visitors before I noticed that Rodney had entered the room. He and Massey nodded at each other. Starfish looked away from Rodney's glance, sort of curled in on himself. Cast Iron paused for a second but then kept his eyes on Rodney while skinning another sweet potato.

Rodney's presence was so familiar to me that I sometimes forgot how massive he was. He was bigger than Massey but lacked Massey's chiseled physique. Rodney's body always looked to me as if he had emerged directly out of a hillside, out of moss and bark and earth. He cut his own hair when it got in his eyes by lifting fistfuls and cutting it as close to his scalp as he could. The look was not uniform. The hair combined with the tattoo made him look feral and strange. Immediately after the Rending, when I first met Rodney, he wasn't garrulous but he was companionable, friendly. But as our fledgling community attracted more and more people, he became less accessible, at least to the new members and to visitors.

Now he and Tenzin, having returned from a hunting trip, stood before the refrigerator door on which we'd drawn a rough map of Zion and the surrounding area. When anyone left the area for a community-prescribed reason, the person was supposed to put a magnet in the general area he or she expected to be. If the person didn't return, we'd know where to start looking. If you left Zion for other reasons and you didn't return, no one would come looking (Rule #3). They clicked their magnets back to the home circle of Zion; Tenzin drifted over to solicit tea from Talia (silly man) and Rodney pulled a chair up to our table.

"Wanna get in on this?" asked Lana.

"Not sure he can handle the intensity," I said.

"Probably not," he said, "but gee whiz I'd sure like to try."

"Gee whiz?" I said.

"Gosh darn that sounds super-duper," said Lana.

"I'm trying to swear less," said Rodney.

"Why?" said Lana.

Rodney shrugged. He had a strange sense of decorum about certain things. He was big on please and thank you but had two hundred ways to describe a bowel movement. It wasn't unusual to hear him telling Asher about the size and shape of the deuce he'd just dropped before asking him to please pass the Philips screwdriver. I'd known him for three years now and I still found myself watching the way his jaw shifted side to side when he was deep in thought, the way he handled the little plastic gingerbread man delicately. I could have written a paean to the veins on the backs of his hands, to my desire to press a section of the vein flat, that tiny soft give of skin. When he started to bounce his right knee and Lana said, "Candy Land earthquake! My ginger man is terrified!" and then, when he didn't stop, "Rodney, quit it," I put my hand on his leg, under the table, to still him. He put his hand on top of mine and we stayed that way for the rest of the game.

Lana finally wandered off to attend to her client. Rodney stayed a few extra minutes to help me put the game away, squaring the cards into an orderly pile. He looked at me, from time to time, green eyes with brown knit in behind. These moments between us were common. He wasn't waiting, exactly; he was creating a pause, holding his foot between the door and the frame, a slim rectangle of space in which I could change my mind. He didn't raise his eyebrows or sputter little half-sentences, he just went about making a pile of the cards: two squares of yellow, one square of red, two squares of green, one square of red. He chose the cards carefully, following a pattern in his head. He was never showy about knowledge, was more apt to tell about the classes he'd failed in high school, how shop had saved him, how he'd completed a year at Dunwoody College, had decided his specialty would be machine tool technology. But, like Chester's, Rodney's mind was always working, and if there wasn't a puzzle in front of him he often created one for himself or a way of organizing things to make meaning out of them. I watched him, smoothing the board with my hand like a freshly ironed sheet. I couldn't fill the space with what he wanted to hear and I couldn't pull myself away either. Finally he put the lid on the box. We both smiled at the tiny gasp of air the lid made going down.

"Thanks for the game, Mira."

"Yes," I said, "of course. Anytime."

Then he was gone and I was left with the two children on the front of the box, a boy and girl with identical blond hair and dewy eyes, chins propped thoughtfully on fists, eyes scooping heavenward, imagining molasses swamps and sugarplum fairies.

I missed Bim.

Bim was short for Bartholomew. Specifically, the Dr. Seuss Bartholomew with all the hats. My parents tried to call him Bart for short but by eighteen months he would point rather sternly at the front of his OshKosh overalls and say "Bim" over and over again until we repeated his chosen name back to him. On the day of the Rending we were at the Mall of America to buy Bim a back-to-school wardrobe. Bim was ten and unenthusiastic about trying on jeans and chinos and choosing between the shirt with the army fatigue pattern and the shirt with flames licking the armpits. He kept coming out of the dressing room with the neck of a shirt over his head like a nun's habit or with the waist of his pants hiked to his upper ribs and his finger knuckle-deep in a nostril. When my mother grew annoyed, Bim turned sulky. Rather than asking when we could go to Nickelodeon Universe, the amusement park at the center of the mall, he took to repeating "pleeeez" in a thin reedy voice as we walked from store to store. Finally, my mother turned, handed me a twenty, and said, "Take him." A few feet from us she turned again and said, "Food court. One hour." I nodded and we were off.

I was aware, in that mall corridor, of every guy my age who walked past. I charted the way they let their flip-flops slap extra loudly against their heels, the way, from the waist up, they were always swiveling—to talk to one another, to watch a girl pass, to gesture to something in a store window. I tried to stay focused, small, narrow. Only my eyes darted everywhere. Sometimes my glance fell against a boy's and stuck, for a second, before we passed one another. It was constant cataloguing and assessment. I was on the lookout, though I wouldn't have admitted it to myself at the time, was searching for the person whose eyes would find mine, catch, and stay with me. Some I dismissed: too much acne, hips wide like a woman's, too much cologne. And I saw from the way their eyes scooted over me that I was being dismissed too, by some of them. I felt the dismissal in my body—the place where my thighs rubbed together as I walked, the tiny swell of fat over the edge of my bra, the hideous knob on my left pinky toe that made Bim refer to me as "witch foot" whenever I went barefoot (which was rarely).

Bim, on the other hand, was busy rolling his body along railings, balancing momentarily on the edge of the pedestrian benches, and jumping against walls. He called this freestyle walking. I saw some of the boys I passed guffawing at him and then sailing their eyes over to me, connecting us. The heat started below my collarbone and by the time we reached Nickelodeon Universe my face was flaming.

I handed Bim the twenty so he could get tickets, then waited while he stood in line for the Log Chute and the Swings. He was saving the Infinity Coaster for last. The line for the coaster seemed to snake into infinity as well. Just across the corridor from where the line trailed off, H&M mannequins flaunted gauzy dresses cinched with slim brown belts.

"I'm going to browse," I told Bim, nodding toward the store. "If you get done and I'm not here just wait."

I wasn't thinking of Bim. I was thinking of Jess, a guy I hated in theory but found myself attracted to in practice, and I was thinking of Liz, a girl who was my friend in theory but a bitch in practice, and I was thinking of the way Liz had curved her head around my locker and said, "Jess says you'd actually be cute if you didn't dress so dykey." I remember, as I said good-bye to Bim, fingering the scarf I was wearing that day, gray with silver filigree, and I remember thinking that maybe the scarf wasn't enough, but maybe a necklace would do it. Feminine with a little edge.

That's what I was thinking when I said, "Just wait."

Then I was in H&M, a necklace with elongated diamonds draped across my palm. I was admiring those little silver daggers. My last thought before the Rending wasn't of Bim, it was of how Jess would nod slightly in approval when he saw me wearing the necklace. How his eyes would dart and catch mine and stay. That's the last thing I remember thinking.

I took a sweet potato from the collection beside the fire pit before I left the Center. Tried, and failed, to leave without Talia touching me (as I bent over the potatoes I felt her hand on my hair, stroking me like a cat: "It's lovely when you wear it down like this, Mira."). I ate it on one of the three blue plastic stadium seats that stood outside between Chester's room and mine, dropping the potato peelings into an orange jack-o'-lantern pail at my feet. I waved to Eleanor and Cassie as they crossed the quadrangle with a load of root vegetables in the canoe-mobile. Figuring out how to attach bicycle wheels to the aluminum vessel was Asher's proudest post-Rending moment. It was a bitch to steer but Eleanor and Cassie were pros.

"Those two look like the beginning of a joke," said Chester, plopping down beside me.

"You're terrible," I said, but he was right. Eleanor was an unbelievably kind person who resembled, according to Chester, a home-schooled heron. She lifted each spindly knee about three times higher than it actually needed to go as she waded her way across the matted grass. Cassie, pushing against a bar Asher attached to the rear of the canoe-mobile, refused all clothing that didn't feature sequins or glitter of some sort. A fashion choice completely antithetical to her personality. Chester picked up the bucket and started to nibble on bits of peel.

"Yuck."

He smiled a jack-o'-lantern grin, having somehow managed to cover a few of his teeth with potato skin.

"Lovely," I said. "Thanks for saving me a trip to the compost."

He ran his tongue over his teeth. Then held out a closed fist. I popped the last bit of warm potato in my mouth, then turned his hand over and peeled back his fingers one at a time to reveal the folded piece of paper, still slightly damp from his sweat. My daily fortune. I opened it and read: "*If you are among the fortunate people who live where choice serviceberries abound, don't fail to notice them this summer.*" I looked up from the paper. "I've always wanted to live where serviceberries abound."

Chester nodded faux-pensively.

"Thanks," I said, rolling my eyes but tucking the fortune into my pocket anyway.

Sometimes I resented Chester. Somehow he managed to make his community work out of not-doing rather than doing. He still talked openly to Lana and me, and to Rodney, Sylvia, and Ida if the occasion arose, but around everyone else he was quiet—and not just quiet like Rodney was quiet; Chester was entirely silent. At community meetings I watched other people watch his face, tracking him for clues about how they should think, when they should grow indifferent or angry or sympathetic. Most of the time, I thought his spiritual guru persona was an act he put on because he could, because it made him feel powerful or useful or permitted him to be lazy. But at other times I felt it too, a more-ness to him, a beyond-ness. I hate those sorts of vague abstractions; they make me feel like I should be selling Enneagram books in a shop reeking of patchouli (perhaps this is my father in me; he had a particular distaste for those who deemed themselves "spiritual but not religious"). But I did find comfort in Chester. Other than Asher he was the only man after the Rending whose gaze didn't veer toward my breasts at some point during the conversation. Maybe Chester was asexual. I never asked. I was just content to be near someone who never seemed to want something from me. Sitting beside Chester, watching the Piles dim as the light turned from heather gray to softened steel, tracking the other community members as they walked across the quadrangle, was like sitting next to a large body of water.

His room was the same as mine, the same as (almost) all of ours, door and window at the front, fireplace at the rear. Though the temperature never sank to a level where fire was necessary for survival, some days the chill worked its way into our bones; on those occasions it was nice to fall asleep beside a source of warmth. So I kept my pallet laid out in front of the fire ring and then positioned a series of shelves, filled with bizarre but useless objects I'd found in the Piles, between the pallet and the rest of the room so that there were two separate spaces. Lana did the same, though her bed and living space were separated by burgundy drapes held back with golden ties with fluttery tassels. Chester kept his bed rolled away during the day. Perpendicular to the fireplace, a long coffee table held a small silver mixing bowl with his most recent treasures. The other mixing bowls (a set) stood in an even line on the counter in front of the window: water for washing, water for drinking, and ghost fruit.

Every Sunday, Ida and Chester went for long walks, Chester with his fanny pack and Ida with a white wicker basket (so that she looked like she was perpetually hunting for Easter eggs). Ida mostly gathered whimsical items—a pinwheel, a Whoopee cushion, potholders with the faces of owls. Chester veered toward the mildly disturbing: retainer shaped to the roof of a mouth we'd never met, glass eye, pin from an artificial leg (the leg itself wouldn't fit in his bowl), hearing aid. Around his coffee table were places to sit; the rest of the room was taken up with his stacks. Perfectly aligned stacks of paper, books, folders, pamphlets.

I don't think Chester intended to stop talking. I think it's that he found that's what people wanted. A sounding board, a silent sage, a sponge. We wanted our mothers and fathers, our confidants and priests, our therapists and friends. When Chester listened to me, really listened, I could shut my eyes and feel like I was with someone from the Before. He helped make a space of intimacy that felt familiar; people came to him again and again for the opportunity to pour themselves out, to fall and be caught. When Chester had heard enough he'd move purposefully to one of his stacks and rip out a passage from a book or a pamphlet, a folder or brochure. Then he'd offer the writing—sometimes just a few words, sometimes half a page—to the lucky Zionite. I'd often see members of Zion removing the scrap surreptitiously, in a moment of privacy, mouthing the words he'd given them like a charm. He took the interactions he had with community members and visitors seriously. However banal their questions or concerns, he never mentioned them to Lana or me afterward. Like Lana with her clients, Chester kept his listening sessions private, holy.

I wonder what my father would have thought of this. He loved literature and poetry. But sometimes it felt eerie to me, sacrilegious somehow, when Chester set the words of a popcorn popper manual or a Thai takeout menu as a seal upon someone's heart, when he made a balm out of crossword clues and vaccination side effects. Of course, considering I'd given up both God and religion, I shouldn't have cared whether something felt sacrilegious; still, watching the profane slide into the sacred (and vice versa) unsettled me.

Religion didn't disappear after the Rending but it went private, underground. We decided early on that the Rules that governed our behavior in Zion wouldn't be religious in nature. They could not be derived from a desire to pacify a driftless, invisible unknown. Or unknowns. Nor could the Rules be premised on why the Rending had or hadn't happened and, based on those ungrounded hypotheses, what we might do to prevent further catastrophe. We were still close enough to the Before to remember cults and to look around at our few numbers and our desperation for meaning and realize we could slide quickly into bizarre behavior meant as a hopeful attempt to keep the unthinkable at bay.

Though religion was banished from the center of our lives, it retained a firm toehold in the peripheries. Marjorie and Sven, our married orchardists, built little altars made of odds and ends from the sorted piles and left them behind their room for Zionites to take free of charge. Most people didn't take them in the light of day, but many of us had one in our rooms, and used it as a place to display whatever objects we'd had on us when the Rending occurred: grocery list, wallet-size photo of a Labrador, Clorox wipes, guitar pick, quarters and dimes piled like little cairns. Items that had no real use in the After other than as touchstones for memory.

Zephyr, our mixture man, had spent two years with the Peace Corps in Nepal as a twentysomething and retained an amalgam of religious habits that, like his mixtures, seemed to have no recipe but still managed to cohere his inner world. He and Tenzin and Talia and

47

a few others practiced meditation in the Center on Tuesday evenings; Lana ushered a handful of Zionites through yoga beside the river three mornings a week. Those who needed a prophet went to Chester. For a while, a small group cobbled together a Christian liturgy, a smattering of prayers and creeds, hymns and blessings. But there was no bread and there was no wine and the substitutes, Marjorie told me, felt wrong on the tongue. And besides, she said, there wasn't anyone to lead them, and Christians like a good shepherd.

It wouldn't have been hard to tell them about my father, but that would have meant admitting that I knew many psalms by heart, that I'd heard my father preach enough sermons that I knew the tightrope walk of law and gospel, knew how to take a Bible story and shape it to the people who were listening, knew that a prayer was exposing the soft belly of fear to light. I knew telling them about my father would mean they would want things from me that I didn't want to give, would mean they would ask things of me that I didn't have answers for, would mean that on a daily basis I'd have to submerge myself in memories of the Before. And, because I hadn't found a Bible in the Piles, I'd be responsible for remembering what was important, I would need to get everything right. And I'd need to pretend I was a person of faith, that I offered prayers to things besides dead cats. I'd need to pretend I believed in an abundant unconditional love that saturated everything, that stalked us everywhere. I'd need to say, with a compassionate face, that resurrection was possible.

I didn't join the Christians, but every Sunday until the group dispersed I spent my mornings close enough to them that I could hear the rise and fall of hymns, the soft, book-shut sound of the "Amens."

I'd never talked with any Zionites about how my belief in God disappeared along with most of the world's population. I'd never told anyone my father was a pastor. I'd never lied either, I simply didn't graft that part of who I was onto the version of Mira that I became when I woke in the Mall of America, the H&M necklace clutched in one hand, the security officer panting above me, and Bim gone for good.

And, stupidly, it didn't occur to me that other members of Zion might have similarly curated their own pasts, track lighting and gleaming pedestals for the parts of themselves they wanted to remember and temperature-controlled basement storage for the parts of themselves they would just as soon forget.

CHAPTER FOUR

TWO DAYS LATER I met Lana on my way out to Larry, the Pile closest to the river. Cal was trailing along somewhere behind me, annoyed that I'd made him push the baby buggy. I'd passed the other members of Lana's morning yoga class already—Paloma and Cassie and Zephyr and Talia—and now here was Lana, rag rug rolled under her arm, blonde hair rerolled into perfect little knobs, cheetah lounge pants, zebra-striped hoodie (she called her yoga outfit safari couture), and a cut that started at the edge of her lip and curled like a fishing hook just above her chin.

"What happened?"

She batted the question away like smoke rising from leftover food on a burner. Annoying but no real cause for concern. "It's fine."

"It doesn't look fine." In fact it did look fine, but there was something about the cut that didn't look accidental.

"Sylvia and Ida pronounced it officially OK."

"You went to the Clinic on your own? Without being dragged?"

"I was dragged a little maybe."

"Who?"

"Rodney."

"Rodney did this?"

"Rodney did not."

"Then who?"

Her voice turned a few notches chillier. "This question from the girl who somehow carries a map of a million objects in her head, whose powers of observation are unsurpassed."

"A visitor?" Massey was gone. Starfish was lame. "The creepy one? With the eyes?"

"Ding ding ding. You win. I'm off. Always something to be done. Always *someone* to be done," she corrected herself. There was bitterness there I hadn't heard before. She started to walk by me but I grabbed her arm. She pushed me quickly, reflexively, and I stumbled back.

"Hey!"

She closed her eyes and took a deep breath. Blew it out slowly. When she opened her eyes again the edge was gone. "Sorry."

"Where is he?"

"Who?"

"Rodney."

"Rodney is escorting a certain visitor hence." She did the little wave again.

"Hence?"

"Elsewhere."

"Alone?"

"I believe Tenzin went along."

"And the visitor did this?"

She shrugged. "He got a little fresh. As my mother would say. Would have said."

"Are you OK? I don't mean the cut—I mean you. Are you OK?"

"Part of the gig," she said. She smiled but the smile cracked open the cut, turning the scab from rust to red.

I took her hands. "Did he rape you?"

She looked over my shoulder. "He did not," she said brightly.

"Did he assault you?"

This time she looked at me and touched my nose as she said, "I'm sorry but you are out of guesses, missy. The vacation to Disney World shall not be yours."

"Why won't you talk to me?" She studied the sky above my head. "Lana."

After a long moment she turned her gaze to mine. Her voice was that of a fifth-grade math teacher, kind but firm. "He was fresh. Rodney was nearby. Now the visitor is hence. That is all."

That night at the community meeting Tenzin distributed our portions of meat from what he and Rodney had collected from the snares. If they returned earlier in the day, Talia usually had time to make a stew, which mellowed the meat, turning it soft and pliable. But Tenzin and Rodney hadn't returned until a couple hours before the meeting so there was barely time to butcher and cook the carcasses and the meat was tough. Sounds of chewing filled the first few minutes of the meeting. I tried to swallow. It had been four days since we'd had any protein and I was hungry but I couldn't get it down.

Lana didn't even try the meat. She spent most of the community meeting that night giving herself a manicure with a red Sharpie I'd found inside a green glass vase on Curly, the tallest Pile, a few days earlier. I breathed in the fumes (a weird sort of nostalgia) and tried to patch one of my scavenging shirts with fishing line. Or I pretended to patch the shirt. Rodney was sitting one row behind me and I felt his gaze on the backs of my ears, on my hair, on the tender skin at the curve of my jaw.

"So please don't take your mug with you," Talia was saying, "otherwise we have no mugs in the Center."

"Tragedy," breathed Lana over her fingernails.

"To help you remember I've marked all the Center mugs with a C and I've made a sign that I'm going to hang above the mugs." She held up a lampshade and rotated it so that we could see the words that wrapped around its pale yellow skirt: ALL MUGS WHO WANDER ARE LOST.

"Thanks, Talia," said Asher. "Anyone else? Going once . . . going twice . . . no more announcements? OK, on to Rules. Any additions or addendums?" Asher fiddled with his baseball cap. He always hung it over the knob of his knee when he was the community meeting leader, revealing the wavy peaks of his thick red hair.

Zephyr raised his finger in the air. Asher nodded. Zephyr stood, right hand cupped around the stick he used to stir his mortars and plasters and glues. "We've been getting a lot more visitors lately seems like. So I think we've either gotta not feed and house them all or we've gotta think about maybe not letting them stay so long."

Rule #4 stated that we would offer food and shelter to any visitor for seven days, after which point he or she either had to leave or join Zion officially. We developed the rule not out of an overwhelming sense of hospitality but as a means of protecting ourselves. Our rationale was that most people who approached with ill intent could be pacified by offers of generosity. So far, it had worked. I glanced at the scab on Lana's chin. Or mostly worked.

"I think Zephyr is right," said Sylvia. She sat with her hands wedged between her crossed legs, back straight, the toe of her black lace-up boot diagramming molecules in the air. At least that's what I imagined she was doing.

"I think the problem isn't so much the number of visitors," said Rodney, casting a glance toward Lana, "it's where we house them." At the moment we had four cots in an otherwise empty room dedicated to visitors. If we had more than four visitors we rolled out pallets in the Center. "Putting them so near to where we sleep seems like it might invite trouble."

"Maybe we should build a whole separate guest facility," said Lana, fluttering her hand in the air, her nails like detached butterfly wings.

Across the room, Tenzin made a sputtering sound. "I don't think we want to make it seem like we're in the hotel business."

"Well," said Rodney, "what if we put up a really simple structure out by the ghost fruit orchard? Barely serviceable but with some kind of bunk system."

"More people but less comfort," added Tenzin, nodding.

"Yep," said Rodney.

"And what if," said Ida, a slow sweet smile spreading across her face, "we put it at the north end of the orchard, within wafting distance of the latrines?"

"OK," said Asher, "let's return to this idea next week. We'll vote then. Any other additions or addendums?"

It was quiet except for the sound of Lana's Sharpie lid clicking back into place. I watched a few of the community members on the other side of the room watch Chester.

Asher readjusted the hat on his knee. "Issues and Ideas then?"

The last part of the meeting was the most haphazard. Initially, it was the time for us to share theories about the Rending. Mostly, it was a way to make sure that no one was turning cultish on us, that no

insane bit of gossip or harebrained theory had a chance to gain trac-
tion as it snowballed from whispered conversation to whispered
conversation.

We were rabid for theories in the first year after the Rending,
desperate to land on a story that could explain the sudden absence
of most of the world's population, the redistribution of goods and
objects into towering Piles, and the ghost fruit. We wanted to know
why we were constantly suffocated by gray sky, why the temperature
hovered between fifty and sixty degrees, why precipitation had ceased
and been replaced by the periodic saturation of the earth from sources
unknown. Toward the end of the second year we added the lack of
children to the mix. We considered terrorism, drugs sent through
pipes and vents, an astronomical event, a compression or expansion
of time. We wondered if the absent people had been taken elsewhere,
if they were being kept. Tenzin once told us he'd had a dream that
the bodies had become a mass in the ocean, like the mile-long pile
of garbage some of us had seen pictures of before the Rending. We
strained the facts, sieved them for truth, looked for patterns, salva-
tion. Zephyr once pointed out at the end of a particularly long meeting
that maybe we weren't the ones who had been saved at all. "I had a
niece who was really into that *Left Behind* series," he said. "Maybe it's
the Rapture and we haven't been brought up."

One meeting we spent offering up details from our lives, looking
for overlap like detectives on *Law and Order* who eventually found
that all the serial killer's victims attended the same health club or had
been born on December 26. But as one year turned to two and two
into three, as we developed a reasonably comfortable way to live, as
our distance from the event dimmed its violence slightly, we stopped
talking about the possible causes publicly. Or maybe we never grew
comfortable, but we tired of continually circling the same questions,
living in a psychic land of dangling conclusions, ellipses trailing off
forever into the distance.

"Nada?" said Asher, slapping his hat against his knee a final time
for emphasis and then replacing it on his head. "Then we is done.
That's all, folks."

We got up from our makeshift benches and grabbed our lanterns. The world had grown dark, its oldest habit, since the meeting began. We drifted to the fire. I lit my red candle stub, ground it into the sand at the base of the coffee can, and walked out the door alone. Chester was listening deeply to Deborah, who was holding on to the cuff of his shirt as she talked. Lana had slipped away with a client; evenings were her busiest time. I watched the homemade lanterns, coffee cans and Mason jars, sugar shakers and soup cans, drift across the quadrangle, each bit of light on its own trajectory.

I touched the notebook that hung between my breasts. The list of what we needed, what we hoped we might find. But at moments like this I added, at the back, my own catalogue of the missing.

Contrails on blue. The drone of plane engines. Stars.

"A litany," my father would have said.

As though naming the things you'd lost could be a blessing. As though he had any say in the matter now.

CHAPTER FIVE

THE NEXT FEW months were different than the previous three years because time began to mark itself, visibly, on Lana's body, like notches in a stick or hash marks carved on a cell wall. The expansion of Lana's frame reminded all of us that each day was not repeating exactly; we were moving forward, into something different.

At thirty-two weeks Lana was proud to announce that she could feel a tiny elbow below her skin, proud to guide Sylvia's hand just there. Lana closed her eyes and smiled a tiny smile of deep maternal satisfaction; Sylvia looked at me as she said, "Yes, there's certainly something sharp growing there." We both knew something was off, not right, but I give Sylvia credit for not sounding alarm bells she wouldn't be able to silence. Ida dutifully recorded all of it in the blue book, often writing far longer than seemed necessary given what had happened in the room.

As Sylvia and I grew more sparing with our enthusiasm, Lana's interest in her belly swelled. She called the fetus Percocet, or Perky for short, because of a gift Chester and I made for her the week we'd learned she was pregnant. Instead of a typical book that compared the size of the fetus to a fruit or a vegetable, Chester and I had created our own version, each week a different object from the Before, something we hadn't managed to find in the Piles. *Your baby is the size of a painkiller! Your baby is the size of a Frosted Flake! Your baby is the size of a scoop of Cherry Garcia!* We'd consulted Ida and Sylvia since we had no idea what size the baby was supposed to be when. Ida had giggled; Sylvia had balanced a heavy textbook on her knees and tried not to. Each week Lana reminded us of Perky's growth based on our crude drawings and ridiculous comparisons.

Though a few of Lana's clients grew more interested in Lana as her breasts and belly took on weight and fluid, many of them came less regularly. But because she'd never announced a father, most of the men still felt obligated to leave small offerings. Gary, head irrigator, brought her a five-gallon bucket of water from the river each morning. Oscar, one of our orchardists, brought jars of ghost fruit jelly. It took him hours to make the jelly; he often did so in the Center, so he could talk to other Zionites while he stirred endlessly, waiting for the fruit to thicken. He bent over the heat so earnestly, Lana and I often joked that there was as much sweat in the jelly as ghost fruit. Without as many clients to occupy her, Lana spent more time trailing me around the Piles like a small directionless blimp, scolding me for failing to collect baby objects. Two hours after her thirty-two-week checkup, she'd pointedly held up a tiny silver spoon and a green sun hat with frog eyes stitched to the top.

"How can you be missing these things?" she asked, propping the hat coyly on her head.

"My job is not to procure baby items for you, Lana. There's a whole encampment here, you know."

"Meow."

"Yes," I said tiredly, "meow." I hefted some panels of linoleum into the buggy.

"I could put these in the corner of my room," she said, fingering a corner. "A nursery."

"I was thinking the Clinic. Easy cleanup."

She took the hat off. "I'm just trying to make the best of this, Mira. Why are you being so bitchy all of a sudden?"

"I don't know," I said. "I'm sorry." I took the hat from her and put it on my head. "I just really wanted the hat for myself." Lana snorted.

Asher and Rodney walked by, carrying a screen door between them. Asher whistled appreciatively. "Hot," said Rodney. He smiled. Sparkler tips in my gut.

When I turned back to Lana she was watching me watch him. She pushed the hat off my head. "It's been crap. We act sometimes like the world wasn't lifted away. The world was lifted away."

"I know."

"Sometimes you act like you don't know. You act like you've been pushing a buggy around fucking Piles your whole life. Like you're not angry."

"I'm not angry."

"You are angry."

"At who?"

"At no one. Everyone. Me. This. Our fucking purgatory in the cloudy armpit of the Midwest. Where I take off my clothes every day for men who close their eyes and whisper the names of dead women into my ear. Where you can't seem to take off a fucking sock for a guy you've liked for three years. What's wrong with you?"

"It's complicated, Lana." I tried to say it kindly. I tried to say it in the kind of tone that would make her understand.

"Of course it's complicated. We're fighting over six squares of puke-colored linoleum." She picked a tile out of the buggy and tried to throw it angrily. It landed with a contented puff of dust two feet away from her. She tried again with a piece of rebar but she couldn't lift it out of the buggy.

I started to laugh. I sat down on the dusty ground and put the frog hat in front of my face and laughed. Lana was beside me then, laughing too. When we were done I put the hat in front of her nose. "It smells like baby," I said.

She inhaled. Nodded. We passed it back and forth for a while like a joint, not saying anything.

"You can't say fuck all the time after the baby's born."

"I know," she said. She inhaled again.

I pressed together and pulled apart the tiny Velcro tabs on the ends of the hat strings.

"I love him," I said finally.

"I know," she said.

Him was Rodney, of course. To say I loved him was an easy thing, a plain truth. But as my father had said repeatedly, from the pulpit and from the couch, love is a verb. The love I had now was a feeling, nothing more. A feeling that could come or go, that I could sweep away or ignore; it didn't mean much. When love became a verb, that's when you got into trouble. Then you started depending on someone, not in the way I already depended on everyone in Zion to shovel out shit or cook turnips or collect ghost fruit or extract possum carcasses from barbed-wire snares. Love with Rodney would mean he'd become my own big fat personal emotional crutch. Not even a crutch. One of those scooters on which someone could prop up a broken leg. And then, when he left or something went wrong as it always did, I'd be left trying to hop around like an idiot. I'd be immobile, emotionally immobile. Ever since the Rending I could see that emotionally immobile woman on a hill off in the distance, a version of myself who was incapable, who wallowed grayly, functionally dim. I knew she existed, this other version up on the hill.

My mom had a version of herself like that. Her curds-and-whey self. That version would come to visit for months at a time. Mom would still fold the laundry and set dishes down with little clinks, but every movement was like she was doing it in a pond of glue. Mostly I remember her face, lit by the computer screen. She'd nestle on the couch with a glass of wine and shop online, often for one of the vases she collected but sometimes for shoes or an immersion blender, car floor mats or coffee filters. If I was quiet and sweet she'd let me slip in next to her—she still smelled the same, like peppermint and sweet Hawaiian bread—and we'd watch the images float up the screen. Sometimes she'd read a review quietly, under her breath. Occasionally she'd ask my opinion and I'd always try to confirm whatever item she was already leaning toward. Whatever darkness was pressing her into a corner, I didn't want to add more. I wanted her to feel right and strong.

My father didn't do much during these episodes. He seemed more tired because he had to pick up so much slack; he didn't complain but I don't think he got her help either. Or maybe he did. Now I know that so much of what happens inside a coupling is invisible to everyone who stands outside it. And my father was so entrenched in dichotomies: death and resurrection, saint and sinner, law and gospel. Both at once, he'd sagely explain from the folds of his alb, always both at once. I think to him my mother's depression was part of the whole, not something that could be excised or transformed.

But I was not yet that version of myself in the distance. The one incapable of anything besides slow, gray grief. To love and lose Rodney, though, I knew that was a sure way to invite that woman to come wandering into my life. To open her suitcase and take out her slippers and curling iron, her lotions and silk underwear. If she came wandering down that hill I knew she'd stay.

I also knew I'd let Rodney down. I would fuck up in some incredible way, a way I couldn't even comprehend now. Just as on the day of the Rending, I had failed Bim so entirely that I'd lost the chance to ever be near him again.

Initially your Final Moment, as we called it, was one of the first things you revealed about yourself when you met someone new. The fragile currency of post-Rending conversation. Like where you were on 9/11. Where you were when JFK was shot. As though history were best constructed by piling together the individual experiences of a singular, tragic event. The only members of the encampment who knew each other before the Rending (besides Sylvia and Ida) were Marjorie and Sven. They'd been golfing when the Rending occurred. Sven's arms had been wrapped around Marjorie, his hands wrapped around her hands, lifting a golf club together, both pairs of eyes on the pocked ball. That's how they described their Final Moment.

Ida and Sylvia had been in S'More Outdoor, a camping outfitter in the Mall of America for those who didn't actually spend all that much time outdoors. The S'More footwear clerks were too busy squatting in front of mothers trying on Tevas and retirees pointing to photos in guidebooks to tend to the twins. Ida finally bent to the floor to press the rubber at the toe of the Bass hiking boot Sylvia was trying on for both of them. "My thumb on Sylvia's toe." That's what Ida would say if you asked her the last thing she remembered before the Rending.

Hands clasped over hands, thumb against toe: they'd been touching. Marjorie and Sven. Sylvia and Ida. They were touching then, when it happened, and here they were, together, now. The myriad ways I could have been touching Bim sifted through my consciousness constantly. Hugging him as he came through the swinging red gate after the ride ended. Rubbing between his shoulder blades as he vomited bits of cotton candy into a green garbage can chained to the ground. His body falling against mine accidentally as he attempted a particularly complicated freestyle walking maneuver. One of my thigh hairs, pinched between his thumb and index finger and yanked as the coaster crested the top of the hill. Swatting his hand away as he tried to dig in my back pocket for the remaining money from Mom.

No one else in Zion seemed to have put this coincidence together. Or maybe they had and, like me, they didn't want to admit the possibility to anyone else. I knew what Lana would say. Or Rodney. Even Chester. That I was being ridiculous and that there had to have been millions of other people touching when the Rending happened and where, exactly, were they? And what good does it do to wonder? To beat yourself up? There's nothing to be done about it now. While debating the possible causes of the Rending might help us to understand our current predicament, lamenting what we could have done differently then, back in the Before, that was useless.

But I couldn't shake my grief or my guilt, couldn't shake the nagging sense that walking away from my brother to buy a necklace for myself was a "teachable moment," as my father would have said. A lesson about narcissism and selfishness and impatience. A lesson about What Love Truly Is, the four words my father often slipped into sermons. Or an example in a book I once saw my newly divorced aunt reading: *What Love Is: Advice from the Front Lines of Marriage*. Love is never going to bed angry. Love is saying yes I will. Love is remembering to put the toilet seat down. I imagined myself in a companion book called *What Love Is Not: Advice from the Post-Apocalyptic Future* that would begin: love is not abandoning your brother just before the end of the world for an H&M necklace.

Inside my room, above the door frame, the necklace with the elongated diamonds dangled. This is what I was touching when the Rending changed everything and so this is what came with me. Ida had Sylvia and Marjorie had Sven. I ran my fingertips over those points each time I left my room, a reminder that I shouldn't have anyone else.

CHAPTER SIX

W E WALKED DURING the first part of Lana's labor as Sylvia had suggested. We walked the path that ran around the outskirts of Zion, wary of going farther since we were uncertain about when the labor might change, when Lana's body might rear into a higher gear. We walked single file and we walked holding hands. We talked about the Before. About the early days after the Rending, how creeped out we'd been by seeing Ida and Sylvia stretched out like American Girl dolls in the back of the Volvo station wagon. How different they looked now, Sylvia whittled to a point, skin stretched tight over her face, hair always wound into a twist and contained with her silver dragon clasp. And Ida wider, softer, her hair in short fuzzy waves over her forehead, the tips of her ears, and the back of her neck—a permanent halo. Ida's speech was like excess throw pillows and Sylvia's sparse like Hansel's pebbles. The perimeter was a fifteen-minute walk; after four loops we'd check in with Sylvia and Ida and then set off again. Sometimes Sylvia had Lana lie on the table, legs spread, so that Sylvia could examine her and declare a number. Two and a half centimeters. Then three. At four centimeters Ida held out a glass of water.

"I like the straw," said Lana. It was blue and loopy. A roller coaster. I imagined Bim, shrunk and sliding inside the thin tube, his face a soft sapphire under the glow of the plastic.

"I found it and saved it for you. For today," said Ida. We sat there quietly for a long time, watching the water snake up and down the straw.

"Can you still talk through the contractions?" asked Sylvia.

"I can even drink through them," said Lana, jazz hands dancing on either side of the straw, her eyes open wide as she sucked.

Sylvia turned to me. "When she can't talk through them anymore, bring her back."

I nodded. We went back to walking.

We were quieter then. We passed the Piles and the Center, the fields that shrouded potatoes and parsnips, carrots and rutabagas below the surface and proffered an anemic, mud-green fuzz of stems above them. When Lana stopped for a contraction I wrote in the back of my notebook: *ferns, edamame, lima beans, limes.* We walked by the orchard, past Sven and Marjorie filling a straw beach bag and a plastic garbage can with ghost fruit. We stopped so that Marjorie could place a swollen mother-of-pearl-colored ball on Lana's palm. We watched as it deflated, the air pulled from the center so suddenly that the skin of the fruit writhed slightly, as if it were alive. Lana placed it on her tongue.

Marjorie nibbled one from her basket that had already deflated. Undone, the fruits looked like prunes or dried apricots without the thick, leathery skin. Over time the deflated fruits also lost some of their flavor; the trick was to move the fruit to a holding vessel before the warmth of one's skin caused the fruit to deflate. Picking ghost fruit required both agility and monotonous persistence.

"Doesn't it drive you crazy," Lana asked, "to have to pay such close attention to each one?"

"They're our babies," said Marjorie, patting Lana's arm.

I'd been so busy being jealous that Sven and Marjorie had each other that I'd never thought about whether they'd left others behind. Kids or grandkids. Since they had each other I hadn't permitted them any other grief.

From a distance we waved to Cal and Tenzin, perched on the side of Curly, the starburst puff of Cal's hair beside the slick black helmet of Tenzin's. At the Sorting Stations Deborah was trying on a tight, fleece-lined canvas jacket that showed off a roll of her white belly. "I could just wear it unzipped, right?" she asked as we passed.

"Tenzin's not going to care," said Lana.

"He's smitten," I said.

"Twitterpated," added Lana.

"Whipped," said Cassie flatly.

Deborah blushed. "I just want to look nice," she said.

"For who? The paparazzi?" Cassie threw Deborah a hibiscus-covered muumuu. "Take this. It'll really complement your shape."

Deborah held it up, completely immune to Cassie's dripping sarcasm. "Really? I think it's a little big. What do you guys think?" She looked at Lana and me. Her face, as always, had the look of dough that's been punched down repeatedly.

"Oooooooohhhh . . . contraction," said Lana, pointing at her belly. "Gotta keep moving." She tugged my sleeve emphatically.

"I hope you're better at faking orgasms than you are contractions," I said after we'd walked another twenty yards.

"Real one," she said in response. She put her hands on my shoulders and touched her forehead lightly to mine. Over her shoulder I could see Asher grinding a handsaw through a lacquered table and Rodney fiddling with what looked like a car engine. Lana blew long breaths through rounded lips and swayed her hips gently from side to side.

"That's a sexy slow dance you guys have going on," said Asher as he sauntered over.

Lana expelled the rest of the breath and looked up. "She's all mine," she said, linking her arm through mine and looking pointedly at Rodney.

"Is that so?" he asked. The left corner of his lip curved up slightly, making the branch on his skin quiver. He'd cut his hair recently and there was an almost-bald patch above his right eye that I very much wanted to touch.

Asher held up his hand to Lana for a high five.

"Looking good, Lana," said Rodney.

"Why is it that when men don't know how to support a woman they simply go into sporting event mode?" Lana mumbled when we were out of hearing distance.

"Maybe they'll dump a cooler of Gatorade on you when the baby's born," I said.

"Mmm," she said, standing still and closing her eyes, "Gatorade."

We stopped to see Chester and he offered Lana a slip of paper and a stone. "I knew I could count on you for something mystical," she said. But she tucked the paper into her bra and carried the stone in her hand while we walked.

We waded in the river below oak and maple, snapped twigs from branches that refused to bud, then threw the twigs toward the deeper water and watched the current helicopter the wood away. We scanned the bottom of Larry and Moe for other baby trinkets and ate more ghost fruit from Marjorie and Sven.

The sky turned from goose gray to cinder gray. Lana began to pause more often for the contractions. She closed her eyes and rocked against me or leaned into a wall. We stopped back at the Clinic. Six centimeters.

"Why don't you take a break," said Ida. "I'll walk with her."

Lana had been leaning over the massage table, her face pressed into her crossed arms while she huffed through a contraction. "I'd like to take a break too," she said.

"You know I'd give you one if I could," said Ida, rubbing a warm circle into Lana's lower back.

"I know," said Lana. She gave Ida a kiss on her pillowy cheek.

While Lana and Ida walked, I lay down on the massage table in the examining room and watched Sylvia. Her hands hovered over a row of instruments on the counter, ones she'd kept covered with a towel while Lana was in the room. Scalpel, black thread, pincushion with spine of needles, kitchen tongs, scissors. Sylvia's hands moved back and forth, sometimes straightening an object but mostly just hovering.

"You look like either you're a magician or you have OCD," I said.

"I'm just making sure I have everything," said Sylvia without turning.

"You can say you're afraid," I said.

"Most births are perfectly normal."

"Were perfectly normal. In the Before."

"The body is made to do the work of birth."

"I know," I said.

She let her hands fall to her sides, then circled them so I could hear her wrists crack. She pulled the straight silver pin out of her hair, let it fall, combed her fingers through it, rewound. Then she placed the dragon clip neatly over the coil, pierced it with the silver pin, and turned to me. "I'll act like I know what to do. That's what the book says: patient confidence in the doctor has a huge effect on outcomes. That's about all I can really do."

"It's more than I could do. No one expects you to do more."

"Of course they do. You do. All of you expect Ida and me to be doctors. Because we had the names of bones on flash cards in our pockets when the Rending occurred we somehow got elected to do this work."

I'd never seen Sylvia angry before. Color filled her usually pale face. The extra blood made her looser, fuller.

I sat up. "You're good at this work, Sylvia." I took her hand. It was thin. I remembered watching my father fillet a salmon. The xylophone of bones. "You're like a robot," I said.

She jerked her hand away. "No!" I grabbed her hand again. "I mean that in the best way possible. That you're able to look at the blood and the mess and people crying and whining and somehow see beyond all that. You see what needs to be done." I took her hand again. She let me keep it. "You see what needs to be done and you do it," I said.

We were quiet for a couple long seconds. She looked at her hand in my hand. Let hers grow heavier, let me hold more and more of her. Then she began to talk.

"We had a cat named Sourpuss. I didn't like him but Ida loved him, he'd even let her push him around in a baby carriage. We would walk with our mother to the grocery store. To Lunds. Mom had a little metal cart she pushed from home. All the other mothers drove, even if they lived only a few blocks away, but our mom grew up in New York and she was proud of the cart. She and Ida always walked ahead; there wasn't room for the three of us abreast since Mother had the cart and Ida had the baby carriage. Sourpuss would look back at me spitefully. I thought they looked ridiculous, but I hate walking slowly and I didn't want to trail behind them. I didn't want to look like the person who came second. So I brought my father's mountaineering compass and a little notebook. I'd stop and pretend to make note of our coordinates every few minutes. Once they were a half block ahead I'd walk very quickly and purposefully to catch up."

I nodded. "That makes sense."

"No. You don't understand. I didn't want to be in front either. I have a terrible sense of direction. I didn't want the burden of having other people follow me. Ida has a horrible sense of direction too. But she'd reach a corner and start to make a wrong turn and Mother would grab the edge of the carriage, pull her the right way. 'This way, sweet pea,' she'd say. And Ida would giggle. Ida was the sweet one. I was the smart one. As I'm sure you've gathered. What I'm saying is that I figured out early on how to cover up the things I didn't know with something that looked like knowledge."

She took her hand out of my grip, but gently this time.

"I guess I thought this was what you wanted, Sylvia."

"Who's allowed to want anything?

"I think we're allowed to want. Within reason."

"Reasonable wants. Yes." She walked over to the basin at the far end of the room. Pressed the pedal that tipped a container on the other side of the wall and spilled water down a tube and into the sink. She placed her hands under the thin stream. "I didn't have water in the Clinic a month ago and now I do. Reasonable. Fulfillable." She turned toward me again. Beads of water dripped from the ends of her fingertips. "What do you want, Mira?"

I didn't like Sylvia much but I almost said it. Her eyes were so clear and direct, like she could absorb a confession without becoming sentimental about it. "I want to be with Rodney. And I want the Before back again," I almost said, the desires so banal and predictable that I felt like a kid asking for a pony. But before I could say anything we heard a groan from outside the door. A groan like time turning in on itself. Then the chipper voice of Ida declaring, "I think she's ready!"

CHAPTER SEVEN

S YLVIA WAS EVERYTHING she said she'd be: authoritative, clear, brusque. Busy when movement was necessary, a static, fixed point of reason when Lana's eyes turned animal and she muttered "I can't do this" again and again.

There were no stirrups so Ida and I each held a thigh open as Lana's whole body went tight one minute, loose and jittery the next. She closed her eyes, moving her head back and forth as though trying to burrow back to the Before or out of the pain or maybe into death.

The pain seemed to come from outside of her and to split her open. I'd heard talk about babies crowning and I'd even watched a video in health class: the blue bruise of a head coming through, scrimmed in a layer of blood. But it was the moments before that fascinated me, the dark opening the pain made in Lana before anything appeared to move through it.

We called the event the Rending after the moment when Jesus died. The curtain torn. The moment of big death, life on the other side not yet known. And we called it the Rending for the way it made us feel afterward: torn, frayed, broken.

But watching Lana I saw that birth was the first Rending, a splitting and tearing of the fibers of life and death. The body itself inhabited by forces beyond the body.

Maybe Lana's body was a version of the tomb. Maybe when this life emerged, when we held it, things would be better. Maybe the birth of this baby would feel like a kind of resurrection. I forgot, seeing her body so alive and inhabited with the pain, what Sylvia and I had intuited a long time ago.

The doll was covered in vernix the way a baby would have been. Arms straight against its sides. Naked plastic. Hair braided. Tiny rubber bands, the kind kids used to attach to their braces, kept the braids from unraveling. Part perfectly straight. Eyelids closed. Dots for nipples. Fingers fixed together into a curved paw. Toes pointed straight ahead, feet at perfect right angles with the body.

Lana let out a long sigh after the Baby emerged, then propped herself up on her forearms. "It's dead, isn't it? Why isn't it crying?" Lana's eyes searched mine. She refused to look down. Refused to see what was there.

"She's not dead," said Sylvia matter-of-factly. She raised the doll gently, passed it between Lana's knees, and placed it on the plane of her chest.

"What the fuck is this? Is this some kind of joke? Give me my baby, Sylvia."

Sylvia took her eyes off Lana's, sat back down, began to check her for tears. Dabbed at her thighs with a washcloth.

"Look at me, Sylvia," screamed Lana. She threw the doll off her, and the skittering sound it made on the floor was too light, insubstantial. Sylvia kept dabbing. "Look at me, goddamn it!" Lana kicked Sylvia's chest with surprising force and Sylvia toppled backward. Ida turned away, tears streaming down her cheeks. She picked up the doll and took it to the sink.

The flame between my ribs flared. Playing doctor, that's what we were doing: there was the doll, the instruments that weren't really instruments.

"Mira!" Lana's hand was around my upper arm. She was sitting upright now. "Get my baby. Find my fucking baby." An orbit of white showed around her irises. The knobs of her hair had become mussed during the birth, a few were fuzzed and one at the top had come unraveled completely. "You need to find the baby, Mir." Her voice rocked back and forth, from anger to pleading.

I took her face between my palms. She was moving it back and forth slightly, side to side, not the burrowing she'd done while giving birth, but just her body denying, denying. "It's not a baby, Lana. It's not a baby. I don't know why."

Ida brought the doll back over to Lana then. She'd wrapped it in a strip of cloth with pink elephants parading on it and she'd opened the doll's eyes. Two blue coals staring into nothing. Lana saw it then. Really saw it. And she started to laugh.

"This?" she said. Her index finger made a circle in the air as she pointed. "This is what I've been making inside me." Her laughter grew louder, hysterical. The room was small with a tin roof and the laughter came back to us, ricocheting off the stove, the sink, the needles, the blades.

Sylvia had righted her chair. Stationed herself again between Lana's knees.

Lana, on her back again, shook with laughter. It was horrible, unstoppable, far worse than the sounds that had torn through her during the birth.

"Get her to stop," Sylvia said to me in a low voice, "she's bleeding too much."

I leaned over Lana. Put my lips to the soft tunnel of her ear. "Shhhhhhhh," I said, "shhhhhhhh."

But she didn't stop. The laugh was a hard, barking scrape. A stick against a barnacled hull.

"Now, Mira." Sylvia's face was still but her hands were quick and serious, moving between rags and gauze and thread.

The blood came in pulses with the laugh. I cupped my right hand under Lana's jaw and my left on top of her head and I pushed. She squirmed but I held tight; I shut the sound up.

The quaking of her body grew more urgent. Then she started to breathe through her nostrils like a horse. Even after her body stopped shaking her eyes still roamed, wild. Keeping my hands on her head, I climbed onto the massage table. Knelt over her so all she could see was my face. My eyes on her eyes. "This is happening," I said.

She shook her head. No, no, no.

"This is happening, Lana," I said.

I don't know how many times I said the words. I knelt until my calves cramped. Until her head stopped shaking. Until she fell asleep.

CHAPTER EIGHT

L ANA DIDN'T WANT to be near the doll. The Baby. Lana didn't want to be near anyone besides Ida. She didn't accept clients, didn't trail me around the Piles, didn't show up for community meetings.

I went to the meetings but couldn't pay attention. The doll lay on an overturned apple crate beside the bookshelf in the Center. The spaces below her cupped hands, her legs, the arch of her back, made her look uncomfortable. While the others talked about what the doll meant, if it was a sign, if it was a warning, if we should treat Lana differently, if we should avoid eating ghost fruit, et cetera, I studied those empty spaces.

We sent things to Lana via Ida. Chester sent his fortunes, the most inappropriate ones he could find, words crossed out or reinserted to make her laugh. I sent her anything I found on the Piles that I thought might distract her: a book of Sudoku puzzles, a pink faux-fur stole, a hideous necklace made of seashells. Into a Care Bear calendar, Chester and I pasted color portraits from a history of WWF Wrestling: Tenderheart Bear offering a plate of cupcakes to Hulk Hogan, The Undertaker riding shotgun beside Funshine Bear, André the Giant sweating onto the unadulterated clouds.

I should have gone to her, should have ignored what she wanted, should have sat beside her, held her hand, napped beside her unwashed body. I should have been the one to empty the gallon bucket she was using as a chamber pot. I thought of my father a lot. Wished I could send him in to her, wished I were brave enough to know how to sit in that kind of silence. But the truth was that I thought I'd be called upon to say something. That she would ask me what to do or to explain what it meant. And I wouldn't have an answer or worse, I'd laugh. That was my biggest terror. One night, after Chester had unrolled his pallet, I lay next to him and we thought up the worst things we could inscribe on a sympathy card:

> *So sorry you gave birth to a doll. At least she'll sleep through the night!*
> *She looks just like you except for the lack of blood, breath, hair, skin, bones, eyes, and internal organs.*
> *When God closes a door, He always opens a window. I'm sure the blessings of your little one will reveal themselves soon!*
> *She is so much cuter than Raggedy Ann.*

On the day I finally spotted Lana walking across the quadrangle toward my room, I ducked inside, hurriedly straightened my room, and began to mash a leftover sweet potato with some ghost fruit. By the time I returned to the doorway I heard the click of the beads on Chester's door. Heard her murmur something low to him. Then silence, for a long time. Just the sound of Chester's rocker and an occasional cough. I know because I sat with my back against the wall that separated our rooms, hoping that, even if I couldn't understand the words she was saying, the vibrations of her voice might come through the wall, might worm their way into my head. I missed her.

After she left I went into Chester's room. He looked at me with his sad doe eyes and shrugged. Ida wasn't much use either, though I tried daily to pump her for information, sometimes subtly, sometimes rather aggressively. She mostly looked at me through her halo of frizzed hair and offered up colloquialisms that made her sound like an aunt in the country: "She's coming along," she'd say, or "She'll get there when she's ready." As though there were a place, a location Lana would eventually reach where she would be fixed, free of the pull of this strange grief.

Experiencing the Rending together had brought Lana and me close, but where she was now, after the birth, was a place so surreal and extreme, I couldn't begin to know how to inhabit it with her.

And I couldn't shake the fact that I'd been so busy not loving Rodney, so carefully avoiding that trap, that I'd placed my affection on Lana. And now she was gone. She hadn't been taken away physically, but she was occupying a different version of the present. She wasn't with me in the way she had been only days before.

Post-Rending grief had felt like a weight in my body, an anchor, the eternal gray of the sky wound into a skein and stuffed into my gut. But the loss of Lana, the birth of the first Baby, didn't feel this way. My grief was heat and anger and motion.

And I want to say that, faced with the loss of my friend, or the loss of the way our friendship had been, I grieved by spending more time on the Piles or by composing sonnets from the list of objects in the back of my notebook, by helping in the orchard or by practicing yoga breaths. But I didn't.

I went to Rodney instead.

CHAPTER NINE

THOUGH I DIDN'T have much of a wardrobe to select from, I'd considered many times what I'd wear if I ever *went to Rodney*. This was the language used in one of my mother's "recovery" books, the romance novels she read when she wanted to recover from her day—books I paged through when I had the house to myself, skipping to the passages that included phrases like *pulsing member* and *gush of warmth*. "She went to him then," the books always stated, the word *went* always the close cousin of *wet*, dripping with desire. There was a bra I'd never shown Lana, one I'd never worn for more than five minutes at a time. It was too small for me really, peach and lace with a little rosette in the middle and underwire that made my boobs look, from my angle, as though they might precariously roll over the edge of the brassiere and off my body at any moment. I kept a clean pair of underwear too. Just in case.

But when the time actually came, I didn't bother with the bra or the underwear. Grief and desire had scrubbed me, momentarily, free of self-consciousness. I put on the necklace instead. Took it down from its peg above the door, watched my fingers remember how to slide back the claw of the clasp, how to fit the small silver circle into its mouth.

Rodney's room was south of the ghost fruit orchards, out near Curly, about a ten-minute walk from my room. He'd built the room on stilts, as though he were expecting a flood or intruders. I'd been there once, after he'd first built it, to see the view, the land scraped clean and brown. In the distance the remains of the real Zion, the one with the real houses we'd scavenged and partially dismantled, the water tower we'd sucked dry after two years.

It was twilight when I got to the bottom of the ladder. Light sifted through the cracks in the floorboards above me. I climbed up

without announcing my arrival, poked my head over the plane of
floorboards. He was standing with his back to me, staring out the
window at Curly or Moe. I thought of my father then (Freud would
be pleased to know), of climbing the utility ladder propped against
our house a month before the Rending. I'd poked my head over the
edge of the roofline, and there was my father sitting on the shingles,
his cell phone pressed to his ear, head bowed slightly between his
bent knees as he listened to whoever was on the other end. He kept
not seeing me and I kept not making myself known. His tennis shoes
were off, socks stuffed inside, bare feet pressed against the warmth of
the shingles. I watched as he reached his right hand to the base of his
neck, watched him run his hand over the fuzz there, where it had
recently been cut. He did it for pleasure, I could see. And I was shocked,
caught by the gesture because it looked natural but I'd never seen
him do it before and whoever was on the other end of the phone
seemed to be bringing it out of him. But even more because he kept
not noticing me, kept not sensing my presence, and I'd thought that
somehow, no matter what happened, he'd always know where I was.
Maybe because when my father spoke of God's promises it was hard
not to hear them as his own.

I looked at Rodney; I hadn't made a sound. One beat. Two beats.
He turned and saw me but he wasn't surprised. He'd known who it
was that was there, knew me before I made myself known.

"Hi," I said.

"Hi," he said. "It's good to see you, Mira." He smiled and the
branch on his jaw moved, seemed to open.

He helped me up the last few rungs of the ladder but then he
just stood, looking at me, hands at his sides.

I glanced down at my dirty Keds and all of my self-consciousness
came flooding back into me. I remembered that the underwear I was
wearing was a size too small, that I'd cut the elastic to keep it from
driving a red hula hoop into my midsection. I longed for the bra I'd
left behind. That little rosette. I'd been so certain that once I
decided to be with Rodney (with all the weight and heat that he
entailed), every gesture and moment would flow easily, a Jacob's

Ladder where one rectangle of wood unfolded into the next and the next and the next.

He was still looking at me. I didn't know whether he was purposely making things difficult out of amusement or spite or whether he truly didn't know why I was there. What would Lana do? Who the fuck knew. She'd told me a few obscene details about her encounters with clients but I'd never bothered to ask about what happened in the moments between when the client entered the room and when he entered her. Crucial, awkward, stupid moments.

I met his gaze. "You're tall," I said, like a complete idiot. I'd always admired Rodney's size but this was the first time I realized my five-foot-three frame made me look like a hobbit beside him, a garden gnome with breasts.

He grabbed an overturned milk crate, lifted me quickly onto it, and then went back to staring at me, arms dangling. He smiled at me, slightly, but didn't move.

I reached out with my index finger and traced the branch along his jaw. He closed his eyes. The line of the branch was graceful but in places it was interrupted by the prick of whiskers poking through. I touched the hollow at the base of his throat; his jaw relaxed and his mouth opened slightly. I ran my palm across his head; his hair was brittle, a little oily. I drew my fingers across his scalp. He sighed and I felt the tiny gust of breath against my cheek. I was crying, I think. I kissed his lower lip, both his lips; I moved my tongue inside his mouth and pressed so close that I could feel his whiskers, his teeth. I had known I wanted Rodney but my brain hadn't really understood what that meant.

My body understood.

Desire made me fierce and ragged. I remember being angry, truly livid about how long it took for his clothes to come off. I hated the fabric for the few seconds it kept my skin from being on his skin. We were on his bed then. This body, his body before me, was a landscape. And it was mine. I was an animal frantic to mark its territory. I bit his earlobes, his chin. I kneaded his thighs and the thick band of muscle and fat around his waist. There was so much of him. I burrowed my nose in his armpit, his neck, his groin. I wanted his scent on my face. I scratched his back and his ass. I covered every inch of his skin with my skin and wound my legs through his, holding his arms above his head, swimming into him, his cock pressing into my belly. Then I slithered down and took it into my mouth so far and so fast that I came up choking, gasping and crying.

The gust of cool air that hit me as I sat up brought with it a recognition of the savage strangeness of my body's behavior. I had meant to be seductive, I had meant to be intentional about each gesture, coy and knowing. Instead I was a boiling mess of need and want and he'd been so still the whole time. Maybe he was just being kind to someone who was the sexual equivalent of a toddler at the end of a tantrum. But when I looked at him I saw that he'd simply been waiting. Being polite. Letting me take my turn.

He put me on my back. He held my face while he kissed me. Then he squeezed my shoulders, my biceps, my forearms, my breasts, my thighs. He worked his way down my body until I was tenderized; not in pain but on the cusp of pain. He put his face between my thighs and he was nothing like the boy I'd slept with before, who'd used his tongue like a quill, raising his eyes to check in with me after delicately carving each letter. Rodney was an animal in need of sustenance; he licked and lapped, his tongue open and rough and wide, as if trying to clean a wound I hadn't known was there. Then he was inside me. Without asking. Without gentle maneuvers or slow insertions. He was outside me and then he was inside me. There. Fully present. Entirely. It hurt and he kept going. I cried out and he kept going, his eyes measuring mine every second so that I knew he would stop if I wanted him to stop. I didn't want him to stop. I closed my eyes. He kept going and going, until the pain sighed into something that felt like pleasure, until the distinction didn't really matter anymore, until something inside my brain tore open. And when I opened my eyes he was there: heavy and emptied and mine.

*

We slept. When we woke in the morning we did all of it again. At the end I kissed him the way I'd wanted to the night before, not with frantic need and desperation, but simply with love. *There is a gold light in certain old paintings.* Words from a poem that I didn't remember until then, that seemed to be written on the other side of his lips.

Then I rolled away from him so we were both on our backs. I put my hand against his chest. "Did you have a dog," I asked, "in the Before?"

"Yep. We had a dog named Patsy."

"Patsy?"

"I got to name him. I don't think I meant it as a joke."

"How old were you?"

"Seven or eight. We got him a few weeks before Halloween. He was a Jack Russell Terrier, a low-key terrier. My mom bought a little pirate costume for him. Patsy even let us put the little black patch over his eye. But then he kept walking into things: table legs, the sofa, the door. My dad kept saying 'fuck's wrong with that animal?' and my mom kept yelling 'language!' from the kitchen. She was in there making caramel apples. She did it every Halloween, twenty-four of them, even though we lived on a busy street and hardly got any trick-or-treaters and the ones that did come didn't want an apple weighing their bags down. But she had this way of sticking the apples into the caramel and then twisting them so the caramel wrapped around just perfectly. It was beautiful. I was trying to guide Patsy around the living room by holding out a bit of bacon so he wouldn't run into things. We figured out later he was blind in one eye. And we'd covered the other eye with the patch."

"That's terrible!" I said. But I was laughing. I'd never heard Rodney string together so many sentences in a row.

"The next morning Patsy came up to my room, his hair all stuck together with wads of caramel. My mom had left the apples out and he'd gotten into them."

I liked watching his profile while he told the story. The tiny dark blades of his whiskers coming in. Adam's apple moving up and down his throat.

"So my dad took him away because he hadn't wanted a dog to begin with; getting Patsy had been some kind of concession to my mom, I think. Dad dropped Patsy far enough away he couldn't find his way back. He told me Patsy was at a farm. I didn't really miss Patsy too much but I missed the way my mom never made caramel apples after that."

"I'm sorry."

I could feel his body shrug beside me.

"Tell me something," he said, "from your Before."

I told him about the way my mother could step delicately through a tangled garden hose, in heels, without looking down. Then Rodney told me about how he and his cousin wore the same size shoes but walked with different gaits. His shoes would wear on the outside of the sole and his cousin's on the inside; every few months their mothers would make them switch pairs. I told him I always licked around the entire rim of a juice bottle before taking the first sip. He described the front window of his house, how it was almost entirely covered with window ornaments, glass flowers because his mother couldn't have a garden.

We went back and forth for a long time. Then he watched as I wrote in the back of my notebook: *Patsy, caramel apples, daffodils made of glass.* Finally he raised himself up on his elbow beside me.

"When you arrived at the gelato place with that douche security guard, I could tell you'd been crying. You had streaks of black down both cheeks. Streaks isn't the right word. Rivers?"

"Rivulets?"

"Yeah, I guess. Rivulets. But what got me is that the rivulets were dry. You'd stopped crying and you looked ready to kick that guy's ass. I had to save him from you." He touched my cheeks where the rivulets had been. Then he touched the necklace.

"I'm glad you saved him," I said.

CHAPTER TEN

I LOVED RODNEY. I love Rodney. But my experience of falling in love with him was different than the way Marjorie or Lana described love. Different than the way my mother had described her romance with my father. Most of the other women I knew had loved a few men, or been deeply infatuated at least, and so they talked about patterns and types. A penchant for a particular body shape or boozy charm or wry intelligence. My divorced aunt with the *What Love Is* book noted through tears that every man she'd ever loved had been born in April. Marjorie's conquests were all big men who couldn't resist adopting stray animals.

My mother had preferred to line up the men she'd loved and describe them as markers on her own psychological journey. *This man taught me to love myself, this man taught me to forgive, this man taught me how to let go.* It was an interesting narrative but I didn't know what this meant about her relationship with my father. Was he simply another stop on her road to self-knowledge or did marrying him mark a moment of Buddhist nirvana, the eightfold path unfolded to a glory bed of matrimonial bliss? But then I thought about my father talking on his cell phone on the roof. His bare feet and a voice I didn't know on the other end of the phone.

And then there were the romantic stories of high school literature and cineplex rom-coms, where love was simultaneously predictable and impossible, the result of a blind God picking two random human beings and banging them together until they sang a Celine Dion song.

But I didn't have other loves before Rodney or after Rodney so I never developed a type. He stood as a singular marker of where I was and would be. The only place he never entered, could never enter, was my Before. This is true of many romantic relationships, of course.

Most people don't have a past that contains the beloved. But the Rending made Rodney's absence in my past more acute. He would never meet my parents or Bim, never hear my father singing "The Riddle Song" while he grilled hamburgers, never watch my mother set out inappropriate snack combinations (a can of tuna and a wedge of cantaloupe; almonds and uncooked asparagus; leftover wilted salad and three squares of chocolate). So we tried, both of us, to make a picture of the Before wide enough for the other to enter. It didn't occur to either of us that the worlds we offered one another were false, mosaics constructed of only the most appealing shards of glass. While I withheld my guilt about the moment of the Rending, the way religion had permeated my life, how desperate I had been for love, it did not occur to me to wonder what Rodney was withholding. I simply received each shard he offered and gazed on each as Truth.

I loved that Rodney had two sides: the version of himself I saw and the version he showed to the rest of Zion. Others saw him as strong, reserved, abrupt. They trusted him to keep anything we deemed a weapon safe, secure. They admired his knowledge of snares, his ability to skin and disembowel an animal. "I mean, I trust Rodney," said Talia to me once in the middle of one of her endless monologues, "but I wouldn't want him mad at me. I think he has a lot of anger. His third chakra is a hot mess. And I just never want to be the one standing in front of him when that anger decides to come rolling out."

I didn't buy into Talia's chakra bullshit exactly but I understood what she meant; there was always a sense of motion below the surface of Rodney, a sense of him being bound by something, as though the branch on his jaw might come undone from his skin. I didn't know that most men who appear to be stoic do so purposely because they lack an internal game. Dumb or charmless, soul-stunned or lazy, these men have nevertheless discovered that women will travel upstream like spawning salmon at the hint of a below, an under, a beneath. So they present themselves as a closed door and women spend weeks, months, even years tapping upon it for access, ultimately finding on the other side an eternity of empty space. To find that Rodney possessed room upon room, each filled with artifacts and ideas, memories and land-scapes I'd never touched—I didn't know then how rare that was.

Here is a truth: After you experience the apocalypse, after you are living on the other side of it, falling in love still feels like its own apocalypse. Even on the other side, you will still use this comparison. And it will not be trite or cliché. Instead, you will know it to be true.

For the first few weeks after my night with Rodney, I was consumed. I went through the usual motions: I climbed the Piles, I delivered items to Tenzin and Sven and Asher, I washed my climbing shirts and hung them on the nails in my wall, I sent notes to Lana and tiptoed through the Center hoping Talia wouldn't look up from her book and notice me, I mended socks at community meetings while visitors told their stories and Zionites whined at each other about latrine care and Sorting Station access, I helped with the construction of the visitor quarters, and from time to time I wiped the accumu-lated dust from Lana's Baby. But my thoughts were always turning to Rodney. I was a dog and Pavlov's bell was ringing, ringing, ringing. There were things I should have been worried about: Lana, her Baby, the increase in visitors, our capricious food supply, the possibility of other Babies and what this might mean. But all of this fell away.

I wanted him. And when I found him alone I fell into him, fell at him. I took him to the top of each Pile and showed him my resting spaces. At the top of Larry I straddled him on a barstool I'd wedged upright between a tire and a huge terra-cotta flowerpot; at the top of Curly he leaned me over a wrought-iron gate, the tips of black iron pressing into the underside of my chin. At the top of Moe I showed him where I'd fastened a crib sheet as a canopy. We didn't make love there. We just lay on our backs, holding hands, looking at the equidis-tantly placed clouds hovering on the baby-blue fabric sky.

CHAPTER ELEVEN

I DIDN'T REALIZE HOW much time had elapsed, or how much my own version of time had been clouded, until the day we watched Deborah bathing in the river. Asher and Tenzin and Rodney were hard at work on the visitor addition so I was on the lookout for weight-bearing framing materials. The ones that proved too heavy or awkward for me to remove on my own I tagged with a scrap of bright fabric so the objects could be collected later when I had the help of another Zionite. Often Rodney was the one who came to help me, which meant that instead we both climbed to the top of Larry and removed our clothes.

One day, as we passed a pitcher of water back and forth between us and ate handfuls of shriveled ghost fruit, we watched a figure with long hair unhitch herself from the tree line and stand at the edge of the water, unmoving. The river switched its hips back and forth, its color flat and dark without the sun's reflection. Rodney started to hum "Down to the River to Pray" and I hummed a few bars with him before I caught myself and stopped.

"Where did you learn that song?" I asked.

"Who knows," he said. "Maybe that movie? With the escaped criminals?"

"*O Brother, Where Art Thou?*"

"Yeah."

The figure removed her shirt and pulled off her pants. Her hair was darker against the pale streak of her body.

"So this is why you sit here," said Rodney.

"I've never seen anyone bathe there before," I said, gesturing with a piece of ghost fruit toward the bank where the figure stood.

"Sure you haven't." Rodney lifted the tuft of my messy ponytail and kissed my neck.

"Who is that?"

He shrugged. "Cassie? I'd be able to guess more accurately if she'd turn around."

I pinched his upper thigh and he tried to tweak my right nipple.

Then she did turn. Just slightly so we could see her enormously pregnant profile. I stopped moving.

"Deborah," said Rodney.

"She's pregnant."

"You knew that."

And I did know that. Or I had known that. Right before Lana gave birth, Deborah and Tenzin had rather shyly raised their clasped hands together during a community meeting and announced that Deborah was five months along. But then Lana's baby was born and I'd spent almost all my time since then either on the Piles or with Rodney. Even in community meetings I barely noted the presence of anyone else. For three months I'd forgotten to look. Forgotten to see anything. The truth felt like a whip end.

"I need to see if Ida and Sylvia need me to look for anything. For the birth." I retied the tails of my climbing shirt, bent to knot my Keds.

Rodney grabbed one of the tail ends. "Mira, it's OK. You don't have to rush off. She's not in labor now."

I pulled my shirt out of his grasp and started down the face of Larry, tracing a path I knew Rodney couldn't follow.

I knew rationally that I had no right to be angry with Rodney, but I was. He'd sealed himself over my eyes like a permanent pair of rose-colored glasses, strung me out on a kind of partial oblivion. I felt suddenly claustrophobic, Jonah in the belly of the whale.

When I arrived at the Clinic I was out of breath. In the waiting area, Ida sat on one of the blue plastic stadium seats, cutting fabric into strips. In the back, Sylvia lifted a pair of scissors out of a steaming pot.

"I'm here to help," I said. "What do you need? For Deborah?"

"You look a little flushed," said Ida, raising one eyebrow and smiling.

Sylvia came out of the exam room, drying her hands on a towel. "How's the view from the top of Larry?"

I rolled my eyes. "Ha ha," I said. That they both knew about Rodney and me, that our romance hadn't been a secret, that my obsession was not buried nearly as deep as I thought—this made me feel like vomiting.

"It's OK, Mir," said Ida, her voice softening. "We're glad you're happy."

"Deborah," I said.

"There's nothing we can do now," said Sylvia, matter-of-fact again. "We'll let you know if we need anything."

"We'll put you on call when she's in labor," said Ida. "Could be anytime." Then she bent her head and, began to roll a strip of checkered fabric around the blue straw Lana had used during her labor, when I'd thought of Bim on the roller coaster, imagined his body slipping through the slim sapphire passages.

I crossed the quadrangle without looking for Rodney, without trying to take note of his presence. Cal and Cassie were hauling a load of ghost fruit to the Center. The red bandana fluttered beside Lana's closed door. Two visitors—a couple—had their belongings laid out in front of the visitor quarters and seemed to be debating the efficacy of various packing techniques. Chester barely looked up from his book when I entered his room and dropped into a sling-back chair I'd never seen before. The glass eye in his bowl of treasures on the coffee table gazed unflinchingly. Beside the bowl was a row of rolled fortunes and a plastic bottle cap filled with a gray liquid. How long had it been since I'd sat here with Chester? Since I'd tried to match my breath to the creaking of his rocker? Since I'd unwrapped a fortune? Days? Weeks? Months?

He was rocking slightly, book open on his lap. I recited, staring at his bowl of strange treasures, the poem I'd remembered when I kissed Rodney on our first morning together:

There is a gold light in certain old paintings
That represents a diffusion of sunlight.
It is like happiness, when we are happy.
It comes from everywhere and nowhere at once, this light.

When I finished, Chester asked me to recite it again so I did.

"It's a nice poem," he said, holding the page of a book taut with one hand as he drew his razor blade around the chosen words.

"I used to think it was such an upbeat poem, when I was in high school. All that light and happiness."

"Sounds upbeat to me."

"Maybe. Maybe it's just thinking about it now. Certain old paintings, not all of them. And the sunlight diffused. Not we are happy but *when* we are happy. As though happiness is something that just happens occasionally."

"Isn't it?" He rolled the rectangle of paper he'd cut into a tiny tube, then dropped the tip of his index finger into the bottle cap on the table. Likely a mixture from Zephyr. Chester slid his finger along the edge of the paper. Sealed it carefully.

"Light coming from nowhere. I thought that was such a poetic idea. I remember saying the line over and over again, 'everywhere and nowhere at once, this light,' while my grandma was dying."

Chester nodded as if I'd told him this before. He set the rolled fortune on the table.

"Which sounds romantic, right? Poetry at your dying grandmother's bedside? But it wasn't. I didn't want to be there but my parents wanted someone there, at all times, the 'death watch' they started to call it. So I rode the city bus after school and did my homework on the little side table in her room, which was usually OK. Except when I had to memorize that poem. I don't even know why I'm telling you this."

Chester shrugged without looking up at me. Pulled the blade across another expanse of paper.

"All the monitors were beeping. There was the shush of a million carts being rolled everywhere. And this old black-and-white film

87

crackling on her television, men in shades of gray stealing a painting. I was trying to concentrate and it was so loud: the rickety dialogue, someone tumbling down a set of stairs, gunshots. I turned it off. My grandmother's nurse had made a big deal of telling me not to but I did anyway. And that's the one time my grandma started to move, to thrash as much as someone with three ounces of life left inside can thrash, the tubes in her mouth making her look hooked, caught. Like she should be clubbed to death so she wouldn't be in pain."

Chester raised his eyebrows.

"Yep, that's what I thought about my grandmother. That she was a trout that should just be put out of her misery. Anyway, the nurse came bustling in. Looked at me with her 'shame-on-you' face, turned on the television, settled my grandmother down. She died a couple days later."

"I'm sorry," said Chester.

"Whatever. The point is that in spite of having that memory attached to the poem I've always loved it."

"Everywhere and nowhere at once."

I nodded. It was a nice thing to visualize in the Before, when light was light and the sun was a marvelous ball that whipped up shadows and glare. "Back then those paintings felt close, like you could go and find one and stand with your hands behind your back and bask in that golden light all day if you wanted."

Chester shrugged. "You don't know for sure you won't find one."

But I knew. I hadn't found art. Not real art. Hadn't found Shakespeare or Donne or Dickinson, hadn't found the Bible or the Koran or the Mahabharata. We'd been given back our cow-patterned sheets and light fixtures, our linoleum and socket wrenches, our books with straight lines of fact and obtuse theories, our magazines filled with train layouts and thirty-minute meals, but the certain old paintings and with them their gold light—those were gone. Even the words I'd memorized seemed fragile. As I pushed Chester's bead curtain aside I wondered if I'd had the poem right or if I'd mangled phrases, switched the syntax, let whole lines sink into a firmament where they could never be recovered.

CHAPTER TWELVE

DEBORAH GAVE BIRTH to three birds. Marjorie was the one to tell me. I was coming back from latrine duty, trying to keep my hands an ample distance from my body until I could get to the river to wash. Marjorie was standing at the edge of the orchard with her gathering basket in one hand, her gray hair floating, rising and falling around her in the wind. She wasn't calling or gesturing but I knew to go to her. We sat on an old air-conditioning unit the orchardists used for storage.

Marjorie took my hand and stroked it while she told me, running the tip of her index finger down the length of each of my fingers, rubbing each nail lightly. They weren't real birds, she explained, they were decorative, the kind you could attach to the boughs of your Christmas tree or your porch railing. There were little bendy wires on the feet of the birds. That was the phrase she used, "little bendy wires," and they had hurt Deborah a little coming out. But she was going to be OK.

"What are they?"

"What are what, sweetheart?"

"The birds. What kind are they?"

Marjorie looked at me a little strangely. Her eyes were blue but the left had a strange brown spot on the iris. "Well, I think there was a cardinal and a goldfinch. I think. Maybe a sparrow was the third? Maybe a thrush. Something red, something yellow, something brown."

"Are they clean?" I couldn't think of Deborah. Couldn't even bring myself to think of her face. But the idea that the birds might be covered in blood or afterbirth made me want to heave.

"I think Ida's taking care of that."

"OK," I said. "Does Lana know?"

Marjorie nodded. If she said anything after that I don't remember. I remember telling her I was fine, over and over again, so that she'd walk away.

CHAPTER THIRTEEN

AFTER TWO DAYS of recuperation in her own room, Deborah staked out space in the Center. For the first few days, she talked with Talia over cup after cup of tea, the three birds lined up on the table in front of her, none of them larger than the teacup Talia offered her, white china with Dutch girls and cows scrolled around the outside in blue. By the fourth day Deborah started to attach the birds to herself. Depending on the hour, the perch for each bird alternated: the bun on top of her head, her scarf, the collar of her shirt. She wore fleece pants and a thick wool sweater to better support the birds' bendy wires. Chummy, Laverne, and Oxtail was what she named them officially but *dear*, *sweetheart*, and *honey* is what she called them.

Anyone who passed through the Center, to get fire for a lantern, to grab a sweet potato or cup of tea, to rest momentarily or browse the library, was introduced to Chummy, Laverne, and Oxtail, was encouraged to stroke delicately from the tops of their heads to their backs, to comment on the softness of the feather, the brightness of the eye. After a week, Deborah was bending her head, birdlike, to listen to what Chummy and Laverne and Oxtail had to say, interpreting and translating for the rest of us, making their desires known. Chummy didn't like loud noises. Laverne liked it if you held your steaming tea just below her beak. Oxtail had a penchant for bright colors and patterns. Meanwhile Tenzin, after having been a dutiful partner for the first few days after the birth, drifted back to work when it became clear that Deborah was stuck in some kind of strange emotional holding pattern.

Rodney and I went together one day, to be formally introduced to the birds, to marvel at them. I'd been avoiding Rodney mostly, feeling as though this wouldn't have happened to Deborah if I'd been paying better attention to the world instead of just to him, even though rationally I knew that made no sense. But I didn't want to be introduced to the birds alone. As we entered the Center a wrinkled female visitor towing a yellow plastic sled piled high with her belongings gave a low whistle. She took a big handful of her short gray hair and motioned her head in the direction of the table where Deborah sat. "Woman in there? With those birdies? Nutso."

Rodney glanced at her duct-taped shirt cuffs, at the old Quaker oatmeal bin in the sled overflowing with what looked like soiled women's underwear, at her widened eyes. "Thank you for the heads-up, ma'am," he said.

"And thank you for the tails," she whispered furtively, nodding toward a ball of fur on the sled.

"You're welcome."

"Tails?" I said as we walked away.

"She saw me skinning those raccoons. She asked." Rodney shrugged.

We sat across the table from Deborah. Her face had lost its saggy, misshapen quality. Instead, the edges of her lips looked like they'd been permanently staked to her cheekbones and tiny red cuts and scratches stippled her skin. She took Rodney's hand in her own, smoothed his index finger over the tiny head of Chummy to show him how to be gentle. "It's not that I don't trust you, Rodney, it's just knowing your own strength and all. You understand." She nodded and we nodded back at her. Ida had done a good job washing the birds; their feathers were slick, almost iridescent, and each dark eye sparked with a bit of reflected light. Stroking the breast feathers with my thumb felt comforting at first; it had been almost four years since I'd touched an animal gently.

Then Deborah was up and before I could resist she was attaching Laverne to the fluorescent string that held my notebook. Attached to such a flimsy resting place, the bird flipped upside down, dangling. Unfazed, Deborah returned to her seat and began winding Oxtail's wires into her sweater. When she was done she held Chummy up to Rodney's face, to the branch. At the ends of the wires, which were almost entirely coated with green plastic, the silver tips protruded, and these Deborah pressed gently against Rodney's skin. "Chummy could sit right here," she said.

Rodney grew very still. He kept his hands around his mug of tea but his eyes held Deborah's. Steam drifted up and parted around the body of the bird. "Chummy would be so happy here, I think, on this branch." As she moved Chummy up and down to show his enthusiasm for the proposition, two thin red lines appeared on Rodney's cheek. Instead of moving the hand that held the bird, Rodney took Deborah's other hand. Laverne's weight, red and dangling from my notebook, felt immense.

"I want to have a branch here too," she moved Chummy away from Rodney's face, pressed the wires to her own. "I want the birds to have a place to rest. I want to be a place for them to rest." She was crying, rubbing Chummy against her cheek, trying to nestle the bird into her skin.

"I think you already are a good place for the birds to rest," I said. I unwound the wires of Laverne's feet from the shoelace, passed her scarlet body to Deborah. "I think Laverne would be happier with you."

"Yes," said Deborah. She took Chummy away from her cheek and tied both Chummy and Laverne to the handle of her coffee mug. "I think they need to sleep now," she said, nodding, and we nodded back at her and then Rodney took my hand and we walked out of the Center, back to his house, and for the first time since we'd seen Deborah bathing in the river, we undressed. I kissed the scratches on his cheek. He cupped my breasts in his hands. Then the knobs of my shoulders. I held his heels. His ass. His testicles. Living skin below my palms.

Cardinal, goldfinch, thrush I wrote in the back of my notebook when we were done.

CHAPTER FOURTEEN

CHESTER WAS THE one who discovered her. He found Deborah hanging from a tree by the river. The slip knot was done with a tidy precision that seemed deeply unlike her. Deborah was hanging from the branch and Chummy, Laverne, and Oxtail were hanging from her sweater, each little body flipped so that its head was hanging down. They didn't look like they were happy to have found a resting place. They looked dead, too.

Chester didn't take the body down. He thought it was important, he told me later, for everyone to see what it looked like to have something haunt you enough to make your own death.

When Lana came to see the body she put her fist to her mouth but she didn't cry.

We'd never buried a Zionite before. A visitor had died a year earlier, just a few hours after arriving in Zion with an infected wound on his upper arm. Sylvia said it looked like someone had tried to saw through him with a bread knife but we never heard how he'd gotten the wound because he spiked a fever and grew delirious before either Sylvia or Ida could coax the story out of him. Tenzin and Rodney were asked to remove the body and they did—and most of us were happy not to know where they disposed of it. Though the next time we ate meat I did ask Lana, only half-joking, whether she thought it tasted like squirrel, possum, or visitor. She said, "One, that's disgusting and two, I think we'd know if this was rancid human flesh. Unless you have some zombie tendencies you haven't bothered to mention. Just ask Rodney or Tenzin if you're so worried." But I didn't ask. Because I was hungry. Because I couldn't afford to lose my appetite.

Tenzin didn't want Deborah buried or burned. He wanted her laid to rest, like some fucked-up version of Sleeping Beauty, in a four-poster bed in a house in old Zion. Apparently, he and Deborah had spent time exploring abandoned houses together and they'd loved this particular one—a two-story Arts and Crafts home, the entire front façade missing. "Deborah thought it'd be just like living in a doll house," he said as we walked over. "We were planning to move here at some point, still be part of Zion but have our own space. She said it felt like home to her."

The ground had been saturated the night before so Tenzin made everyone remove their shoes when we arrived; then he forgot to remove his own and most of what I remember about Deborah's funeral (though it seems strange to call it that) is the imprint of those boot marks on the beige rug of the bedroom suite. At least fifty of us fit into the suite, though we were careful not to stand too near the wall-less side—the other twenty or so Zionites stood or sat in the hallway. The room had been cleared of most useful items when we did our scavenging in the year after the Rending. There was a lighter patch of paint on one wall where a work of art or framed family portrait must have hung (I imagined matching checkered shirts, a field of winter wheat). Divots in the carpet marked where a dresser had stood, and maybe a love seat or a desk. The nightstand was still there, dusted and empty except for a pair of flesh-colored earplugs set upright like nipples. Under the window at the far end of the room was a lithe, taxidermied mammal—a weasel or a pine marten—and a fan with two blades hung above the bed. On the pillow, Deborah's hair was arranged in an unnatural-looking sunburst.

Everything felt wrong and strange. Not the house, exactly—all the houses after the Rending felt wrong and strange; that's why most people chose not to inhabit them. It felt wrong and strange that this space felt like home to Deborah and Tenzin, two people I didn't know well but had lived with for almost four years. And the whole room—the pristine carpet and the earplugs and the weasel and the empty walls and the divots they hadn't bothered to snub out with their feet—all of these were choices they had made about the room and yet the space felt like nothing I understood, had understood, about either of them.

Tenzin sat on the edge of the bed and took Deborah's hand. He told us about her summers on Cape Cod, her memorized store of facts from the Guinness World Records book (longest fingernails, fattest man, largest number of offspring), that she'd sung "You Are My Sunshine" to her belly. He said that each evening they'd asked one another if they'd rather die but be given a last meal or keep living forever on sweet potatoes and ghost fruit. He said that he loved her. He chose not to offer prayers but when he was done speaking no one spoke or disrupted the silence for a long time. Finally, Chester offered a rolled fortune, which Tenzin pressed between Deborah's stiff fingers. Ida cleared her throat and began singing "You Are My Sunshine" and we all jumped in and the second time through we started to file out. Tenzin stayed behind to clean his own muddy footprints; when I knelt beside him to help, he batted me away.

I cried on the twenty-minute walk back to our Zion, slow, steady tears. Rodney's hand was at the small of my back, tender but firm, guiding me forward. I cried for Deborah and for Tenzin, for the always-ache of hunger, for my mother and my father and Bim, for the distance I still felt from Lana and the strangeness of the earplugs on that night-stand. And I also cried because as strange and fucked up as that room had seemed, Deborah and Tenzin had gone off in search of something that felt like a life together. For the first time, Rodney's touch felt insubstantial, as though if I quickened my pace even slightly we might lose contact altogether.

CHAPTER FIFTEEN

THE FUNERAL WAS on a Monday. Two days later, a few hours before the community meeting, Lana found me at the bottom of Larry unthreading ribbons woven through the spokes of a child's bicycle. The tires I'd give to Asher, in the hope he'd make me a cart instead of the baby buggy I used for collecting purposes. I wasn't sure who the ribbons were for yet but I was enjoying the ribbed, waxy feel on my fingertips, thinking of the way my mother would whiz ribbon over the flat side of a scissors blade to create a froth of curls.

"Hey," said Lana.

I turned to look at her. Stopped myself from really looking at her and turned back to the bike.

"Can I help?"

I scooted over slightly. Patted the ground next to me. As she bent over the tire her hair, undone and unwashed, brushed the spokes. When she handed an unthreaded ribbon to me it was slightly sweaty from her palms.

"Thanks," I said. "Are you OK?"

The question hung there, laundry saturated with rain.

She shrugged. Rubbed the tread of the tire with her thumb. "Kind of. I will be."

I stood to put the ribbon in the buggy. "Your hair looks like shit."

She smiled up at me from the ground. The first smile in almost four months. "I know," she said.

We walked to the river, to the place where Deborah had been found, where the water slummed itself over a sandbar to make a six-inch-deep pool. Lana, on her hands and knees in the water, bent her head so that her long hair fell forward, the tips like the legs of water bugs skimming the surface. *Water bugs, dragonflies, pill bugs, centipedes.* Words I'd add to the list at the end of my notebook. Insects I hadn't thought to miss until now. She didn't flinch when I poured the icy water over her head, when it ran down the sides of her neck and soaked the collar of her Dodgers sweatshirt. Her belly hung loose and soft. I wanted to pull it up, cajole it back into its former place. When her hair was saturated I wrung it out as best I could. Then back in her room I braided it. Not the tiny knots she'd worn for as long as I'd known her, but a braid that started at her left ear and wound itself over her forehead, past her right ear and around the back of her head to end where it began. A crown. It took a long time to get it right.

We walked to the community meeting together.

At the front of the meeting room, beside Lana's doll, Chummy, Laverne, and Oxtail lay on their sides. They had not been tucked into bed with Deborah. They looked stunned by a recent flight into a window, as if they'd mistaken a world behind glass for their own.

Zephyr was the meeting leader. We breezed through Announcements and Rules; when it came time to move onto Issues and Ideas, Zephyr took out a card on which he'd written a few questions to start the conversation, questions so bland I don't remember them now, though I do remember feeling sorry for him. Deborah's absence was palpable. Across the room, Rodney was sitting next to Tenzin but not too close; there was enough room between them that Deborah could have squeezed right in. Since she was often late to our meetings, often entered saying "oops, oops, oops" under her breath, there was a sense in which we were all waiting for her, hoping that there was a different Deborah, one whose body wasn't rotting in a four-poster bed, one who would enter as herself, who wouldn't even recognize the goldfinch, the cardinal, and the thrush lined up in a row on the crate in front of Zephyr.

"Is there a way to know if all the babies will be like this now?" Cassie's hand was in the air when she spoke but Zephyr hadn't called on her.

Beside me, Lana focused on trying to tuck loose strands of hair into her braided crown. Asher swiveled the brim of his hat, front to back, back to front, and Rodney focused on unclogging bits of mud from the treads in his left boot.

"Sylvia?" asked Zephyr finally.

Sylvia was sitting in front of me, across from Cassie, her hair secured in the silver dragon clasp, her spine a scalpel line. "I'm not a fortune-teller. I don't have a crystal ball." She spoke carefully, clearly, as though we were strangers in town and she were offering directions. "It is likely that in certain cases I'll be able to tell there isn't a human baby developing inside."

"But you couldn't tell with Lana." Cassie stood then, likely to offer the effect of her five-month-pregnant belly.

"I thought there was something wrong with Lana's pregnancy," said Sylvia, not turning her head to look at Lana, "but I'd never delivered a baby before. I'd never done a prenatal exam."

"So you were withholding information, then," I said suddenly, heat rising up my neck, though I had intuited the exact same thing. Lana had pulled her hands into the cuffs of her sweatshirt. She was pointedly not looking at Cassie, Sylvia, me, or her Baby.

"I know," said Sylvia, still not turning, "that stress is bad for a pregnant woman. What could I have done? Even if I'd known."

"And Deborah?" said Cassie.

"Deborah too."

Cassie stared at her. We wanted her to ask the inevitable question about her own pregnancy. But she didn't.

Ida raised her hand, just to the height of her shoulder. Zephyr nodded. "I understand why Cassie's concerned. Obviously." She waved her hand in the direction of Cassie's belly. "But we don't have much control over that right now. We don't know enough. But it seems to me that we do have some control over what happens after the Babies are born, after they come out."

Talia's hand shot up into the air. Zephyr ignored her. "Say more, Ida."

"Well, I don't think we helped Deborah very much. I don't think she knew how to relate to her birds. To her Babies."

Beside me, Lana leaned forward, forearms on knees. I put my hand on her back. Her breath was fast.

Ida continued with her eyes on Lana: "None of us knew how either and I'm not blaming anyone, I'm just saying. Being with them all the time, being with the birds—"

"Chummy. Laverne. Oxtail." Tenzin said it quietly but Ida heard him.

"Thank you, Tenzin. Yes. Chummy and Laverne and Oxtail. Being near them all the time didn't seem healthy for her."

Lana stood suddenly, her hands still pulled into the sleeves of her sweatshirt. When she spoke her breath was ragged, asthmatic. "It makes me feel crazy to be near her," she said, pointing at her Baby, "and it makes me feel crazy to be away." She started to cry, big sobs that she didn't try to hide in her hands or wipe away; instead she looked at each person while she cried. "Either way it is impossible. Being close or being far away. It could have been me in that tree. Just as easily. It could have been me." I tried to take her hand but she pulled it away. Looked at me when she said "it could still be me in that tree."

She sat again and I took her hand. She let me hold it but kept it soft and lifeless. No one else spoke. Not even Zephyr to officially bring the meeting to a close. It was as if a light had gone out in the room, as though someone had given the order for us to leave in silence. I thought of Maundy Thursday and the stripping of the altar. We left the room that way. In ones and twos and threes. Lighting our candles from the fire. Disappearing into the night.

CHAPTER SIXTEEN

RODNEY WAS WAITING for me outside the Center. He tried to steer me to his room but I wasn't interested. I stood on tiptoes and kissed him on the edge of his lips where the tiny buds at the end of the branch were stenciled into his skin. He smelled like fire and sweat and himself. "I'll see you tomorrow," I said. Then I walked across the quadrangle, through the curtain of beads, and into Chester's room.

Chester wasn't there so I sat on an embroidered footstool and studied his bowl of treasures. In the light of my lantern the ridges pressed into the retainer looked lunar and the false teeth resembled a Paleolithic zipper. When Chester entered the room he seemed, as usual, completely unsurprised by my presence. He washed his hands in one of the silver bowls on his counter, dried them on his shirt, settled down across from me in his rocker, hands on the arms, gazing at me until I was ready to speak.

"I hate not doing anything. To help. I hate not being able to help her."

Chester nodded. "I need a fortune," I said, in the way cowboys in Westerns said they needed a shot of whiskey or rich housewives on reality shows professed their desire for wine.

Chester leaned back and reached into the small pocket above the regular front pocket on his jeans. I'd always wondered what that tiny pocket was for and now I had the answer: that little pocket was for holding fortunes after the apocalypse. He handed it to me.

I unfolded it and read without a trace of sarcasm: "Oh Mister Sun, Sun, Mister Golden Sun, please shine down on me."

Chester whistled a little of the Raffi tune.

"Fuck you, Chester," I said. "Seriously?"

Chester stopped whistling but kept rocking. "You know, Mira, Raffi suffered from debilitating depression."

"Really?" I said.

"I have no idea," said Chester, "but it would make the song better, right?"

This time I was the one not to answer. I stared at him. Didn't realize I was crying until I wiped the tears off my cheek with the back of my hand.

Chester came around to my side of the coffee table, sat cross-legged beside the footstool, took my hands. "Mir," he said, "we're all broken. Or if we're not yet we will be. Lana's broken in a different way than she would have been in the Before, but it doesn't have to be the end."

"You mean she won't end up killing herself."

"I was going for vague and poetic. But yeah. That's what I mean."

"So you don't think she'll end up dangling from a branch."

"I think Lana's more of a pills kind of girl."

"So we're safe because she can't buy any Vicodin on the street?"

"Maybe." Chester offered a half-smile. "I don't know, Mir, I think Lana's stronger than you think."

I picked the false teeth from the dish, pressed them against my knee. "I can tell she's hurting but it's like I can't get inside it. I don't understand it." I pressed harder on my knee until I could feel the bite of the teeth through my jeans. I wanted to leave a mark.

On the other side of the wall, in my own room, lying on my pallet, I couldn't get the Mr. Sun song out of my head. I thought of the sun: reprinted on logos for cereal, anthropomorphized in children's books, scalded onto tourist paraphernalia. That's when I thought of the wallet: ARIZONA with the fluorescent setting sun, the one in which I'd stored our ridiculous baby names, the scraps I knew I needed now.

CHAPTER SEVENTEEN

I WENT TO ZEPHYR with a tray I'd found in the Piles, about eighteen inches in diameter. Into the tray he poured his thickest sludge, a slurry comparable to cement, and around the circumference I placed spokes from the bike Lana had helped me de-ribbon; they dried splayed out from the tray like the rays of a silver sun. Once the cement was dry and the spokes were fastened I wove the ribbon, waxy and ribbed, through the spokes, followed by all the fabric scraps I could find: nylon from pink ballet tights and the polyester shimmer of a woman's emerald blouse, thuggish canvas and wraithlike silk. Onto the sharp tip of each spoke I pressed a child's eraser, nubby seahorses and starfish, and then into the fabric I nestled the names, some of the scraps showing and others layered within creases and folds until I'd made a place where Lana's Baby could rest.

CHAPTER EIGHTEEN

L ANA STOOD IN front of the Nest for a long time, hands dangling at her sides. Her breath came slow and even. The doll, her Baby, lay nestled in the fabric at the bottom. Without turning her head to look at me she said, "I know she's not alive, Mir. I get it. I know that. But she looks happy there. Do you think I'm bat-shit crazy if I say that I think she's happy there?"

"I don't think you sound bat-shit crazy."

"She does look kind of cold."

I nodded. Then she said, "You should make one for Deborah too."

By the next community meeting I'd made a Nest for the birds as well. I twisted twine and metal coat hangers into a kind of birdcage. I affixed the cage to a silver hubcap but didn't add any sort of lid or cover; inside the cage I placed the yellow skeleton of an old Connect Four game and around and through and into these holes I wound the bendy wires attached to the feet of Chummy and Laverne and Oxtail. Upright, they looked wry and alert, alive.

The meeting didn't start on time because everyone wanted to get a closer look at the Nests, and strangely everyone—not just Lana—seemed more at ease, more content in the presence of the Babies now that they were placed, contained, resting. Over her Baby, ostensibly so that she looked less cold, Lana had placed the red bandana that had hung above her door for the last three and a half years. I watched Gary and Oscar and even Zephyr look at it and look at her, as though her gaze might suggest that she was still available, that her use of the bandana was simply a coincidence; but she refused to look.

Paloma, the meeting leader, finally got everyone to sit down by clearing her throat multiple times. Though her figure was soft and feminine (full bosom, wide hips, a ponytail tied at the base of her neck that gave way to a cascade of straight black hair down the entire length of her spine), her voice was gruff and her gait masculine (she led with her shoulders, raised and tight, her pelvis pressed backward). Her family, originally from Guatemala, had raised free-range chickens in the Before to sell to hormone- and pesticide-conscious upper-middle-class families in Minneapolis. They sold the eggs to local co-ops and she'd had one in her hand at the moment of the Rending. She described how one minute there was an egg and the next moment her hand was "full of yellow, full of yolk." She often did this when she talked, initially forgetting an English word and substituting a description instead, then remembering, correcting.

"We'll go backward today," she said. "Issues first. Announcements last. We need to talk about these." She gestured to the Babies in front of her. "What's going on here? No one would say what they thought the last time."

Though the theories began tentatively enough (no one wanted to offend Lana or frighten Cassie), they quickly accrued and gathered a strange and twisting momentum: we were being punished by a supernatural being; we were lab rats below an invisible dome; it was some sort of side effect of the ghost fruit (like Adam and Eve!); a particular trigger or gene had been removed and the women were like the buildings we'd seen on our way to Zion, parts missing and absent, deformed in a way that was impossible to see or define. Talia suggested that the Babies were somehow the manifestation of inner fears and Zephyr suggested, as he often did during Issues time, that maybe this was all just a dream.

Finally Paloma cleared her throat a few more times and said, "Enough. Rules now."

Lana's hand rose quietly, an unlit wick. The crown of hair made her look less whimsical, more mature. Paloma nodded at her.

"I propose three rules," said Lana.

The room grew quiet. "First, I think you—I think we—have to take the Baby—or the Babies—away from the mother within twenty-four hours. If the Baby is like this I mean," she said, gesturing to the Nests. "Otherwise it's dangerous. Something in you wants to take care of it, of them, and you can't. But the second rule is that they should each be given one of these, one of these Nests so that they have a place to go. So the mother—or the father," she looked at Tenzin, "knows that the Baby is safe."

"The third rule?" asked Paloma.

"A name. I think each Baby should be given a name. I think that should be Chester's job."

A look of surprise crossed Chester's face. But he looked at Lana and nodded.

There were no exceptions to the Rules, no addendums. All of us were glad to push a little order toward the chaos. We held the first Naming Ceremony, for Lana's and Deborah's Babies, at the next community meeting. Asher, Rodney, and Tenzin began construction on the Nesting Facility soon after that.

As much as I hated to admit it, given the distance I felt from both God and Christianity, the Nesting Facility was necessary not only as a physical space to hold the Babies, but as a place we could call holy, where the air particles could shift slightly, where spirits and questions could hover. After Deborah, we realized that things beyond our explanation, if not named and given a place to live, could harm us, could drive us to enter an unspeakable place too.

Lana helped build the Nesting Facility. She was so thin and wiry it never occurred to me she'd be able to lift anything. But she was strong. Her sweatshirt lying in a gray pool on the ground, Lana worked in a white wifebeater, which on our first Valentine's Day she'd decorated with a red-nail-polish heart. The muscles in her biceps were quail eggs, shifting below her skin as she lifted. The best part of fifty-five-degree weather is that it's conducive to working long hours—and we did. Rodney and Asher and Tenzin did much of the work but other community members stepped in to help when they could: Paloma and Zephyr and Marjorie and Sven and Kristen and Chester and Oscar and Cassie and Eleanor. There was an odd sense of cheer in the air as we worked, as though we were at an Amish barn raising or filming a Folgers commercial. Asher complimented our efforts without a trace of irony, Tenzin whistled tunes he invented that reminded me of gliders catching updrafts higher and higher, spiraling into the air. Occasionally Lana, who had spent ten days on the cheerleading squad in high school, would shout out an appropriately mangled cheer. Mostly, I think all of us were glad to be doing something tangible in response to the unseen, the unknown.

We built the facility in the middle of the quadrangle, a central, circular room from which three rectangular rooms extended, like a Mercedes symbol. One branch pointed toward the Clinic, the other two pointed toward the spaces between where the Center ended and our rows of rooms began. The rectangular rooms we lined with shelves to hold the Nests; the central room would be used for the Naming Ceremonies or as a place to sit. "Quiet contemplation" were the words Talia used, though I'm not sure anyone had quietly contemplated anything within a twenty-foot radius of Talia.

We still needed a pedestal to hold the Nest in question during the ceremony but none of the objects I'd brought forth to serve that purpose had pleased Lana. Instead she decided we needed to build the pedestal ourselves out of forlorn objects from the Sorting Stations. She declared this would be artistic but so far it just looked ugly.

"I'm trying on gratitude today," said Lana as she attempted to adhere an answering machine to the preliminary base of the pedestal.

"That sounds promising," I said, slathering a Zephyr mixture into the cracks between the answering machine and what looked like the former base of a streetlight.

"Maybe not gratitude exactly. I've just had a lot of time to think lately." She pulled her hands gently away from the pedestal. The objects didn't move. "I'm trying to be positive. What if Zephyr and the others are right? What if the Babies are a kind of sign or signal or opportunity or something?" She stood, brushed the dust off her cheetah-patterned lounge pants, and gave me a crooked smile. "What if they represent a kind of, I don't know, potential?"

"Potential?" I said, perhaps a little too cynically. I wedged the grill from a barbecue below a splintered trough to give it more support.

The edge of her smile fell. She nudged the answering machine gently. It held. "Forget it," she said.

"I'm sorry," I said. Say more." But she was already walking away with the empty mixture bucket while I remained at the base of the pedestal, holding the grill, waiting for what held it to harden.

Later I added the word *potential* to the list at the front of my notebook, as if it were an object I could find in the Piles, as real under my fingers as fishing line or a Rubik's Cube or a string of pearls. I hadn't thought of our bodies, of the Babies that way. I'd only thought of our wombs as damaged, maligned, wrecked. Like the buildings we saw in the Cities, stripped of shutters or gutters or bricks, I'd assumed something crucial had been taken from us—a genetic sequence, an army of white blood cells, the favor of a higher power. I carried the word *potential* in my head as well as between the sea-blue lines of my notebook, chewing the notion that the Babies weren't a botched version of a human but were their own kind of cog in a machine we had yet to understand.

Unlike the extra visitor quarters, a fairly simple construction that had taken four months to complete, the Nesting Facility took only a month. By the time Cassie gave birth to a honey bear filled with sand, we had a place to put its Nest and a way to welcome it into the world.

It seems absurd, in retrospect, that after the birth of the first few Babies, we didn't stop having sex. Why didn't we make a rule, simple as where to shit or where to dispose of your half-eaten potato, that said, in less vulgar language, Things Get Weird When We Fuck So No More Fucking?

The answer is relatively simple: We were living in the backwash of the former world. Although we found—*were blessed to find*, Talia often said—objects in the Piles, we were without a great deal too. We missed ice and Netflix and aspirin, tampons and coffee and soap that sudsed into a mountain of lather between our palms. We missed things we never thought we'd miss from the old world: car alarms, the scent of Indian food woven into the fabric of our clothes, the lurch and hiss of the city bus, grapes, granola, Christmas carolers, the fuzzed roar of a packed stadium. We missed the way newscasters spoke into their microphones, the sound of a particular footstep on wooden stairs. We missed stairs.

And we had no mothers or fathers. I had no Bim. And so, almost four years after the Rending, although we had created a fairly stable world in which to live, we still sometimes walked around for weeks at a time looking as though our eyes had been scooped out with spoons, sockets brown and purple with sadness or insomnia.

The sky was gray, yes, but this phenomenon was more than a weather pattern. Those of us that had started with white skin turned almost translucent. Those that had darker skin seemed to lose pigment, an ashy deep-green color rising up below. Depression stopped being a cause for concern and became the status quo; the steady ebb and flow of our loss, the gulping cavernous depths of it, went on and on. The story lies in who we were in spite of all of that. The beautiful veins on Rodney's hand, the raised life tracking above the skin.

But the unrelenting ache of loss is what made sex necessary. A small moment of pleasure coupled to a draft of oblivion was the closest heaven we could hope for. Pleasure and oblivion and, in my case (and likely the case of other women in Zion), the hope that my body might be different, that my body might be the one that would behave correctly, sprouting a twining umbilicus to feed fingers and toes and liver and kidneys and heart.

Sex wasn't the only way to find pleasure or oblivion in Zion, of course. A few people cut themselves. Gary and Kristen and Oscar ran the road, loop after loop, until a passable version of bliss swept their faces. Marjorie and Sven sometimes came to community meetings with soft smiles and bleary eyes, prompting rumors that they'd found a way to ferment the ghost fruit. And once Tenzin had explained to us, eyes lit, how he and Rodney had found a buck (the meat of which we were currently eating) tangled in the barbed wire of a fence; how they'd had to heave rocks to stun it, how he'd sliced the jugular and literally seen the life drain out of the eyes. Deborah had set down her plate then and walked from the room. Tenzin hadn't ever spoken of what happened on their hunting trips again and I rarely asked Rodney for details. If butchering animals brought him pleasure, I didn't want to know.

There was much we could regulate in Zion, but no one was willing to suggest that we remove whatever small sources of pleasure might be left to us, even when it became clear that the result of those couplings had the potential to cause all of us harm.

CHAPTER NINETEEN

T HIS IS WHAT is important to know about the next year, the
fifth year:

There were four births and seven new Babies. In addi-
tion to Cassie's Baby, Esther, there were three sets of twins. Paloma gave
birth to a set of ivory chopsticks, Nairobi and Phoenix; five months
later, Eleanor birthed a set of salt and pepper shakers that Chester
christened Azure and Tallow. Kristen's twins weren't identical. Homer,
a curling cable bike lock, came easily but it took Sylvia a long time to
coax Ezra, four skateboard wheels on a chain, from Kristen's womb.
Each Nest was different: Nairobi's built in a single night, a stack of
newspapers crinkled and bunched and bound with strips of green
cloth from a May Day banner; Tallow's created over the course of a
week, a wooden bowl I left in the Center so Zionites could add candle
drippings to it, the wax thickening into time-stopped tears. The
Naming Ceremonies were awkward at first, but by the time Ezra and
Homer were born a pattern was in place.

We came after the community meeting, our lanterns dotting the
dark quadrangle like salt scattered on black ice. We entered the Nesting
Facility humming. Sometimes a tune, sometimes simply the note that
was buzzing inside us. Sometimes our note attached to others when
we entered and our hum became a low drone and other times a melody
formed, something from the Before or something we invented in the
now, between us. Some of us held hands. The Baby rested in the Nest
at the top of the pedestal Lana and I had made. Then there was usually
some sort of breaking—a breaking of the weight, of the heavy importance of the moment. Someone would walk in late, someone would
cough or fart or belch, Chester would make too much noise uncrin-
kling the paper he'd brought, or a sound in the distance would remind
us that someone hadn't come to the ceremony and we'd exchange

smirks or eye rolls. The mother and father, standing near the Nest, would visibly relax at that point.

And then Chester would hand the paper to Ida and Ida in her homey voice would say, "Here's what Chester thinks we should call this Baby." And then she'd read the name and the mother and father would nod. Or sometimes laugh. Then the mother or father sang a lullaby or asked us to sing a lullaby. We did "Rock-a-bye Baby" and "Hush Little Baby" and other less likely numbers like "Raindrops Keep Fallin' on My Head" and "Rudolph the Red-Nosed Reindeer." Usually someone cried. A few left as soon as the lullaby was finished. Many went to the Baby and touched it and said the name. I suppose I should have thought of baptisms in those moments but instead I thought of the tiny stone frog on the doorstep of our neighbor, Mrs. Parker. It sat on its haunches, rubbery lips pulled into a permanent smile, and waved at passersby. I high-fived it on my way to school each day, the tip of my index finger pressed to the center of its palm. I did it for luck most of the time but I think also for the tiny possibility that there was a bit of life buzzing underneath there, a bit of spirit that might charge out through my skin. We touched the Babies to honor the mother and father and in the hope that we might sense something there, coursing below the surface of plastic or ivory or leather. After everyone was gone, Lana placed the Nest on a shelf, straightened the cushions that faced the shelves, and wiped the top of the pedestal with her sleeve. She was mistress of this place now, rather than playing mistress to anyone else. It suited her.

Rodney and I fell back into one another but this time I knew to come up for air. Lana and I edged toward one another, slowly at first, but gradually things between us felt comfortable again. For a long time after the birth of her Baby, Lana was so fragile that it would have been impossible for me to ask her to hold any burden of mine. Any complaint I had felt small, dust at the foot of her Kilimanjaro. So I kept my mouth shut. But then one day Lana found me in the Center, fastening and unfastening the magnets to the Zion refrigerator map, and she asked what was wrong and I told her it was Bim's birthday. He would have been fourteen. I told her I felt like I should be able to imagine what he'd look like now, that it was my job to grow him up in my imagination at least. I made him taller, broader, gave him bigger feet and boxers instead of tighty-whiteys—but his face always remained the same. The head of a ten-year-old on the body of a fourteen-year-old. "I feel like I fail him all the time," I said. "Even now."

She didn't placate me or tell me it would be OK. She took me to the Nesting Facility and made me sit on a pillow and all afternoon she did gentle things, painting my nails with the Sharpie, brushing my hair, massaging my hands, all the while asking me questions about Bim. What game did he like to play and how did he walk and who cut his hair and what was in his room? And she let me talk and talk until he came back a little, until I was able to bring a version of him into the room long enough to wish him well.

There were more visitors the fifth year. They had heard about the extra spaces in our visitor quarters, I suppose, and many of them wanted to stay longer than the week allotted them.

Zion lay between Highway 77 and Interstate 35, two thruways that ran south from Minneapolis–St. Paul—or what had been Minneapolis–St. Paul. Most of the visitors used I-35; savvy entrepreneurs had set up hostel-type facilities at fairly regular intervals along the blacktop. Because the only weather the post-Rending world boasted was gray skies, mild temperatures, and a wet saturation of the ground every couple days, structures didn't need to be particularly stable to be functional.

But Zion wasn't a way station. We were an encampment built, as I have said, near the bones of an actual town. We were two miles away from 35 and one mile from 77, so the visitors we received weren't the standard travelers. They were those who needed substantial rest or medical care; or they came to see our version of life lived after the Rending.

Some visitors kept to themselves. Others sat in the Center for hours, drinking ghost fruit tea and half-heartedly working on a jigsaw puzzle (on a day when I was feeling particularly unpleased with the world I'd combined an incomplete puzzle of kittens with one of a castle in Scotland). All of the visitors washed in the river and all visited the Clinic at some point. Sylvia and Ida treated blisters and cuts, sprains and exposure. Many of the visitors wandered around Zion and, finding the place where Rodney or Asher was working, would stand, twenty feet away, watching. Eventually, Rodney would approach the visitor with a hammer or an axe, a croquet mallet or a length of rebar, and say, "Here, lend a hand." The visitor would pitch in then or wander far enough away not to be distracting.

We gave them food and shelter for a week. The return currency was story. In previous years we'd pestered visitors for information, for news from elsewhere, but now that there was a steady stream of strangers we made the process official. Our Friday-night entertainment. Most Zionites showed up to listen although, unfortunately, most of the visitors weren't natural storytellers. Almost all were men who by choice hadn't found a home after the Rending. They were loners, the type of men who, in the Before, would have stretched their cash indefinitely on beaches in Thailand or lingered in coffee shops with a copy of Kerouac on the table in front of them and a dog tied to the bike rack outside. They weren't generally elegant about speaking and they didn't think in terms of narrative or climax or character. Information had to be pried out of them and they spoke in spurts, as though used to spitting out wads of tobacco in between phrases. So this was how we heard the news. In scraps, in bits, in bullet points:

"Decent people don't live in the Cities."

"Sure, there's regular folks in the Cities, but they keep to themselves."

"You'd think people would hole up in million-dollar lofts or Victorian mansions but they don't for the most part. People get creeped out pretty easily, living in those spaces."

"Women stay in. Women cover up. Women travel in groups."

"I haven't seen a gun but that doesn't mean there aren't guns out there. The question is who has the guns. Where are the guns being kept? Are the guns in the Piles? There are knives though. I've seen more knives in the last four years than I saw in my forty years in the Before. I've got a buddy who makes sheaths for knives. Nice ones attached to belts. People will trade him a can of expired *tuna* for a sheath. Can you believe that shit?"

"You've got some nice Piles here. A lot to use. I've seen Piles that are just junk. Nothing worth looking at."

"I haven't seen anyone killed but I've seen people who look like they want to kill. And I've seen a lot more people who look like they wanna die."

"The Zoo. I was there a year ago. Real fucked-up setup there. There was a man with a suit, real clean. Nice enough but kind of strange. When I talked to him his voice had this way of swinging back and forth, couldn't even really tell you what he said."

"People kill for food, mostly. Not always the people you'd expect. I don't wanna say more."

"In the south they use the stadiums for trade. People bring all sorts of things. What they've scavenged. What they've found in the Piles."

"Is there a better place? Depends on what you're looking for I suppose. The amusement parks. Six Flags and whatnot? Those places are fucked up. Stuffed animals hanging from the top of those game tents? Looked like some movie right before the zombies come out and tear you up. I got out of there real fast. This is pretty good. What you have going here."

By the fifth year we knew what to listen for, because we were interested in what we didn't hear. No widespread disease. We heard: death by knife, by rope, by falling, by drowning, by asphyxiation, by choking, by board with nails still protruding. Death by human hand— hand of the self or hand of the other. But no death by bacteria, by germ, by virus, by cancer. No slow pain sprouting on the inside that couldn't be quelled. Sometimes I wondered if our new world was an arena and this was a version of gladiators. If you take away 95 percent of the world, will the pain kill off the other 5 percent? Will they kill each other out of fear and loneliness?

The visitors came and we listened. The visitors went away and we went on with our lives. Until Michael arrived, at least. The fifth year ended on the day that Michael arrived.

PART TWO

CHAPTER ONE

L ANA ENTERED BREATHLESS. Rarely since the birth of her Baby had Lana been breathless because rarely did she feel like moving at a pace that required her heart to step up its motion. I was sitting on the floor of my room, fastening metal odds and ends to the rim of a Nest for Paloma's next Baby, though she wasn't due for another four or five months.

"Who do you think the father is?" I asked Chester, who'd been offering me unwanted construction advice.

Chester started to hum "Santa Claus Is Coming to Town" around the mouthpiece of his pipe. I rolled my eyes. "Nice, Chester."

"What's nice?" asked Lana as she breezed through the doorway and, without waiting for a response from me, did some sort of ballet combination through the detritus on the floor, at one point using my head for balance and at another swooping her toe in a rainbow over Chester's head. Then she collapsed on the couch, panting gently.

"Your enthusiasm seems to be greater than ours," I said drily. "What's up?"

Lana sighed, closed her eyes and let one arm dangle over the side of the couch as though she were boating in a Manet painting.

"Well?" I said.

She opened her eyes and turned on her side, using both hands to pillow her head so she looked very much like a seventh-grader at a sleepover. "Well?" I said again.

"He. Is. Here."

"Who? Jesus? Have you had a conversion experience?" I was only half kidding. Her eyes were darting everywhere, lighting on an object and then lifting off again, as though looking at something for too long burned her retinas.

"Jesus?" She batted my question away with a hand. "Not Jesus. Michael."

"Michael?" I felt like we were playing "Who's on First?" Chester had gone back to flipping through a *National Geographic*, theoretically looking for fortunes or Baby names or both.

"Just listen."

"Okay. I'm listening."

"I went into the Center because I needed to light my lantern" (she gestured to the Mason jar she'd left near the door) "and when I walked in there was this guy, this visitor, by the fire. Talia was stroking his arm, of course. And he was beautiful, Mir, he is beautiful I mean, he's tall—so tall—but not scrawny tall. Rodney tall but without all the brawniness. No offense. You know I love Rodney. But Michael has these perfect proportions and all this dark wavy hair that actually looks clean. I was looking at him from the side, first, and his nose— my God, I've never noticed anyone's nose before but his was perfect. Can you believe I'm saying this, that I'm talking about a guy's nose?"

"No?" I said, trying to be helpful.

"I was honestly thinking they could put his face on *Sesame Street.*"

"That doesn't seem like a very high compliment," muttered Chester without looking up.

"I wasn't finished, Chester. I mean, do you remember, when they'd show a scene like a park or a row of buildings or a street sign and then a voice would ask you to find a shape? Octagon? Rectangle? Whatever. OK, so his nose was—is—a perfect isosceles triangle!" Lana paused as though she'd come to a punch line.

"Wow," I said rather feebly. "Did you talk to him?"

"Of course I talked to him. I'm just trying to give you a sense of—well, whatever, forget it. I guess you'll meet him soon enough."

"I'm glad you're excited."

"Thanks, Mom."

"Seriously, Lana. It's good to see you happy."

"You don't even understand what made me happy yet. Well, you kind of do. The point is that he saw me and our eyes met and then he lit my candle for me—" Chester covered his hand with his mouth to stifle a laugh. "What? Chester, what?" Chester just shook his head but I made the mistake of making eye contact with him and had to cover my mouth too. Lana closed her eyes so she wouldn't have to see either of us. She lifted her chin and told the rest of the story like a martyr about to be executed: "So then he lit my candle and he told me his name and I told him my name. And he said, 'It's so very nice to meet you, Lana.' Then we stared at each other until Talia cleared her throat and asked if we wanted tea." Lana lowered her chin and opened her eyes. Chester and I had gotten hold of ourselves but were studiously not looking at one another.

"That sounds really, um, romantic," I said.

"It's not even about romance, Mir. I mean it sort of is. He's beautiful, but the point is that he's not like any other visitor. He looked so comfortable, like he already belonged. He didn't seem lost. All the other visitors always seem lost or like they're looking for something."

"You could put that on your Match.com profile," suggested Chester.

"What?"

"That you love Candy Land, turnip pottage, and men who don't seem lost."

"Hilarious."

"Also, men who know how to light a lantern," I added.

"There was no way to say that without sounding ridiculous," said Lana. "I tried to think of a way to tell it that wouldn't sound cliché. But there aren't a lot of ways to say that he lit my candle . . ." This time Lana laughed too. She rolled over on her back and laughed until tears came, the wisps of hair loosed from the crown making her face look softer, gentler.

It was good to be this way. The three of us, laughing. Chester's blue eyes wide and alert, petals of red at the tops of Lana's cheeks, my own particular purpose here spread out around me on the floor, the glints of metal reflecting back pieces of the room, doubling us in fragments.

CHAPTER TWO

I WISH THERE HAD been something in Lana's voice, something in the recounting of the perfection of Michael's nose or the way he helped relight her lantern, anything to set off a tiny bell of warning. But there was nothing.

And so I left Chester and Lana in my room, left Paloma's half-finished Nest, and headed to the Piles to do a little more scavenging before it became too dark to see. More and more, Tenzin was assuming the role of scavenger so that I could work on the Nests, but it was hard to communicate to him exactly what was in my brain, the memory of the placement of each object. I'd tried diagrams but mostly I realized he'd just have to figure it out for himself as I had. So Zionites still came to me with requests and I still kept the List around my neck. And then there were the staples, the things we always needed—screws, nails, ball bearings, a flywheel: objects I'd never thought about in the Before that now I dedicated whole days to extracting.

I was on the far side of Moe, peeling back the faux greenery of a Christmas wreath to see if the wiring that bound it was worth salvaging, when I felt Rodney's arms around me. Breath on my neck. I remember thinking *breath on my neck*, and how much it sounded like a moment from one of my mother's recovery novels. I turned to face him.

"Hey," he said. Two days' worth of stubble was pushing through the lower half of his face, the branch on his jaw visible but fading.

"Hey," I said. I was thinking of Lana, and that flush of excitement, her palpable moony desire. It had been a year since I first went to Rodney with that chain of silver daggers clasped around my neck. Already lust had been replaced by the comfort of predictability. Here were his hazel eyes flicked with lashes. Here was the tiny scar above his eyebrow that no one ever noticed because everyone looked at his jaw. Here was his hair, chopped into uneven clumps. Here on my fingers, after touching his hair, was the particular oil of his scalp. Here was his plaid shirt, maroons and blues, and the green wool vest he wore over it because the shirt had lost every button. Here was the stain on his vest from the packet of soy sauce I'd found and brought to him months ago. Here was the invisible place around the stain where I'd tried to suck the taste from his sweater. Here was a sliver of potato peel wedged between his upper incisors. Here the fine fuzz of brown fur that grew along the rim of his ear. Here the shoulders and here the hands, easy on my waist.

Maybe it was feeling that difference, between the fragility of early lust and the secure warmth of now, that made me unbutton my pants and turn my back to him. He lifted the back of my shirt, enough that he could kiss a small "v" of skin while he entered me. For the first time since being with Rodney I closed my eyes and pretended it was someone else fucking me. No one I knew or remembered, no face plucked from a tabloid or a history book, just someone anonymous. Clean.

And then I was pregnant. Just like that. I didn't know it then, of course. But I knew within a few weeks. Had I met Michael first I never would have let Rodney near me that day. But it wasn't only Rodney I blamed for everything that happened next. It was also my own thoughts, my own desire. I wondered what I had ushered into my body, what I had permitted to grow.

CHAPTER THREE

RODNEY PUSHED THE buggy to the Sorting Stations and helped me set the clothing and household items and building materials in the right places. Then we walked to the Center together, not hand in hand, but each pinching a bit of the other's shirt, a bit of his green wool vest between my fingers and a section of my checked button-down between his.

Lana and Michael and Talia were sitting at a table, a bowl filled with carrot peelings between them. Not the dirty scabs of the carrot skin, but sweet damp curls of inner carrot flesh that were apparently meant to be a kind of delicacy, as evidenced by Talia's proud smile. She wasn't smiling at us, she was smiling at Michael, who was setting a curl onto his outstretched tongue as we entered.

The first thing I noticed about Michael was the way that others stopped noticing anything else when he was in the room. He raised his eyes as we approached but Talia kept her eyes on the disappearing carrot curl and Lana, in the process of re-braiding her hair, watched Talia watch him. Without realizing it, I'd let go of the pinch of wool held between my fingers; Rodney had let go of me, too.

Michael stood to meet us. He shook our hands; his nails were clean and his grip was stiff, as though the bend of his fingers were fixed. Below a suit coat he wore a shirt buttoned all the way to the top. His dark hair lifted off his forehead and backward in a time-stopped wave, and impossibly long lashes framed blue eyes. From the height of his cheekbones the rest of his face fell down and inward, narrowing to the point of his chin. The eyes and cheekbones and hair and lashes were so striking it felt like the top half of his face was trying to distract you from the bottom. When he spoke, his teeth came as a shock, small and stunted but impeccably white. His Adam's apple was an arrowhead buried below his skin. He felt starched in a world where starching was no longer possible.

"Welcome," I said. I think I said. Rodney mumbled a greeting, too. "I'm Mira. This is Rodney."

"Michael."

"I told them already," said Lana around the bobby pins she was holding between her teeth. She hooked a nearby stool with her leg and pulled it closer, motioned with her head for me to sit. I sat.

I don't remember what we talked about exactly. I remember Talia peppering Michael with questions and Michael easily turning most of them back to her so that we learned almost nothing about him right away. I do remember the way we were seated: Michael on the old wooden dining room chair, Lana and Talia slightly lower on two metal chairs that looked like they belonged to a 1950s-style diner (I'd found one upside down on top of the other, like someone was about to come through to mop), me on an old-fashioned milking stool and Rodney standing, arms across his chest, working his jaw side to side as he listened. I remember this acutely because I felt small and young and dumb, my held tilted upright to listen to the conversation; Rodney looked too big somehow, hulking and awkward. Only Michael, set slightly back from the table, right leg crossed over left, looked comfortable and at home. As though this had been his home from the very beginning.

I know he didn't tell us about the Zoo then. He simply listened and asked questions of us. I didn't really notice him eating the carrots after that first piece but by the time all of us rose, the bowl was empty.

"I promised Michael a tour," said Lana.

"You are going to *love* the Babies," said Talia.

"I've heard about the Babies," said Michael.

"We'll get you settled in the visitor quarters first," said Rodney. "Where's your stuff?"

By the time Rodney finished asking the question we were outside, where we could plainly see Michael's stuff, or rather the carrier of Michael's stuff: a bike trailer fitted with a human harness.

Talia immediately pressed her head against the mesh cover while Rodney fingered the harness straps appreciatively.

"You have so much paper!" said Talia. Somehow every sentence Talia ever spoke sounded like it was being read from a children's book. I sauntered over to the Burley and tried to gaze inside from a more respectable distance. Paper, clean paper, was one of the most difficult objects to find in the Piles.

"Smart," said Rodney, "affixing a waist strap to the frame."

Michael nodded.

"It looks like it's all covered in writing. Was it like that when you found it?" Talia spoke with her cheek still pressed to the mesh. Michal didn't move to open the bike trailer but he didn't ask her to step away either. Lana was assiduously fastening and unfastening a button on her jade blouse, trying her best not to stare at Michael but failing miserably.

"It's my writing," he said. "Stories." He looked at Lana as he said it. The skin of her neck turned red.

"Like, novels?" said Talia.

"No, Talia. The stories of others. I collect them. Share them. This is my work." Still, he didn't move to unfasten the cover.

"Like a library?" Talia's fingers slid over the metal buttons that held the cover closed.

"Not exactly."

"I'd love to read all of this," said Talia.

"I'd be glad to read all of it to you, Talia." Talia smiled. The fact that she was imagining her own body cat-curled next to Michael's as he entertained her with a private story was clear.

"I'd be glad to read it all to everyone," Michael clarified. Talia's face fell. "I'd like to listen to your stories and add them to my collection."

Talia's face brightened again. "I had a lot of premonitions about the Rending before the Rending." This was new to all of us. "And my mother was part Gypsy. And my dairy allergy has disappeared entirely."

"We don't eat any dairy," said Lana.

"Gone. Entirely," said Talia, raising her eyebrows.

Michael nodded. "Show me the Babies," he said, reaching out his hand to Lana. She took it and we all followed, Talia a half stutter-step behind them, Rodney pulling the trailer, and finally me, a flame of panic rising between my ribs for no reason I could quite understand. To calm myself I took out my notebook, wrote: *unicycle, motorcycle, the silver ding of Bim's tricycle.*

Michael didn't touch the Babies. He reached his hand as close as humanly possible without touching. When Bim was little and couldn't sleep we'd play a game where he'd close his eyes and raise his shirt. I'd hover my fingertips close to his skin, over the blue-veined root system across his chest, or the puckered mouth of his belly button, or the tiered plateau of his ribs to see if he could guess, from the heat of my fingertips alone, where exactly I was in the dark. I hated the idea of the Babies haunted by the heat of a stranger. And then I hated myself for caring, for believing the Babies could feel anything.

I raised my eyes from his hands to his face; Michael returned my stare. And I swear he moved his hand a few millimeters closer to the Baby to watch the way my disdain increased. I swear, even then, he was measuring the way he changed me.

Talia prattled on about the Naming Ceremonies and about who had given birth to which baby when. With the sleeve of her jade blouse, Lana dusted off the pedestal. Michael listened to what Talia said, nodding. He nodded almost constantly, as though each swing of his head inserted a new piece of information into his system. But even as he listened I could tell a part of his mind was elsewhere. My father had a friend who visited us once, an older woman who had studied geology before women really studied geology. She sat stiffly through dinner, elbows off the table, salmon extracted methodically from the bone. The rest of us pulled the white slivers we missed from our mouths but she was surgical about the process. There were no mistakes. And though she engaged in conversation I could see that what we were talking about (my gross science partner, whether the aid to Haitians was proving sufficient, how Bim got to be Aquaman that day and Freddy had to be Spiderman) was not enough to occupy her mind, that it was always reaching and sprawling its tentacles into other caverns and depths. She couldn't help herself. I hadn't seen someone like her, someone that fiercely intelligent, since the Rending.

"These carriers. These beds. Who made them?"

"They're Nests," said Talia. Lana smiled encouragingly at me.

"I made them," I said, stepping forward, toward Michael, as though I were volunteering for something. I wasn't physically attracted to Michael, I didn't want him in the way that Lana and Talia clearly did. But I could tell from the easy way he held himself, from the cleanliness of his hair, from the reams of paper in the bike trailer, that Michael carried with him real knowledge of elsewhere. I wanted him to see me as the person most worthy to receive this information, wanted, when he looked at me, for his brain not to be distracted by any other thing.

Rodney stood behind me in the doorway wearing the harness, an ox still yoked to the Burley, maintaining a silence that, beside Michael, looked a lot like stupidity.

CHAPTER FOUR

MICHAEL'S STORY UNFOLDED on the following Friday when, true to form when we had visitors, many of us gathered in the Center to hear stories of elsewhere. But unlike the visitors who had come before, Michael was a storyteller. Not the hyper-engaged, roly-poly, perspiring and spit-flecked kind of storyteller like the one who used to come every year to our elementary school, a sixty-year-old white woman who told us about Anansi the Spider while shaking a gourd rattle. Michael didn't need to lean forward. He sat as he had that first afternoon: settled, legs crossed, one arm slung over the back of the chair. The hand on the other arm was always in motion though, a fist carving fossils and fissures and wounds in the air.

Lana sat next to him, on an old La-Z-Boy recliner, her legs dangling over one arm, her back resting against the other. She kept her hands busy that whole first night, re-braiding her hair or inefficiently mending a shirt or shuffling and reshuffling an incomplete deck of cards. (The queen of hearts and jack of spades were missing; Lana always suspected an illicit affair.) The rest of us sat on the motley assortment of chairs and benches, blankets and pillows. And Cal, as always, on his pool float.

I can't capture Michael's storytelling on paper, the whip-stitch of his voice, the gestures wormed into the air, his perpetual ease. But this is what he told us that first night.

People went to the Zoo initially for the same reason people went anywhere just after the Rending: to see who or what had been left behind. Most of the animals were gone, of course. A sea otter remained in the Russia's Grizzly Coast exhibit; a fruit bat, a cockroach, and a puffer fish on the Tropics Trail had survived the Rending but all quickly died because no one was willing to feed the animals, not when human survival was uncertain and it was unclear how much food remained on the earth.

The habitats themselves were mostly intact: A few faux boulders had disappeared, strips of vegetation and portions of barriers (glass, railings, walls) had been erased. At first the people Michael saw step into the habitats did so out of curiosity, to see if the boa was still curled below a log or out of a sense of dark humor, miming apes or warty pigs. Then people staked out the habitats as territory. This was a few months after the Rending, around the time we formed Zion, when settling began to feel more sensible than wandering.

Things went on that way for a few months, Michael told us. The majority of the community constructed dwellings on the fields where the camels and pronghorn used to putter. Labor was divided and seeds were planted. They found, as we did, that root crops did well but anything that grew above the surface did poorly. In addition to ghost fruit they had stings, a hard, brown, marble-size fruit that grew on gnarled vines, bitter with a touch of sweetness at the core. People sucked on stings constantly; like coca leaves or chewing gum, stings gave a flavor to the gray of life after the Rending. To stand near someone in the Zoo was to hear the tiny clicks of stings against teeth.

Unlike here in Zion, the people who inhabited the Zoo were aggressive and methodical about the two Piles close by, enlisting everyone available to dismantle them. Early on, a woman had suggested that maybe there was something or someone below it all, her words conjuring up footage of earthquake devastation in which the camera reveals a sudden hand or foot, twitching below mounds of rubble. So they spread the materials over a mile-wide stretch to the south of the Zoo. They started by trying to sort the objects into smaller piles, as we did, but they quickly found that most of the objects were too random, too useless, to afford use in any pile. The sorting pile in which they were supposed to place all the "useless" items grew larger and larger as the original Pile grew smaller.

But there was nothing. Below the objects were more objects and finally just dirt. And because they hadn't really developed a system, hadn't catalogued or kept track, they ended up with a field studded with crap and a new Pile two-thirds the size of the original.

(How was it that in all my years of climbing the Piles, I had never had this thought, never wondered if there was something at the bottom, something below? I was grateful that it turned out not to matter, glad that Zionites had avoided wasting their energy on a fruitless task, but it made me wonder what other possibilities I hadn't considered, what other explanations all of us had failed to imagine.)

By that point it was late. So we asked Michael to continue the story the next night. So he did. And the next night. And the next night and the next.

It was in the second year that the Zoo began to turn. That's what Michael called it, a turning. By then there were around two hundred curious pilgrims, with more arriving all the time. Those newly arrived always wanted to walk the trails and paths, to tour the Zoo as they would have in the Before. But now instead of staring at snow monkeys, they watched the new human Inhabitants: a bearded man sewing together kids' clothing to make a blanket, or a guy with a mustache tattooed on his biceps trying to construct a laundry line from wires he'd ripped out of the bowels of a stereo.

From there the newly arrived could move on to the old tortoise enclosure, where an elderly woman washed other people's undergarments—only undergarments because they weren't too heavy—and hung them on the remaining bits of vegetation to dry. She'd come to the edge of the barrier wall to talk, resting her forearms on stone. Though the temperatures on the Tropics Trail were no longer tropical, she always wore tank tops, the wrinkled white skin of her arms mirroring the drying fabric behind her.

Then one of the newly arrived made the mistake of feeding one of the enclosure Inhabitants. Michael didn't see it happen himself. He thinks it was something simple, a bag of Fritos volleyed over the dry moat of the tiger enclosure or maybe a can of cream of mushroom soup left on a rock in the porcupine habitat. Suddenly, those who had made their homes in the enclosures realized that others would pay for the privilege of observing—pay in food or supplies, in pages of naked women folded into paper airplanes, in nail clippers, in soap. Those who arrived and had nothing to offer simply had to walk the half-mile to the nearest water source and offer a refilled can or bottle to the Inhabitants.

Michael paused at that point in the story. "When I was a kid," he began. I remember he said this because it was so strange to consider that Michael had ever been a kid. I could only imagine him exactly the same but smaller: same suit coat, same swept-back hair, same studded white teeth and nodding head, fisted hand moving delicately through the air. "When I was a kid," he said, "we'd try to divide everyone in the world into two categories. Those who love summer and those who despise it. Those who could swing across the creek on a rope and those who couldn't. Those who could eat a jalapeño without pissing themselves and those who could not. It seems like a silly childish pastime.

"But it turns out we weren't far from the truth. The Zoo proved that the world can be divided into two categories: those who like to watch and those who like to be watched. And the more interesting you were, the more worthy of being watched, the more you were paid."

Cal interrupted: "Is this how it is still, now, today?" (Cal had moved from his pool float over to Lana's recliner so she could try to twine his hair into dreadlocks.)

Michael nodded his head. "Probably. I left six months ago to collect stories. But yes, as far as I know the men are still in the snow monkey cage. They're usually paid the least but sometimes pulling down their pants, or singing a drinking ballad, arms wound around each other doing Rockette kicks, sometimes that amuses people. And the woman who used to wash undergarments doesn't do it for food anymore. She only washes her own. But she comes to the wall and if you want she'll take your face between her hands and tell you how proud she is of you. People leave her food and also things that remind them of their grandparents. So her enclave is now filled with sachets, with owl figurines, with glass birds and embroidered pillows.

"The Tropics Trail aquarium is drained. Inside, four women who call themselves the Furies go topless, cloaks around their shoulders.

They take requests if the requests are sent on paper that contains a blank side. Or if the request is inscribed inside a book that looks appealing. They'll do what's asked—lick each other, spank each other. The red-haired one will put her pen in the anus of the brown-haired one. The brown-haired one with the curls will be absolutely still while the red-haired one urinates on her breasts. The one with short blonde hair will bend over, close to the glass, and press her bottom against it. They will not hurt one another; nor will they feign delight or excitement. They'll do all of this for paper, to write or draw on, I suppose. No one knows exactly because as soon as the act is done they retreat to the far reaches of the aquarium, behind a barrier they've constructed. Only the backs of their bare shoulders, or a swatch of fabric or a swirl of hair, is visible.

"On the Minnesota Trail it's rare to actually see any of the Inhabitants. The Watchers come because they like the challenge. The Inhabitants have constructed amazing blinds—large forts, really—scraps of fabric sewn together and jerry-rigged into what looks like a childhood version of a stage. Except the curtains never part and through the gaps in the curtains you can sometimes spot a flash of skin, the undulation of a different colored fabric, or the press of a body shifting the curtain outward. Every so often an Inhabitant at the far end of the enclosure begins a song or a chant. The next in line picks it up, changes the tune or carries the note until the next Inhabitant picks it up. Sometimes it takes thirty minutes for the sound to travel all the way up the line, sometimes only thirty seconds. It's quite amazing, really, to hear."

"And what were you," said Rodney, finally. "When you lived at the Zoo, before you began this story-collecting business. Were you a Watcher or a captive?"

"They aren't captives," said Michael, "they are Inhabitants. They are free to go at any time."

"What were you?" Rodney asked again.

"I was the keeper," said Michael.

*

133

The next night Michael picked up the thread again in a more professorial mode. He stood instead of sitting, hands plunged into the pockets of his suit coat. The gestures that he couldn't contain lifted the coat up, revealing the shine of the silky interior.

"I know all of you have questions about the Zoo. You should have questions about the Zoo. I can imagine how strange it seems. How horribly unnatural."

There were nods and murmurs.

"The Watchers don't spend all their time watching. I don't mean to suggest that. Most of their time is spent the way you spend your time: figuring out how to eat, how to build dwellings that won't collapse, how to dispose of waste and sewage, trying to determine what can be scavenged, what will likely never appear. They've distributed tasks, delegated work, formulated rules for sharing resources. They try to make their lives more efficient. They're reinventing the world. The same inventions again: how to make an oven, how to irrigate plants, how to—" and here Michael rolled his hand through the air so we could see how the list went on and on.

"But it's still appalling, isn't it? All of this? Even with everything we do to make life manageable it's still only that. Manageable. You can't go more than three minutes without feeling loss. Without wondering for the fiftieth time that day what happened. The Watchers want to turn away from their work and see something that isn't loss or a half-assed attempt at resurrection. The Zoo is a strangeness that isn't this strangeness.

"Human beings, it turns out, are deliciously simple and deliciously stupid. Whatever world we are in, we want to imagine a different one. In the Before this manifested itself in a variety of ways: for the religious it was heaven, for the climate activists it was the return of bucolic arcadia; most of America believed in a world created by advertisements; academics spun out their other intellectual planets of thought. Even the children wanted yellow brick roads and talking pigs. You may have forgotten but I guarantee you were not happy with the world you were living in before the Rending. You were imagining an elsewhere then, too. But you've forgotten. The

Before has become your Eden, the land to which you long to return. It wasn't better then. Not really. It was simply different."

Michael stopped talking but kept looking at us, at all of us in turn. Ida, who was sitting against the wall making a mobile for the Nesting Facility, let out a sigh pitched somewhere between contentment and consternation. It was quiet enough that I could hear Sylvia's pen scraping over a page in her notebook, Asher unsnapping the plastic fastener on the back of his hat, the muted thump of Paloma's braid as she swung it over her shoulder.

Tenzin cleared his throat. "We should probably move on to the meeting." Then, when no one spoke: "It's Wednesday."

"Is there really much to discuss?" asked Zephyr. "Seems like discussing the best way to dispose of potato peels or who pissed who off could wait a couple weeks. What he's saying"—here he nodded at Michael—"seems more important. We know almost nothing about what the hell is going on out there. Most of the visitors tell us jack shit. Maybe it's time to listen for a while instead of talking about what maybe didn't cause the Rending for the five hundredth time."

Talia stood abruptly, tucking her hair behind her ears. "I think Michael has a lot of wisdom to offer. I think we should listen."

Zephyr nodded and then spoke again as though Michael weren't three feet from him: "I'm not saying we do anything except hear him out."

From where I sat near the door at the back I could see Asher shrug, could hear the sound of Sylvia's neck pop as she tilted her head to the side. Eleanor, glasses pushed to the top of her head, nodded slightly though her eyes were closed. Rodney, beside me, squeezed my thigh, but I didn't know what he meant by it—that he agreed with Zephyr? That we should proceed with caution? That I should keep my mouth shut?

Though there was nothing I wanted to say, I felt like there should be. Like something was being decided.

"All in favor," asked Zephyr.

A muted chorus of "yea"s.

"Against?"

No one said a word. But in the darkness of the back of the room I watched as Chester turned and walked out the door.

For the first time since the Rending, Chester looked surprised to see me enter his room. He wasn't in his rocking chair, didn't have a book open on his lap or a pen at the ready. His owl eyes looked so startled that it took me a second to notice that he was holding a gun. He was holding it in front of him, cradling it with both hands, palms open, as though about to offer it up to something or someone.

"Chester," I said.

His eyes were on mine. He was giving me one of his I-will-crawl-deep-down-inside-you-and-rummage-around-to-see-what-I-find stares. He didn't say anything.

"Where the hell did you get a gun? How long have you had it? Did you find it in one of the Piles? Why didn't you tell me? Why didn't you bring it to a meeting? Chester."

He squinted slightly and I noticed the tiny lines around the corners of his eyes. I stepped closer.

"Chester, give it to me." It was what I thought I was supposed to say, perhaps because I thought he was going to do damage to himself or to me. He offered it to me abruptly, with both hands, and I received it with both of mine. I sat down on the stool with the embroidery on top.

It felt the way a gun is supposed to feel, heavy and cold. There were raised rectangles on the grip. For decoration? They made it look reptilian. As did the trigger, which emerged like a pointed tongue, floating in the empty space made by the trigger guard. The barrel was slightly darker on the top than the bottom. I ran my thumb gently over the raised letters that spelled out KEL-TEC.

"Front sight. Rear sight. Muzzle. Magazine release." Chester whispered the parts almost reverently as I touched them.

I looked at Chester again. He sat down in the rocking chair. Between us, on the table, the sight of the dental X-rays, of the impression of human flesh on the retainer, made me feel like I'd touched my tongue to the tip of a battery. In the toothbrush holder, four rolled fortunes sat unclaimed; I had no desire to unroll one. I set the gun on the table; beside it, the other objects looked horribly familiar.

"I had it," he said after a long time.

I waited for more.

"At the Rending."

"At the Rending."

"Like you had the necklace. I had the gun."

"I didn't see it."

"I had it. Tucked in the back of my jeans."

"We walked for weeks, Chester."

He nodded.

"I would have noticed it."

He shrugged. "You didn't."

"Someone would have noticed it."

"Rodney did."

"Rodney knows you have a gun? Rodney knows you have this?"

He nodded.

"I don't believe you."

He nodded again. "I can understand why you wouldn't."

"Don't put therapist psychobabble onto me, Chester. You had a fucking gun. You have a gun."

"Does it matter?"

"Of course it matters."

"I don't have any ammunition. It's not loaded. It can't be used. How is it any different than your necklace?"

"If it didn't matter—if it doesn't matter—then why not tell everyone? Why not hand it over?"

"What if you did find ammunition, Mira? We've heard from more than one visitor that no one has found a gun in the Piles but what if there is ammunition? What if it could become a weapon?"

"Then we'd deal with it. We'd figure it out." I heard my voice climbing. "Don't you trust us, Chester? Don't you trust me?"

"Mira."

I fixed my gaze on the gun.

"Mira, look at me."

I looked at him briefly, then away, like I was fourteen again.

"I trust you. If you want me to go over to the Center right now, I will. I'll turn it over to everyone. We can have a meeting about it. If that's what you want." He stood up so forcefully the rocking chair almost tipped, then swung back, with equal force, banging the backs of his calves. He didn't flinch. He held out his hand to me. "Come on, let's go."

I thought of Michael. The swept-back crest of his hair. Lana's arm, beneath his suit coat, hugging his waist. I thought of men in the Zoo pulling down their pants, jiggling their dicks for a jar of Tang.

I shook my head. I left his room without looking at him again. I hated the damn beads for not being a door that I could slam.

It was only after I was back in my room, alone, that I realized I hadn't asked him why he had the gun in the first place. Why Chester, with his collared shirts and Birkenstock sandals, with his silences and scribbled fortunes, why this boy-man I had grown to love as a brother had been holding a gun at the moment of the Rending.

It was easy, after that first skipped meeting, to postpone the next one. And the next. There was nothing urgent to discuss and everyone seemed content to gather and listen to Michael. When he finished the story of the Zoo he was more than happy to read other stories from his collection, eight-and-a-half- by eleven-inch memoirs of other lives. After seven days no one mentioned that his time as a visitor was officially up.

During the day he used Lana's room to record the stories of Zionites. Ida went one day, curious, and shrugged a lot when we asked her how it had gone. Said it was nice to be listened to, that he had asked good questions, that every once in a while she'd looked at him and he'd be staring over her head where Lana's mirror fed his reflection back to him.

Chester spent more time sitting in the blue stadium seats between his room and mine, a Packers blanket thrown over his lap, watching the steady stream of Zionites enter and leave Lana's room. Michael's presence rendered Chester's own skill set considerably less useful. Chester listened too but he didn't ask questions and he didn't write anything down. He was a sponge. Michael was the Rosetta stone. It turned out that people who had no interest in having their lives documented in the Before wanted to be known, remembered, and catalogued in the After. We had no children to carry on versions of ourselves, no families to stretch our DNA across the country. We wanted—we want—to be remembered; Michael offered this and Chester did not.

But it wasn't just stories; Michael participated in community life in other ways, too: turned compost, collected wood, helped Cal check the lines for fish. He even accompanied Tenzin to old Zion, ostensibly to scavenge building materials, though I'm certain Tenzin showed him Deborah's resting place, stood with Michael in front of the house without a face.

It seems strange, in retrospect, that none of us called Michael on the seven-day rule or talked more openly about feeling disconcerted by his presence. Lana and Talia were infatuated, but Chester and Rodney were certainly more savvy and suspicious. But whatever lurking premonitions we carried, Michael was different, different from all of us, and we couldn't turn away. Until we met Michael we hadn't noticed it in ourselves: the way we'd been worn down by the last five years, our edges scuffed, need rippling always below the surface of our skins. Michael was like an upper-middle-class person from the Before. He moved through the world as though he knew pumpkin pie and TiVo and a hot tub awaited him at the end of the day. A confidence born of sufficiency. We all wanted to know where that came from, that perpetual sense that he had enough.

Those were the early days of my pregnancy and they passed in a blur of objects and stories. I was the one on Sylvia's examining table once a month, I was the one Ida spoke to softly while Sylvia measured the growth of my uterus, while she palpated my abdomen and jotted notes in a blue exam book with my name written on the front. I told

Sylvia I wanted to climb the Piles until I was on my hands and knees, pushing this piece of kitsch out of me, but Sylvia sternly forewarned me that after the fourth month I'd have to stop, said that if I fell the object could break, could leave sharp edges inside of me. So I tried to prepare for this future restriction by focusing my attention on the base of the Piles, searching for small objects, mostly for the Nests, which could be extracted without shifting the structure of the Pile itself. I found a set of nesting dolls for Marjorie and a wide-brimmed straw hat to keep the nonexistent sun off of Sven's face while he picked ghost fruit. He was forever checking the moles on his balding scalp with a handheld Gucci mirror.

From the top of Curly or Moe I often saw Lana and Michael walking. From that distance Lana's skirts made her appear wider, more grounded, while Michael rose up, a lever with the potential to move the earth. If they were close enough, I could see the thin line that connected them: outstretched arms, hand to hand. There wasn't a rule about how far you could wander from Zion. Zionites had left and returned before, often to trade on the I-35 corridor or sometimes just to be gone, away from the rest of us for a week or more. But the third rule did state that if you wandered more than a mile from the Center and you didn't return, no one would come looking. Lana and Michael were pushing the edge of that boundary on their walks. Lana knew it. I didn't say a word. Instead I offered her a skirt with gingerbread trim, a belt that buckled in a snug heart across her belly.

CHAPTER FIVE

"Don't put all your weight on that," I said. Cal was twenty feet above me, bouncing up and down on a railroad-crossing arm, holding on to a protruding rain gutter with one hand to keep his balance. He kept bouncing. "Cal! We want the whole thing if we can get it. Can you slide it out?"

He shook his head and continued to bounce.

"Cal! Don't!" I hated how much I sounded like my mother. Hated that as I yelled at Cal I reflexively touched my own small belly and willed the wobble of the crossing arm into my uterus. Nothing.

"For this to work you actually have to listen to me," I continued, but I'd already climbed halfway to where Cal bounced by the time I said it. I grabbed the crossing arm and took a minute to catch my breath. "You're right not to try to slide something out if it's going to upset the balance," I said, trying to keep my voice light and positive, "but if you do need to break it, get a tool. Get Rodney to give you a saw from the shed."

"I don't want a fucking saw," said Cal. He was generally sweet and passive. This rage was new. Cal whined pretty continually about having to do work; he wanted his work to be art (sculpting elephant figurines from Zephyr's leftover mixture material, creating mosaics on the walls of the Center from broken ceramic shards) but since he had been fourteen when we formed Zion, the initial consensus was that he needed to be an apprentice to the adult community members.

"What's wrong?" I asked.

Lana's attempts at taming his hair into dreadlocks had mostly failed; Cal's hair was nappy, fuzzed into chunks that made it look like he'd been hibernating. "Nothing," he said. He wouldn't look at me. From just above his right elbow he pulled a bowling shoe out of the Pile. Size ten and a half. He chucked it as far as he could.

"Your shirt's on backward," I observed.

He pulled his collar forward and saw the tag. Then he pulled the shirt off, balled it up, and chucked it, too. It opened in flight and caught on the edge of a kidney-shaped table. Cal crossed his arms in the sudden cold. Goose bumps flared across his shoulder blades.

"You can tell me," I said quietly.

"He's a perv," he said—or I thought he said—before he climbed down. He left his shirt on the Pile. Walked back to his room with his arms stiff at his sides, hands balled into fists as if he could keep the chill contained within them.

I tried to extract more out of Cal later, both surreptitiously and overtly, vague inquiries about his "OK-ness" as we sat in the Center popping ghost fruit and direct interrogation as we circled the bottom of Moe, checking for tagged objects. Had he said perv? Did he mean Michael? Had Michael done something? But by then Cal's sunny disposition had returned, as had his cheerful capacity to ignore me.

CHAPTER SIX

RODNEY CUPPED MY swollen breasts. I kissed his palm, right in the center, and then took his fingers in my mouth when he entered me. When he paused I took up the rhythm on his fingers. He burrowed his face in my hair, pressed his teeth into my neck, tried to pull his fingers from my mouth, but I held them tight and then rocked back suddenly against his still, held body. When he came inside me I thought of Michael, not naked or undressing, not touching my skin or his. Just Michael's gaze, unwavering, on me. Fixed on me until I became a singular sun, purposed, chosen.

Rodney rolled me on my back and kissed the soft brown line from my navel to my pubic bone, measuring the length with his mouth, measuring me with his mouth until my whole body tightened, my abdomen rock-hard, a seismic shattering on my skin.

Afterward I used my teeth to rip open a new pack of Bic pens I'd found on Moe. Tried to spit the plastic out of my mouth in a celebratory fashion.

"Doesn't this belong at the Sorting Stations?" he asked. "Are you being naughty?"

I blushed. "I'll put them there eventually."

He rolled me so that I was sitting on top of him. "Seems like you're taking advantage of your position."

"Maybe I am," I said, rocking my hips back and forth suggestively—though since we'd just finished, the suggestion was a little half-hearted.

"Lemme see one of those." I handed him a pen. "Close your eyes." I did. The light slide of the tip over my breasts, my belly made me feel like a rink. *Ice skates, hockey puck, Zamboni.* "Now open."

I looked down. He'd drawn eyelashes around the tops of my areolas, cat's-eye glasses around the swell of my breasts, and a nose on my swollen belly. My belly button was a mouth pursed into an "O" of surprise that now sported a Hitler-style mustache.

"Very funny," I said. "My turn."

He handed me the pen. "I'm keeping my eyes open," he said.

I wiped my hand over the top of his left thigh where the hair was sparse. "Lizard or frog?"

"Lizard."

While I drew I told him about my conversation with Cal, about all of my suspicions. He nodded or said "sure," his favorite stale-wafer word. Rodney tended to give people the benefit of the doubt until he didn't. His judgment suspended and hovered but when it fell it fell hard and there was no changing it. I chattered while he drew a constellation on the back of my hand (just the points of light; to connect the dots would be cheating) and a twining branch of ivy around my right index finger.

"Well, what do you think?" I said finally.

"About what?"

"About Michael."

Rodney paused. He traced the connections between the dots on my hand with his finger over and over again. "I don't trust the guy."

"But . . ."

"I also think he's been spending a lot of time with Lana."

"What's that supposed to mean?"

"I know things are better between you two, but they're not back to the way they were before."

"Things between us are fine."

"OK," he said, "I'm sure they are. I just know she's your friend and you haven't been seeing each other as much."

"You're saying I'm jealous? Do you think I'm twelve? Have you been listening at all to what I've been saying?"

"I have."

"Cal? The Zoo? Being a keeper—whatever the fuck that means? Having these little secret meetings with everyone in Zion? The way he holds forth with his stories? The way everyone just flocks around him? Just eats up whatever he says?" I didn't like the way my voice had risen to a squeak. He tried to do another dot-to-dot and I pulled my hand away.

"What do you want me to say, Mira?"

"I want you to say that you don't think I'm crazy. That you agree with me."

"I don't think you're crazy."

"But you don't think we have anything to be worried about?"

"I don't trust any of the visitors, Mira. I think they're all fucked up. Michael doesn't seem any different to me." He shrugged. "I think you miss Lana."

"Screw you."

He got out of bed. Dressed without saying anything. I pulled the covers to my chin, curled onto my side, pressed my hand to the side of my belly. Willed movement, a fluttering.

He started down the ladder. One rung, two, three, four. He stopped. I didn't turn. "I'm sorry I have an opinion that's different from yours, Mira. I guess I forgot that's not allowed."

Then he was gone.

I dressed quickly and headed out to Curly without bothering to find Cal or grab the buggy. I needed hay or straw, something to finish the nest for Paloma's Baby, soon to be born. Maybe crinkle-cut paper, the packing material that nestled the vases my mother ordered from Crate and Barrel and Williams-Sonoma. When the first few had arrived my father had asked whether we needed so many vases, but my mother had said she was collecting them, that she was allowed a collection. She didn't display them anywhere. She'd re-nestle each vase back in its bower of crinkle cuts and close the box and then take the box down to the basement.

At four months, at the cusp of when I was supposed to stop climbing, my own belly wasn't incredibly noticeable. Some women, even early on, grew bellies that seemed only thinly connected to their frames, swollen and pluckable, not a part of them at all. Mine looked like the vague swell of an ancient burial ground.

The small of my back was wet; I was panting. The oxygen felt thinner, less satisfying. I was looking for straw, but each time I pressed upward, calf lengthening, hand groping for the next handhold above me, I noted the drawing on my right index finger, the ring that wasn't a ring, the ring that was on the wrong finger, that with each day would become less visible, less able to hold any meaning. What would my parents have thought of my relationship with Rodney—known but unspecified, joined but not promised? We hadn't vowed anything to one another, hadn't brought up the future—was this failure on my part? Or his? Or was this just the way we needed to live now that the future was perpetually uncertain, now that God had disappeared into the ether? Was this the way things always should have been anyway? Had marriage always been a stupid patriarchal tradition? Was my creeping desire for marriage, for some kind of promise, was it a result of our fight or just a desire for faux certainty in a world that would no longer ever be certain? Or was it that the combination of Michael's arrival, his story of the Zoo, Chester's gun, Lana's naïveté, and the strangeness inside my own body made me want to hitch myself to a fixed point? But then I thought of Deborah and Tenzin, ready to set up their lives in that strange broken house; a part of me ached for that kind of declaration, if not in words then in a singular, solidifying act.

He was standing on a green chalkboard, the only flat space on top of Curly. He was strange among the items that were now familiar: a behemoth of a machine I thought had been used in the Before for adhering emblems to clothing, a coatrack, a stopped clock with an anchor at its center, a treadmill, the torso of a mannequin.

"Hello, Mira," he said, and I remember that instead of feeling shock or anger, instead of feeling violated or vulnerable, what I felt most strongly upon seeing him there was shame. Shame for the grime on my shirt, shame for the sweat at the small of my back, for the scent of my own body and Rodney's body, shame for the way we'd fought, shame for the face penned on my skin, shame for all the questions sifting through me.

"Hey," I said to Michael as I hefted myself into an upright position. I carefully stepped onto the belt of the treadmill, wiped my sweaty hands on my shirt, tucked back the lining of a pocket that had come unstuffed. "What are you doing here?"

"There aren't any others," he said.

"Any other what?"

"Babies," he said.

"Live babies? I know."

"No," he said, "these Babies." I watched his eyes trail down the side of the pile to the Nesting Facility.

"So you've said."

He stared at me then and his gaze was so similar to the one I'd imagined in my head only hours before that I bent my head to my notebook to hide the heat that was creeping up my neck. I wrote CRINKLE CUTS in letters as epileptic as the objects themselves.

"What do you write in there?"

I wrote CRINKLE CUTS again, in cursive this time because I couldn't think of anything else to write.

"It's a list."

"It must be an important list. You're certainly assiduous about it."

"Things we need," I said.

"Ah," he said. He turned away from me then and for the first time I noticed that the line of hair across the back of his neck had been cut unevenly, that at the bottom of his coat there was a pattern of small dark stains, dirt or mud splashed in its own constellation.

"It's quite the view."

I nodded. Realized he couldn't see me nodding. "It is."

He turned back to me and studied me again without reservation or explanation. As if I were an exhibit. A light in certain old paintings. Only I wasn't a small winged god splashing into a lake or a bonneted woman pressing a book into the dappled light on my petticoat. I stared at the blue rubber bands that bound the bottoms of my pants so they wouldn't catch on anything as I climbed, at my Keds that were no longer even vaguely white, at the stains that spread like ripples from the toe toward the laces. I forced myself to look at him again.

"I love her," he said. He'd been studying me so closely that for a moment I thought he meant me.

"Her?"

"Lana."

The ground had been saturated the night before and I remember being surprised I could smell the scent of wet earth so far from the ground.

"Good for you," I said finally.

"She feels the same."

The world tipped incrementally, became a floor raised slightly, everything running toward a drain clogged with hair and gum wrappers and paint shards.

I shrugged. "Whatever you say."

"You don't believe me."

"I believe she probably thinks she's in love with you."

"But it couldn't actually be so."

"She doesn't know you."

"She knows enough."

"Why are you telling me this? It doesn't matter what I think."

"Your opinion means a great deal to her."

"Lana does what she wants."

This time he was the one to shrug. "Of course she does." He sighed and put his hands in his pockets. "But as her best friend you can imagine how difficult this decision could be for her."

I nodded because I had no idea what he was talking about and I refused to give him the satisfaction of asking. The decision to love him? Was that even a decision?

"But also," he nodded knowingly back at me, "how potentially healing. Given her history in the Before."

I kept nodding. I closed my mouth when I realized it was hanging open slightly. A pin in his lapel sparked, though it couldn't have since there wasn't any sun. Then he stepped closer, reached out his hand. Stupid puppet that I was, I held out mine.

We shook hands, then, his right hand in my right hand, his left hand cupping my elbow. His hand, I noticed again, strangely stiff amid the ease of his demeanor. Shame filled me again, this time for whatever it was I had just agreed to lose.

CHAPTER SEVEN

I couldn't write a word in my notebook anymore without
wondering whether that word might be the object growing inside
me. Whether to write was to conjure. I touched my belly for clues.
At night, lying perfectly still beside Rodney's even breath, I imagined
I felt movements. I thought of *James and the Giant Peach*, all those
insects in the pit of the peach with their tiny legs, miniature motions
undetectable on the surface of the fruit. I thought of reading the book
with my father in our hammock one summer, a citronella candle
burning beside us, the scent of beer on his breath. How when the day
began to dim and the bats to snatch movement out of the air above
us he'd set the book on his chest and close his eyes. Then he'd hum.
Some mash-up of Beatles tunes and hymns and whatever ballad had
been blaring on the radio that week. Sometimes melodies I hadn't
heard before, made up on the spot or pulled from another time. This
was the closest I ever got to observing my father's train of thought.
He always chose his words so carefully, square paving stones continually leading somewhere. I loved the humming for the imperfections,
for the way it all blurred together into a lullaby.

I should have begun collecting materials for a Nest for my own
Baby. But I couldn't do it. To do so felt like abandoning hope altogether.

Two days after my conversation with Michael I had a checkup, during
which Sylvia told me in no uncertain terms that I couldn't climb the
Piles anymore.

I rolled my eyes. "Fine," I said.

"I'm asking others to keep an eye on you," said Sylvia. Ida nodded
in agreement. "I know you'll be tempted."

"What is this, *1984*?"

"It might be," said Ida, too quickly, pressing her lips together against a snorting giggle. This time Sylvia was the one to roll her eyes. Ida tried to contain her laughter by slipping both hands over her mouth but the soft waves on her head were shaking so hard that soon I was laughing too.

"It might actually be nineteen eighty-four. She's right," I noted. "We haven't actually considered that possibility in all our meetings." Sylvia shook her head. "I mean," I said, framing my face with Madonna "Vogue" hands, "this just kind of feels right to me."

Ida jumped out of her chair and proceeded to go through a series of choreographed moves that must have been learned from watching *Flashdance* or *Footloose* a few too many times. "I'm feeling it!" said Ida, still laughing.

"I'm feeling like I'm having the time of my life, actually."

"Nobody puts our Babies in the corner," said Ida, pulling me off the table for a quick twirl.

"I'm feeling like this appointment is over," said Sylvia. But I swear I saw her smile before she pulled back the curtain and left the room.

It only took about five warnings—two from Asher, one from Tenzin, and one each from Marjorie and Sven—before I realized that climbing the Piles was actually not a good idea. (The fifteen warnings from Rodney didn't count. I just flipped him off and kept going.) All the same, climbing the Piles offered physical distance and perspective from the rest of Zion as well as the deep physical satisfaction of pushing the strength and malleability of my own body; staying grounded felt like failure.

It also meant I needed help, and since I wanted to find out what the hell Michael was talking about, I enlisted Lana. All the strength and verve she'd exhibited when we were building the Nesting Facility seemed to have dissipated; she climbed delicately, often taking fifteen minutes to reach the item we actually needed because along the way she had ideas about fifty other objects she passed. It was like taking Bim to Target.

"How about this?" she said, holding up a NO PARKING sign.

"For what?"

She turned it horizontally. "Dinner plate?"

"When was the last time you used a plate?"

"Maybe we should work on being more civilized." She extended the pinky on the hand holding the sign.

"The plastic bin. Up and to your right. You can do it, Lana."

"Ooooohhh!" She held up a two-inch-long dangly earring made of either rhinestones or diamonds, I couldn't tell. She turned to me, perched unsteadily on the edge of a radiator, fit the earring to her lobe, and then mimed eating delicately from the NO PARKING sign. "See, Mira. Civilized."

"You can mine the Piles for civilized objects anytime you want, Lana. They're always here."

"It's more fun with you."

"The plastic bin. Please."

She finally reached the bin and with a little yanking managed to unearth it. Then she turned and unceremoniously dropped it down the side of the Pile. By the time it reached me it had a thin gray crack running across the bottom, a telephone wire across an eggshell sky.

"Oops. Shitty plastic, I guess."

I didn't say anything. I picked up the bin, stuck it in the buggy, and walked away from Moe, though we had at least four or five items on our list to collect from the Pile.

She caught up with me. Grabbed the handle of the buggy. "I'm sorry, Mir. It's just a bin." One of those apologies that wasn't really an apology. "You can still use it."

"Not for water. Not for mixtures. Not for anything remotely resembling liquid. Not for anything heavy."

"You said Marjorie wanted it for ghost fruit."

"That's not the point."

"It isn't?"

"No."

"Then what is the point, Mira?" She dropped the buggy handle and stretched up to her full angry-dancer pose: chin slightly raised, chest out, flat and forward like a shield she was about to pirouette into battle. She hadn't re-braided her hair that morning and so the crown looked like a fuzzed halo. At the corners of her eyelids, the palest smudge of blue. She didn't wear the shadow much anymore since she barely had any left. It was reserved for days that she deemed special. Or days when she needed a little perking up. "Enlighten me," she said.

"Are you leaving?" The question surprised even me. I hadn't let myself consider that might be what Michael had meant.

Lana deflated. I almost laughed because she truly resembled a party balloon in her sway and crumple to the ground. She put her arms around her knees and looked up at me.

"Maybe," she said. "I think so. I don't know."

"Why? Because of Michael?"

"Kind of. Yeah." She picked at the faux jewels I'd watched her stick to her sandals the night before during Michael's nightly oration. "I love you, Mir. You know that. I love everyone in Zion. Well, almost everyone. But I love Michael too and he doesn't want to stay here. Since he left the Zoo he's not a stay-in-one-place kind of guy. He wants to collect more stories. And I want to see what the rest of the world is like now."

I sat down on the ground beside her. "It's mostly like here, Lana. Or it's a violent shit hole. That's basically what all of the visitors have said."

She shrugged. "Maybe."

She slid her feet out of her sandals and I took them into my lap. Touched the red lines where the straps had pulled too tight. Her calluses. The nails that had fallen off and grown back thick and yellow.

"You have disgusting feet."

"I know." She pressed the balls of her feet gently against my belly. "I'll come back in time for this."

I nodded. Tilted my head toward the sky in order to keep the tears from spilling. Clouds the color of the Apple glow on my father's laptop.

"There isn't anything here for me the way there is for you, Mira. You have Rodney and your work making the Nests. People need you, they listen to you."

"Right," I said sarcastically, thinking of my fight with Rodney. "Anyway, they listen to you, too."

She shrugged. "I'm the one who used to be the prostitute and popped out a doll. I don't know what to do here anymore and no one wants to accuse me of laziness or not participating because they're all afraid I'll go off the deep end again. They think I'm fragile and weak."

"I don't think that," I said, but my voice wasn't as convincing as it should have been. "And you take care of the Nesting Facility."

"Yes, Mira. I dust. It's critical work. Whatever. The point is that this isn't the person I want to be anymore. The person I am here."

"By which you mean it's actually the hot sex, right?" I said, pinching her big toe and smiling. But she didn't smile back. She pulled her feet from my lap.

"That isn't it." Then, after a pause, "We're not having sex."

"Oh."

"I don't want to and he doesn't ask that of me." Her answer sounded like a line she'd been ordered to write over and over on the chalkboard so she might be convinced of its veracity.

"Huh," I said.

"Don't be judgey."

"I'm not being judgey." I wasn't being judgey, in fact, because I had no idea how to judge this new piece of information.

CHAPTER EIGHT

L ANA AND MICHAEL left two weeks later. I don't remember the good-bye all that well. I was trying to get through it as quickly as possible. I remember that the backpack Ida crafted for Lana looked huge and unwieldy on her frame, that as the Zionites released Lana from bear hugs, she'd step back and then almost topple over. No one hugged Michael but almost everyone shook his hand. Asher and Tenzin had tried to put together a farewell band: Oscar and Kristen and Cal banged on tubs and pieces of sheet metal, Talia hit a tiny gong she'd taken from the Zen Center the first day we met her, Eleanor shook a Mason jar filled with broken plastic, and Tenzin blew into a panpipe he'd jerry-rigged out of empty bottles and leftover pipe ends. I think they were trying for "Yankee Doodle" and "When the Saints Go Marching In," but everything sounded like a dirge. Cassie hung back, arms wrapped around her metallic blue shirt. Paloma clucked something I couldn't hear into Lana's ear.

I hugged Lana until she drew in her breath, until I could feel her ribs, how much smaller she'd gotten below her billowy blouses and sweatshirts. Chester gave her a Band-Aid box filled with fortunes. He cried steadily without bothering to wipe away his tears. Lana kissed them away, then looked him in the eye and said, "I'm coming back, dummy." Sylvia offered a tiny first-aid kit. I gave Lana the necklace. She protested but I tucked it into a pocket at the back of the huge pack where she couldn't reach without taking it off.

"Bitch," she said affectionately.

"You better bring it back," I said.

They headed west, toward I-35. I tried to climb Curly so I could watch them go but Rodney caught up with me, said, "Mira, you can't," and I said, "Fuck you, I can," and I tried to climb and he grabbed me below my swollen belly and I clawed and pushed and sobbed but he wouldn't let me go. So I didn't see which way they went when they got to 35. I didn't get to watch them disappear.

About a week after Lana left, Paloma birthed a canteen, covered with camouflage fabric and filled with a handful of coins. The coins were rubbed free of faces, of letters, of buildings or animals, anything that might connect the metal to a country or a moment in time. I was there just after the birth when she shook the coins out onto the skin between her breasts, covered with a fluttering of moles, when she rubbed a few of the coins with her thumb as though she could bring the markings back. Then she returned the coins to the vessel, handed it to me, and turned her head to face the counter, to stare blankly at the haphazard instruments arranged on a tea towel.

"Mmmmm," she said, "mmmmmmmm." A sound made almost entirely of breath, a teakettle at the end of its whistle. No tears, just the aching whine and her bare thighs shaking.

Ida put a blanket over her chest and while Sylvia cleaned away the afterbirth I massaged Paloma's calves, her feet still housed in socks and the pair of duct-taped Crocs she'd worn since the Rending. I thought of sitting beside my mother while she shaved her legs in the bath, shaving cream foamed into a perfect ball and skin revealed in perfect swaths cut through the white. My father cleaned the windshield at the gas station using those same methodical strokes, making bird shit and the dried corpses of bugs disappear with even sweeps of the squeegee. In the Before I was certain my parents loved each other but since the Rending, when I remembered them, it was separately. They were always in different frames. When I tried to remember them touching or what love had looked like between them I couldn't find a memory. So it was a small kind of comfort to connect them through this motion, as though an entire marriage could survive on the way a couple swept a surface clean.

When Sylvia was done cleaning her, Paloma dressed, wrapped the blanket around her, and walked to her room, shoulders back, looking half-regal and half-homeless. I remember how she didn't hunch into herself, how much dignity there was in her posture.

As tempted as I am to pretend things fell apart after Lana left, they didn't. Community meetings resumed, a leader guiding us through Announcements and Rules and Zephyr suggesting during Issues and Ideas that maybe the Rending was really just a complicated reality show and didn't we remember that movie with Jim Carrey where his life was actually a television show but he didn't realize it and did we remember signing some kind of consent form in the weeks before the Rending because he recalled some kind of form.

Chester named Paloma's Baby Sonata and Paloma requested that everyone hold hands at the Naming Ceremony while we sang "Santo, Santo, Santo." Most of us didn't know the words but the tune was familiar because, I realized partway through the singing, it had always been on the edge of Paloma's breath, a humming that existed at the fringes of her like an aura.

A month passed and then another. I got bigger and then bigger again. Began to watch for Lana's return, occasionally thinking I saw her out of the corner of my eye and then turning to find Kristen or Cassie instead. I compulsively checked my belly for edges, for outlines, pressing into the skin to see what I could feel. There weren't any other Babies on the way, or no one who was admitting to being pregnant or showing the signs, so the only Nest I should have been working on was my own. But I couldn't bring myself to do it. So mostly I helped Cal and Tenzin, spotting items for them from the ground while they scrambled on the Piles. Sometimes I sat with Ida, cutting unwanted pieces of clothing into neat squares for her to quilt. I spent one day transferring the smaller containers of ghost fruit Marjorie and Sven collected into the larger plastic bin, each load further testing the thin plastic crack that ran the length of the bottom. Still, Lana did not return.

Visitors continued to trickle through. A man with a crutch and a Bob Marley T-shirt told us he had come from the east, from a town where prayer was currency. Prayers of thanksgiving for any semblance of food, for the dull gray light that woke them in the morning, for the saturation of the crops. You couldn't pass anyone else without offering and receiving a blessing. He thought the prayer was supposed to release them or comfort them or make them feel more secure but he said he just felt like the sky kept getting lower. Pressing down. Then one day he heard a guy say a blessing over the shit he'd just taken in the woods and he couldn't take it anymore.

Then there was a couple, a woman and a man who called themselves peddlers. Inside their floor-length coats they'd fastened travel kits, the kind you can open and hang up when you arrive somewhere fancy, the kind that reveal your toiletries in separate zipped plastic sections. And the bizarre thing was that the pouches contained all of those things, all of the items you'd expect: razors and toothbrushes, floss and fingernail clippers and Q-Tips with fuzzed heads still white and unsullied.

"Where did you get these things?" asked Paloma. We were in the Center. She sat on a chair and touched delicately the plastic that covered the objects. The female visitor stood very still, her coat outstretched like she was a wire display rack we could turn to pull other objects into view. "Where?" asked Paloma again.

"No one place," said the woman.

"Takes time," said the man.

"We could make a trade," said the man. He took out a razor and removed the safety guard. The blade was bright, unmarried with whiskers of hair.

"What do you want?" asked Paloma.

The corner of his lip twitched; he raised his eyebrows slightly then tilted his head a few degrees toward the Nesting Facility.

"No," said Paloma. She placed both her hands on the table and heaved herself to her feet.

The night before my thirty-six-week checkup a man arrived from the north. He didn't speak. We weren't sure if he couldn't or wouldn't. His tongue was too big for his mouth and it was always moving, creeping out around the edges of his lips, worrying the tender skin so that it grew red and chapped. Instead of speaking, he drew. He wore a navy apron with the outline of Kansas on the front and his name, Willis, written in white chalk underneath. In the pockets of the apron he kept writing utensils: stubs of charcoal and chalk, a ballpoint pen he could coax ink out of via persistent licking of the nib, a purple pencil, a burnt-sienna crayon. Instead of helping pick ghost fruit or harvest root vegetables or sweep walkways he drew sketches of people or scenes. We had a few mirrors but no visual recording of our lives since the Rending. We'd left behind (mostly without much withdrawal) selfies and Instagram, photo booths and Photoshop, computers crowded with thousands of images of where we'd been and who we'd loved. We mourned the absence of any visual catalogue of our personal worlds in the Before, of course. A few Zionites were lucky enough to have pictures in wallets or purses that survived but for most of us the images we carried were memories, blurred with nostalgia, changed permanently by the simple act of remembering.

But until Willis arrived, we hadn't realized how hungry we'd been for physical proof of this life. Michael had gathered written proof but he'd taken all of the stories with him; the Zionites who had poured out their lives to him had felt momentary gratification but retained no evidence for themselves. Willis used Lana's room for the portraits just as Michael had for the stories. I dragged Rodney in one afternoon; I wanted to see him on a page through someone else's eyes but I also wanted to see us together in a frame, caught and held. And I trusted Willis's perspective far more than Michael's; whatever version of ourselves he offered us, however awkward and imperfect, I knew it wouldn't be manipulated to serve another purpose. Willis was a brilliant artist but his muteness kept him from offering us any direction. We sat on Lana's turquoise fainting couch, Rodney's arm slung over the back. I put my head on his shoulder and we both smiled widely. We held the pose for about fifteen seconds. There was no click, no flash, just Willis's tongue searching out the edges of his lips as he peered at us and then back at his page. I crossed my legs and uncrossed them. Thought about the bodily fluids that had likely permeated the fabric below me. I'd taken my hair down for the picture; it came to my shoulders now since Lana hadn't been around to trim it for me. I checked for split ends. Opened my notebook to the back and wrote *curling iron, hot rollers, hair dryer.* Rodney bit at his cuticles, rubbed a patch of hair he'd cut shorter than the rest. Then he started slowly sneaking his hand behind my back and down the waist of my pants.

In the final image we look slouched. Our knees are huge. My head is on his shoulder but my gaze is turned down to where I study a splayed-out portion of my own hair on his green vest. Rodney is looking over my head, at something in the distance (as though there were a distance to examine in that space). From the way his head is turned the branch is invisible; each time I examine the picture, even now, I feel like I'm looking at a different version of him. His right arm, thrown over the back of the couch, is easy, loose. His left hand, on the sofa beside him, is balled into a fist. I tucked the drawing inside the plastic sleeve of a three-ring binder and propped it up on a table in my room.

But Willis didn't just draw our portraits, he also unfolded his crumpled representations of the rest of the world. Unlike Michael's well-ordered library, Willis kept his drawings in a decapitated plastic snowman lawn ornament, each image crumpled into the smallest possible ball. By the time he got around to opening them, some were smudged beyond recognition. And he wasn't possessive about the drawings, the way Michael was about his writings. While Willis was in Zion he left the snowman on a table in the Center. No matter how much we asked about the drawings, he wouldn't offer context. It was just glimpses: a water park with a half-finished (or half-disappeared?) slide hanging open in the air, a row of evergreens, an army barracks with a smudged face in each window, a plate with bits of unrecognizable food, a skyline, a beetle on a CD case.

On the fifth evening of Willis's visit, Rodney and I sat uncrumpling the drawings while Talia hovered nearby, offering tea. I spread out a large sheet of paper. On one side, a flyer posted information about a spaghetti dinner to benefit Luke Owens, a five-year-old with a heart defect. On the other side, Willis had divided the paper into four sections, like a window. In the upper left portion a few men perched on an outcropping of rock. Something about their positions was strange; they were in a state of repose, somehow too relaxed for the wilderness that surrounded them. Stalactites hung from the upper edge of the right quadrant. In the lower left a woman stood behind a low fence; Willis had swirled wisps of hair around her head so that she looked like a dandelion gone to seed. Beside her in the lower right frame was a woman I first assumed was supposed to be a younger version of the woman to the left. This woman was also behind a barrier, but she had one hand out to steady herself while the other lifted her right leg up and toward her face. Atop the open scissors of her body, her face was turned away from the viewer, but along the back of her head Willis had noted, with a few deft crosses of his pencil, a braid that encircled her head like a crown.

I tried to pull in breath but my throat had narrowed to the width of a thread. I tried to hold onto the edge of the table. I tried to say her name aloud.

CHAPTER NINE

WHAT WAS INCREDIBLY and ridiculously obvious to me was not incredibly and ridiculously obvious to anyone else in Zion. Anyone else besides Chester, that is.

When everyone had gathered for the community meeting that night I stood before them all, shaking, feeling bad I had to present the news to those who hadn't seen the image yet. "Lana's in the Zoo. She's there against her will. We have to get her." I paused between each of these revelations, making eye contact with each person in the room who would look at me.

Asher took off his hat and frothed his red hair. Tipped back in his chair. Didn't say anything. Ida gave me a half-smile and nodded encouragingly, as though I had a more complicated argument to present. Talia was busy watching everyone else, trying to weigh the feeling in the room so she could decide how to feel.

"Did Willis tell you this?" Zephyr asked finally.

"No. Not with words. In the picture." The picture was already circulating. Watching people put their fingers near the image of Lana, touch the outline of her form, made me want to vomit.

Zephyr cleared his throat. "I'll give you that it sure looks a lot like Lana, but how do we know it's really her?"

Tenzin, usually quiet, placed his elbows on his knees and looked up at me gently. "And how do we know she wants to be rescued, Mira?"

Paloma, who had the picture on her lap, added, "She doesn't exactly look unhappy."

"She's not happy." I was crying now in front of all of them, something I'd never done before. "She said she'd be back. She said she'd be back in time." Even as I said the words, I could see myself the way they saw me: a hormonal pregnant woman. They nodded, friends who knew the truth but couldn't quite bring themselves to say it.

"Mir," said Asher finally, "she chose to leave. We have a rule about this. Remember? We don't go looking."

Then there was quiet again. The sound of me sobbing and no one quite willing to call the meeting off. They waited patiently for me to give in, to adjourn, to admit my insanity. They were trying to give me the dignity of doing it myself.

"I'll go." It was Chester. The first two words he'd spoken in public since the Rending. He didn't repeat himself and he didn't elaborate. I stopped crying.

"I'll go too," said Ida with a sigh, like she was volunteering to make the cranberries for Thanksgiving dinner. "I want to know what it's like to be a Watcher." She winked at me.

I looked at Rodney then: arms crossed, the branch on his jaw fuzzed beneath a week's worth of stubble. He nodded his assent at me but he didn't speak. He nodded but I'm not sure everyone saw.

"Fine," said Sylvia suddenly, hands folded primly in her lap.

"You can't go," said Zephyr.

"I can't?" said Sylvia, swiveling her head to face him.

"Especially not if Ida's going. You're our medical care."

"I think you can handle the sprains and splinters for a couple of weeks. Mira is the only one pregnant right now. She's the one at greatest risk. If she goes it's my duty to go."

Her logic made me feel deeply stupid for not thinking of it myself.

Suddenly there was the reverberating tinny ache of the gong. Talia held the mallet a little sheepishly. "That was the sound of me saying I'll go too."

There were two routes to the Zoo. The first was via the I-35 corridor, the road most itinerants traveled, where every few miles one could barter for shelter, food, and water. But more travelers meant more of the kind who marauded their way through the remnants of civilization by taking what they needed from others. Sometimes the marauders left bodies behind, violated beyond what was necessary to procure the kettle of stew, the jar of artichoke hearts in oil. Travelers on 35 kept some food easily accessible and the rest squirreled away in the linings of cloaks, the double bottoms of bags.

Given that we hadn't heard of pregnancies outside of Zion we didn't know how strangers would react to my visibly pregnant belly, so we opted to travel north up Highway 77 instead, a road that ran parallel to 35 but provided none of the way stations; as a result, our journey consisted of long stretches of boredom interrupted by pangs of fear. The people who chose to travel 77 did so because they didn't want conversation or help, because they wanted to escape notice and, in many cases, weren't afraid to protect their anonymity.

I resolved to collect items for my own Nest as we traveled, filling in the gaps of time, the stretches of anxiety as we moved into the unknown, by looking for objects that might provide a resting place for my Baby. Looking for objects for the Nest also kept my eyes closer to the road, stopped me from scanning the horizon and wondering if the next approaching traveler might want to do us harm. Unfortunately, Talia caught on and fluttered around me like an amicable bat, picking up an empty Mars bar wrapper, the jellyfished cowl of a plastic bag, a hair rubber band affixed with a turquoise star. "How about this, Mira? Something about this feels right to me." Mostly, I ignored her.

We knew the walk would take us five days or so. We didn't hurry ourselves because, though we were determined not to wallow passively in Zion, none of us was exactly eager to reach our destination. Sylvia and Ida collected leaves from unfamiliar plants, tucking them inside *French Cooking in 60 Minutes or Less*, a title no one had claimed from our bookshelf in the Center. Rodney and Chester walked faster, stopping at the remnants of buildings to kick through the detritus, to see if there was anything worth salvaging. Usually by the time the four of us caught up to them they were shaking their heads and moving on.

It was impossible those first few days not to think of our walk almost six years earlier: the raw blisters below Chester's Birkenstocks, the anatomy flash cards Sylvia and Ida passed back and forth, Talia's Costco-size jar of almonds, the curl of my own body against Rodney's, how I'd feigned sleep just to be near his warmth and scent. Now I didn't even notice his scent when I slept beside him, now I shifted often enough in my sleep, moving my belly from one side of the bed to the other, so that by the time I woke Rodney was often already awake and gone. We usually slept in my room since the ladder up to his was the kind of mild inconvenience that felt melodramatically large in my current state. I assumed he went back to his own room to sleep sometimes, too, but I didn't ask. I was afraid that starting that conversation might lead to some truth about how he felt about my body or this pregnancy that, once spoken, could not be recalled.

I thought, too, about Lana. Somehow, of all of us, she'd always seemed the most ephemeral, the least practical. It was tempting, in Zion, where we needed everyone to be of use, to see Lana as superfluous, her dalliances and effervescence as a waste of human muscle and problem solving. But now, in memory, her presence felt crucial, a levity and warmth and vulnerability that all of us needed; she wasn't secretive about her weaknesses and we all gained confidence and strength from caring for her. I felt an overwhelming fondness for all the Zionites.

Then Sylvia bent to pull the leaf off of what looked like a fairly standard piece of clover and as her shirt rose in the back I noticed what looked like the beginning of a tattoo to the right of her spine, just above the band of her navy skirt. It looked like a disembodied tentacle, the gesture of an aquatic creature beckoning for something. And I wondered whether it had been there all along or whether this was something that had been done to her, that she'd asked to be done to her, since we arrived in Zion. Maybe it was only ink, like the ring Rodney had playfully sketched on my finger, but it looked permanent—though incomplete, interrupted. If it had been Ida I would have asked but I knew if Sylvia thought the tattoo was any of my business, she'd be the first to tell me.

Sylvia's tattoo. Chester's gun. My father's bare feet on the warm shingles. My mother's thumb on the edge of those vases. Behind all of these gestures might be stories I didn't want to hear. Or maybe they were just gestures, empty of consequence beyond themselves. But sitting all those years in the front of my father's church, coloring book spread across my knees, pressing crayon wax onto the faces of Abraham and Isaac or Adam and Eve, all that passive listening had prepared me to see everything as layered. Behind wine was blood, behind a broken body on a cross was unconditional forgiveness and love. Water might quench your thirst, but Jesus promised endless water of the spiritual variety. It wasn't just the parables, which were supposed to have a lesson; it was every story in the Bible. Each needed to be decoded so the pew-bound could know how to behave. How to discipline their kids. Where to send their money. How often to turn a cheek. No matter how much my post-Rending consciousness denied the presence of God or affirmed the arbitrariness of Christianity, the truth was that my religion wasn't just belief, it was the way I'd been trained to see the world.

And I realized, seeing Sylvia's half-finished tattoo, that my refusal to ask her about it had nothing to do with her and everything to do with the fact that since the Rending, I hadn't really wanted to see beyond the surface of the present. I loved Sylvia and Ida, Chester and Rodney and Lana. I even loved Talia. But I loved what I knew: the present-tense flesh-and-blood bodies that stood before me. I knew bits and pieces of their Before stories, but most of the time, I didn't ask because thinking about my own past was a hedgehog in the brain. Needles of pain everywhere.

But how much of who we are now is bound up in who we have been?

Rodney, who had stopped to wait for me, took my hand. He didn't look at me. He was busy scanning the Piles, the horizon, the periphery, his gaze positioned on everything I didn't want to see.

Choosing to travel up 77 meant that after three days of crumpled cornfields spotted with the occasional Pile and a few farmsteads (one missing the roof of the barn and another the east-facing wall of the farmhouse), we came to the outskirts of suburbia, to the remains of Home Depot and Old Chicago, Wendy's and Red Robin. We stopped to rest at a movie theater where rows of blue cushioned seats stood neat as soybeans in the open air. The six of us sat side by side, not speaking, staring at the place where the screen would have been. Instead we had the rise of a few naked trees and a sweep of horizon that we couldn't bind into a fixed box. Saturated the night before, the warm earth steamed in a mellow haze near the ground, a blur below the sharp line where the knife-colored sky met the earth. The ground and sky were interrupted only by the trees and a red plow, its right side listing toward the ground.

"I like what the artist has done with the foreground," said Chester.

"Yeah," said Ida, nodding, "the use of such dull colors really brings that tractor thing into bright contrast."

"It was painted during his postapocalyptic period," I added.

"Looks more like his bored-as-fuck period," said Rodney, flicking a blue pen cap at the nonexistent screen.

"Good use of line," said Sylvia.

"Are we pretending this is a painting?" said Talia.

Chester rolled his eyes and offered his hand to me. I heaved my body up with a groan like a keeling ship.

Rodney and Sylvia headed to the Home Depot on the off chance something useful might remain; Chester, Ida, Talia, and I made our way to Barnes and Noble.

Dust was everywhere. Dirt skirted the corners of the windows. The tiled café floor and the silver counter were grimed with a sticky residue and coated with ash, the same ash that filled a metal garbage can. The ceiling darkly reflected someone's attempts at heat.

Ida was the only one brave enough to enter the restrooms. They'd been used as such long after the toilets stopped functioning, as if whoever lived inside the store had been afraid to go outside or as if he or she couldn't bear the thought of constructing a new system by which to live.

Most of the books were gone but a few sundry items remained: a cat calendar, a book on Roman mythology with the cover removed, *Mortgages for Dummies*. At the back of the store, below looming cutouts of Frog and Toad, Olivia the pig, and Alice in Wonderland, we found a pile of blankets, a row of planters filled with dirt. A few thin brown stalks wilted over the edges. At a child's table a stuffed alligator sat on a chair; between its outstretched paws, a *Lyle, Lyle, Crocodile* book was open to a picture of an apartment building with a whirlwind of smoke emerging from an upper window. Facing the alligator, a row of Thomas the Tank Engine cars stood stiff as the Von Trapp children.

I remembered the feel of those small train wheels on my thigh while trying to read a Nancy Drew book on the couch. A crust of toast sat on a blue plate beside me. Chugging noises inside Bim's mouth. How long did I let him play before I sighed him away, before I turned to curl on my other side, toppling the entire Thomas family to the depths of the carpet?

I was thankful that fluorescent lights weren't possible, that the only way of seeing what remained was via the pale light bleeding through the floor-to-ceiling window. Taped to the window were a few bleached pages from a Richard Scarry book. Holding the swell of my belly with one hand I touched the specters of Lowly Worm and Huckle Cat. A pickle truck. A dog, ears whipping behind him with the speed of his motorcycle ride. Watermelons tumbling down a winding road. I dug the tips of my fingers into my belly. Nothing pressed back.

Though the books were gone, most of the shelves were cluttered with objects. It took us a few minutes to realize that someone had curated the objects based on the genre cards that remained. Below the Romance sign: an empty perfume bottle, the top of a lipstick tube, a tiny green plastic trident, the kind used to hold a greeting card in a bouquet of flowers.

In the Mystery/Thriller section: a red plastic magnifying glass that looked like a McDonald's Happy Meal toy, a piece of yellow twine looped into the shape of a noose, a Polly Pocket doll lying on her back, her tiny plastic body outlined with chalk. The dum-dum of the *Law and Order* scene break chimed in my head.

In Biography/Memoir were faces—from photos, books, flyers. A teenage girl in a white sweater holding a flute and a poodle; a man with a beer belly and a red bandana wrapped around his forehead raising a walleye above his head; a middle-aged woman with owly glasses and a pixie cut half-smiling in front of a blue background studded with fake clouds. Some of the faces rested in frames, some were torn and taped to the back of the shelf, some were held in place by a makeshift weight, a few had drifted to the floor. Most of the shelves held faces.

More unbearable to me than these faces was the thought of a person or people moving through empty houses and apartments, choosing to keep or collect the one thing that the rest of us automatically passed over. I couldn't decide whether this was creepy or beautiful.

The Self-Help section was small and less understandable. It consisted only of a wad of cotton balls, a single flip-flop with a rainbow strap, and a 4H trophy featuring a golden goat.

"It's not that different from our Nesting Facility," said Ida, touching the goat's tiny tail.

"Except," said Talia, "no Nests."

"Maybe these are Babies," I said.

Chester shook his head. "Too many. And plus, they left them behind."

Did Lana miss her Baby? Was it easier for her to be away from it? Is that why she hadn't come back to Zion? For the first time the possibility that perhaps she didn't want to return coated my stomach like an oily sheen. The lurch I'd felt in my heart when I saw Willis's drawing—I'd trusted that it was connected to Lana's suffering but it suddenly dawned on me that perhaps the only suffering I'd ever understood was my own.

We waited for Sylvia and Rodney in the parking lot. Ida and Chester rifled through parked cars though we knew the chances of finding anything useful were slim. I sat on a curb, paging through a mildewed road atlas, roads and cities taken over by splotches of brown, names smudged beyond knowing. Talia stood in mountain pose, eyes closed, absentmindedly running the bristles of a snow scraper over her neck, down her left arm. Her half-smile caused a sudden rush of pity; I saw how much she was enjoying that touch, the sensation of something on her skin other than her own two hands.

"Anything?" I asked Rodney and Sylvia when they grew close enough to hear.

Rodney shook his head.

"People had been living there," said Sylvia simply.

"Could you tell why they left?" asked Ida.

Sylvia shrugged. "No signs of struggle. Hunger maybe? Loneliness?"

"They didn't leave anything valuable behind." With that, Rodney turned and started walking again.

It's not that we didn't see other people. Two women I initially thought were mannequins watched us from inside an Arby's, playing cards at a table just behind the empty window frame. One woman raised her hand as we passed, as if to show us her flush or full house, but she didn't open her mouth and we didn't either. In the lot of an old Shell station a man in a huge navy sweatshirt stood poking at a fire on an aluminum sheet. Our view of his face was blocked by the hood, white draw-strings dangling like tusks. I wondered how he'd managed to keep them so clean. He didn't look up, though he must have known we were there. At other times we were watched by people we never saw, but whose presence we registered nonetheless. Talia wanted to talk to everyone, of course, but Rodney and Chester and Sylvia were all adamant that we remain anonymous, neutral.

"Don't you believe that people are really good at heart?" Talia asked plaintively.

"People might be good at heart, Anne Frank," said Rodney, "but people also want things. And when you stop to talk to someone it's easy to get messed up in their wanting."

"Fine," Talia said, crossing her arms over her chest, "but I think you are mistaken."

To keep Talia from radiating her perpetual good cheer toward the women in the Arby's, I asked her to sing a song, told her I needed a little pick-me-up. She immediately started in with "Eye of the Tiger," a song to which she knew only two actual lines. Rodney and Chester, only a few steps ahead of us, quickened their pace. Sylvia and Ida grew suddenly interested in a vine of ivy twined around the Galaxie Avenue sign. Talia moved from "Eye of the Tiger" to "Holding Out for a Hero." Up ahead, Rodney and Chester turned right, onto McAndrews Road. The Zoo was only a mile ahead.

"I keep thinking about that woman." Talia stopped abruptly, both the walking and the singing. She'd been using the snow scraper as a walking stick; now she planted it in the cement beside her and turned it in little half-circles.

"What woman?"

"After the Rending. How I sat in that supply closet in the Zen Center. How she just kept crying."

I touched her wrist. "I'm sorry that happened, Talia."

"I'm just starting to feel really strongly that the Zoo is not a good place."

I sighed and put my hands on my lower back to stretch. "Well, you're probably right. It's probably not such a great place."

"Aren't you afraid?"

I shrugged. "I'm trying not to think about it."

"I think you need to think about it. I think we need a game plan." I could hear the faint grind of the nub of the scraper against the concrete.

"I don't have a plan exactly. I thought we'd wait and see."

"Wait and see." She stared at me; stepped closer. Tiny whiteheads framed each of her nostrils. Her dark eyelashes were short and her eyes were the kind of brown that in sunlight can appear golden. But there was no sunlight. "I thought you were brave. I came because I thought you were brave." She let out a gulpy little laugh. "But you just don't get it. You've always—you've always been safe."

"Not always," I said. I thought of the dead cat's tongue, the cast-iron eyes of the visitor, of Doug pressing caramel corn into my mouth and Michael's stunted teeth and the sound of Lana laughing after her Baby emerged. "I've been scared before, Talia." But I had to look away from her in order to say so because I also knew that not all fears are equivalent, that her experience of terror was greater than mine. I stared to the left of her head, at the roof of a nondescript office building, the kind that would have housed an orthodontist or podiatrist in the Before.

"This is a long way to take us without a plan. This is a lot to ask of us without a plan." She pushed her chin toward me and put her fists on her hips. The tiny bells on the hem of her skirt jingled emphatically.

I closed my eyes. The full force of the emptiness of our planet swept in: no whirring of humidifiers or air conditioners or generators, no rumble of vehicles over gravel or asphalt, no drone of airplanes arcing across the sky, no low buzz of fluorescent lights or neon signs, no clocks ticking forward or an automated voice telling you it was OK to cross the street. Though we sometimes heard the occasional animal sound from the few that remained (a rustle, a squeak, a chirrup), there was no uniform pulse of crickets, no chorus of somnambulant frogs. There was the sound of Talia's breath, a slightly nasal wheezing, and the tinkle of her bells. More distantly, the sound of Rodney hacking mucus out of the back of his throat and Sylvia or Ida turning the pages of their book. But mostly, nothing. I opened my eyes.

"I don't have a plan, Talia. You're right. I should have a plan. I'm sorry."

Talia relaxed her chin slightly and shifted her weight to one hip. "OK. But you need to think of something, Mira."

"OK," I said.

She picked up the scraper and for the first time since I'd met her, Talia walked away.

CHAPTER TEN

I WISH I'D CALLED Rodney and Chester back at that moment, wish I'd followed Talia's advice, made us stay put until we had some kind of plan, until we had agreed upon a single story, a single explanation for why we were there. As it turned out, the only credential we needed was my belly.

Once we turned the corner onto McAndrews Road, we were no longer mostly alone in the world. McAndrews ran from the Zoo, about a mile down the road to the east, to the I-35 corridor, about a mile and a half to our west. And McAndrews was filled with people. At least, the couple dozen people we could see from where we stood made the road feel full. Most of the people were traveling in packs of two or three, though a few were solo. They still obeyed the driving rules of the Before: those headed toward the Zoo stayed on the right side of the median, those heading toward 35 stuck to the left. At first, no one paid much attention to us. But then the two men directly in front of us stopped briefly and as they did so one turned idly in our direction. He nudged his partner, who also turned. Neither moved.

We gained on them steadily. Fifty yards. Thirty yards. Rodney and Chester were still a bit in front of us so they must have been the first to see the knives hanging from the belts of the duo.

"Rodney!" Talia cooed lightly, jingling the bells of her skirt a little to try to get his attention.

"Rodney!" I hissed.

He and Chester turned. "It's OK, Mir," he said, "but you can stay there if you want." Then he kept walking. Ida, who had caught up to Talia and me at that point, put her hand gently to the small of my back. "Come on, sweetie," she said softly. I thought of Rodney's same touch on the day we met, guiding me away from the security guard; I thought of the sharp punctuation of Lana's elbows in the air as she made my first and last cappuccino.

Foam. Frothed milk. Shaving cream: I wrote the words in the back of my notebook as I walked, hands shaking, so I didn't have to watch the knives grow bigger.

Chester was offering a fortune to one of the men when we caught up. Rodney had his head down and was smiling slightly as he listened to something the other man said. Each was a good foot shorter than Rodney or Chester with skin the color of freshly saturated earth. Their arms were short, made shorter by the way they held their shoulders high, almost to their ears. They introduced themselves as Knight and Drake in voices that sounded like swooping swallows; they spoke over and around one another, sometimes finishing one another's sentences, sometimes leaving fragments of thoughts hovering in the air. Drake's left eye was cloudy and wandered. Knight's hair was shaved just as closely as Drake's and was just as dark except for a streak of rust that ran from his left temple to the back of his neck. The right halves of their bodies were completely identical.

Both of Knight's eyes and Drake's right one were focused on my belly.

"Is it?" asked Drake.

"Is it a, you know?" added Knight.

I nodded. "It is," I said.

"We'll take you," said Drake.

"You wanted the Zoo?" asked Knight.

"We can take you to the Zoo."

"Is it the Zoo you wanted?"

"The Zoo is a place we can take you."

I nodded. Knight took my right hand and Drake took my left. Their hands were small but warm and each exerted the same amount of pressure on my hand. I felt held but not suffocated. Though both Knight and Drake were a good six inches shorter than I and though I'd known them for only three minutes I felt strangely protected.

A power-walking woman bypassed us on the right, then caught sight of my belly and slowed her pace. "I'm Mona," she said, pointing to a piece of red electrical tape that functioned as a nametag on her pink athletic jacket. Even though she'd slowed her pace she still moved her arms with vicious pumping motions; her legs were bound and thickened by three or four pairs of gray exercise tights. "And you're pregnant," she said matter-of-factly.

"I'm Mira," I said, "and yes, I'm pregnant."

"I'm Talia!" piped up a voice behind me but Mona didn't even glance back. She pointed to the underside of her visor to which she'd affixed a glaringly bright piece of yellow fabric. "If there's no sun you bring the sun to you," she said.

I nodded.

"Hi Knight. Hi Drake," Mona puffed. Drake and Knight nodded without looking directly at Mona.

"I live with my sister in the Zoo," said Mona, as though I'd asked her a question. "No, she's not really my sister, she's a second cousin. I met her at a barbecue. No, not after the Rending, before the Rending." She stretched out the word "before" as though my intelligence were in question. "Someone's anniversary or retirement. There was one of those ice cream cakes." She suddenly tilted her head to the sky and yelled loudly, "ICE CREAM CAKES!" Then she looked at me again. "And everyone squeezed into a screened-in porch watching a rented white tent flap around in the rain. You don't care about this," she added matter-of-factly. "I'm not immune to social cues."

I looked at Drake. He squeezed my hand and shook his head imperceptibly. Knight let out a tiny sigh.

Mona took a suck out of what looked like a homemade Camelbak. "But after the Rending—and this is what kills me—we found each other. Harriet and I. We found each other in Athleta" (she drew out the worth for emphasis the same way as before). "We just kind of nodded at each other but then, four days later, we ran into each other *again* at REI. The big stuff was gone. The tents and the kayaks and the bikes." She abruptly looked up at the sky again and yelled, "BIVY SACK!" and then leaned toward me and put her hands on either side of her mouth. "But Harriet and I, we knew it was about the clothes." She took her hands down from her mouth and ticked off the types of important clothing on her fingers: "Stuff that dries fast, stuff that traps heat, stuff with a little thermometer built into the cuff."

This woman was like Talia on crack. "I'm not immune to social cues," she said again. "But when that baby is born you're going to want a coat with thermal heat technology. You're going to come to Mona and Harriet. And maybe we share and maybe we don't." She raised her eyebrows at me and picked up her pace. Her fluorescent body and swinging ponytail disappeared into the bodies in front of us.

I'd been so busy listening to Mona that I hadn't really paid attention to the other bodies. Ones who had slowed their pace or quickened it, ones who had crossed over from the other side of the road to walk in the opposite direction with us. The people in front of me walked forward while turning occasionally, their faces like cottonwood leaves catching sun. There were the faces and also the smells. Body odor that was dull and musky, thick and fruity, sweat that had soured and sweat mixed in with earth. Thin remnants of manufactured scents, too. And dust and oil and rust and age, the scent of clothes folded in upon themselves for too long, new organisms taking root in the creases.

Of course I'd been surrounded by Zionites; I hadn't forgotten people. But this press of newness was a scene I could only absorb in tiny bits: a pink rose embroidered onto denim, an unraveled hem, moles and pearl earrings and blue eyes large behind thick lenses; black Converse sneakers with yellow laces, a head scarf, a thinning red beard. It was as though one of the Piles had come alive and I was in the center of it.

My instinct was to cover my belly with my hands, to protect it. But Drake and Knight held my hands firmly. And then something else began to happen. The people began to reach out to touch me. Sometimes just fingertips, once what was certainly a palm. A brushing, a rub, a poke. When I turned, when I looked down, there was nothing, no hand; I couldn't see who had reached out. Although I knew rationally that those sensations were coming to me from outside of my body, the lack of a visible contact made the sensations feel like they might be coming from within. And so, I stopped looking. I fixed my gaze above their heads and let myself imagine, for that half-hour walk, that what

I felt was a human being, kicking, turning, finding purchase on the inside of my skin.

When we reached the outskirts of the massive Zoo parking lot, Drake and Knight stopped abruptly.

"We'll take her now," said Drake.

"Now we will be the guides alone."

"You can go back to your places."

I turned to look at Rodney. He was less than a foot behind me. "I'm here," he said simply.

Around us, the crowd dispersed.

Chester, Ida, Talia, and Sylvia were gone.

My mouth opened to speak and Rodney pressed his own words in to stop me: "I'm here," he said.

CHAPTER ELEVEN

THE CROWD MOVED off along the road at the back of the parking lot and when everyone else had gone, Drake and Knight dropped my hands. Oddly, the sudden absence of the crowd and the touching felt deflating, like absence in the worst sense of the word. I felt untethered, consciously aware of the vast amounts of air around my limbs. Below a sky the color of dirty dishwater, we moved through a maze of forgotten cars, doors hanging open like broken jaws, past the one parking sign that remained of a bottlenose dolphin curled into a gray comma.

We followed Drake and Knight into the Zoo, through a door marked PERSONNEL ONLY and down a hall of gray cement and white-washed walls. A series of thick skylights turned the space dim and drowsy. We reached an unmarked door and Drake bowed slightly, his right eye staring firmly at my face and his left eye wandering toward the door I was ostensibly supposed to pass through.

"You alone," said Knight.

Drake made a tsk-tsk sound and wagged his index finger at Rodney, who shrugged at me and then slid to a sitting position against the wall. Satisfied, Knight and Drake headed back down the hall the way we'd come.

I wanted to kick Rodney. Hard. I presumed it was Michael behind that door, presumed that Michael wasn't violent, that this would be a quick matter, settled through rational conversation. I realized that had been my plan all along. That I would come and ask nicely and Michael would give me what I wanted. But who the fuck knew. Talia was right. Somehow I'd managed to skirt through the first five and a half years after the apocalypse in relative safety. But the knives on the belts of the twins were knives. And a mob of people is a mob of people. And the fact that I thought I had to ask anyone to *return my friend to me* was incredibly fucked up. The fact that Rodney would let almost-thirty-seven-week pregnant me into a room of unknowns made me want to grind his testicles under the heel of my dirty canvas Keds sneaker. I stared at Rodney and for a split second I took in not only the familiar forest-green vest and unlaced work boots but also the dark shadows below his eyes. Sitting on the floor, all the height and girth taken out of him, Rodney looked weak, surmountable, human. How much of my bravery and confidence came from the simple assumption that he would protect me? He studiously rolled his hands on the tops of his wrists, as though the cracking of the bones and ligaments gave him some kind of comfort. He didn't look at me.

I pushed open the door.

I went in expecting something akin to the Cave of Wonders in Aladdin. I went in expecting Persian carpets, Ming vases, golden ashtrays, and spittoons or perhaps Tiffany lamps, a silver tea service, peacock-feather accents. What I found was a room similar in aesthetics to the hallway. The cement floor, the white walls, the large square drain in the center of the floor—all this was visible because the wall on the right side of the room was missing. The room bordered a Zoo path, providing an unobstructed view of a shitty-looking duck pond. A few electrical cables hung from the ceiling and from these cables dangled dream catchers and prisms and a few small trinkets. In the middle of the opening sat a card table covered with piles of neatly arranged papers; a cup held a few writing utensils. Michael's hands were poised over the keys of a typewriter. He didn't turn when I entered; instead, he began punching down the keys with exclamatory fervor. I thought of a documentary called *INSECTS!* that Bim liked to check out from the library. One scene featured a katydid eating, the sound of its jaws cutting through leaf magnified one thousand times. Munch, munch, munch. Munch, munch, much.

Above Michael a naked Barbie dangled from a cable, its torso inked bright red, half its hair shorn. Against the opposite wall stood an uncomfortable-looking wicker rocking chair. I concentrated on imagining Michael as a katydid. Munch, munch, munch. Munch, munch, munch.

After a few minutes he pulled the paper out of the typewriter with a whiz-zing flourish and turned to me. "Mira," he said, nodding empathetically, as though he'd worked me in for an emergency therapy session. "You're probably wondering what I use the industrial-size freezer for."

I hadn't been wondering that at all. I hadn't really even noticed the freezer that lined the back wall of the room until he mentioned it, had assumed it was simply counter space.

"Food prep," said Michael in answer to my gaze, "for *los animales*. When *los animales* existed." His Spanish accent felt precise but strange, as though it had been soaked in French or German first. He lifted the top of the freezer. "Not anymore. A different kind of preparation for a different kind of *animal*."

The inside was filled with paper. His stories. The stories of others, theoretically, though who knew how the words spoken by others had been altered as they slid through his brain. He didn't leave the lid open long but I could see that the papers weren't haphazardly stuffed in; they were organized. Some in files, some in milk crates, some papers clipped, some sheaves bound with actual safety pins.

"That's that," he said, letting the lid slam shut. He licked his thumb and rubbed at an errant spot on the lid, but behind the rubbing motion there was a shaking. Something about the way his other fingers clenched and curled, the way the movement ran up through his wrist. He noticed me watching and abruptly stuffed his hands into the pockets of his suit coat.

"Where's Lana?" I asked.

"She's here, she's here."

"I know," I said, "but I'd like you to show me where."

He stepped closer and put his hands on my shoulders. I tried not to flinch. "Let me look at you, Mira."

He studied me carefully but he paid almost no attention to my belly. He looked over my face as if he were studying a map. He looked at me for what felt like a century, though it must have only been five minutes or so. Longer than I remember anyone ever looking at me. I tried to imagine what he was seeing: my brown eyes that wouldn't possess even the slightest hint of green in this light, the masses of freckles that covered my nose and cheeks, my hated cheeks that had always made me look slightly cherubic, thick brows and thick lips (unplucked and chapped, respectively). And framing my face all the little wispy hairs that slipped out of whatever knot I wound my hair into, hairs that curled and framed my face. And of course I couldn't help looking at Michael: his upper lip curled around the row of tiny white teeth, his frozen black hair, and those blue eyes with lashes that looked like they could embrace you all on their own. He studied me sincerely, curiously. I vacillated between wanting to spit in his face and wanting the moment to continue. How long had it been since Rodney looked at me this way? Maybe that wasn't fair. The gaze wasn't that of a lover, it was the gaze of a compassionate scientist, someone engaged in observation but who isn't too caught up in his own hypothesis, someone wise enough to learn from whatever events unfold.

Michael released his grip on my upper arms and plunged his hands into the pockets of his coat again. He rattled the pockets energetically and whatever he was carrying inside made a happy little clicking sound. Then he took out one hand and put his thumb and forefinger on my upper back, one fingertip on either side of my spine, to guide me toward the door. I thought of Rodney's hand on my lower back when we first met, the warmth of his palm guiding me away from danger. Michael's thumb and forefinger pressed against knots on my back I didn't even know were there. I gasped and hated myself for gasping. I opened the door.

Rodney stood as we exited. Nodded at Michael, who returned the nod. But Michael kept his fingers against my back and Rodney didn't tell him not to. Rodney did not take my hand, but then again I didn't offer it to him.

And there was no one to tell me what this gap, this lull, this dead space in our relationship meant. I understood that relationships went through rough patches. I wasn't an idiot. When, months earlier, I had seen Lana fall obsessively in love with Michael, I realized Rodney and I were no longer there, no longer in the confettied-rose-petal days of early courtship. But that change had felt natural to me, a shift from excitement to contentment, a shift from turning obsessively toward one another to turning back outward to see the world. But somehow that place of comfort and ease had slid into this other place where we now resided, this place that seemed a graveyard of a million tiny deaths of affection: the way he hadn't spoken up for me at the last community meeting, the way he had walked ahead with Chester, the twenty times he could have grabbed my hand and hadn't. And it wasn't just him. It was me. Why hadn't I gone to him first when I saw the picture of Lana? Why hadn't we discussed a plan together? Why hadn't I talked to him more openly about the Baby, about my inability to build a Nest for it, to give up the hope that it might be a living being, full of breath and shrieking? As the ring he inked on my finger faded I should have asked for something more permanent. Why couldn't I admit to myself that I wanted permanence?

Michael touched those two places on my back and I thought of my parents and their particular distances. I would never be able to go back, would never understand exactly what those distances had meant, would never know for certain whether they had loved one another. And I'd never be able to go back to the way they'd loved me or the way I'd felt loved by them, in the Before. Love ended, just like everything else—so I hated myself for wanting the endless, unconditional kind from Rodney anyway.

Michael increased the pressure on my back. There wasn't room for uncertainty now.

CHAPTER TWELVE

THE SCENT OF the Zoo had thinned considerably in the years since the Rending but it hadn't disappeared entirely. The Tropics Trail no longer boasted tropical temperatures but it still retained the ruddy odor of hay and excrement, the kind of scent that climbs inside your nostrils and then collapses lethargically. The flashy tropical plants were all dead or had disappeared but some of the filler plants remained, casting shaky stems toward the half-glass, half-cloud sky.

The last time I had been at the Zoo I was twelve and Bim was five. It was his fifth birthday, in fact, and he'd been permitted to bring five friends along. I was supposed to be helping my mother and father keep an eye on the hyperactive mass of Boy but I mostly sulked, complaining about the smell and occasionally striving for a moment of communion with some raisin-eyed creature behind the glass. Bim and his friends each wore a neon-green shirt with an electric blue poisonous dart frog on the front. Theoretically the T-shirts were party gifts but really they were a way for my parents to keep an eye on six bodies in constant motion.

Bim and his friends had ducked and darted, staining a railing with sticky fingerprints before spinning off to crawl through a faux hollow log or rail their knuckles against the glass to summon a shrug or snort from a tapir or gibbon.

Now, ten years after that birthday party, the Watchers moved placidly, casually along the same paths. There was none of the frenetic energy of the Before: no strollers, no waving of errant grandmas into photo frames, no children climbing onto statues of extinct creatures, no disappearance and reemergence of tiny heads. No tiny heads. It wasn't the Inhabitants I noticed first, it was the Watchers.

The trail sloped downward and curved slightly to the right. To our left as we rounded the bend was the former tortoise enclosure. At the back of the habitat, curled into one of the indentations in the wall meant for amphibian bodies, an older woman sat with her tank top pulled over her knees. She pressed her mouth and nose into her shirt so only her eyes were visible, staring at a focal point somewhere in the sand a few feet in front of her. Her white hair was so thin that even her slight rocking motion made it waver in the air.

A fiftyish woman with her hair in low pigtails was bending over the railing, shaking a package of oyster crackers at the Inhabitant. "Here you go! Crackers! Crunchy crunchy crackers!" She shook the cellophane again. "Yum yum! Crackers!"

The Inhabitant raised her chin, spat, and then buried the lower half of her face in the shirt again. Pigtail Woman set the crackers on a rock near the railing then swept her sleeve across her eyes.

"Maybe she doesn't WANT the crackers," said Michael, too loudly. He reached over the edge of the enclosure and with an index finger pressed one of the crackers into oblivion. The Inhabitant was surprisingly quick. She scuttled out of her resting place, grabbed the crackers, and crept back in five seconds. Michael began to smile and then bit his lower lip to keep the smile at bay. I saw the dark nipples below her filthy tank top, the skin wrinkled and sagging from her upper arms. Her eyes did not invite pity.

Other Watchers lingered to see if the Inhabitant would eat her crackers, but Michael's fingers pressed me on. Rodney trailed a few feet behind us.

Another forty feet down the path, on the right, the glass of the former crocodile enclosure was darkened, covered with some substance on the inside. I quickened my pace. Where the hell was Lana? But Michael grabbed my upper arm. "Watch," he instructed.

A line made its way through the darkness on the glass. The line rose and fell, rose and fell. Then another line, beneath, following the same pattern as the one above.

"Someone's writing," I said.

"Drawing," corrected Michael.

Above the first wavy line a bowl appeared. Then a mast. A sail. Into the middle of the boat, a circle. The Inhabitant holding the tool then focused—her? his?—attention on the circle itself, picking away at the substance (was it just dirt? dried excrement? clay?) until the entire circle became transparent.

Then there was an eye. Staring at us through the porthole. It wasn't Lana's eye. Then it was gone.

Pigtail Woman applauded, wiped away a few stray tears. She stepped up to the glass and pressed her eye to the porthole. "Hello?" she said. "Hello?"

"She had triplets in the Before," Michael whispered, nodding at Pigtail Woman with his head. "All boys. She'd sent them out to do their chores. Mowing, Sweeping, Weeding: that's what she calls the boys now. In case she talks to you. That's what she means."

I nodded.

"You're OK in there," she was saying to the form behind the glass. "You're OK."

"This way," said Michael. "Almost there."

Lana was in the former Komodo dragon enclosure. The Komodo dragon was perennially every child's least favorite exhibit in the zoo because the Komodo dragon did absolutely nothing. It was usually either doing nothing on the large faux fallen tree that stretched the length of the space or doing nothing below a warming light.

It wasn't the lack of Komodo dragon I noticed so much as the lack of the warming light and the absence of the log that had formerly occupied so much of the ground. The sand was different too, swirled into stops and arcs, zigzags and divots. At the back of the enclosure, Lana was working a pair of ballet shoes onto her feet. I called her name. A number of Watchers stopped their leisurely progression to stare at me. I called her name again, loudly.

Lana looked up. She found my face among the row of faces. Then she looked at Rodney. Finally, at Michael. Then she turned away.

"You're not going to get her to dance that way," whispered someone conspiratorially. I looked into the face of a mousy, balding man whose small brown eyes were framed with red cat's-eye women's glasses. "She's very unpredictable. But I try to do all her patterns." He held out a napkin covered with scribbles that vaguely resembled the patterns on the floor of the enclosure. "It looks like chaos, I know. But there's chaos *theory*. There's a pattern here. It will all become clear soon enough." He looked at Michael.

"Lana!" I shouted again.

"Right, Michael?" asked the man with the napkin.

"Exactly," said Michael.

"Lana! Look at me! I'm right here. Look at me." I waved frantically, pressing against the rail like a Titanic passenger who knows what's coming. "Lana!" She stood. Turned her back to me fully. Gently pulled her head to the right to stretch her neck. "Lana!" She pulled her head to the left. "Lana!" Her arms overhead. Then circling backward, windmilling. The man in cat's-eye glasses was now looking at me studiously. The mother of the triplets sucked the end of one of her pigtails. Michael was rocking back and forth, his gaze moving between Lana and me. His face was opening in this strange way. Eyes widening, nostrils flaring. I tried a different tack. Kept my voice light and sing-songy. "I know you see me. People clearly think I'm crazy. I bet you're loving this. Ha ha ha! Really funny, Lana."

"Laaaa-naaaaa," sang the woman with the pigtails. "Laaaaa-naaaaa." More Watchers were gathering.

"La-NA," said the man, clapping his hands in her direction with each syllable. "La-NA!"

"Laaaaaa- naaaaaa," Pigtail Woman continued.

I tried stern, raising my voice so I could be heard above the gathering murmurs: "Lana! We're here. We came a long way. You need to look at me. You need to turn around. Now! NOW!" I shouted, loud enough that pain rose up the back of my throat.

But the "now" was lost in the cacophony of other voices. "Lana, Lana, Lana," they murmured and shouted and whispered and crowed. Not one chant but a terrible noise that had her name buried inside of it.

Lana lana lana lana lana lana lana: the press of noise and the press of bodies, leaning toward her and toward me, hungry for whatever was going to happen between us, not curious not interested not rubbernecking but hungry. Something here they needed as sustenance. The neon yellow of Mona's visor. The cast-iron eyes of the visitor. A snatch of a navy-blue security uniform. Buzzed blond hair.

Lana lana lana lana lana lana: no longer her name, only a sound. Bodies so close I couldn't turn, belly pressed hard against the rail. "Lana, lana, lana," they called and yodeled and whooped and screeched. Sweat on my shirt, on my lip. Sweat running down between my breasts. I opened my mouth, so dry, and couldn't find her name, couldn't hear my own voice anymore. She stretched out one leg, toe pointed. None of this touching her.

CHAPTER THIRTEEN

THE GRAY ARMOR of the sky hung above me. I lifted my hands to my belly. Still pregnant. I touched gently my face, my neck, my breasts, my arms. Nothing hurt.

"Look who's awaaaaaake!" That voice hurt. I turned my head. Talia stood with her hands on her hips. "Good morning, Mira!" Behind her, Chester, Sylvia, and Ida sat around a small fire.

I pushed myself to my elbows. "Where are we?"

"Don't try to move too much yet," said Sylvia. She came over and helped me work myself into a seated position. I felt dizzy but OK. Ida brought me a mug. The ghost fruit tea, which I'd come to despise, actually tasted good. Familiar and warm, like Sven and Marjorie. The way they moved and communicated like a single being, how much was unspoken between them.

"Where's Rodney?" I asked.

"Poking around," said Ida, resting her hand on my knee.

"Collecting intel," said Talia.

"Whoring," said Chester. He raised an eyebrow at me. I should have laughed. But everything felt so strange and fucked up, so like the Rending all over again, and I felt so far away from Rodney that whoring seemed just as likely as anything else he might be doing. Rollerblading. Crocheting. Scrapbooking.

"Where were you guys? Where did you go?" I finally managed to ask.

"Rodney and I thought it would be better if we arrived separately. So that if anything happened . . ." Chester trailed off. Then he looked at me squarely. "I'm glad you're OK, Mira."

"I'm fine," I said. "Where are we?"

"On a hill," said Talia, as though I was incapable of noticing the slope in front of us.

"Former camel enclosure, sweetie," said Ida. "It's where all the cool kids hang out." She squeezed my knee gently.

"There are also camps in the other fields," said Sylvia, "pronghorn, wild horse, gazelle."

The scene in front of us made me think of documentaries I'd seen of refugee camps: a patchwork of color, matted grass, smoke lifting from a smattering of fires. Rising along with the smoke were the sounds of life lived close together: the low murmur of voices and the reshuffling of belongings punctuated with the snap of wood breaking or a bark of laughter or a shriek of delight or fear. Talia's initial greeting to me had been ironic; it wasn't morning, it was late afternoon.

Chester prodded a wrapped sweet potato out of the fire; Talia and Ida wandered away to get water and then wandered back again. Sylvia held the French cooking book open on her lap, though whether she was memorizing the veins of a leaf or the recipe for bouillabaisse, I couldn't be sure.

"How did I get here?" I asked finally, of no one in particular.

Sylvia laid down a finger to mark her place before looking up. "Rodney brought you after you passed out. An anxiety attack, I assume." Then, more kindly: "It sounds like it was a very stressful situation."

I stared at the fire.

"It looked really romantic from a distance," added Talia, "Rodney staggering up the hill with you in his arms. But less romantic with the belly."

"Right," I said, running my thumb over the tiny indentation my belly button still made. "Definitely less romantic."

Haze turned to dusk and dusk to gloaming. A man walked by with a squirrel hanging like an extension of his arm. Farther down the slope a man and a woman carrying a roll of carpet between them paused to adjust their grip. Chester wrapped another potato and nudged it between the coals. Rodney did not return. When I yawned, Ida led me to a nest made from the blankets we'd brought; above the blankets hung the cloud sheet from the top of Moe.

"You brought this?" I said.

"Rodney did. Lie down, sweetie."

I obeyed and she sat beside me, hunched slightly below the sheet. With gentle fingers she unrolled my hair from its loose knot and used her fingers to comb it over the blanket I'd pulled to my chin. Then she set to work with her fingertips, smoothing all the tiny curls along my hairline.

The sobs seemed to come up from whatever I was growing inside me, and once they started I couldn't stop. There was a fault line cutting me in two and I was shaking as everything crumbled down and in.

I fell asleep crying and when I woke again in the middle of the night Rodney was beside me. Without stars or moon, without city lights refracted by the clouds, darkness after the Rending could be absolute. But I'm almost certain that when I opened my eyes, Rodney was studying me, his eyes trained on the contours of my face. I closed my eyes again and by the time I woke in the morning, he was gone.

The next day, I still couldn't bring myself to talk about Lana, to tell them about the way she had refused to turn, though I'm sure they'd already heard the story from Rodney. I couldn't bear to think about the way my own voice had cracked, how desperate I had sounded, how painful it had been to watch her refuse me. The terrible sound of all those voices echoing her name. I was too tired to think about what my failure meant or to consider the hovering guilt I felt for having dragged my friends to this sad, strange place.

They didn't ask me to tell them. They told me in stops and starts what they'd learned in the few hours I'd been away from them the day before: the food was grown over by the former farm, mostly the same root vegetables we produced. They had ghost fruit too, though it tasted slightly different from our varieties, and stings, the fruit Michael told us about, which looked and grew much like grapes but were rock-hard and dissolved into bitter threads of saliva. They explained where the latrines were, where the dismantled and reinstated Pile lay, and pointed down the hill at figures moving slowly in the morning light: who talked too much, who seemed OK, who was hoarding food.

I nodded and sipped at my tea. Tried to eat a little reheated carrot-turnip pottage from the night before. Thirty-seven weeks today. At one point I caught Sylvia measuring me with her eyes but she didn't say anything.

"We're just going to try to make ourselves useful," said Chester. "Sylvia and Ida are going to offer medical services and Talia and I are going to check out the farm."

"Turnips!" said Talia, "Yay!"

I shoved myself to a standing position. "I think I'll just walk around a little," I said, "try to get my bearings."

And just like that we dispersed, eased ourselves down the hill and into the rhythms of a community completely unlike our own.

I N MANY WAYS the Zoo was exactly as Michael had explained. There were Inhabitants and there were Watchers. The gifts of food and water and supplies that the Watchers provided kept the Inhabitants alive. But the Watchers didn't just watch to be entertained and though the Inhabitants might have been free to leave on a practical level, I also knew now that something held them where they were. Something kept Lana from acknowledging us.

The Zoo layout was a giant loop. The large indoor building, which formerly housed the Minnesota Trail, the Tropics Trail, and Discovery Bay and now housed the majority of the Inhabitants, was at the opposite end from our paltry campsite. The rest of the loop was outside and wound through the remains of grassy hillsides and playgrounds, ponds and amphitheaters.

At the bottom of the hill I took a left and wandered past slopes studded with tents and lean-tos, structures that would have fallen at the slightest hint of inclement weather. They looked delicate and fragile, like the forts Bim and I used to make by attaching blankets to door frames with masking tape. People stopped to watch as I passed— mid-stretch, mid-conversation, mid-bite. Some of them smiled or nodded, others stared slack-jawed or clucked to get the attention of a friend who hadn't yet noticed my elegant waddle. Most people, however, watched me with a gaze reminiscent of Michael's: studious, patient, controlled.

Sound felt different, too. The Zoo was mostly quieter than Zion but occasionally a sudden noise or series of noises pierced the fabric of calm; Zion had more of a low, steady rumble.

I paused to open my notebook: *lightning, lightning bugs, heat lamps.*

When I paused, footsteps behind me paused too. I turned; behind me, a bald man with a red beard balanced a basket on top of his head. He met my gaze, blushed, and averted his eyes to a trash can chained to the ground. "Hey," he said softly.

"Hey," I said. I moved to the side of the path slightly and made a your-table-is-right-this-way gesture. He nodded and walked by me quickly.

I missed Asher: his patched khakis, his appreciative winks, his plaintive requests to find him a decent wrench in the Piles because the lack of one really was about to kill him.

The carousel was mostly just a disk of poles, stripped of their animal counterparts. A tapir and an ostrich remained. I climbed on the tapir and pressed my forehead to the pole. There was a bit of sticky pink residue behind one of the ears; I wondered if someone in the After had scraped it off, just for the taste of chewing gum again.

I ghosted my way past the moose enclosure, where people were harvesting stings. Then the bird amphitheater, the tiger enclosure, the central outdoor courtyard where kids used to frolic through geysers that sprang up under the watchful gaze of bronze bears. There were no bears. Around the edges of the courtyard were piles of smaller objects. It looked like a flea market, without tables or any kind of organization. The man with the red cat's-eye glasses was squatting in front of a microwave, holding the glass plate up to the sky as though checking for the manufacturer's stamp. A few yards away a dark-haired woman unloaded objects from a yellow gym bag: a funnel, a pinwheel, a PlayStation controller.

"Davis," said the cat's-eye man, waving his arm rather robotically.

"Excuse me?" I said.

"I'm Davis," he said. "That's Kim." He gestured at the woman with the gym bag.

Kim flinched just slightly as though the mere gesture were an assault.

"Have you seen all of it?" asked Davis.

"Most of the Tropics Trail," I said. "And we're camped over in the camel enclosure. I'm just poking around I guess."

"Have you been over to the Minnesota Trail yet?" I shook my head. "Kim." The woman continued to dig through the bag. "Kim!"

Davis shouted. She flipped her head up as if she'd been tasered. "Do you have anything for feeding or offering, Kim?"

"Why?" Three different headbands kept her hair pressed tightly to her scalp.

"So we can show her," said Davis.

"Mira," I said.

"So we can show Mira," he confirmed.

She eyed my belly quickly then zipped the gym bag closed. "OK, but I need to go to the Pile first." She slung the bag over her shoulder; as she walked, her body crumpled slightly, though I couldn't tell whether it was the weight of the bag or an injury that caused the limp.

Davis and I followed. It felt strange not to be carrying anything; I was used to pushing the buggy or bearing the weight of my collecting backpack whenever I headed anywhere in Zion. Davis didn't carry anything either but he compulsively patted his pockets—jeans and shirt, front and back—where he'd stuffed the napkins with his scribbled notes. Neither spoke but each glanced at my belly so often that by the time we arrived at the Pile I wished that I could simply remove the swell from my body, offer it to them as Show and Tell.

Kim made a beeline for two chairs with torn bottom cushions but pristine backs. She removed a butter knife from her bag and set about trying to unscrew the bolts that held the backs in place.

"It's hard to find textiles," said Davis, pushing one of the napkins farther down into his front pocket. "Pillows, blankets, clothing, batting. Most of it's gone. Picked over. Kim's smart. She'll use those backs as pillows or trade them."

"Offer them," said Kim through clenched teeth.

"Offer them. OK. Offer them," said Davis.

The Pile was about two-thirds the size of Curly. Because it had been undone and reconstituted it had less height but more girth, as though it had begun a slow melt into the ground. Fewer colors and textures. Heavier, more industrial objects. Though sometimes I found only a portion of an object on Larry or Curly or Moe, rarely was there rust, splinters, serrated edges. Our objects were dismantled but many of these looked broken, worn beyond use.

"Smaller stuff that people don't want they take to the market," said Davis. "That's where we were when you found us."

Kim finished unscrewing the last bolt from the second chair back and managed to stuff both pieces at least halfway into her bag. "OK," she said, sitting up.

"Who're you going to offer it to?" Davis asked.

Kim shrugged. Her middle headband, made of silver sequins, sparkled against the frieze of her face.

Davis and I followed Kim's determined limp from the Pile to the Minnesota Trail.

"Kim used to be an Inhabitant," Davis whispered.

"What happened?"

He shrugged. "I wasn't here yet. Probably she wasn't showing any signs so people stopped watching."

"Signs?" I said.

"I don't know why she doesn't go. Doesn't seem like she likes to be here. But she's really good about bringing offerings to the other Inhabitants."

"Signs?" I asked again.

"Here we are," said Davis.

Unlike the Tropics Trail, which was missing most of its roof, the Minnesota Trail remained the dim tunnel it had been in the Before. The enclosures on the right were open to the gray sky beyond (and so not truly enclosed at all); the enclosures on the left still backed up to walls darkened with dead foliage or faux branches. Had I raised my hands above my head I could have grazed the ceiling. In the Before, this made the experience with the animals feel close and exciting; now it was simply suffocating.

From a distance the eight or nine women in the former wolf enclosure looked like apes checking each other for lice, a flurry of hygienic bonding, like Lana's care for me after I told her about Bim's birthday. But really the women were cutting each other: gently, carefully, methodically. Thin, inch-long openings of red. They searched out skin that wasn't already thickened with scar tissue and cut with an X-Acto knife they passed from one to another with a heavy reverence. The ones who weren't being cut or doing the cutting bent over the wounds with ointment, salves, and poultices. They kissed one another often: temple, scalp, forehead. On the wound or near it. It wasn't the cutting I couldn't bear—it was the tenderness. A few Watchers stood quietly, their faces open and vulnerable, earth newly pocked with rain. Kim placed a spice jar full of rosemary on the ground in front of a woman pressing a navy bandana to her shin. Davis opened a piece of paper from his breast pocket and drew a few hash marks in a curving design, an image of the cuts without the bodies below them. Bile rose up the back of my throat. I started walking again.

"To your left is the most peaceful one I think," said Davis from behind me.

In the former porcupine enclosure stalactites dripped from the ceiling, icicles of rock formed out of millions of tiny pebbles. Davis took the wads of napkins out of his front pockets and dug until he came up with a fistful of pebbles and a few stings. He popped a sting in his mouth and offered one to me. I shook my head. "Suit yourself," he said before placing the pebbles on a bar table at the far right side of the enclosure. The man who emerged from behind the hanging garden of rock was hunched, one side of his back considerably higher than the other. He took one of the pebbles on the table and moved off toward a stalactite. "He's got rubber cement today," Davis noted. "That's rare." The man affixed the pebble and then returned to the table and chose a different stone.

"Always one at a time," said Kim. She took two carrots out of her bag and placed them on the table. When the man returned, he took the carrots instead of a stone and disappeared through the maze of rock, returning a few seconds later empty-handed. He didn't raise his eyes to us.

"Sit down or move out of the way," said a voice like a rusted bedspring. Behind us, a man wearing an army beret and sunglasses flicked us on our way with his wrist. "If you're going to watch, sit down and watch," he said again. "Don't block the view."

We obeyed. The tunnel curved to the left. After we rounded the bend there were no enclosures on the right, only bare trees stenciled against the gray sky. The Inhabitants of the enclosures on the left, a long row of them, were blocked from view by blankets and sheets, paper bags ripped flat and taped together, netting stuffed with newspaper and magazines. I remembered Michael's story about these Inhabitants just as the first sound started up.

A quiet moaning on one end dipped into a rhythmic "yah, yah, yah," a low beat that carried the sound farther, "yah yah yah, yah, yah, yah," a drumbeat made in the diaphragm, passed where we stood, where it morphed into a sound like a Disney princess in ecstasy. The high note of finding the prince at the wishing well held, one voice after another taking up the exact same pitch until the sound was a shiv in the skull, until farther up the room it transformed again into an agonized groan of mourning and then collapsed in a single, hysterical shriek. Then there was silence except for the sound of metal against rock, a scraping I couldn't see.

Kim left the two cushions in front of the newspaper-stuffed netting. Davis and I followed her onward through the strange silence into the open light of the atrium where the Minnesota Trail and Tropics Trail met, where there used to be an information booth and picnic tables. A zoo employee had painted a seahorse on my cheek during one visit. I remembered the cold bristles of her brush on my skin, the gentle way she held my head to keep me still. Her care had been simple, straightforward, neat. Nothing seemed straightforward anymore: the tenderness between those women mixed into the pain they were causing one another, the beauty of the stalactites beside the bent man who wouldn't raise his eyes, the horror of those sounds behind the curtain, Lana's unwillingness to face me, and Rodney's careful distance. This place felt so wrong, so broken, but what, really, did I know about what people needed to survive? About love or sex or desire? I'd been a privileged, white, suburban girl before the Rending and, as Talia had pointed out, I'd been mostly shielded from violence after the Rending. There were the Babies, sure, but I'd made nice little

Nests for them and I felt so proud about myself for that. And my little job collecting objects from the Piles. I'd felt so useful. But I was three weeks away from giving birth to my own Baby and my moral compass felt broken.

Davis and Kim left me at the entrance to Discovery Bay, where clearly Michael held court. The room featured two large former aquariums, one that had once held dolphins and another that had held coral and fish and a few sharks that swam near the surface, showing the children below their perpetual razor-sharp overbite. Michael stood in the middle of the room where, in an interactive estuary, rays and tiger sharks used to swim in slow rotations, children bellied up to the water on rocks, hopeful fingers pointed toward the dappled bodies below. The water, of course, was gone and so were most of the rocks that had once framed the pool; the setup now resembled the kind of stone circle you might find in Ireland, a worn attempt at magic.

There were one or two people consulting with Michael within the circle; others sat on a few remaining benches. Many of them held papers or objects in their hands and cast occasional glances toward the center of the room.

Knight and Drake were on their knees, tinkering with a large dog kennel. When Knight turned to reach for a roll of duct tape he saw me, raised his arm, smiled. Drake noticed his brother's movement and did the same. I raised my arm and wiggled my fingers halfheartedly. Then I turned and headed for the Tropics.

The woman in the tortoise enclosure was dozing with her head resting on an arm stretched out in front of her, winning at the five-hundred-meter freestyle in her sleep. As I rounded the bend in the trail, I noticed that the waves and boat and porthole were no longer etched in the glass; the mud or excrement covered the pane again, thick and unyielding. In the Komodo dragon enclosure, Lana was stretching. Lifting each leg, one at a time, pressing knee to nose. Then she rotated each leg in its hip socket, each foot at the ankle, each hand at the wrist, her head on the spindle of her neck. She did all of this facing away from the Watchers, a few feet from the faux stones at the back of the enclosure. From time to time she bent to drink from a fluorescent-pink water bottle at her feet. Along the back of the wall, disposable plastic water bottles, dented, labels peeling, stood like a row of sentinels. I held onto the railing and imitated some of her movements, raising myself up onto my toes, lowering my body slowly until my heels touched the ground. I tried a plié when she pliéd. I tried to remember fourth position and fifth. I didn't call her name or try to get her attention, I just tried, in the smallest possible ways, to make my body like her body, to put myself in her shape.

This was ridiculous given the current state of our bodies. Her naturally willowy frame had been further whittled by the dancing; my body looked like an advertisement for words like *ample* and *full* and *abundant*. For Halloween she could be Jack Sprat and I could be his wife, the one perpetually unable to eat any lean. *This is happening*, I told myself. *This is happening.* I opened my notebook and wrote *JACK SPRAT COSTUMES* in large block letters. Then Lana started to dance.

She was liquid and fragile, bow and scythe, angles and languor. With her toes, with her heels, with elbows and knees, sometimes on her back with the knives of her shoulder blades, she etched the dance into the sand of the enclosure. The movement was symbol, was emblem and totem, was myth and open door. Watching Lana wasn't like watching ballet in the Before. There was no clear pattern of rhythm or structure, no narrative woven into the unfolding from slouch to roll to leap to stretch. Ironically, it was like watching fish in an aquarium or the sleek otters that used to roll against each other in lithe piles on the other side of this very path. I was watching an animal move instinctually through her world, and the otherness of that move-ment was mesmerizing.

As she finished, something of a half-smile swam across her face. Or maybe it wasn't a smile, maybe it was simply that the weight that had been pulling on her features had been momentarily lifted. She looked at me then and I thought I saw an opening, a tiny uprush of hope in her eyes. Then she turned away.

CHAPTER FIFTEEN

A WEEK PASSED. EACH day I circled the Zoo until the space became almost familiar. Talia and Chester helped out where they could: washing root vegetables, carrying loads of stings to storage spaces in the old Zoo cafeteria, shoveling out new latrines. Chester returned to his mute genius status and learned what he could by listening to the Watchers, who talked at him almost perpetually. Ida and Sylvia joined forces with the only medical personality at the Zoo, a chiropractor unfortunately named Greg Cracker. He was the only person I'd encountered since the Rending who elected to use his last name. He wore gray sweatpants and a Christmas sweater (with real tinsel somehow woven into the perky-looking evergreen tree) and he looked completely incapable of manipulating the human skeleton. But Sylvia was in heaven. She would have split open his skull and stepped inside if she could. Instead she started sleeping with him. When I, upon learning this news, made a little retching noise in the back of my throat Ida looked at me seriously and said, "He's a nice man, Mira. He's a nice man."

Which was more than I could say for my man at the moment. It wasn't that Rodney wasn't nice. But most of the time Rodney wasn't there. Sometimes I saw him helping Drake or Knight with a project or unloading or packing up objects from the market in the central courtyard, but mostly during the day he was absent. In the evenings he sat with us around the fire. Ate, held my hand, rubbed his thumb down each of my fingers. He fell asleep beside me every night, often aligning the edge of his foot to the edge of mine, but he didn't touch my belly or my breasts, didn't snake his hand up under my shirt, didn't press his body against me in the morning. He didn't want to enter me but he didn't leave me either. I didn't know what the silence between us meant. He didn't shave. Day by day, his whiskers covered the branch on his cheek until it disappeared completely.

I had thought that once we reached the Zoo, there would be clear sides, an obvious battle, that the plan Talia had asked for on the road a week earlier would assert itself. But the fact that Lana refused to communicate complicated everything; she didn't look happy but she also didn't indicate any desire to be rescued. Meanwhile, while no one particularly liked the Zoo, though we all used words like *creepy* and *horrible* and *messed up* and *strange* to describe it, though none of us wanted to stay for long, we were all compelled by difference and mystery. I think we fancied ourselves ethnographers, anthropologists, international travelers; benign and patient observers of a different land. Taking Lana would almost certainly change our benign status.

And there was the small matter that I was thirty-eight weeks pregnant and I had no desire to give birth anywhere near the Zoo.

"Maybe tomorrow we should just go into the enclosure and tell Lana we're leaving. Just be direct. Maybe she's just waiting for our direction." I said this abruptly on the seventh night. I was scraping all the gunk off a piece of aluminum foil we used every night for wrapping sweet potatoes and laying them in the dying embers of the fire.

"That seems unwise," said Chester. He was trying to cut his fingernails with embroidery scissors. Mostly unsuccessfully.

"Why?" I said. "I want to touch her. I want to be near enough to her that she has to respond."

"And if she doesn't want to go?" said Rodney.

"We convince her to go." I folded the cleaned foil around a potato.

"And what, exactly, is everyone else doing while we're in the enclosure communing with Lana?" Chester flicked a cut nail into the fire.

"They can watch," I said, shrugging. "They like to watch, remember? It can be like an episode of *The Young and the Restless*. I'll pretend to wake from a coma and Talia can be my evil twin."

"And you think, assuming she wants to go, that everyone will just watch that happen. That Michael will just wave as we all happily skip off down Highway 77 into the sunset."

"Well, technically there is no sunset," said Talia.

"The Inhabitants are free to go at any time," I said, sounding like a mini Michael.

"Sweetie," said Ida, "most of these folks think Lana's got some secret stored up inside her. They think one of these days she's gonna dance it out. You think they're going to let her walk away?"

"I think 'secret' is a bit of an exaggeration."

"Mira." I could feel Sylvia's level gaze from the other side of the fire. "Ida's right. These people aren't just watching for entertainment the way that Michael claimed. He said it was all about wanting to be in another world. It isn't. They're taking notes. They're looking for signs."

"About what?"

"Who knows exactly. What the Rending meant. Why it happened. Whether it will happen again. Probably the same questions we ask in Zion. Only they think they have evidence."

"Why do you think people wait to talk to Michael all day?" added Rodney.

"I understand that the Watchers are paying close attention," I said. "I get that. Maybe even obsessively close attention. Fine. If they think Lana's so important, it's not like they're going to kill her."

"Mobs are strange things, Mir," said Chester.

"A lot of these people are strange things all on their own," said Rodney. "Belief makes people do crazy shit."

Chester shrugged. He was holding the tiny scissors between his thumb and index finger, letting it swing back and forth. Firelight ticked off the metal. "Lack of belief in anything makes people do strange things too."

I tossed the wrapped potato into the flames. We watched the fire pucker and splutter. Another sheet of foil lay open across my knees, a shadowed square of light.

"So we'll get her at night, then. When the Watchers aren't watching."

"And none of the hundreds of people in the Zoo will notice? Drake and Knight won't notice? This isn't *Mission Impossible*, Mira." I had kind of been imagining *Mission Impossible*.

Talia started humming the *Mission Impossible* theme.

"Shut up, Talia."

She shut up. When she spoke it was in a voice entirely devoid of light. "I notice you still don't really have a plan."

I sighed. Crumpled the foil around another potato. "What's your plan, Talia?"

Her response was quick: "I think you should talk to Michael. He's a reasonable person. Convince him it's a good idea for her to go."

"You think he's reasonable because you still want to get in his pants," I retorted.

I waited for further scoffing remarks from the others. There was only silence. Somewhere down the hill, the sound of poured water. Hammered wood.

"She has a point, Mir," said Rodney finally.

"I agree," said Sylvia, her words like a ballot slipping in a box. "It's worth a try."

"If it doesn't work he's on to us," I protested pathetically.

"On to us?" Rodney laughed, scorn at the back of his throat.

Chester added, more gently, "Mira, he's been on to us since we set foot in the Zoo. He knows why we're here. He knows what we want. We need to have a real conversation with Lana and it would be best if Michael could facilitate that."

"Fine," I said. I threw the half-wrapped potato into the flames. As I stood up the patches of exposed, dry skin caught and flared.

Rodney followed me to bed soon afterward. We lay below our blankets, not touching, not sleeping. I didn't like that I was breathing in the same air, molecules from his lungs filtering into mine.

Though we'd placed a tarp below the blankets to keep saturation from seeping upward and into our dreams, the cushion between our bodies and the ground was thin. A rock sliced into my left shoulder blade. The right part of my lower back was on distinctly higher ground than my left. I blamed these discomforts on Rodney. My belly, though it didn't even create that much of a disturbance in the duned waves of the blanket, felt huge and monstrous. Above us, on the sheet from Moe, the contrast between the white of the clouds and the blue of the sky was barely discernable.

Farther away, someone was trying out notes on a flute or a recorder. There was a rustling as Ida and Sylvia crawled into their sleeping space. Talia's voice breaking a whisper to say, "But then what I said was." The scraping sound of Chester's pocket knife against a stick as he listened. Then there were the softer sounds, difficult to place: a blanket snapped open? Leftover tea splashed onto the earth? The hinges of a lawn chair expanding? The cap of a water bottle raking into its grooves?

"I think you should go alone tomorrow," Rodney said. "I think I make things worse."

I didn't respond. This was the man who'd quieted Massey and the other visitors just by walking into a room. This was the man who cleaned animal carcasses in sure, quick motions. This was the man whose body was a plow, who entered me with the force of reined thunder. I'd seen doubt in Rodney but never cowardice.

"He wants to have a conversation with you, Mira. I don't know why. But I can tell he's waiting. He's not going to hurt you."

Mira of a year earlier might have believed that. But I thought about Cal's anger and Kim's limp and Lana's back as she refused and refused to turn and face me; I thought of the screeches echoing down the Minnesota Trail, of the slices of blood, of the blue eye peering through glass stained with excrement.

"He isn't a good man," I said. Then I rolled away and sank my breaths deep and slow until they resembled the rhythm of sleep.

CHAPTER SIXTEEN

I FOUND MICHAEL HOLDING court in Discovery Bay. He stood in the middle of the circle of stones; on the floor in front of him, a woman wearing a beige velour jogging suit was arranging pieces of green construction paper into a pyramid shape. Each sheet of paper had a Roman numeral drawn on the front. When I entered the circle of stones she jumped to her feet and splayed her arms and legs out as if that might prevent me from seeing her project.

"It's OK, Oakley," said Michael, but Oakley maintained her posture for a few seconds longer, her eyes like thistles in the middle of her smooth, round face. Finally, she crossed her arms on her chest and leaned her weight over her right hip as if to say I had some explaining to do.

"I need to talk to you, Michael."

"There's a protocol," said Oakley. She nodded her head in the direction of the three other Watchers who were sitting on the nearby bench.

"I don't really care," I said. I put a hand on my belly and Oakley shrank back a bit.

"These are writings from the Furies," said Michael. "I'm sure you've encountered them on the Tropics Trail, Mira."

I purposely hadn't encountered them because I remembered Michael's story about them. I didn't want to watch.

"Oakley numbered the papers ahead of time," Michael continued, "and then had the Furies write a few words on the back of each sheet. Now she's organized the pages again and we were just about to see what the words might reveal to us. Weren't we, Oakley?"

She nodded weakly, wiped the sleeve of her jogging suit across her nose. I could see the swaths along both forearms where the fabric was crusted, white and dry.

"Let's finish looking at this later today, OK, Oakley? We'll leave the pages right here. Knight and Drake will make sure no one disturbs them. OK?" The tenderness in Michael's voice felt genuine.

Then it was his hand on my back again, those two places on my spine. And this time in the midst of feeling disgusted and manipulated there was a tiny part of me that felt glad for touch from someone else, felt glad to have someone direct my path, someone for whom the way through this particular world was clear. The world Michael moved through was a dot-to-dot. There was an image on the page and figuring out the image was as easy as moving a pencil from 14 to 15 to 16. My life felt more like pointillism gone wrong. Dots scattered and layered to form recognizable images but only when you stepped away, only after a long time. Or maybe all those dots formed nothing at all.

Michael guided me out of Discovery Bay and back to the room I'd found him in when we'd first arrived. The desk with the typewriter had been moved against the wall. Below the dangling dream catchers and trinkets and inked Barbie doll, the wicker rocking chair sat beside a lawn chair, its crosshatched mouth open to the view of the brackish pond. We sat.

The armrests of my lawn chair had been white at some point but dirt or mold had worked its way into the pattern imprinted on the plastic. I busied myself trying to clean the grime out with my thumbnail.

Michael crossed his legs and rattled the stings in his pockets. "I imagine you are eager to depart with Lana."

"Yes," I said simply.

"I'm fond of Lana," he said, rocking back and forth gently.

"You love her," I reminded him drily.

"Yes," he said, nodding. "I do."

"I love her too," I said. I was embarrassed at how thick my voice sounded, how easily the tears came. On the other side of the blur, a red flare. A cardinal, ten feet away from us, happily pecking at something.

"I've got a feeder tucked in there," said Michael.

"You watch the birds? For pleasure?"

"I do."

"I thought your pleasure came from other things."

"What kind of a person do you think I am, Mira?"

It took every ounce of self-control I possessed not to say "sociopath." I let the question hang between us and focused on the armrests instead.

Eventually, Michael took his hands out of his pockets and held them out in front of himself. He stretched his fingers out, two pulsing stars, but they didn't entirely straighten. When he tried to relax them they didn't loosen either; instead, the fingers curled back toward his palms, searching for an offering.

"What's wrong with your hands?" I asked.

"Rheumatoid arthritis," he said, "treatable with medication but often debilitating without it. No new diseases since the Rending, I'm sure you've noticed, but some of us can't shake the old ones." Then he stuffed his hands in his pockets again and looked at me directly. "I'm not forcing anyone to be here."

"So you say."

"Hope isn't a thing with feathers, Mira. Hope is a thing you manufacture. The Zoo is my way of manufacturing hope."

"Hope?" I thought of Oakley, her arms crusted with snot, of Knight and Drake, of the woman curled into the tortoise enclosure. "Then let Lana go," I said.

"I have a responsibility to these people, Mira. Davis is pretty certain he's on the cusp of a discovery with Lana. Have you noticed the extra bounce in his step? It would be unkind of me to withhold that particular hope from him."

"So you'd keep Lana in a pen so Davis can experience some fucked-up sense of hope."

"I'm not keeping her. Remember. She likes to dance." His voice had an edge.

"I know she likes to dance. But you've messed with her head somehow. She's not right."

"I gave her an audience. And a purpose. Some people would see that as kindness."

"She needs to go. She's going to go. She's coming with us."

"Didn't go so well last time you tried to convince her of that."

"Let her go."

"I'm not sure what you mean."

"You know exactly what I mean. Say whatever it is you need to say. Unlock her brain."

"Unlock her brain?" He threw back his head and laughed, a clapping bark. When he was done he left his head tilted backward, gazing at the floating objects above him. "Unlock her brain," he repeated. "That's rather marvelous. I like that." He reached up and batted the Barbie doll. She sailed through the air like a trapeze artist in a murder-victim circus. We both watched until she slowed and then stopped. Michael stuffed his hands in his pockets. "Unfortunately, Lana's really the most compelling Inhabitant I have right now." He turned and looked at me fully then. Rattled the contents of his pockets so loudly I could almost feel a hard sting dissolving into threads of bitterness on my tongue.

And then I understood: he wanted me. I was the real freak show, the one about to give birth. And whether it was a squalling baby or a teacup that came out of me it didn't matter. Both would be exotic, both could be trembled and turned in the minds of these people until my Baby became hope and sign and signal. But Michael was smart so he'd been biding his time, waiting for me to offer myself.

He smiled when he saw the realization cross my face. "Aha! There it is. I knew you wouldn't disappoint, Mira." And then he reached across the space between us and with his stiffened index finger he traced a line: temple to cheek to neck to breast to belly. At the base of my belly he stopped. Pressed his finger into the crease of my thigh, all the while never breaking my gaze.

I held his gaze and I did not shrink back from his touch. One of the proudest moments of my life is not shrinking back from that touch.

It was only when he drew his hand away that I said, "OK. You can have me instead."

He lifted his hands to his mouth in mock surprise. "I was expecting a bit more anger and tearful deliberation. You continue to surprise me, Mira."

I was tired. So very tired. And Talia was right. We needed a plan. My body for Lana's body. That was a kind of plan.

CHAPTER SEVENTEEN

I HAD OFFERED UP my body for Lana's body because I loved Lana but also because I was overwhelmed by Michael's creepy intensity and Rodney's emotional absence and my own failure to devise a rescue plan. The gesture of martyrdom felt right and heroic but in truth I hadn't thought I'd need to go through with it. I thought the idea would be so appalling to the others that another plan would be brainstormed, devised, implemented. They were appalled that I'd said "yes" to Michael's idea but they were not, in fact, appalled enough to invent another option. It would be easy to free me, they conceded, if I was in on the plan. Inhabitants, after all, were free to go. Sylvia would insist on staying as my midwife—it would look strange if she didn't—meanwhile, Ida and Talia would return to Zion and find a different place to house the Babies. The Nesting Facility would be turned into something innocuous. If the Watchers followed them to Zion, there'd be nothing to see. We'd turn Michael into a liar.

Rodney and Chester and Lana would stay while I was becoming established as an Inhabitant. Within twenty-four hours of being placed in the Komodo dragon enclosure I'd fake some labor pains, Sylvia would fake concern, and I'd be transported to their clinic. From there it would be easy to slip away. We assured each other that from there it would be easy to slip away. I nodded from time to time but mostly I didn't speak. All this needed to happen soon, before I went into labor. Obviously. Obviously. Then Ida and Talia were kissing me on the cheek and stuffing blankets and food into bags and they were gone in what seemed like minutes. It might have been hours or days. I can't remember.

*

Trauma returns to us in snatches, in bright, painful bits that burn and die, the pop and fizz of orange flares against a starlit sky. The moments between are dark or blurred.

The next thing I remember it was twilight and Rodney was kneeling in front of me. I was sitting on a chair. I remember it as antique; turquoise cushions with a rhapsody of golden stitchwork, but this can't be. Rodney was going to read to me from a sheet of paper. From sheets of paper. Like a bedtime story, I remember thinking fondly. But first he explained to me how he had come to acquire these papers. Some kind of subterfuge. His explanation was complicated and I wasn't listening carefully because I knew I was going soon, to stand where Lana stood, and though I knew it would only be temporary, that I'd be rescued, still I couldn't quite concentrate on what he was saying. A freezer chest. A lock. Sheaves and sheaves of paper. But he found it finally. "I found it," he said, "and I need to read it to you"; and I remember thinking *reed* not *read* because his voice was coming through like that, thin and wooden, and then he began to read and that's when I began to listen. That's when everything swerved into sharp focus, words and images lined up on the inside of my brain.

And the story he read to me went lilting along in Michael's words like this:

"Once upon a time Lana was a dancer and she practiced in a studio that smelled of wax and oranges. And beside the studio (housed rather unromantically in a strip mall), workers were turning a Verizon store into a nail salon. The dancers liked to whine about the noise on the other side of the wall while they bit off long stretches of athletic tape with their teeth and they liked to eye the men when they smoked after their classes; the curves on the biceps of the men looked like they'd line up so perfectly with the swell of the dancers' own calves. And there was one worker who was younger, who wasn't there every day, whose eyes looked less dull, as though there were something he could see on a horizon, somewhere he wanted to arrive.

Lana offered this worker a cigarette and he accepted and eventually he asked if she wanted to go for a drive and she said yes. He took her to an empty quarry and showed her how you could roll bits of junk from the top down that incline, and the sound that it could make, and he smoked and laughed while the dust rose up over her flip-flops, over her gnarled toes, over the gray shorts she wore pulled low over her almost nonexistent hips. Another time he took her to a field of corn out beyond all the suburbs where a farmhouse had been uprooted, moved completely, and they stared into the hole in the ground, the empty foundation, at the washer and dryer and roll of insulation and plastic dinosaur and exercise bike. The blaring horn of sun quieted behind the corn and out came the fireflies and they lay down together in the back of his truck. The sex wasn't beautiful because he was nervous and a virgin and so finished too quickly and she didn't seem as reverent as he'd expected and the next day and the day after the pull between them was gone, just wasn't there like it had been, and he timed his breaks differently and she tried to ignore the sound of sinks being installed on the other side of the barre. And it wasn't really hard to ignore. It was easy enough. And all would have gone on just as before except—because all good stories have an 'except'— except she was pregnant. That age-old twist. And he didn't want her to get rid of the baby and she wanted to get rid of the embryo. He called it a baby. She called it an embryo. She couldn't be a dancer if she had a baby so she had an abortion. He wouldn't go with her but they met at a café in the mall afterward so that she could say that it was done, so that they could part amicably, so that he could give her one last dry kiss on the cheek. Right as the Rending happened. Wouldn't you know. Everyone you care about gone except for the one person you were just saying good-bye to forever. And then how do you say good-bye to that person, the only one that holds the thinnest thread of your past?

"And then up walks a girl in a lopsided scarf, her cheeks dirty with mascara and a sweaty security guard holding her too hard on the upper arm. Her jeans are a little too tight on her curvy frame and her hair looks like it would be gorgeous if she'd just let it down. She looks like she's busy trying to hide some parts of herself and trying to flaunt other parts and on top of all of that she looks pissed and terrified."

Then the story shifted away from Michael's telling and into a direct transcription of Lana's telling: "And I think we both just loved Mira, right away. Rodney and I did. She looked as broken as we felt and she also looked like she knew how to put herself back together. And we never told her. The Rending, when it happened, was the best chance not to say anything you didn't want to say. And by the time I wanted to tell her it had been too long. And by the time the Baby was born, my Baby—how to explain what I thought it might have meant? I couldn't."

When he finished reading Lana's story I took his face in my hands. He had shaved, finally, and I was pleased about this. I kept running my thumb over the branch on his jaw. The three tiny buds near the edge of his lip. His eyebrows. His cheekbones. I remember holding each of his earlobes between my thumb and forefinger and feeling embarrassed that I'd never noticed the bump of tissue in the right lobe before. I don't remember any people on the hill below us. I don't remember Sylvia or Chester. Only Rodney. Around us, on the ground, were the pages.

"You don't have to do this, Mira," Rodney said and I said, "Yes I do," though I didn't believe that. Only that there was nothing else left to do. My father used to say that the moment with Jesus in the Garden of Gethsemane, hours before his crucifixion, his grief and prayers and fear, the purpose of that scene is to show Jesus as human. But now I realize that moment is when he realizes he can't go back, can't get off the ride. The story is stronger than he is.

Rodney's jaw. His ears. The purple stains below his eyes. His eyes that finally, finally met mine. "I love you," he said. And I knew that he was being truthful.

"I love you," I said, and he was crying because I was saying the words with the sound of good-bye inside them.

I remember this moment: his face in my hands.

CHAPTER EIGHTEEN

T HE NEXT THING I remember is being watched.

Michael followed up on his promise, and Lana was released. I'd imagined taking her place exactly, precisely, amid the swirled and divoted sand. I'd nestle to sleep where she nestled to sleep, I'd add misshapen water bottles to her row of misshapen water bottles. But I was put in the empty dolphin aquarium instead. Knight and Drake lowered me down in the dog kennel I'd seen them tinkering with a week earlier.

Was put in. I say it as though I had no agency, no volition. I was playing a role: Willing Participant, Happy Inhabitant. Or maybe it was that I was already turning inward, already feeling the first tightenings, from my lower back around my waist. Either way, I knew as soon as I reached the bottom of that empty tank that there would be no sauntering out arm in arm with Sylvia and my feigned labor pains. I had to hope that Rodney and Sylvia and Chester would find another way.

In the hours before I recognized my contractions for what they were I remember being watched. The aquarium was no longer completely empty; it now looked like the set of a low-budget play. A burgundy recliner had been positioned next to a pink circular rug with elephants parading around the perimeter. From two tires filled with cement sprang two metal poles, a hammock slung between them. Wrapped into the cocoon of the hammock was a plastic ball the size of a grapefruit, Disney princesses posed coyly around the perimeter. At the top of one pole a net-less basketball hoop, a poor man's eclipse. I raised my hand to write *eclipse* and *tiara* in my notebook but my notebook was gone. When had they taken my notebook? I hated the idea of Michael leafing through it, finding Zion's practical needs beside my own list of desires. Words that betrayed my ache for the Before, for a way back.

I spent what felt like hours shooting the ball: from the hammock, the floor, the chair. I tried to move the chair to a more favorable angle and received a banging warning from the Watchers on the other side of the glass. I was pregnant so I was not to move heavy objects. I gave them the finger and pushed harder. Then there was a tightening ache that made me release my grip on the chair and slide to the concrete behind it so that for a moment their view of me would be blocked. Until I realized they were above me, too. The actual aquarium stadium seats didn't permit the Watchers to see into the depths of the whitewashed pit so they sat along the edges, legs dangling, heels kicking the sides. A constant irregular pattering like drops scattered from a branch at the end of a storm. And above those legs, the familiar nothing of the sky. Margarine without color.

I shot the ball until I noticed a few of the Watchers taking notes, carefully counting the number of times Tiana and Cinderella sliced through that circular wedge of air. Then I stopped abruptly and studied the ball; the row of tiny smiling faces and half-inch cinched waists filled me with histrionic fury.

It took me a long time to figure out how to deflate the ball. It was a tough little fucker, but I did it. Then I put it in the green five-gallon bucket in the corner that had presumably been left for me as a toilet. I climbed into the hammock and fell asleep.

But there was a moment—if I am honest with you, if I am honest with myself—sometime into the second or third hour of shooting when I enjoyed the watching. The woman with the low pigtails, the one who'd offered the oyster crackers, she was there. Forehead pressed to the glass. She'd nod whenever I made a shot. Nod when I didn't. Either Knight or Drake was always watching from somewhere around the rim of the tank, their comings and goings marked by the scratch of their knives against the plaster. Mona with her neon visor, chewing the end of a straw. The man with the red beard, on his belly, arms dangling toward me as though I were offering warmth. Sometimes I thought I saw Sylvia; once Rodney—I can't be certain. There were so many faces, static and in motion. I tried not to look at them but always they were looking at me. So many people, thinking I might have an answer. And maybe I did. It was intoxicating. To feel beloved, to be of use. Is this why Lana stayed?

Then the contractions started in earnest. Sylvia came. Was lowered in? And there was some time, between contractions, when I asked her what we would do now and she said *I don't know*, she said *we'll figure it out*, she said *this is your only job right now. Just this.* Her hand was warm on my back.

Then I was on my knees on the floor, face pressed to the burgundy cushion, burrowing into it. There was a dark tunnel and the darkness was material, consumable. With each wave of pain I gnawed into it, made a portion of it disappear. I ate and ate the darkness. There was no Lana or Rodney. There was no Chester or Ida or Talia. No Zion or Zoo. No Nests or Piles, stings or ghost fruit. No Deborah dangling from a branch; no disembodied eye pressed against the glass. The pain came and I burrowed into it. There was no Rending except for this.

CHAPTER NINETEEN

WHEN I WOKE it was dawn. I was huddled under a tartan blanket on the recliner. Below the blanket my belly was deflated, wrinkled flaps of skin crouched on top of one another. I was wearing a pair of mint-colored granny panties with sprigs of baby's breath pocked across the surface. The panties were stuffed thickly with rags. My breasts were hard, the areolas darker. The feel of my body was all wrong, hard belly turned soft, pliable breasts turned to rocks. My knees. I touched each gently. My knees were still exactly the same.

But my Baby, whatever it was, had been taken.

Had I somehow been drugged? Had I simply passed out from the pain? Had there been some moment of trauma that I was repressing, followed resolutely by sleep?

I looked away from my own body. No one watched from the other side of the glass. No legs dangled from above. Hanging over the hammock was the collecting shirt I'd been wearing and a new pair of pants, beige linen with an elastic waist. Had I soiled my other pants? With blood or fluid or shit? Had the Watchers seen me that way? When had they left? No more questions.

On the floor, on a tray, a cup of cooling water and a Lipton tea bag. Real tea. This must be my reward. Beside the tea, carrots cut and cooked. This was a gesture of kindness too, the way they were arranged on the plate, dominoes fallen in a perfect circle. I uncurled myself from the chair and dressed. I waddled over to the bucket in the corner and expelled urine and clots of blood the size of golf balls. I replaced the soiled rags with new ones I found beside the bucket. I ate the carrots; drank the tea. Tried to be practical and patient. Someone would come soon. I closed my eyes and tried to exhale slowly, thinking of Sylvia's warm palm on my back. *You have not been forgotten,* I whispered to myself. *Everything is under control. This is happening. Rodney will be here soon. Lana will be here soon. They have your Baby. You will make a list of items for the Nest. Then it will be easy to make as soon as you're back to Zion.* I reached again for my notebook but my notebook was gone.

Then the feeling reared up in me, a door kicked open by hooves. I wanted my Baby.

I don't know what it felt like in the Before. Of course I'd heard about a mother's love, but I'd expected some gentle stirring. I'd imagined Mary's sweet face turned toward a plump and docile Jesus.

The feeling was not gentle. It did not come on softly. It was violent and abrupt: the sudden roar of an airplane right above your head. One minute you see the airplane and the next minute you belong only to that sound. I belonged only to the sound of wanting my Baby.

I was feral.

The last hours of labor are still a blur. The first hours of wanting my Baby are not.

I screamed. I screamed the obvious. *Give me back my Baby! Give me my Baby! My Baby, now!* I banged on the glass with my fists. I banged until I felt the hardness of the glass in the bones of my wrists and my forearms. I tried to break the glass with my foot, with my body. I directed the screaming upward. I stood on the chair so that my voice could be that much closer. I went to the drain in the middle of the floor. I dug around the edges until the metal cut my fingertips. I called them what they were: *cowards, fuckers, oblivious motherfuckers, baby stealers, Nazis, psychopaths.* I took a break to sob with my cheek pressed against the floor. Whenever I moved, my whole undercarriage hurt. I reached through the piss and blood in the bucket and grabbed the deflated ball. I smeared my own blood across the glass. Wrote FUCK YOU on one whitewashed wall. I tried to push the poles over; when I failed I shoved the chair under the hoop and tried to rip it from its condescending place at the top. I screamed and screamed. I yelled at the God I no longer believed in.

Finally, I curled back into the fetal position in the chair. My effort of moving and screaming had made me bleed through the shitty mint-green underwear and onto the cushion. Wine on wine. I went to the bucket again. More rags. The spot on the cushion looked like Louisiana. *At least this place isn't filled with crocodiles*, I said to myself. I could smell the blood in my hair, on my skin. *Cleanliness is next to godliness*, I said in my brightest Merry Maid voice. Then I flipped the cushion over. There was Chester's gun.

I know now where they were, why they didn't come, but I didn't know any of that when I picked up the gun. At any given moment, no one knows the whole story. We act with limited information, from bias and belief, from memory and hope. My story is only part of a story. But my story is mine.

I pressed the cushion down again. Looked at the glass, at the rim of aquarium above, at the open shell of sky. No one.

Sylvia must have hidden the gun during my labor. One hand pressed warm against my back, the other concealing a firearm in a recliner. A hideous laugh started in my chest but I choked it off. The gun was just the same, but this time touching the trigger, the muzzle, the reptilian grip evoked nostalgia rather than fear: Chester's blue eyes, the toothbrush holder filled with tiny scrolled fortunes, the thin waxy skin of his forehead. The comfort of his presence.

I knew what the gun meant: we are not coming for you. We won't or we can't. This is the best we can offer. Good luck.

I ejected the magazine. I was not surprised to find that it was loaded. I was not surprised that he had lied to me, back there in his room. No one goes into a shopping mall with an unloaded gun. He had meant to do harm. I would have known this then if I had let myself know it. I slid the magazine back into place.

I don't know how long I held the gun in my hands before Michael appeared, don't know if he knew the gun was there all along, if he'd been waiting for me to discover it, observing me from a distance. Or maybe it was a surprise to him as well; Michael was delighted by surprises as long as they didn't unsettle his authority. As usual, he did not look unsettled. He stood a few inches from the glass, black hair slicked into that strange crescendo, hands clasped behind his back, mouth at the precipice of a smile. Pleased to observe his Inhabitant.

He took time to note every changed detail of the panorama before him. I watched his eyes take in the smear of blood on the glass, the chair pushed below the basketball hoop, the graffitied expletives, before his eyes finally came to rest on the gun in my hands.

I leveled it at his face. He held up both his hands, tried to uncurl all of his fingers into a full gesture of surrender, but his expression didn't change. I tried to remember everything I could from the physics class I'd almost failed junior year: speed and velocity and acceleration, force and mass and angular momentum. A year before the Rending a bear at the Minnesota Zoo threw a rock at its partition and only partially succeeded in breaking it. But maybe gun beats rock. Maybe bullet beats acrylic glass.

Michael wiggled the tips of his raised fingers, as if he were waving to me from the side of some fake battlefield.

My Baby. My Baby.

I took a breath. Refocused. Released the safety. A tiny click. Like an instrument case shutting or a lock sliding into place, a turn signal snapped off, a fingernail clipped. The first sound since I'd woken that hadn't come from me. A little break in the middle of emptiness.

I fired.

When I opened my eyes a split second later, the acrylic glass was gone but Michael was still standing. I raised the gun again and took a few steps toward him, hoping that my aim might be better at closer range.

I pointed the gun not at his heart, but at the place where the gold pin glistened on his lapel in spite of the lack of sunshine.

He nodded. As though he'd been expecting this all along. "I'm not afraid to die, Mira."

"I want my Baby," I said.

He nodded again. "That can be arranged," he said.

"I don't want it arranged. I want it. Now."

"It's not here."

"Where is it?"

"Why don't you give me the gun and I can show you."

"Fuck you."

"I'm not going to show you your Baby with a gun pointed at my face. That's not negotiable."

I lowered the gun. He reached out his hand.

"No," I said.

"It seems we're at a bit of an impasse then. You know I don't offer things without expecting something in return."

"It's my Baby."

He shrugged. "That may be. But right now I have it."

I considered his hands. I wasn't even sure they could hold the gun properly.

"Where's Lana? Rodney. Sylvia. Where's Chester?"

Michael stirred the dust motes above his head with his fingertips. "Off," he said. "Elsewhere."

I felt that elsewhere in my body. Felt that I had stepped into a different version of myself altogether. Not just my loose belly, painfully huge breasts, the aching pulse of blood between my legs, but this gaping uncertainty. Had I been loved? Had I been abandoned? The grief was so great that there were no tears, only a great trembling that moved through my limbs until it felt like the whole room was shaking, quaking open.

"The gun," he said again.

"Send Drake," I said. "Tomorrow. There's a Barnes and Noble off of Galaxie Avenue. I'll give him the gun once I see the Baby."

"Fair enough," he said. Perhaps too quickly. "Let me escort you out."

And he did.

*

When we got to the road, it was mostly empty. He handed me a water bottle. Clapped me once on the shoulder as though he were my mortgage broker. As though he'd gotten the financing he'd promised.

I looked over my shoulder twice; he was always watching.

The people I passed veered out of my way, tried not to look at me directly. I'd unloaded the gun by then; bullets in my pocket, gun itself tucked into the waistband of my pants. It slipped farther and farther until it was somewhere in the bloody mess of rags I carried with me, until I couldn't take a step without feeling metal poking my ass and blood drying on my inner thighs.

There was a bit of gummy residue on the water bottle where the label had been. I concentrated on adhering my thumb to that residue and plucking it off. I concentrated on not thinking a single thought until I had ripped my thumb away one hundred times. Two hundred times. Three hundred times.

Without the commentary of Talia and Chester, the Barnes and Noble felt even more empty and eerie: the stuffed crocodile, the faded pages taped to the windows, the stain of smoke on the ceiling. Hardest of all, the photos in the Biography section, each face a living human being now gone. A story, kaput. I looked at the pictures and let myself cry. Not the angry tears I'd cried in the aquarium, but the wrung-out kind. All of those people gone.

And the version of life I'd lived since the Rending was gone too, because whatever had happened with my Baby, I had to carry this wanting, this attachment with me. I hadn't understood before. The cruelty was not that women were giving birth to objects; the cruelty was that we felt for those objects something akin to what mothers feel for living babies.

The problem with love is that it craves an outlet. Love is a verb, as my father said, and so love makes us act: notes scribbled, roses purchased, hair brushed, ointment administered. Simple acts and tremendous ones. Offering a cup of tea, a fortune, a visor to block the nonexistent sun. There was no way to love the Babies. To birth a Baby was to learn to suffer in a new way.

I studied the photos again. All those people gone and no way to love them anymore.

I fell asleep in front of all those faces. A bloody mess curled around a gun. Aching with love I wasn't sure I'd be able to offer to anyone else again.

CHAPTER TWENTY

I WOKE A LITTLE when he scooped me up. I turned to him after he kissed my forehead. He told me later I murmured that I must taste like blood. There were whiskers on his cheek but I could see the branch, even in the dimness of the night.

When I woke again the light in the room had edged closer to dawn. Chester was staring at me from the kiddie chair beside the children's table. The stuffed alligator lay in his lap. He offered it to me and I took it. It was soft and smelled oddly of laundry soap. Rodney lay sleeping beside me. Chester scooted the chair closer and took my hand. I fell back into sleep holding on to him.

I think I could have slept for days but Rodney and Chester roused me fairly early.

"Drake could be here anytime," Chester said by way of greeting.

"Here's how this will go," said Rodney. His voice, so tender and certain, made me start crying again.

"Are you in pain?" asked Chester.

I shook my head. "Just glad to see you both," I choked out. Chester winked at me.

"Here's how this will go," said Rodney again.

"Where have you been?" I interrupted.

"Later, Mira. I promise. We don't know when Drake will be here."

"Where's Lana?"

Rodney sighed. "With Sylvia. Heading to Zion."

"Is she—is she herself? Does she—"

Chester shook his head. But I didn't know whether that meant she was still closed off, shut down, a cipher of her former self, or if it meant that we didn't have time to talk about this now.

Rodney began again. "Drake will be here soon. Chester's hidden the ammunition. I'll do the exchange. You can watch but you need to be hidden outside somewhere. Chester will be with you."

"That doesn't sound safe for you." I was thinking of the knives on Drake's belt, all those dangling points.

Rodney shrugged. "We're giving him what he asked for. We didn't promise the bullets. We promised the gun."

"But what if he won't give you the Baby?"

"I'll get the Baby, Mira."

Chester and I waited in a silver Volvo on the far side of the parking lot. He sat in the driver's seat and I sat in the backseat behind him, beside a car seat he told me not to look at. Rodney sat in front of the Barnes and Noble, on a chair that had once been used in the café. One of the chair legs was missing its rubber tip so if I stared hard I could see the motion Rodney made, rocking back and forth against that tiny imbalance.

As time crept on I peppered Chester with questions he wouldn't answer: Had he seen my Baby? What *was* my Baby? Where had everyone been after I gave birth? How did Lana and Sylvia get away? Had he seen my Baby? With each question my throat constricted more tightly until Chester simply said, "Mira, breathe."

To quiet the want that pulsed in every breath I took I distracted myself by reading the driver's manual aloud to Chester, by poking the back of his seat, by shaking the little monkey rattle attached to the car seat's strap.

Chester shot me glances of annoyance in the rearview mirror and then occupied himself with sorting through the fortunes he kept in the drawstring Tibetan purse he'd found in the Zoo courtyard.

"I wouldn't be good at stakeouts," I observed.

"That's an understatement," said Chester.

"Why won't you tell me anything?" I asked him, catching his eyes in the mirror.

"Because I'm supposed to be keeping you calm."

"Then how about why you had the gun in the first place. How about that story?"

He was quiet. We both stared at Rodney, his almost imperceptible rocking. A bird landed on an oil stain a few parking spaces over.

"Sparrow," I said quietly.

"I wasn't a happy kid, Mira."

I tried not to move. The sparrow pecked at the stain as though the residue contained some lost nutrient.

"Have you ever had a dream where something terrible is happening to you and you open your mouth to scream and nothing comes out?"

I nodded. Realized he wasn't looking at me. "Yes," I said.

"That was what my waking life felt like."

"Why? Was someone hurting you?" I asked.

"Not exactly. Sort of. Other kids ignored me or harassed me. Light bullying, I guess you'd call it. Not one person in particular and nothing drastic. But I felt it all. Every minor aggression, every interruption, every time someone turned away from me or ignored me. My mother called me hypersensitive and I thought maybe she was right. So I started to document them, all of the strikes against me. Seeing the slights and unkindnesses, even the few moments of brutality, seeing them written down made me feel justified in my bitterness. But then the bitterness turned to rage and the slights seemed to be growing, part of a greater plan. I really felt like people were trying to slowly grind me into oblivion. Trying to extinguish me."

"I'm sorry," I said.

"I know," he said simply. "I see now that my world was not closed. I see that there were ways out, people I could have asked for help. And there were a couple times when I tried. But it was like that dream. Nothing coming out of my mouth. Maybe because there was no big story to share. My parents were shitty and distracted but they weren't abusing me. I was bullied some at school but not particularly aggressively; I wasn't singled out. But I had this notebook full of grievances. And I decided that once I got to the end of the notebook I would do something. I would fight back. I wouldn't be extinguished."

"So you brought the gun to the mall."

"I did."

"And then the Rending."

"And I thought, Mira, I really thought I had done it. One minute this place was bustling with people talking to one another, touching each other. A mother helping a boy with his shoe. A high school kid touching a girl's necklace. I remember seeing you, Mira. Your little brother was bouncing off the walls and you were kind of looking at him but mostly looking at the boys. Those assholes."

"Those assholes," I murmured in agreement.

"Your eyes slid over me. Your eyes and the eyes of hundreds of people. They did not register me. Not with pity or attraction or disdain. Nothing. I was like carpeting. And then the Rending. I opened my eyes and the world was the way I thought it should be. Everyone gone."

"And we saw you."

"And you saw me. You actually wanted me with you."

"Of course we did."

"No, Mira, not of course. That's what I'm telling you. 'Of course' came after the Rending. I became a human being after the Rending. For the first year I had to hide my glee. Everyone was grieving and I was just so happy I got to be a part of the world."

"I'm sorry, Chester."

"You don't have to be sorry. I still feel guilty that I don't regret it, the Rending. I have never wished it away or wished for a return to the Before."

The sparrow lifted from the ground, flew out of my range of vision. Behind its departure there was another movement. Drake was approaching. I could see the knives on his belt and the burlap sack he carried over his shoulder.

"Chester," I said.

"I see."

We watched the scene in complete silence. I held on to the handle on the inside of the door as though we were taking turns at eighty miles per hour, as though there were an embankment we might go tumbling down.

Rodney stood as Drake approached. Drake set down the sack gently and then opened it. Rodney squatted down and looked inside for what seemed like a long time but didn't reach forward to touch. He straightened up again, nodded, reached around behind his back, and pulled the gun from the waist of his pants. He held it out to Drake with his hand wrapped around the muzzle. Drake tucked the gun out of sight. They shook hands and then Rodney lifted up the sack. Both of them turned and walked away. If there were words exchanged, we didn't hear them. The whole interaction took a few minutes at most. Chester made me wait ten whole minutes before opening the door of the Volvo, before flying across the parking lot to Rodney. To my Baby.

CHAPTER TWENTY-ONE

M Y BABY WAS beautiful. My Baby was a blue glass vase, eight inches tall, made to hold only a handful of blooms. My Baby was a crush of cold from Lake Superior, cousin of the Grecian urn, companion to the vases my mother tucked away in boxes. The body fit perfectly into my palm; my fingers curved naturally around her, my thumb fit into the rise of her neck. I ran my thumb around her lip the way my mother would have. There was nothing but air inside but that air smelled faintly like saltwater. Holding my Baby felt like holding everything on my list I'd been missing: stars and foam, blue raspberry slushies and the scent of a sun-warmed dock. My Baby was buoy and plum, pinecone and letterhead. All of it returned to me and was in me when I held my Baby.

It took all the strength I had, all the kindness, to offer the Baby to Rodney and Chester, to let them feel what I felt. They each took her in turn and I could see that nothing entered them. I could see from their faces that what they held in their hands was a vase. This made me a little sad but also pleased; it meant they wouldn't want to hold her, wouldn't need to touch her.

I held her while they sat me in a chair in the middle of that parking lot and washed me. I held her while Chester ran a wet rag over the bits of blood on my forehead, my cheeks, my thighs, while Rodney held out underwear, pants, shoes for me to step into. I held her while Chester gathered our supplies, while Rodney held a water bottle to my lips. I held her while we walked and all of those things I'd missed were spun, patterned, dappled inside me: my father's mixed-up lullabies and his gaze holding mine while he bandaged my knee; Bim chugging a Thomas train down the length of my calf; my mother brushing my sweaty bangs aside to plant a kiss on my forehead. These weren't just memories. This was the Before springing up alive and living inside me.

I held her in my right hand and Chester took my left arm. I held her in my left hand and Rodney took my right. When we stopped to eat, I placed her on my lap. I smiled a full smile. I saw Rodney and Chester cast concerned glances back and forth and I let their concern float away from me.

We camped for the night and I curled on my side and pressed her to me, against my pliable belly. Rodney was near me but his warmth was a different kind of reminder than hers. I wondered if this is the way mothers felt in the Before, as though a baby were a transmutation of all that they had loved before that moment. Is that what my mother felt when she held me?

The next day was the same: the walking, the road. Except I fashioned a sling so that I could hold her against me without using my hands. All the questions I had thought to ask, everything I'd been rabid to know had vanished. The Baby was enough.

When I woke on the morning of the third day an emptiness was whistling through me. I was a wind tunnel of doubt and grief; a persistent throaty loneliness sailed along my being. Rodney was holding the Baby. He was studying her bottom, as though it contained a sign or clue. Her base was thicker glass and there were a few scratches there. The Watchers would have tried to decipher them as clues. Everyone so intent on the surface of things when it was the essence that mattered.

"I'd like my Baby back now," I said carefully. I kept the anxiety out of my voice, knew that might cause him to keep her from me.

"OK," he said. He handed her to me carefully, a little sadly.

Chester hefted his backpack onto his shoulders and Rodney helped me to my feet; we kept walking.

It was the afternoon of the fourth day, when we were about three miles from Zion, that we saw them. We had just crossed a set of railroad tracks, climbed the steepest hill that Highway 77 offered the flat

Midwest landscape. We were eating turnips we'd cooked in the fire the night before. She was in her sling, lightly against my chest; there was nothing I needed.

"There," said Chester, pointing.

Rodney stood. He sighed. "They're coming."

"Who?" I said.

"The Watchers."

I stood too. I could see people. A group of them. Ten? Twenty? It was impossible to say. But enough that this was not simply a band of travelers. I squinted to see if I could decipher Michael among them.

"They want her," I said.

Chester nodded.

"They want my Baby."

Rodney ran his hand through his hair, pulled it upward as though trying to detach it from his scalp.

"But you shook on it. I saw you and Drake shake hands."

"We did."

"And Michael promised."

"Mira," said Chester. "You can't tell a bunch of people who want a sign to forget the most obvious sign they've seen in the last five years."

"You think Michael's told them about Zion? About the other Babies?"

"They were always going to come," said Rodney. "It was just a question of how long we had before they arrived."

"They're not moving," I observed.

"I don't think they want a confrontation," said Chester, "at least not here."

"They want her," I said again.

"They might want you, too." Rodney put his hand protectively around my shoulders. His touch was fine. Neither welcome nor unwelcome. My Baby hummed her warmth against my chest.

"They want all the Babies," said Chester.

"It will be fine," I said. "Let's keep going."

"We could try to move at night. Head in a different direction. Find a place to hide out. She's less obvious now that she's not pregnant." Rodney spoke as though I were a five-year-old or a dog, someone incapable of making rational decisions about her own safety. I knew I should be furious but my Baby broke up the anger and replaced it with the drip of a strawberry milkshake down the side of a tall glass, my mother's lap full of clean but unmatched socks, the feather-light pages of my father's Bible.

Chester nodded, staring at the Watchers as he spoke. "I could go on to Zion. That's true. Maybe they'll be ready for this by now."

Rodney studied Chester's profile. "But you think they need me. You think I'd be abandoning them."

"I didn't say that."

"This isn't the time to speak in fucking fortunes, Chester. Tell me what you think."

"I think you'd be abandoning Zion, yes, but you'd probably be saving Mira and your Baby."

"Probably?"

Then something passed between them that I felt but didn't see because I was studying the reflection of the sky on her, canoes of lighter blue that skimmed up her sides.

"Let's build a fire." Rodney sluffed his backpack off his shoulders.

"It's four p.m.," said Chester.

"It signals to them that we're staying here for the night. We'll go the rest of the way tonight. After they're asleep."

"Presumably asleep," Chester interjected.

"That should give us a couple hours, at least, before they find us tomorrow."

"If they find us," I countered.

"Mira, there are roads. The distance from here to Zion can be summarized in a description of two turns. They know how to get to Zion." Rodney's voice had an edge but my Baby rounded it out. Smoothed it down.

"Just don't let them take her," I said.

Chester squeezed my hand. Rodney had already turned to look for kindling.

For me, walking at night was not so different from walking during the day. I carried her in the sling and the feeling of fullness, wholeness remained. Images swished through me, not simply as memory but as essence. Bim laughing, the edges of his lips tinged with chocolate milk. My father, letting me practice tying knots using the rope of his alb. Over, under, around. On my mother's palm, three small piles of spice: cumin, cinnamon, salt. I am wrapped around her hip and she instructs me to add the spices to the pot of chili in any order I please.

And then came images untethered to any certain moment: snow squeaking below boots, our garage door pulled up and lowered, the sun casting squares of light on floorboards, couches, tiles. Before I had her, to remember meant to see the image but also to feel the distance between that moment and the one in which I resided. I couldn't conjure the Before without conjuring sadness or nostalgia, grief or guilt. But now the distance had collapsed. Everything that I remembered inhabited me: chilled cantaloupe, cheeks rubbed with dandelion petals, the pull of the tide around my ankles, the rattling of change in pockets.

The rattling. I heard it now. The way a dream changes to reflect the waking sounds around it. Chester was beside me. Had there always been that rattling? The last few days? Had I only just now noticed it?

I stopped. Whispered because night seemed to ask for whispering. "What is that, Chester?"

"What is what?"

"That rattling sound?"

He looked at Rodney, who shrugged. Chester reached into his pocket and pulled out the bullets. The four remaining bullets he had pulled from the chamber of the gun before returning it to Drake.

"They weren't stings," I said.

"No. They're bullets."

233

"In Michael's pockets. He was always rattling them. I assumed they were stings. But he never put a thing in his mouth. Never once." I bent over and as I did, the Baby fell away from me slightly. The place where she had touched my chest felt raw.

"That's why Drake didn't check the chamber," said Chester quietly.

"What?" said Rodney.

Chester was standing very still. Arms at his sides. Eyes closed. "When you gave Drake the gun he just took it. He didn't check. It's because it didn't matter. Michael had ammunition all along. He only needed the gun."

I straightened up and felt the bulb of the vase lodge back between my ribs. "We keep going," I said, as though someone had presented another option.

Rodney threw his head back then and screamed. A scream mixed with a groan. Like some superhero unable to emerge from his human form, his transformation curtailed. Chester kept his eyes closed.

I began to walk. At some point, they followed.

CHAPTER TWENTY-TWO

AND THEN THERE was Zion. At first it made me sad to see it. The Zoo, for all its internal monstrosities, still occupied structures that were substantial, tall. An aura of permanence drifted around them although, like all structures post-Rending, they carried the signs of absence. But we'd made Zion from scratch. I'd forgotten how low the buildings were, how insubstantial. The Center, the Clinic, the cobbled walls of the barracks where we slept—all huddled within reach of Larry and Curly and Moe. Zion looked like a shantytown, a sulking child. In spite of my Baby's presence against my chest, when I first saw Zion again, I felt despair.

But as we grew closer, the familiar began to exert itself. In the orchard, picked ghost fruit covered the bottom of the bin with the thin gray crack. I touched the scabbed bark of a tree, picked a piece of the fruit and let it shrivel to nothing on my tongue. At the edge of the orchard stood the baby buggy, its wheels slightly sunk into the saturated earth. There was Rodney's house, stilted and dumb. There were the Sorting Stations. In the household pile a few Tupperware lids and plastic cups, strands of Packer football lights, a silver toaster in which someone (probably Cal) had placed two torn cereal boxes, likely to suggest decorative possibilities. There, pressed to the outside of the Clinic, was the garbage can Asher and Rodney had been attaching the day Lana told me she was pregnant two and a half years earlier. There were the blue stadium seats that bridged the space between Chester's room and mine. There, in front of me, the Nesting Facility. And a single, familiar figure holding vigil in the gray half-light of dawn.

Lana was wearing her Dodgers sweatshirt and a pair of polyester bell-bottom pants. A lantern dangled from her arm. Her hair was down, long and frothy around her shoulders.

"You're here," she said.

"I'm here," I said.

She set down the lantern.

"They're coming," I said, gesturing vaguely behind me.

"Who? Chester and Rodney?"

"Yes. And the Watchers."

"Are you sure?" she said. "We thought—" she let her voice trail off. The presence of my Baby made me feel benevolent but not particularly interested in what she or they thought.

"Because of my Baby," I said.

"May I see her?" she asked. And you will think it absurd but when she said "her" she said it with the right weight, with the understanding that the object possessed significance, importance. Rodney and Chester had not understood this.

I pulled her out of the sling. Lana stood very still, looking. I turned her in my hands, touching the curve of the neck and the edge of the opening, running my thumb over the scratches on the dark blue bottom.

"She's beautiful," said Lana, her voice lined with velvet.

"We need to have a meeting." It was Rodney, behind me.

"Hi Lana," said Chester.

"Hi Chester," said Lana quietly. Then: "Hi Rodney."

Rodney didn't say anything. If he made a gesture to acknowledge her presence, I didn't see it.

"We need to wake people up. We need to meet," he said again.

"We have to do the ceremony first," said Lana.

"We don't have time."

"If we don't do the ceremony, the rest is no good." Lana took my hand. "This way," she said. Rodney and Chester headed toward the living spaces.

A Nest was on the pedestal in the center room, but behind the pedestal the shelves of the Nesting Facility were empty. Each shelf had been extended so it could serve as a bunk for a visitor instead.

"Where are they?" I asked, gesturing at the shelves.

"They're safe," she said.

The Nest on the pedestal was a lampshade turned upside down. The shade itself was dark gray but Lana had cut slices out of the fabric: stars, a sun, a comet, even a collection of tiny holes that I took to be rain. She'd backed each place of absence with a piece of fabric in a different color so that the celestial figures stood out as yellow and red and gold and blue against the gray. Inside the Nest the pieces of backing hadn't been trimmed but instead padded the base, loosely swirled together to create a place of bright comfort. Lana reached her hand into the Nest and moved the fabric to the side so I could see that the base itself was one of Zephyr's mixtures, not smooth but peppered with little indentations. "Those are fingerprints," said Lana, "everyone in Zion."

"How did you finish this so quickly?" I asked.

"I had help," she said.

I held my Baby to my chest with my left hand and touched the tiny indentations with my right.

"May I hold her?" asked Lana, so quietly and tentatively that I wasn't sure I'd heard.

I took a deep breath and handed the Baby to her and the world came back to me as I knew it would. The complex mixture of anger and grief and fear I felt so acutely that had Lana not been holding the Baby I probably would have hugged her until her ribs cracked. Because I loved her and I also wanted to hear the sound of her breaking.

She looked like the same Lana who had put her feet in my lap, who had touched my belly and said *I'll be back for this*. But she hadn't come back. And when I'd tried to rescue her, when I'd gone all that way, she hadn't even looked at me. And she hadn't told me, ever, that she'd known Rodney. Or that she'd had a baby, an embryo, growing inside her. Or what it had been like to lie on a table having that embryo sucked out of her.

I had thought that when I got back to Zion there would be time for all the questions. But there wasn't time. There was the press of the Watchers approaching; as Lana held my Baby I felt that press acutely, like a reminder of Chester's gun digging into the small of my back.

Now Michael had the gun and it was loaded and he wanted things we didn't want to give him. Fear webbed its way across my skin.

And then the humming began, the sound of Zion gathering. Chester and Rodney must have gone and woken them. The humming first and then the spots of light. Not like at night when the lanterns looked disembodied, detached from a human form. In the dawn the sparks of fire simply looked like a portent of what was to come, a reminder that no matter what we did, day would surely arrive.

Ida came and put her arm around my waist, kissed my cheek. Talia scratched my back a little too vigorously. Asher sauntered over and rested his hands on my hips, squinted into my eyes. "You look good," he said, his voice full of comfort rather than flirtation. Tenzin smiled sadly. Paloma nodded at me and swayed in place. Marjorie took my face in her hands. She smelled like ghost fruit and suntan lotion. Sven tipped his straw hat and winked. Cal strode over purposefully and lifted me off my feet in a hug. There were tears in his eyes when he put me down. Zephyr took my hand and squeezed it for a long time. All of them gathered around the pedestal.

Here were all of the people I loved, and here also was all that I didn't know about who they were. Here was the unknown. Here was the complexity of loving someone who has betrayed you. Here were people I loved who would both hurt me and love me, intentionally and unintentionally, again and again. Here was the far-off approach of people who were damaged, who thought violence might offer hope. Here was brokenness. Here was the After.

All the while Lana held my Baby. To hold my Baby was comfort, an infusion of unconditional love, an all-access pass to the feathered metaphorical wings of the God my father had offered me, the God I was certain had abandoned me. All I wanted was my Baby and the safety of the old world thrumming through me. But to hold on to my Baby would also mean isolation. My body would be among these people but I would perpetually be elsewhere. I would exist in a world none of the people around me would have access to, I would live in an ocean of contentment they would not be able to touch. To hold on to my Baby forever would mean abandoning Lana and Rodney and Chester and Ida and Sylvia and Talia. It would mean abandoning the complex and broken world of the After to live in a place of contentment alone.

"What do you want to sing, Mira?" Lana asked.

"'The Riddle Song,' I think. Does anyone know that one?"

"I do," said Paloma. And because I couldn't start the song, she did. The hesitant voices of the others rose up, slowly but surely, and found the tune. "A cherry when it's blooming, it has no stone. A chicken when it's pipping, it has no bone." Paloma sang the words my father loved but the words were cloaked by the voices of those who loved me, imperfectly, now. "A baby when it's sleeping, there's no crying. And when I say I love you it has no end."

I looked around the circle of faces, at our wavering ring of light.

I took my Baby from Lana and I laid her in the Nest.

PART THREE

CHAPTER ONE

T HEN LANA TOOK me by the hand again. Her skin felt like gauze, like a Styrofoam communion wafer that's supposed to be bread. Human touch was absurd after the rush and swell of my Baby against me. Lana took my hand and Kristen took the Nest and they led me toward the river. Had I been paying attention I would have registered the canvas duffel bag slung over Paloma's shoulder and the briefcase of medical supplies in Sylvia's hand. I would have noticed that the baby buggy Cal pushed was filled with ghost fruit and sweet potatoes and a container of smoked meat. But I didn't think about it. I assumed it was part of a ritual I didn't yet understand.

We walked to the spot along the bank where Rodney and I had seen Deborah bathing more than a year earlier, the place I'd washed Lana's hair, willing her sagging belly to reattach itself to her willowy frame. I touched my own belly, still swollen, misshapen.

On the shrug of sand stood our canoe-mobile, its wheels now removed. Beside it bobbed three jerry-rigged rafts I'd never seen before. The vessels were loaded with supplies—and with the Nests and Babies. Paloma plowed through the water in her duct-taped Crocs and positioned herself on a milk crate at the back of the first raft; Talia joined her. Eleanor climbed onto the second and Cassie and Kristen helmed the third. Sylvia lifted her skirt and stepped delicately through water in her black boots to the canoe.

"What is this?" I asked no one in particular.

"This is a plan, Mir," said Talia, not unkindly.

"Spot for you right here, sweetie." Ida stood beside the canoe, holding it steady. In the center, a few cushions and a blanket had been nested together in a way that was clearly supposed to look appealing.

I looked at Chester, who seemed equally baffled and shrugged. Rodney was already thigh-deep in the water, checking the rafts for buoyancy or whatever word means not-likely-to-fall-apart-in-the-middle-of-a-river.

"What is this?" I asked again. "We just got back. I don't want to go."

"He wants the Babies, Mira. He probably wants the women of child-bearing age, too," said Lana.

"Michael," I said, the word like a bird flung against a windowpane.

Lana nodded.

"And this . . ." I gestured at the vessels. "This is supposed to stop him? Running away?"

"They're well made. You did a good job," said Rodney appreciatively, nodding at Tenzin and Asher and Cal.

"Why wouldn't we fight? Why wouldn't we stay and fight?" But my body no longer had energy to put behind my questions. All the urgency in my voice had fled.

"Mira," said Paloma from her position on the raft, "you need to get into the canoe. They're coming. We'll talk later."

Lana took my face in her hands and looked in my eyes. I was reminded of the day she gave birth, only this time it was me with the heaving chest, me snorting breath through my nose like a horse. "I know you have no reason to trust me right now, Mira." Her hands were cold but strong. "But this is happening. This is happening, Mira, and we have to go now. He is coming." On the word *he* her eyes flashed in fear and I saw there was a story there. Things I didn't know or understand.

"OK," I whispered back to her. But still I didn't move.

So Rodney waded through the water back to shore and scooped me up and carried me to the canoe. I didn't fight. I felt the heavy weight of each of his steps through the murk of the river bottom. He deposited me gently and pulled a blanket around my shoulders. Then he kissed me. He smelled like Rodney and tasted like Rodney. I didn't kiss him back but I didn't pull away. I closed my eyes and there was that brief golden glow. A stooped sunset. Words rubbed soft as stone. *It is like happiness, when we are happy.*

"I don't know what this is yet, either," he whispered, "but I trust them. I do." The branch was glossy on his skin. "Be good," he said. Maybe he said. The words came only half-loose from the back of his throat.

Then he and Tenzin and Asher and Cal pushed us off that shrug of sand and my last glimpse of home was Rodney, chest-deep in the middle of the river, the current cutting paths around his skin.

CHAPTER TWO

THE RIVER FLOWED south at a manageable pace. Most of the time, people didn't use the river as a conduit for travel because it made the traveler into an easy target, a sitting duck. One visitor had told us about an encampment in the south that set hooks and snares just below the waterline. "They were fishing for people," he said, "fishers of men. Not what Jesus had in mind I don't think."

The first hour or two all of the women were busy, maneuvering us away from fallen logs and snaggle-toothed rocks. The minute we caught (or seemed to catch) on a sandbar there were shouts about who should get out to push while poles and oars were used to gain purchase and leverage. Floating gently was not sufficient, we needed to be moving forward with purpose. I didn't try to help. I barely watched. I was still wearing the pants and shirt Rodney and Chester had held out for me in the Barnes and Noble parking lot. Two days ago? Three? The shirt was red and advertised a reindeer run, Rudolph's nose disappearing against the flush of the background. A failure in advertising. Encasing my feet were hiking books with purple laces—which should have been practical but instead made me feel heavy and immobile. Over the red shirt, a wool sweater thick with the scent of alpaca oil. I touched my chest. Where was my notebook? Did Michael have it? I couldn't remember, and my interest in the answer to the question waned just as quickly as the question had waxed. I watched the backs of Sylvia's arms as she paddled in front of me; when she removed her cardigan I watched a slow bloom of sweat move from the small of her back upward along her spine. I watched the banks: matted grass and snarls of bramble. Sometimes the silver wink of a candy wrapper.

I knew I should want answers. Where we were going, for starters. Or how the other Zionites, left behind, were supposed to fare against Michael and the Watchers. I should have asked about the fear in

Lana's eyes. Or why she hadn't acknowledged me in the Zoo. Why she hadn't told me about Rodney or the abortion. What she thought our Babies meant, if they were signs or warnings, absolutions or punishments. But even the huge, consuming desire to hold my Baby had passed. They'd put her on Paloma's raft and now that she was snug and secure in her Nest the desire to hold her, to have her against me, had eased. I was unnecessary, a shell without sea sound. And I was so very tired of caring. I was so very tired, as if I'd come to the end of a marathon and been told it was a triathlon instead.

Was I hopeless? That's difficult to say. I think I simply didn't know who I was anymore. When the Rending occurred I was seventeen, still toeing the ice of my identity, checking for soft spots, for bubbles and cracks and fissures. That's what being a teenager often is: not so much asserting yourself as trying not to fall through the ice. But since the Rending I'd become a citizen of Zion, collector of objects and builder of Nests; I was Lana's best friend and Rodney's lover. For a few brief days I'd even been some fucked-up version of a mother.

Now everything was different. The Piles were still there. So were Zion and Rodney and Lana. My Baby bobbed along merrily a few feet from where I sat cross-legged in the base of the canoe. But it all felt wilted and sullied and fetid. *Nowhere at once.*

The Mira of a week and a half earlier would have been peppering Lana and Sylvia with questions, would have been consumed with worry about Chester and Rodney and those we'd left behind. But this woman in the canoe, the only thing familiar about her was the way she resembled my mother on the nights she fell away, glass of wine in one hand and the computer screen scrolling in front of her. That version of my mother stretched her arms down the length of my arms, coaxed the sky into coming down and spreading its gray foam in my brain.

And so I watched the surface of the water for objects that might catch, claw, or destroy us. But I didn't watch in fear; I watched in numb expectation.

CHAPTER THREE

A NOTHER HOUR PASSED. The next time we snagged on shallow ground, Paloma called out, "Food!" and instead of prying the vessels free, we passed provisions to one another, containers of turnip pottage. I ate enough that no one would confront me about not eating.

We started up again but I didn't offer to paddle. Lana and Sylvia settled into a rhythm, taking turns. On one of Sylvia's turns, Lana began to speak from behind me.

"We're going to an encampment of women, Mira. They live down the river."

I had no desire to respond.

"They call themselves Noons. One of the women was a visitor once. When Ida and Talia got back to Zion a week ago and told everyone about the—the situation at the Zoo, Paloma remembered this woman and she and Kristen went down there and I guess, you know, asked if we could stay. Booked us a reservation. Mud baths and hot-stone massages."

She paused and I could tell she was waiting for me to chime in or turn and roll my eyes, to acknowledge her forced attempt at humor in some small way. I stared at the purple laces in my boots. They weren't entirely purple. There were black threads woven in, too.

She sighed. "So the plan as I understand it is to camp out there until the Watchers get bored with Zion and depart. Then we head back to Zion. The Zionites will give us an all-clear signal. Something Tenzin and Asher worked out with Paloma. A red flag tied in a tree?" Even though my back was to her, I could see her waving her hand in the air to fan away the logistics. "I don't really remember. Just that while they were talking I kept thinking about pirates. Anyway. We'll see the all-clear signal, do an all-clear dance, and then go home. It will all be OK. You'll see."

"Your turn," said Sylvia. She rested the paddle across her knees. The leftover drops of water slid like loosed pearls back into the brown river. When Lana spoke again I could hear the effort of the paddle strokes in her voice.

"I know what you're thinking, Mir. You're thinking that's a shitty-ass plan. You're thinking what if Michael sets up shop or what if he turns Zion into a pilgrimage site or what if there's a skirmish, a small one but a few folks take a bullet. What if Zion becomes a little Zoo? What if the Watchers figure out where we've gone? Yadda yadda yadda. You think I don't know what you're thinking but I know what you're thinking."

I felt a poke on my upper back to the left of my spine. I didn't turn. She pressed the edge of the paddle against me again.

"That's fine. You know what? You can not talk as long as you want. You can ignore me. I get it. Tit for tat. I slept with your boyfriend before he was even your boyfriend. I didn't tell you I had an abortion. I HAD AN ABORTION!" she shouted. "TA-DA!!!" Eleanor and Ida turned around briefly and then went back to paddling and steering. We were starting to drift to the right, toward a half-submerged log. Lana poked me again, harder, but still I didn't turn. Sylvia started to paddle even though it wasn't her turn yet. We narrowly missed the log.

"And then. AND THEN. You come to rescue me and I won't even participate. I'd been so good at being the flimsy princess. Or the prostitute. Though we didn't use that word, did we? You didn't call me the Whore of Zion. At least not to my face. And then I didn't do the damsel in distress role right either. I couldn't even let myself be rescued properly. I get it, Mira. I'm the fuckup and you're the hero." Then, more quietly: "I get it. I know how your brain works."

It was quiet then. I could feel the others purposely not looking in the direction of our canoe. Sylvia lifted her paddle out of the water and let us drift.

When Lana spoke again her voice was a knot of tenderness and pain. "I love you, Mira. You know I do. But for all the complicated maps of objects in your head, you also have a pretty good ability to ignore things you don't want to see."

Mira of a week earlier would have fought back, pleaded her point of view, prodded the empty spaces in Lana's argument. But the Mira I was in that canoe let Lana tell me who I was: self-absorbed, self-righteous, blind. That version of myself felt just as true as any other.

CHAPTER FOUR

T HREE HOURS LATER, as the sky began to dim, Paloma called out, "There!" Up ahead, the river curved to the west; on the right bank two saplings arced unnaturally toward the river like fishing poles heavy with trout. Paloma heaved herself over the side of the raft she was steering, the first in our flotilla. As water sloshed around her hips, she pulled the raft through sheer force of will toward the left bank. The other two rafts followed suit. A string of profanities from our canoe brought us within reaching distance of the rafts; Sylvia held out her paddle and Talia grabbed it and pulled us close.

Somehow or other, we secured the flotilla to the bank, a bramble-covered bank that stretched fifty feet to the left and fifty feet to the right and twenty feet almost straight upward. Paloma called out a name—Maisy or Dana or Daisy, I couldn't quite make it out—and a section of the branches, about ten feet above us, shifted slightly to reveal a face and an arm.

"You and Perky walk the boats down to the launch," said the face while the arm gestured to Paloma and Kristen. "The rest of you come up here."

Paloma and Kristen (who admittedly was on the annoying side of attentive some of the time) began to guide our vessels along the bank, using a dim, muddy path; the rest of us clambered our way to the opening in the undergrowth.

When I finally reached the opening I saw that behind the hole the bank leveled out; the branches that stretched ten feet farther above me weren't growing out of the riverbank, they'd been constructed purposely to give the appearance of insurmountability. I slithered through the crackle of branches and onto a bed of moss.

Moss. Green ground alive and soft and growing. Rather than standing up I stayed on my knees, pressing my face to the floor like an animal rooting for a scent. Not just earth but green sparking newness. Spring. Clear and full. The scent of a billion plants manufacturing chlorophyll at once. The almost alien green of minuscule new leaves, taut with moisture.

"Keep it moving," said the voice, a voice with the subtlety of grinding machinery.

I obeyed; stood and moved to the side. The moss was everywhere. A carpet stretching across a space the size of a gymnasium but shaped like a horseshoe. We were standing on the arch of land that tucked into the bend of the river. All around us, branches rose up, woven into a crosshatched covering. Only the center of the room was completely open to the sky, though the gray light worked its way in between the slats of the branches as well. Hanging from the walls of branches were what looked like huge baskets; scattered on the floor were a few pallets, also knit from strips of wood. Though the craftsmanship was impressive it was the moss that had all of us goggle-eyed and gulping. It was a patchwork carpet, forest green and lime green and fluorescent green and every Crayola green in between. Ida crouched down like a kid playing marbles, running her hands back and forth over the fuzzed green skin, tears sliding down her cheeks.

Since the Rending we'd encountered green in the crocodile hue of the root vegetable tops or in the sheen of a potato dug up too soon. But abundant green, the green that swizzles inside your chest and spreads out its parachute arms in springtime—it had been five years since we'd been inside that kind of green. And you will likely find it absurd when I say that the green washed out the gray foam that had clouded my brain—but it did. I don't mean that everything was made right, just that the green made me want to be in the world again.

"I think we made it to Oz," Lana whispered.

"We're not in Kansas anymore, Toto," I whispered back, pinching a section of her Dodgers sweatshirt between my fingers.

"Hootey-tootey book metaphors later, ladies." It was the voice again, coupled with a poking sensation against my ass. I turned and for the first time actually really looked at our hostess. She was the visitor with the yellow sled and Quaker oatmeal containers, the one with duct-taped shirt cuffs and short gray hair to whom Rodney had given the dead animal tails. Who'd said Deborah was cuckoo. I'd been poked by the glitter star at the end of a child's fairy wand.

"I'm Daisy." She smiled, tongue pressed to a gap in her upper row of teeth. "The name is meant to be ironic. You two come with me. Cora, you too." She pointed the wand at a woman with short blonde hair who'd been repairing a portion of the wall. The woman nodded. "The rest of you get cleaned up. Abigail?" A girl no older than Cal with protruding ears and angry skin moved out from the shadows at the edge of the room. "Tell 'em what to do." Abigail nodded.

Daisy turned abruptly on her heel; Lana and I followed her toward the other side of the room. The branch wall gave way to a tunnel, presumably made of branches, though in the darkness I couldn't tell. I pinched the edge of Lana's shirt again to keep track of her in the dark. The tunnel was only about twenty feet long; at the end we ducked under a burlap coffee sack while Daisy made impatient clicking sounds. We blinked in the brightness of the gallows sky. I turned.

Behind us wasn't the wall of branches I'd expected but a Pile, one of the shortest I'd seen, only about fifteen feet high. Although short it stretched for almost the length of a full city block. Half a mile or so to the north loomed another Pile of more average stature.

"Concept by me, design by Cora," said Daisy, flicking the wand toward the smaller Pile.

"She means we made it," said Cora. Her voice was lilting; it made me want to hear her sing.

"She may look stupid," said Daisy, poking Cora with the wand rather fondly, "but she actually has a degree in how to make shit that doesn't fall down."

"Engineering. MIT," said Cora, reaching out her hand toward Lana and me. "And welcome. Sometimes we forget to say that around here."

"If we let them in it's assumed," said Daisy.

"I designed the tunnel first," Cora explained. Then we just transferred objects from Dumbbell over there," she waved her hand in the direction of the larger Pile, "and thus Junior was born."

"So if you didn't know the course of the river, you wouldn't even think there was anything behind Junior besides water," said Lana.

"Yep," said Cora.

"She's maybe not so dumb either," said Daisy to Cora. Then, to us: "This way, before it gets dark." We walked south for about half a mile until Daisy turned abruptly into a sparse line of saplings, stunned into a sort of half-life since the Rending. Like most of the trees, they had no leaves, but there was still the bend of life in the branches. Beyond the saplings was a large holding pond in which our vessels bobbed. Our Babies were unmoved but the rest of the supplies lay in a pile on the bank.

Kristen was bent at the waist, the tuft of her ponytail sweeping the ground. Paloma was wiping sweat off her neck with a red bandana. Her usual upright posture looked slightly deflated but she smiled when she saw us. "Good timing," she said.

"Load us up," said Daisy.

We divvied up the belongings among us.

"The Babies?" I asked hesitantly. Though the urgency to hold my Baby had dimmed ever since I'd laid her in the Nest I still felt her presence, a soft blue heartbeat beneath my skin.

Kristen wrapped her arms across her chest as if to keep herself from reaching for her own Babies. Paloma sighed. "I think we should leave them here for now. They'll be safe. If we want to move them we can do it in the morning."

I nodded.

We headed back to the moss room through the ashy drowse of twilight. No one mentioned Zion, but worry had worked its way into the press of Paloma's mouth, into the dark saddles below Kristen's eyes. I knew they were both exhausted so I tried to take on more weight—but I'd underestimated my own lingering physical exhaustion from the trauma of giving birth and the walk back from the Zoo. By the time we'd returned to the mossy cavern my thighs and arms were shaking.

Inside, a blue tarp had been spread out under the opening at the center of the room. The Zionite women, who looked cleaner but not entirely relaxed, and about a dozen other women I didn't

recognize—the other Noons, Lana had said they called themselves—
sat around the edges of the tarp, sipping from identical white mugs
that looked like they'd been plundered directly from a church basement. As soon as we stepped out of the shadows, five or six of the Noons
stood up and took the bags from our shoulders and backs. What seemed
like a gesture of hospitality turned when they immediately began
pawing through our bags and setting out food items on the tarp: turnip
pottage, sweet potato pottage, Ziploc bags of smoked fish and meat,
ghost fruit, and even a little container of ghost fruit jam (I suddenly
felt a spark of gratitude in my chest for Oscar and the sweat he'd poured
into the jam for us). They didn't ask permission and they didn't set
aside anything for later. They put it all out, offered everyone a spoon,
and then started passing the containers of food around the awkward
rectangle of bodies.

"Well, step up to the trough," said Daisy, poking Lana and me
with the wand.

We obeyed. The sound of chewing and swallowing filled the
space. The Noons varied in age and appearance. Some eyed us shyly
and a few stared openly, unapologetic about the hanging silence. They
seemed comfortable with the quiet, as if it were an object they gathered around, simple as the flat blue tarp.

The looks I exchanged with Talia and Ida and Sylvia and Lana
and the other Zionites suggested that we were not so comfortable with
the silence but were equally uncomfortable with beginning a conversation. There seemed to be habits and gestures that framed this place
that we didn't yet understand. Exhaustion and a still-present Midwestern
sense of propriety kept us, I think, from peppering the Noons with
questions or offering them portions of ourselves they didn't seem
particularly interested in receiving.

I should have felt gratitude that we had been welcomed into
their community, but instead I felt a sliver of disdain as these women
we didn't know ate our food without contributing anything of their
own, not even conversation. The sounds of eating grew louder as the
daylight diminished, our hearing amplified by the absence of our
vision. There was the sound of the Noons rising, then the outline of

Abigail's ears before me as she gently took the mug and spoon from my hands. To my left, someone cracked her back. Someone else let out a belch.

"Where would you like us to sleep?" I asked finally, both my voice and question sounding somehow ridiculous in the dark.

"I don't give a donkey's dick where you sleep," came the raw grind of Daisy's voice from somewhere behind me.

"The moss? Is it OK to sleep on the moss?" For the first time I identified with the tremulous whine in Talia's voice.

"Yes," came Cora's lilting voice from what felt like above me, though that couldn't have been possible. "You're welcome to sleep on it. It's hard not to when you first arrive. We all did. But you'll wake up feeling like a frozen piece of clay."

I heard the crinkle of the tarp as Kristen and Paloma opted to follow Cora's advice. The rest of us curled up on the moss, sweaters and jackets pulled close. In the dark it was impossible not to feel the immensity of all we'd left behind. Had the Zionites just let the Watchers come? Had they brought out our collection of knives and axes? I thought of Michael stretching his hands open again and again. Then traded Michael's hands for Rodney's. Squared fingertips, the calluses at the top of his palms and the whorl of softness in the middle. Rodney in his stilted house, framed by his single window. I held him there in my mind, safe inside that frame, until finally I fell asleep.

CHAPTER FIVE

I woke feeling the way Cora had predicted but I had slept deeply; the chill hadn't reached into my dreams. Paloma and Kristen were no longer on the tarp. Abigail was busy setting out the identical coffee mugs and the spoons, still glistening a little with what I supposed was river water. An abused cooler stood at the center of the tarp, the kind with wheels and a long handle for the easy transportation of raw hamburger and Popsicles from the back of a minivan to the grill at a picnic area. Beside the cooler, a straw beach bag held empty food containers.

A woman with black, tightly curled hair cropped close to her head was poking at the hanging baskets with the silver wand. I heard groans from a few of the baskets and saw Cora's eyes peer blearily over the edge of one hanging just above where I'd been sitting the night before. I'd been right about the trajectory of her voice in the dark.

"The baskets are hammocks!" Talia said with stupid delight.

Daisy whistled the first few bars of "Rock-a-Bye Baby" before opening a container from the cooler and sniffing its contents.

Everything felt looser and more familiar in the light of day. There didn't seem to be a ritual to breakfast the way there had been at dinner the night before. And there was mumbled conversation in various parts of the room. Maybe everything would be as straightforward and simple as Lana had suggested. The sign would come today and by tomorrow we'd be back in Zion, everyone accounted for, everyone safe and sound. A feel-good postapocalyptic after-school special. But the tightening across my chest suggested that even my body didn't believe things could work out that easily.

The cooler contained turnips and carrots and potatoes, ghost fruit and stings and smoked fish. There was even a fruit I'd never seen before with red, damasked skin about the size of a kumquat. The red skin collapsed into a burst of cotton-candy sweetness on my tongue but the inside was mostly filled with seeds that tasted like anise. Abigail watched my face turn from joy to annoyance as I chewed. "They're terrible to chew," she said sympathetically, "but we think they have protein."

"Does all this grow near here?" I asked, gesturing to the stings and ghost fruit and my full mouth.

Abigail shrugged. "The ghost fruit is from Zion. The stings are from the Zoo. The goose fruit," here she pointed to my mouth, "is from an encampment a few miles southeast of here that calls itself Big City."

"It's ironic," Cora added as she thrashed around in her rocking bower. She was either struggling to put on pants or strangling a mongoose.

"How'd you get the ghost fruit and the stings?" asked Lana. Behind her, Eleanor was busy twining Lana's blonde hair back into its crown, her thin, quick forearms jerking like knitting needles.

"Oh, Abby'll tell ya how," said Daisy, clicking the edge of the spoon against her teeth. "Tell 'em, Abby."

"No one pays attention to a crazy," Abigail recited in a singsong voice.

"Absofuckinglutely," said Daisy. She smiled at us grandly with her tongue stuffed into the tooth gap.

"You stole, you mean," chimed in Talia, who was attempting to pick the seeds out of a goose fruit but only succeeding in staining her fingers with red juice.

"Unbundle your undies, honey. You've got a place to sleep and food to eat. You're safe from Señor Dicko. Calm down. Go weave some baskets."

"Kristen and I will head out and climb your Pile. Dumbbell it's called? See if they've signaled yet," said Paloma.

"Nope," said Daisy, "we'll be taking care of that. You'll stay here. Simone and Abigail and Cora'll keep you busy. You could use a little work. You all look like you're auditioning for a show called who has the biggest stick up her ass."

Like sock puppets, all of us opened our mouths slightly—but nothing came out. We couldn't afford to make enemies of our hosts.

After breakfast, we divided into groups. Paloma and Talia and Sylvia headed off with Abigail. Eleanor and Kristen went with Cora. Lana and Cassie and Ida and I followed Simone, the woman with the curly black hair who'd been waking people with the wand, to another entrance near the one we'd slithered through on the previous day. We walked downriver on a trail parallel to the one Paloma and Kristen had used to pull our flotilla to the holding pond. Above and around us the branches spread out their woven designs. It reminded me of an arbor, one that should have housed women in petticoats and powdered wigs, whispering behind fans about betrothals and betrayals and the cost of calfskin gloves. We were so far away from those women: in our dress, in our speech, in the cadence of our steps. Even our wombs were different, turning semen and egg into vases and canteens, chopsticks and honey bears.

Two hours later that gap did not feel quite so large. I wasn't any closer to the women of laced bodices and candled chandeliers, but I felt connected to their peasant sisters, the ones for whom a gesture, spinning or scrubbing or churning, was repeated and repeated until it became housed in the very marrow of their bones.

We arrived at a body of water similar to the boat pond. But this one was much smaller and perfectly still since it contained no direct access to the river. There were no branches above the pond itself but they stood sentinel around the perimeter along with a pair of navy green waders and a bag filled with supplies. Around the edges of the pond were piles of branches, some half in and half out of the water; on the surface of the pond floated a few plastic ducks. Simone showed us how the Noons used thread attached to the ducks to keep track of the soaking branches.

"Willow or bamboo would be best to use but we don't have a lot of willow and bamboo," said Simone, resuming a lecture she had never officially started. "We find that if we soak elm and maple and birch we can weave them well enough, but they need to be thin and uniform. Otherwise it's a huge pain in the ass." She hauled a thin, lithe-looking branch out of the pond and pointed it limply at Lana and me. "Try to get those," she said, gesturing at a pile of thicker branches to our left, "to look like this." Then she gave us each a kitchen knife. Cassie and Ida were given the task of transporting the properly soaked and cut specimens to the boat launch, which currently lacked the camou-flaged structures the Noons deemed necessary. Simone put on the waders and spent the first hour slogging around, pulling out piles of wood and re-sorting into those that needed more soaking and those that were ready to be cut or transported.

Once Lana and I figured out our task (the right pressure to put against the knife, the best way to brace each branch as we stripped it), we developed a rhythm that was both soothing and boring. Once my mind was no longer occupied in making sure I didn't slice off my thumb I began to think about Zion and the Zoo, about the patter of heels against the walls of the aquarium, the gun in my hands, the sticky residue on the side of the water bottle. I tried to visualize the Zionites safe but all I could imagine was injury. So then I waded through my memory, trying to remember all the fortunes Chester had ever given me, trying to walk backward through the last times Rodney had touched me: carrying me to the raft, taking the Baby from my hands, cradling me in the Barnes and Noble, holding on to the knobs of my knees as he told me Lana's story, touching his foot to mine below the cloud sheet in our tent. When was the last time we'd made love? Would I ever get to touch him again? I tried to keep my anxiety in check. Tried nursery rhymes and hymns, recipes and poems.

Eventually Simone came over and sat beside us, correcting what-ever mistakes we'd made, trimming and slicing and whittling with strokes that were gorgeous in their grace and accuracy.

"Did you arrive here knowing how to do that?" I blurted out.

Simone looked up and laughed. She had a sloping forehead and wide cheekbones and a dimple in the middle of her chin that made her look both regal and childlike at once.

"Not even a little," she said.

"How did you get here?" I asked rather lamely. I wanted to know and even more I wanted to get out of my own head.

She watched Lana for a bit and suggested that she position her hands differently. Lana massaged her palm a bit, shook her fingers out, and then started up again. Once we had all turned back to our work, Simone finally responded to my question.

"When the Rending happened my husband was holding a fistful of my hair and a pair of scissors. We were about to go to a benefit. The kids were at my parents' house. I had a new dress: emerald green with a row of rhinestones right under the boobs. Maybe now I'd think it was too gaudy, but then I didn't. I had a matching necklace and earring set, too. It was my benefit—not for me, for the Museum of Contemporary Art, but I was putting it on. I'd been a social worker for fifteen years but I went back to school and got a degree in arts administration. It's not all that uncommon for social workers to burn out; I was so hopeful when I started but the system was so broken. After a few years I started going to museums on my lunch break, for the quiet and for those flat, clean floors. Pretty soon the art took hold and I wanted to be near it. I'd minored in art history at Beloit, I knew a Rembrandt from a Rubens, but it was the contemporary work that got me. Paintings that looked like photographs and dollhouses covered in sod and religious icons soaking in jars of urine."

She bit her bottom lip as she used her knife to split a branch I thought was already remarkably thin; it parted into symmetrical boughs. "My husband, Raphael, was this tireless community organizer, so beloved and charismatic. And that night he had my hair in his fist. I'd straightened it like those flat, clean floors and he accused me of trying to be a fancy white bitch. Of abandoning everything that was most important. Of selling out."

"And then the Rending?" prompted Lana.

"Then the Rending."

"Was he gone?"

"He wasn't gone. I thought I'd just blacked out momentarily from fear or pain. He cut my hair—which I don't actually remember that well. I do remember pawing through my daughter's jewelry box for her dress-up rhinestone bobby pins. I remember spending another half hour twisting my hair up so that no one would know. And then we were driving through the streets and started noticing cars, empty and abandoned, and the awning missing from the corner mini-mart and the skyline different, too, though I don't know if I knew that consciously. I remember saying that the world suddenly felt like an art installation."

Ida and Cassie returned then and we helped them load more of the trimmed boughs into their sacks. Simone slogged over to the other side of the small pond, bundled some of the large dry sticks, and then dragged them into the water. When she had resituated herself on the bank she offered Lana and me a few stings from her pocket. We both declined but I felt the bitter threads of saliva fill my mouth anyway, Michael's finger tracing its way from my breast to my thigh.

"I stayed with him. Raphael. For a year and a half after the Rending, I stayed with him because, you know, the familiar."

I glanced at Lana but she didn't look up.

"Raphael wasn't violent. Not exactly. Just squeezing my arm too hard or yanking something away with too much force. Stupid little things: drinking the rest of the water when he knew I was thirsty or telling other travelers we met that I was on the rag if I hiked my voice above a whisper. Then we met Daisy and after only a couple hours she saw it. All these moments I thought were invisible. And she said why don't you come with me? And I did. And there was this." She raised her knife and the branch she was working with to encompass the whole area. "The Asylum."

"The Asylum?" I repeated.

"Yep. No one pays attention to a crazy." Simone's voice took on the same singsong lilt that Abigail's had earlier.

"What does that mean exactly?" asked Lana.

"It means that no one pays much attention to older women who seem a little batty. They're not a threat. They're not, as Daisy would say, 'pluckable.' Their information is suspect. They're unlikely to have anything that anyone else might want. So Asylum. The place for crazies."

"And safety. That kind of asylum too, right?"

"Yeah," said Simone. "Most women don't stay too long. Some, like Abigail and me, stay for months or years. And many who leave come back, bring us gifts, offerings. The waders we got from a woman who was here for a year named Sarah Ann. She was Sarah Ann because there was another Sarah here at the time. Ann wasn't even really her middle name. Sometimes women come back and bring another woman who needs—this."

"And Noons? Where did that come from?"

Simone shrugged. "Daisy. Who else. Because we're nuns without the God part." Simone rolled her eyes. "She wanted all of us to choose a saint name. Like the Benedictines. She chose Daisy and the rest of us refused. But if she calls you something random—Birch or Cardamom or Samosa—it's a throwback to that idea. She still thinks it's hilarious."

Simone measured the bough she was working on against the perfectly slim and whittled branch she'd offered us as a prototype. She sliced off about an inch at both ends and with a few more swipes of her knife along the length the two boughs looked almost identical. The eight or ten branches Lana and I had worked on looked like they'd been mauled by a drunk beaver.

We were quiet for quite a while. Lana began to speak, picking up a dropped thread of conversation. "Michael was like that, too. I mean, seeing what I thought was invisible." I looked up at her but both Lana and Simone just kept up the steady motion of knife against wood. "He was such a good listener. He is, I guess."

I thought of his epic speeches punctuated with the gestures in the air, the way the Zionites had emerged from telling him their stories flushed and proud. I tried to imagine him truly listening to anyone in Zion now.

"He listened to my story," Lana continued. "I hadn't shared it with anyone, not entirely, since the Rending." She looked at me and then peeled her eyes away. "It was so liberating. He said he saw my pain so clearly; my wounding was like a neon sign to him. He told me that pain is easily written but not so easily erased. 'Look at your Baby,' he said, 'What must that mean? Maybe it means you haven't moved beyond anything.' He had ideas for healing, and dancing was one of them. I'd done ballet since I was three," she explained to Simone. "And that actually did help a little. Then, this was at the Zoo, then he thought maybe a rocking chair would help, that the motion would unlock something. I don't know."

Lana set down the bough she'd been stripping and flexed her hands. Then she picked it up again and ran her thumb along the knots and fibers. "So for a while he had me going every day to his little room. You saw it, right, Mir? With the Barbie doll swinging from the ceiling?" I nodded. She sniffled a little and drew her sleeve across her nose. "I'd do my rocking therapy every day for an hour. Two? I don't really know. Back and forth. Back and forth. I know it sounds crazy but he had this way of talking to me. He said, 'I think you're so much better than who they wanted you to be in Zion, Lana.'"

"Who we *wanted* you to be?" I broke in; but Simone looked at me and I closed my mouth.

"He'd say, 'I see your real spirit and it's trapped inside all this wounding and it's such hard work to be free of it but you are doing such a good job.' And he told me I could go. Every day. It was part of the ritual and he made a production out of it, out of actually opening the door and making the offer." She gave a little scraping laugh. "Then he caught a cardinal."

"From the feeder he had out there? Has out there," I corrected myself.

She nodded. "He put it in a cage and didn't feed it. He said it was part of the therapy. So I rocked and, day after day, watched it starve to death. When it died he wrapped it in a rag and had me hold it while I rocked." She gave that barking laugh again. "It's so absurd. I know. I thought of Deborah's birds, of course. Then he took the cardinal away and had Horace come in."

"Horace?"

"The man with the stalactites. Did you see him? So big and sweet and also hurt. You could see it behind his eyes. And Michael convinced him—I don't know how—to—" Lana made a gesture toward her sweatshirt, her pants, "—on me. On my skin. And I was supposed to rub it in so I wouldn't be afraid of what semen could do. 'A healing balm' were the words Michael used." She wiped her hands on her pants as though that would erase the memory from her skin.

Then she walked down to the edge of the pond and raised her arms above her head and then let them float earthward. Folded her body in half and then raised it up halfway. Flat back. Then down again. Both Simone and I stopped to watch. It had been a long time since I'd seen Lana do yoga and her body was a perfect instrument. It felt like it belonged here; the lines she made with her arms, her legs, her back were an echo of the latticework of branches that curved around the place. Salutation finished, she took a deep breath but still didn't turn to face us.

"And what happened was that I lost track of what I deserved. Did I deserve punishment or penance or humiliation? Did I deserve friendship or love or any kind of answer? Does any of us deserve anything after the Rending?" She turned around to face us, her face washed clean of everything besides her own truth, spoken plainly. "I think that since the Rending, since surviving, I haven't been certain I deserve anything else. I'm still not sure. I feel ashamed that I'm here. That I even exist at all.

"Then Michael started to talk about you, Mira. That he had a feeling you were coming. How excited he was to have the opportunity to help my friend. Especially when you were so close to giving birth. And what I could see clearly was that you didn't deserve whatever this was. So I didn't turn, Mira. When you came to see me in the Zoo I didn't turn. I thought maybe there was still time for you to walk out the door."

*

That night, after another quiet dinner around the blue tarp, Lana climbed into one of the hanging baskets. I walked over and nudged the basket into motion gently.

"Is this more rocking therapy?" I could hear the strained smile inside her voice.

"No," I said. "No more dead birds."

"Promise?"

"Promise."

Branch flexed against branch, a raw creaking. I wondered whether the wood was dry enough for a fire to start from the friction. Wondered, if the Asylum burned down, if the moss would remain.

"I'm sorry," I said.

"I know," she said.

"You deserve to feel safe, Lana."

And then she finally started to cry.

TWO DAYS PRESSED into three and then four. A week passed and then another. I'd assumed our time at the Asylum would be brief. I'd assumed that Michael's arrival in Zion would trigger a confrontation that in turn would decide everything quickly and entirely. In my most comforting—but highly cartoonish—fantasy Michael arrived in Zion, looked around behind cots and under the tables in the Center, and then threw up his hands in consternation. He then turned on his heel and departed, the Watchers trailing dutifully behind him. In my nightmares, Cal and Chester were stuck on top of Curly and Michael was pushing Rodney around in a wheelchair, soaking the bottom of the Pile with gasoline. My only comfort when I woke was that if something had gone wrong, truly wrong, I would know. Against all reason, I was certain of this.

Each day one of the elder Noons, Pearl or Daisy or Laurel, climbed to the top of Dumbbell, the Pile just to the north of the Asylum, to see if the red signal flag had been flown. Each day they returned with a few useless objects but not the news we longed to hear. All I wanted was to climb the Pile myself as though, from that height, I could will the red flag into existence. But the "pluckable" women had to stay inside. Pearl and Daisy and Laurel were the only women currently living at the Asylum who were old enough to fulfill Daisy's notion of what a crazy looked like. The three of them left during the day, sometimes alone, sometimes together, pulling sleds or wagons or bumbling under backpacks that betrayed them as ridiculous, even from a distance. They returned with food and supplies most evenings, though occasionally they stayed out for a day or two or even longer if the encampment was distant.

"We only take the excess, dear," Pearl told Talia one afternoon when she caught Talia's expression of disdain. Pearl was pulling ghost fruit and a knotted bundle of shoelaces from a backpack. "And we even try to leave something behind. If we can. Your friend there," and here she shook the bundle of shoelaces at me, "was quite thrilled with a bit of flexible tubing I left in a cookie jar a few years ago." She smiled. Her eyes were almost Disney-caliber in their size but her cheeks hung down below her jawline like sacks of marbles. I remembered the tubing and also the slice of the knife in my palm. I wondered if she'd left the blade, too.

As time passed, we fell into rhythms, steady as the sweep of our knives down the length of the branches. I became accustomed to the soreness in my forearms, to the silence around the crinkling blue tarp in the evenings, to the sound of wood creaking as women turned in their sleep. The sound of the river, the loamy scent of the moss, even the poke of the glitter wand in my upper arm (or thigh or ass depending on who was wielding it). I learned to gut fish and to hang the meat on lines along the river to dry it. I braided Lana's hair and watched as my hips shrunk back to their regular width and my breasts regained their normal heft. One night I even woke myself with my own groaning: The rocking motion of the basket had worked its way into my hips and Rodney was above me, inside me, throat flecked with whiskers, chest hair curled like fiddlehead ferns. When I woke I was ashamed of desiring him when I didn't even know if he was alive.

Although I know she was also worried about Zion, Lana was happier than I'd ever seen her. Ever since our conversation at the holding pond, much of her effervescent airiness had returned. She went back to inserting yoga poses and dance steps into random conversations and she was full of good-natured banter and chitchat. But she also dedicated herself to the work, whatever it was, in a way that went beyond the debt we owed the Noons. I'm not sure if it was the moss and the branches, the company of the Noons, or simply the feeling of safety, but Lana thrived at the Asylum.

Meanwhile, I began to shrivel. And as much as I loved the safety, the delicate sprigs of moss, the latticework of branches, and the company of Simone and Daisy and Abigail and Cora and the other

Noons, I hated being confined, hated feeling like I was living inside a chess game abandoned at its crisis. Strategy and loss and danger all cloaked in a frozen calm. And there was nothing I could do but wait.

CHAPTER SEVEN

O NCE WE HAD accumulated enough branches, we began work in earnest on the boat pond, the only part of the Asylum property that wasn't camouflaged from prying eyes. Although there was a row of birch trees to the east of the pond and the river to the west, the I-35 thruway was only a quarter mile beyond the river and there was little vegetation on either bank, leaving a view of the pond mostly unobstructed if a traveler happened to wander a little off course to camp or take a piss. One day, about three weeks after we arrived, Daisy accompanied Ida and Talia and Paloma and me to the pond, convinced that there was a high probability that we would mess up the construction if we went without her.

The Noons had a collection of cloaks, many in the style of cheap ponchos, stitched together from pieces of fabric that knit the wearer to the earth—browns and grays and greens with all the life sucked out. We all wore them, since this area was more exposed.

Ida and Talia and Paloma ferried themselves to the other side of the river to begin digging holes into which the major posts would be inserted. Daisy was "pretty sure they couldn't fuck up a hole in the ground," though her expression suggested that she remained doubtful. On the east side of the river, where the posts had already been established, she and I began affixing crosspieces to create a grid that would support the camouflaging branches.

Behind us in the pond bobbed our rafts and canoe and a paddleboat with a swan's neck curving into half a graceful heart. A few sunbleached life vests lay on the bank around the pond like mourners at a viewing. Oddly, we had never taken the Nests and Babies out of the vessels; they bobbed beneath the sky, just out of reach.

I held a smaller branch against a post where Daisy had chipped out a space for it. She had a rope made from rubber bands woven together three or four thick. Bim used to have a loom on which he'd make bracelets out of rubber bands. I'd scratched him across the cheek once when he stole the bands I used for my braces and made a necklace out of them.

"One of those yours?"

Daisy had never asked me a question and it took me a second to gauge what she was talking about.

"What? The Babies?"

"No, the fucking flamingos."

"Oh. Yes."

Her hands were surprisingly quick, wrapping the rubber-band rope under and around and through the cross the wood made.

"The blue vase," I added.

"Is that why you're still here? That vase have your number?"

I cleared my throat. "We're here for safety, because of Michael and the Zoo. I thought that was clear."

She shrugged. "Whatever you say, sugar."

I stared at her but she kept busy with the rubber bands. I waited for her to say more. To explain herself. When she didn't—or wouldn't—I finally spoke using my best I-am-annoyed-but-trying-to-contain-it-professionally voice: "Wait. I'm confused. Are you saying we're being cowardly?" She kept winding the rubber rope. "I've wanted to leave. To climb the Pile. Dumbbell. You're the one who wants us to stay hidden all day."

"Huh," she said.

"Am I lying?" I pressed.

"Not lying. Just choosing your story."

"What's that supposed to mean?"

"You were a mess when you got here. Probably still bleeding. Wavery inside. You needed this. I saw that. But I also see the story you've got inside your head now. And that story has to do with needing safety because you're weak and powerless."

"I don't think that."

"You do. Who knows what's happening to your friends right now. Even your lover boy, the man with the tails." She smiled, tongue placed in the empty notch, and made a little sucking sound. "A fine specimen." She winked. "And the tails weren't bad either. Did you see 'em? Over on the east side of the moss room. About yea high." She paused in the wrapping to gesture to a place in the air at chin level. "It's a compelling story, defeat is. And it will get here eventually, if you wait long enough. You'll be a person who suffers defeat. Gracefully probably. That's a good story to tell yourself. Plaster."

"What?"

"On the rubber bands. Plaster."

"Oh." I unscrewed the peanut butter jar at my feet and dipped a knife into a concoction that looked like a combo of mud and grass and smelled vaguely of feces. I started to smear it on the rubber bands. Daisy walked off to the next post, whistling. I finished slathering and hurried after her.

"But this is your whole deal here," I said, failing to keep the wheedling sound out of my voice.

"Hold it up," she said. I dutifully lifted the branch and she reached into her back pocket and pulled out another sort of rope, this one fashioned out of scarves and rags and other strips of fabric. She began to wind it around the place where the post met the branch.

"This is what you do here," I tried again.

"The Asylum is for safety. Yep. But too much safety makes you crazy. Or it makes you mean. We get pushed out of the womb for a reason. You pushed *that* out of your womb for a reason." She gestured with her head toward where my Baby bobbed.

"Why?" I asked quietly. She kept winding, so I grabbed her arm and squeezed. "WHY?"

Daisy pulled her arm out of my grip and wiped her face against her shoulder.

"I don't have a fucking clue," she said. "I can't give you your why. It's pretty clear all of you think they're special. You've built those Nests and you hauled them all down here on those parade floats." She tied the ends of the cloth rope together and tested the hold. When she was sure it was secure she rested her forearms on the branch and looked at me. "But then you left them here, bobbing in this little swamp we call a boat pond. Are these your totems? Your icons? Your sacred flutes? Your voodoo dolls? Do they bring you luck or misery?"

I thought of the press of my Baby against me, that rush of love, that purified version of the Before sailing through my limbs. The impossibility of living, really living, with my Baby attached to me and the cavernous loss of letting her go. I didn't want to cry in front of Daisy and I was sobbing in front of Daisy. "I don't know," I said. "I don't know what they mean."

She kept looking at me. Not angry, not bored, not really even compassionate. As if I were an aquarium and she were waiting for a shark to make another pass. "I don't know," I said a bit more loudly in case she was hard of hearing. She kept her gaze steady. "I DON'T KNOW!" I shouted so loudly that a fleck of spittle landed on her cheek. She didn't wipe it away. She let me keep crying like that for a long time, saying the words over and over until they became a mantra. Finally she took my chin in her hand and raised my eyes to hers. And this time in her voice was a deep kindness. "No," she said quietly, "you're probably never going to know why. The only thing you get to decide is the story you're going to tell yourself about what's happened. You haven't figured out your story yet." Her tone switched back to the gruff Daisy. "So you're holing up here like a little larva waiting for someone to tell you your boyfriend's dead and your home has been pillaged. Then you'll accept that as your story. Defeat. And so will they."

"I'm not in charge of them," I said. "The other Zionites are free to do whatever they want. It was their idea to come here in the first place."

"Whatever you say," said Daisy, "whatever you want to tell yourself." Then she turned, put her fingers in her mouth, and whistled at the others. Paloma lifted her arm and waved it to show they'd heard.

"Sometimes I think I'd rather fuck a python than eat another goddamn sweet potato," she said, apropos of absolutely nothing. I started to laugh then and Daisy joined me, her laugh a pointed cackle and mine a revving, sputtering engine. It had been a long time since I'd heard my body make that sound.

CHAPTER EIGHT

ONVINCING THE OTHERS to leave was different than trying to convince people to follow me to the Zoo, though I'd stood before them with that plea less than two months earlier. But this time I wasn't pregnant, wasn't shaking, wasn't desperate for volunteers. I knew I would go alone if I had to. The Asylum was a necessary place but it wasn't my place. I'd laid my Baby in the Nest so that I wouldn't be lost forever in a spun sugar version of the Before, so I could live with the people I loved in the place we called home. The Rending took home and family away from us without offering us a chance to fight to save them. Now I finally had that chance and I was weaving baskets and tiptoeing around on moss. I knew I would go alone if I needed to but I also knew I would need the others for my plan to work.

After most people had finished eating dinner that night I stood and clinked my spoon against my coffee mug, a gesture that immediately felt too formal. "I'm going to leave," I said, in a voice too loud for the quiet of the moss and branches.

"You're what?" said Lana, swiveling out of a spinal twist so she could see my face.

"I mean," I said, "I think we should all leave. Not the Noons. I didn't mean—" I was waving the spoon around like a laser pointer. I put the spoon and cup down and stood again, reaching to my chest out of habit to grab my notebook and finding only my breastbone. I thrust my hands into the pockets of my Guatemalan sweater instead, pinched little clumps of wool at the bottoms. Cora wiped her nose with her sleeve. Paloma finished securing a rubber band around the end of her braid but otherwise everyone was still.

"I can't add any more words," I said finally. "I can't add any more words to the list of what I've lost. I know we'll continue to lose things, to lose people. I get it. But I won't sit here while it happens and document it. We're acting like this is another Rending, like we have no choice about what's taken from us. But that's not true. We had a choice and we chose the Babies over Zion.

"We have to give up the Babies. Whatever the Babies might mean to us—Zion means more." I waited for someone to protest but no one did. "So we take the Babies to a neutral location," I continued. "Then we go back to Zion and we tell Michael where the Babies are. The Babies are what he wants. I vote that we give him what he wants and take back what we want: our home."

Sylvia had been nodding along as I spoke but now her eyes narrowed. "You really think he'll believe us? When we show up and tell him this?"

"I don't think our pinkie swearing will be enough to get him out of Zion, sweetie," said Ida.

"We offer proof. We take one Baby with us. As a sign of good faith."

"Because good faith is certain to work with Michael," said Lana.

"I have no idea if this will work." I looked at each Zionite in turn then, the way my father used his gaze to cross the distance between us when I was hurt or afraid. "I don't know if it will work," I said again, "but I know I can't stay here any longer."

We were ready to leave by dawn the next day. We packed our Babies into backpacks and satchels. The Noons offered us food, a few cloaks, and a basket with straps that Abigail helped Ida heft onto her shoulders when it was time to go. Abigail gently untucked Ida's hair from where it caught below one of the straps then offered, quietly, to come with us. She and Ida walked beside one another, pinkies intertwined, for most of our journey.

It took us two long days of walking to reach the Barnes and Noble. We were only about thirty miles away as the crow flies but since we were attempting some level of subtlety we didn't travel on Highway

77 or I-35, instead slopping our way through newly saturated fields and the rough stubble of uneven ground.

As we walked we talked about the Babies, really talked, for the first time. It was Abigail who asked a question, something simple and innocuous like "who had the first Baby?" and the story unfolded, each of us picking up the portion of the story that was ours, Ida chiming in with images of Deborah's birds and her strange funeral in the open-mouthed house.

"Nairobi and Phoenix," Paloma began and then, turning to Abigail, "the ivory chopsticks. My first Babies." Abigail nodded encouragingly. "They were also from my Before, they were in my third-grade teacher's house. Her name was Mrs. Moustakas but she had us call her Mrs. Mouse. A few of us were invited to her house at the end of the year, as a treat, when we'd taken the tests and she knew who had done well, succeeded. My mama had plaited my hair so tightly the pain pulled the day into focus, you know?"

Many of us nodded. Paloma stopped walking abruptly and pulled out her roll of duct tape. She applied a bit more to her left Croc where she must have perceived some weakness, though there was none that we could see. But we stopped and watched her, took sips from water bottles. When she began to walk again, we did too.

"Mrs. Mouse made tea sandwiches. Everything so clean, no wrinkles, shining—elegant. Everything so elegant. We were all girls, all five of us, but my dress was the only one with the netting fabric. What do you call it?"

"Tulle?" Ida supplied.

"Yes, tulle. Satin and tulle. I made so much noise, every time I moved. The other girls wore dresses too but theirs were cotton with bright stripes or polka dots; some of them had big-eyed animals stitched to the front. I looked ready for my first communion. Next to the plates on the napkins were chopsticks that Mrs. Mouse said she collected. Each pair was different: some were wooden, some were plastic, but mine were ivory. She said we could try to eat with them, that it was good to try new things. I don't remember whether there was meanness in her voice when she said it or not."

"Eating tea sandwiches with chopsticks?" said Sylvia, "That's absurd. Why would someone make third-graders try to do that?"

Paloma shrugged. "I don't know. But we couldn't do it. The cucumber kept sliding through. But we kept trying. Over and over. For a long time it went on, just the sound the chopsticks made as they lost their grip. All this click click clicking."

"It sounds terrible," said Abigail sympathetically.

"It was and it wasn't," said Paloma. "I'd worked so hard to do well on those tests. *Mi hermana* Adriana smoothing her arm over practice pages after dinner every night. So I was proud to be at that table and also humiliated by how overdressed I was, by the way my dress kept swishing. But we were all making that same sound with the chopsticks, the clicking. And there was comfort in that. I remember thinking this is what it means to be grown up, that's what I remember most about that day."

Kristen coughed lightly then and gestured with her head toward Highway 77, about a quarter of a mile away, where a few figures were visible on the road. We sank down to the ground as a group, pulling our hoods up, and the cloaks close around us. Once we were entirely quiet I could hear faintly the voices of the other travelers, though not what they were saying, only that their voices were loud enough that they weren't suspicious, hadn't seen us.

Once we stood and started walking again it was Ida who asked, "And the canteen, Paloma? What about that Baby?"

"That's a different kind of story," said Paloma. She tucked her chin in toward her chest like a bird settling in and we didn't ask her any more questions.

Cassie, who'd been mostly quiet on the journey, picked up a stick and began to swing it at high grasses, trees, and fence posts as we walked, scything her way forward. "We didn't have much money," she said without prompting. "After every spring break all the kids would bring in something for show and tell. Sand dollars and shells and Mickey Mouse ears and little bottles filled with ocean water and even plastic hotel room keys. I never had anything because I spent spring break watching TV and eating cereal while my mom worked. One year on the day I was going back my mom gave me this little honey bear filled with sand. And at breakfast she showed me this magazine picture of Tahiti and we talked about what I would say. This whole elaborate lie. How I ate lobster and butter dripped off my fingers. And there was a big yellow water slide. And every night our towels folded to swans on our pillows." Cassie took a big swing with the stick at a bent sapling.

"Did it work?" asked Talia.

"It did that day. Those kids believed that I had a dazzling life and there was a minute I believed it too. But by middle school kids knew; the ones with money could smell it on each other, they sniffed it out like dogs."

No one said anything for a few minutes. We were in the middle of a field of what had been soybeans and even Cassie's stick didn't make much of a sound. Eventually, Eleanor talked about how her twins, salt and pepper shakers, were gifts she'd registered for with her first husband. The only things they'd ever actually agreed upon. And Kristen explained that Ezra (four skateboard wheels on a chain) and then Homer (a cable bike lock) were reminders of her boys. Until that moment, I hadn't known that Kristen had been a mother in the Before. Her constant peppy optimism made that kind of grief seem impossible.

We stopped for the night in a small copse of birch. We lay side by side for warmth, staring up at the skeletal branches.

"After the Asylum, these branches look so disorganized," said Lana.

"I keep thinking about how much knife-work each would require before it would meet Simone's standards," I murmured.

"Are you going to tell the story of your Baby?"

And so I finally did. With the sky darkening between the lines of the branches I told them about my mother and her vases. About the aquarium and my labor and seeing my Baby finally in the parking lot with Rodney and Chester. And when I talked about the feeling of her against me there were murmurs of assent and "yes," little bits of sound rising up like smoke from snuffed out flames.

We arrived at the Barnes and Noble late on the second day and slept in the children's section where the blanket Chester and Rodney had covered me with still snaked its way across the ground. One of the chairs was still turned toward the blanket and the sensations of Chester's hands around mine, of Rodney scooping me to his chest were so strong that I had to point to the stuffed crocodile and say something stupidly ironic to keep from crying. We slept that night like puppies, one mass on the floor.

In the morning light, wiping the grit of sleep from our eyes, we carried the Nests over to the shelves. Lana had found the Baby/ Parenthood category marker and we affixed this above the Nests because we hadn't lost our senses of humor entirely. And it was at that moment, Nests on the shelves, gray light steeping the room, that I realized that all of the Zionites were looking at me, that they were waiting for me to say something or do something or offer a signal of some sort.

So I started to sing "Away in a Manger" because it's the only song I know that's about birth and death at the same time. And it was nice to think of mangers and cattle lowing and mothers bending close to hum the tune on Christmas Eve. Then I said the name of each Baby and the others echoed it. At first it was just mumbling repetition, but by the end, it was a litany.

"Tallow."
"Tallow."
"Esther."
"Esther."
"Phoenix."
"Phoenix."
"Azure."
"Azure."
"Ezra."
"Ezra."

And on and on.

And when we had said all the names I said "Deborah" and they said "Deborah" and we stood in the quiet.

Then I said, "We loved these Babies. We loved the world they came from. We miss that world. But we live in this one now."

Paloma and Kristen wiped tears away; Lana blew a breath out slowly between pursed lips; Kristen and Eleanor held hands; Cassie folded her arms across her chest and rubbed her own skin as if she couldn't quite get warm enough.

"Amen," I said.

"Amen," they repeated.

Amen. Truly. So be it.

As we filed out of the Barnes and Noble and headed toward Zion the sound of the Amen echoed like a soft clap of thunder. It felt like a gift. My experience of religion when I was seventeen had been so tied to an expectation that God would manifest himself—or herself or itself—as a miracle or overwhelming comfort or a sense of safety. We used the word *savior* for a reason. Or so I thought. But I never felt saved; I kept waiting for God to show up and God kept not showing up. But now I realized that if an all-knowing being existed, it would be unlikely to make itself known in exactly the ways I expected or desired. My father's promises and explanations of God's behavior weren't wrong, they were a way of helping people tell a story about themselves and the world that emphasized life instead of death, hope instead of despair. It was a great responsibility, this coaxing of people toward a story, because if you did it without compassion, without concern for your flock, then you were no better than Michael.

But if you did it well—and now I knew my father had done it well—then you opened a space for people to see all of the little deaths— the betrayals and job loss, the miscarriages and divorces—to see them as part of the story but not the end of the story. My father preached that the days in the tomb were the middle, not the end. He said if you paid attention, resurrection was everywhere.

I had understood this promise of resurrection as a constant divine provision of gold light, signals of new life at precisely the right times, comfort at every turn. But it was the paying attention that mattered. In the end, looking closely, without judgment or expectation, is one of the few things we can control, and it is the one act that reveals the heart of the world, regardless of whether that world is imbued with divinity or not.

CHAPTER NINE

AL SAW US first, from the top of Curly. He scrambled down and came running, hair swelling up around him. I thought of the fourteen-year-old boy he'd been, head bobbing on a body that seemed too slight to support it. Now his grown body had arrived and the breadth of his shoulders fit the width of his face, the grace of his eyes. He ran with steam moving through him, arms pumping like pistons. It wasn't until he reached me and embraced me that I could finally hear what he was saying: "You have to go, you have to go." By which time it was too late, of course. Not that we would have gone anyway.

Close behind Cal came Drake, who'd been supervising Cal's movements from the bottom of the Pile. Drake didn't run, just a brisk walk. Still, those knives. He smiled when he reached us and shook our hands, his cloudy left eye wandering beyond us. "Welcome back," he said, like a concierge at the Waldorf Astoria.

Drake took my hand again, the way he had when we'd entered the Zoo. It was still warm and light and strangely comforting—which was absurd given that he was squarely on the other team. "Michael will be so pleased," he said, like the servant who sees the prodigal son returning first, who gets to lead him through the fields to the benevolent father.

As we made our way to the Center, both Zionites and Watchers appeared to observe our procession. Sven approached from the direction of the ghost fruit orchard, pushing a wheelbarrow I'd never seen before, but he stopped when he saw us, didn't wave or call out. It was the same with Tenzin and Zephyr and Asher. Each Zionite seemed held by an invisible electrical fence while the Watchers trailed us, matching our pace.

At the base of the ladder leading up to Rodney's house were two pairs of shoes I'd never seen before. One was missing laces and the tongues had been pulled out in a way that made me shudder. Those are just shoes, I tried to remind myself. Canvas and rubber. But when Cal tucked his thick hair behind his ears I could see delicate scratches laddering their way from chin to temple; Cal's skin was not made of canvas and rubber.

Chester stood in front of our blue stadium seats; as we passed he lifted just his right hand, from the wrist, and wiggled his fingers. I responded in kind. Rodney did not appear.

Someone must have alerted Michael because he came to the door of the Center as we began to cross the quadrangle. Now there was a herd of us, ten cloaked women and a couple dozen Watchers behind and around us. *Our beautiful quadrangle*, Lana had said, her navy dress spinning around her hips. Now she took my hand. "Cobblestone installer," she whispered.

"We don't have any cobblestones," I said, desperation edging my voice.

"You'll find them," she whispered back.

Michael looked the same from a distance but markedly different close up. Shoulders raised, elbows pressed to sides, mouth tightened into a hyphen: It seemed as if he were trying to press the entirety of his body into a smaller space. His blue eyes were still as stunning as the small white teeth were disturbing but his hair was no longer slicked back into a crested wave. Now it hung in long greasy strands across his forehead. His hands were plunged into the pockets of the same blue suit coat but one of the pockets was stained a rusty brown.

"Ladies' night out has ended, I see," he said. The words sounded like Michael but he'd lost his easy, I-have-everything-I-could-possibly-need tone. "I can't say the new couture is particularly appealing, but we can fix that. Or perhaps someone just neglected to tell me that cloaks are making a comeback."

Knight appeared then beside Michael, smiling at me with the same warmth as his twin brother, which almost made up for the fact

283

that about a foot below his lips he was leveling a gun at us. The gun I'd given him.

"Have you missed your friends? I think your friends have missed you. But we've been happy here, just business as usual. Cal loves to climb the Piles and he's still climbing the Piles. Aren't you, Cal?"

Cal nodded without raising his eyes from the ground.

"And Sven! Look at him. Can't separate that guy from his ghost fruit. Really. Happy as a clam."

As much as I tried not to, I couldn't help breaking my gaze from Michael's to scan the periphery of the quadrangle for Rodney's shape.

Michael caught my gaze. "Yes, well, except for Rodney. Rodney grew a trifle belligerent. Which isn't a way to treat your guests. Guests should feel welcome. So I shot him."

My chest clamped shut. A low buzz started up in my ears, a plague of locusts.

"Oh, he's not dead. Well, not yet. He's 'between the worlds,' as my grandmother used to say."

"You can have the Babies," I gasped. My plan was to be remote and precise, icy. But there was that buzzing and I needed to quiet it. Also I needed to somehow get more air into my chest.

Michael looked caught off guard, as though his teleprompter screen had gone suddenly blank. "Your Babies?" he said finally. "Why would you give them to me?"

"Because we want you to leave," I said simply.

"Ah," he said, his smarmy tone returning, though it still sounded pressed through a sieve. "So after three weeks in the bush you've decided that the lives of real people are more important to you than the lives of these objects you birthed. How very forward thinking. I'm sure your friends will be just tickled pink to find out you reached this conclusion."

"Pack your things," said Paloma. Her voice was a herd of animals moving across a plain. "Pack your things and round up your people and we'll tell you where the Babies are."

"You really think I'm going to parade everyone out of here because you assure me the Babies are nestled in some secret location?" The

Watchers tittered their support around us. "First of all, dear—I'm sorry, I don't remember your name."

"Paloma."

"Paloma. That's beautiful. Dove, right?"

Paloma just stared.

Michael continued, "Well, Paloma, first of all that assumes that I'm incredibly trusting and second of all it assumes that I'm eager to depart from Zion, that the Babies are the only reason I'm here. Surely I must be a little bit more complex than that." Michael drew his right hand from his pocket to emphasize the "little bit" and I saw how grotesque his hands had become from the arthritis, the fingers curling like roots. It was pain that was tightening his voice. "Mira, you certainly thought I was more complex than that, didn't you? After all we've been through?"

His voice came to me through the screen of the buzzing. "Was this really your plan?" I heard him say. And for a second I couldn't remember. Had I thought the Babies were all that he wanted? That he would march good-naturedly away as soon as they were offered?

"We'll give you one now," I heard myself say. Because suddenly I understood it wasn't just the Babies he wanted. The Babies might satiate the Watchers, but Michael wanted the Babies for the way they offered him control over us. If they were just objects on the shelf of some Barnes and Noble they were worthless to him. He wanted marionettes. He wanted to make us dance. The only way to win was to refuse to dance.

"Drake, take a peek in Mira's backpack," Michael said, his voice strained again, but this time against excitement, not pain.

Drake grabbed for my backpack and Lana tried to stop him. Drake pulled a knife, suddenly and effortlessly, and sliced Lana's arm, then the backpack straps from my shoulders. Ida and Sylvia and I bent to Lana. She held the wrist of her injured arm as though it might fall off. I pressed the corner of my cloak to the wound.

"It's OK, it's OK, we've got it," said Ida. She let Lana lean against her. Sylvia gently lifted my cloak and pressed hers to the wound instead. She nodded at me, her eyes snapping.

When I stood again, the buzzing had gone. My backpack and the Nest were at Michael's feet. Michael was holding my Baby. Michael cupped her, cupped the vase in the palm of his left hand. He ran his finger down the length of her side. And I felt his finger down the length of my side, the spot he'd pressed against just below my hip. At the top of my chest, the base of my throat, the swell of vomit.

He looked at me. "She's quite beautiful." He raised her to his cheek. "Is it a she? Did you choose a gender for your Baby? Or was the gender just known to you?"

I curled my fingers into fists and made myself uncurl them. She wasn't my Baby. She was a vase. Just a vase. A vase like any of the ones my mom had unpacked from squiggles of cut paper. An object with a return slip. Something manufactured not once but a million times. A vase, a vase, a vase. I tried to take deep breaths. Do not dance. Do not dance.

"You know," he said, eyes still fastened on mine, "she feels very female in my hand like this." He held her up at eye level as if checking his own reflection and then he gently, very gently, licked her side. "She tastes female too," he said.

Tears boiled at the corners of my eyes. My nostrils flared. I could feel a flush rising up from my breasts to my neck, my cheeks. Do not dance for this man. Do not give him this.

"Look away," whispered Lana.

I could not look away.

Michael smiled. Without taking his eyes from mine he held her out in front of him horizontally with his right hand. He sucked the gnarled fingers on his left hand and he squeezed them inside her. I could hear his breath coming faster. And I could see his fingertips on the other side of her, inside of her, smearing arcs on the glass.

And I could not be still.

I screamed and I ran at him. I was only instinct.

As soon as I moved I knew he had been waiting for this because he drew up his arm, the one inside of her, he drew it up above his head as I rushed at him and he brought it down against the ground with an incredible amount of force.

She shattered.

And I had to stop, abruptly, before I reached him, so that I would not step on the broken pieces of her. My Baby was a hundred pieces on the ground.

The buzzing filled my head again, the insistent shuddering of life at a frequency so high it burned against the deep insides of my ears. It entered my vertebrae, doubling me over until I thought I was going to vomit the sound onto the matted grass. But I righted myself and I looked him in the eye.

His eyes were glassy, shining, he was on the verge of true relief from his pain. He needed me to plummet into some unknowable pit of grief so he could ascend into ecstasy, and we were both tottering on this edge together. He removed a handkerchief from his jacket pocket and he bent and wrapped it around the biggest shard of what had been my Baby and as he handed it to me I could see him mouthing the word *token*. I took what had been my Baby in my hand and fragments of the Before came rushing through me, torn and disembodied, appearing and disappearing in the freight rush of a flood: the base of my ballerina lamp and oil glistening on a silver platter; the heft of a hymnal in my five-year-old hands and drips from a grape Popsicle on the tops of my bare feet; there was the sun and Orion, there was the moon and a pot of dead hydrangeas, there were my mother and father and Bim and here—

—here was Michael waiting for me to crumple and so I drew back and I plunged the fragment of her into Michael's chest, I plunged it in with all the force I had in my body, just below his ribs.

I stabbed him with my Baby in the place from which God might have created a woman—if this were a different kind of story.

CHAPTER TEN

IS FACE CHANGED. Transmuted from the cliff edge of ecstasy across the flat plateau of numbness and back to the obsidian valley of pain. His tongue touched his top lip as though he were trying to taste the sensation.

Then he crumpled down, backward, away from me, with the glass, my Baby, still inside of him. My hand was gulping or sobbing, I couldn't tell. I just remember thinking it should have made a sound but it didn't. I closed my eyes so the darkness could help me hear.

When I opened my eyes again I was in the same place but Michael was gone. Lana was cradling my upper body in her lap while Ida wound strips of her cloak around my throbbing hand. After wearing the cloaks the last few days it was strange to see Ida's actual clothing, a navy button-down shirt with tiny white flowers. An amethyst stone nestled at her collarbone. "That's beautiful," I said, reaching up to touch it with my left hand.

"Be still, Mira," said Lana, and she took my raised arm and brought it firmly back to earth.

Around us, Zion had come alive again, as though the pulsing crickets between my ears had been turned out onto the landscape where they belonged. I felt strangely happy, a bee in the middle of her hive.

"Let's get you to the Clinic," said Ida, tying the final strip of fabric into a satisfactory knot. Lana used her uninjured arm to gather me up and somehow raise me to my feet.

The moment I stood, his absence crashed into me. "Rodney. I want to see Rodney."

"Your hand first, sweetie," said Ida.

I shook my head and pulled my injured arm away from her. The jolt sent an extra throb to my palm and a brief flash of darkness across my eyes. I cradled my hand against my chest. "Not until I see him."

While Ida and Lana exchanged glances and shrugs I turned in a slow circle. There was Asher, guiding a Watcher I didn't recognize out of Lana's room and toward the Center. There was Cal, herding a few other Watchers forward from the Clinic. Just outside the door of the Center, Sven stood beside a plastic bin into which Knight was reverently placing his knives. Mona and Davis sat nearby with the other collected Watchers, bags and backpacks at their feet, as though ready to hitchhike to Baja. Tenzin, exiting the Nesting Facility, offered a thumbs-up in Asher's direction. "Check the Piles," called Asher in response.

And in the space between where the Center ended and where the barracks began I could see a wheelbarrow, the one I'd seen Sven pushing earlier. Drake stood beside it, his silhouette strange without the bloom of knives around his waist. From the side of the wheelbarrow dangled an arm and a leg and I knew that the body inside the wheelbarrow was Michael.

"This way," said Ida.

Lana and Ida guided me to Chester's room, the strings of beads still dangling from the door, still refusing to cast prismed rainbows on the bare walls. The piles of papers, the bowl with Chester's treasured objects, even his rocker: All of it was gone. In the middle of the room, on the embroidered stool, sat Sylvia. Her left hand pushed the bare flesh of Rodney's upper right thigh together while her right hand tried to work a needle through his skin. She glanced up at us when we entered but didn't say anything.

Rodney lay on Cal's pool float, my cloud-scudded sheet beneath him. His whole upper body arched upward, his head thrown back, eyes closed and body rigid against the pain. His right hand squeezed my necklace, though I couldn't tell whether it was supposed to bring him comfort or, in the press of those daggers against his palm, offer distraction through another avenue of suffering. And when Lana had decided to give the necklace to Rodney—I couldn't even begin to piece that together in my mind.

Then he made a sound, his voice tearing open, and I went to him and knelt beside him and covered his mouth with my mouth. He didn't kiss me back, not at first, not exactly. His lips simply opened and closed gently, the way Bim, as a baby, would mouth the air as he slept, searching his dreams for the comfort of our mother. But then he opened his eyes. "You," he said. I nodded. I touched the branch on his cheek and kissed the buds at the corner of his lip and then I put my uninjured hand on his chest and he deflated, he let his body down.

I heard the sound of the necklace falling to the floor and then the warmth of his hand cupping my neck. He was crying and so I laid my head against his body. I pressed my ear to his chest so I could hear the hitch of his grief and so I could also hear the heartbeat that moved him forward, that moved us forward, steadily, steadily, into a certain kind of light.

EPILOGUE

Here are the other shards of the story, the pieces you might still want to possess.

The wound did not kill Michael, at least not while he was still in Zion. Sylvia and Ida patched Michael up—not so that he'd live but so he wouldn't necessarily die. The arm and leg I saw dangling from the wheelbarrow belonged to him but they weren't lifeless. At least not then.

After Michael fell, Knight dropped the gun. I don't know whether it was shock or whether he'd been wanting to give it up for a long time, but it turned out the other Watchers weren't interested in fighting. The Zoo collapsed soon after that. One visitor told us that Michael had hanged himself from the basketball hoop in the aquarium, that for a week the Watchers observed his dead body, thinking that his suicide might contain a sign. When he began to decompose, like any other body, most of them left.

Though I'm glad to know there are no longer Inhabitants and Watchers, I'm also certain Michael couldn't have tied those knots on his own. I know now there will be other Zoos. I know now that we carry pain from which even a Rending cannot separate us.

I have a scar across my palm, deeper than the life line and the love line. When I spread my right hand open fully I can feel the scar stretch, too. I am never entirely away from that act of violence and that is as it should be.

Lana decided to return to the Asylum. I see her every few weeks. I take ghost fruit or willow branches. She's working on making me a hanging basket, a cradle.

Things in Zion are much as they were. Before Lana left we took the fragments of my Baby and we began to make a mosaic on the outside of the Nesting Facility. Tenzin and I stay on the lookout for objects that are broken or useless and Zephyr makes his mixtures and Cal turns the broken bits into beauty. Or the remnants of beauty.

Abigail and Ida still intertwine their pinkies at our community meetings and Greg Cracker, the chiropractor with the horrible Christmas sweater, showed up in Zion after the Zoo deflated. He's adjusted something in Sylvia and now she shows a bit more flexibility. Not much, but some. Talia still reminds us to return our mugs to the Center and Chester distributes fortunes with solemn ceremony. Things in Zion are much as they were before. Except that I am no longer hoping or preparing to arrive anywhere else.

Rodney survived, of course, and it was he who said, when I felt the first flutterings of you beneath my skin: "Mira, you need to give our child her story. Start from the very beginning."

This is the story I choose to tell about the world and who I was inside of it at a particular moment in time. Like all stories, this one contains gaps and flaws, omissions and embellishments—and scenes I'm sure you'd just as soon forget.

The most dangerous thing of all is the absence of a story.

I cannot give you yours so here is mine, dear one, until you are ready to write your own.

ACKNOWLEDGMENTS

Thank you to Barbara Poelle: agent, cheerleader, therapist, whip-smart reader, and my personal superhero. Thanks especially for noticing that twenty thousand words were missing from the end of the book. Thank you to Brita Lundberg, who offered both wisdom and calm at critical moments.

Thank you to Lea Beresford, editor extraordinaire, who is as watchful about unwieldy verbs as she is about wobbly character arcs. The book is so much better because of you, Lea, and I'm a better writer, too.

Thank you to all of the other folks at Bloomsbury who poured time and energy into the novel, including Nancy Miller, Nicole Jarvis, Sara Kitchen, Sarah New, and Janet McDonald.

Thank you to Supergroup (Kate Schultz, Jana Hiller, Sarah Hanley, Sean Beggs, Coralee Grebe, Kristi Belcamino, and Brian Rubin). What would I do without you guys?

Thanks to those who filled in my knowledge gaps: Emily Carroll, Dan Hernandez, Martha Schwehn, Jennifer Wolcott, and a huge number of friends on Facebook.

Thanks to Pastor Charlie Ruud for chats about law and gospel.

Thanks to the Loft Literary Center and to the members of the "Double-Take" class (slutty bears, all) and especially to Heather Herrman for her keen eye and gracious support.

Thanks to the folks at Brick Oven Bakery and especially Jenna Huberg, who provides dollops of beauty and caffeine on a daily basis.

Thanks to my colleagues at St. Olaf College and to my students, who ask the very best questions.

Thanks to Jessica Peterson White and Tripp Ryder and all of the literati at Content Bookstore who offer our little town an abundance of good words.

ACKNOWLEDGMENTS

Thanks to my mom, Ricki Thompson, who has supported my imaginative life in millions of practical and emotional ways for decades now.

But most especially, thank you to Thisbe and Matteus, who always return me to this world, and to Peder, who read countless drafts of this novel and whose support was truly unending. Thank you for believing when I couldn't; thank you for always seeing a way forward.

A NOTE ON THE AUTHOR

KAETHE SCHWEHN'S first book, *Tailings: A Memoir*, won the 2015 Minnesota Book Award for Creative Nonfiction and her chapbook of poems, *Tanka & Me*, was selected for the Mineral Point Chapbook Series. In addition to holding MFAs from the Iowa Writers' Workshop and the University of Montana, Kaethe has been the recipient of an Academy of American Poets prize, a Minnesota State Arts Board Grant, and a Loft Mentor Series Award. She teaches at St. Olaf College and lives in Northfield, Minnesota.